Michelle Smart's love affair with books started when she was a baby and would cuddle them in her cot. A voracious reader of all genres, she found her love of romance established when she stumbled across her first Mills & Boon book at the age of twelve. She's been reading them—and writing them—ever since. Michelle lives in Northamptonshire, England, with her husband and two young Smarties.

Louise Fuller was once a tomboy who hated pink and always wanted to be the Prince—not the Princess! Now she enjoys creating heroines who aren't pretty push-overs but strong, believable women. Before writing for Mills & Boon she studied literature and philosophy at university, and then worked as a reporter on her local newspaper. She lives in Tunbridge Wells with her impossibly handsome husband Patrick and their six children.

CROWNING HIS KIDNAPPED PRINCESS

MICHELLE SMART

MAID FOR THE GREEK'S RING

LOUISE FULLER

MILLS & BOON

First published in Great Britain 2022
by Mills & Boon, an imprint of HarperCollins*Publishers* Ltd,
1 London Bridge Street, London, SE1 9GF

www.harpercollins.co.uk

HarperCollins*Publishers*
1st Floor, Watermarque Building,
Ringsend Road, Dublin 4, Ireland

Crowning His Kidnapped Princess © 2022 Michelle Smart

Maid for the Greek's Ring © 2022 Louise Fuller

ISBN: 978-0-263-30089-5

07/22

MIX
Paper from
responsible sources
FSC® C007454

This book is produced from independently certified FSC™ paper
to ensure responsible forest management.
For more information visit www.harpercollins.co.uk/green.

Printed and Bound in Spain using 100% Renewable Electricity
at CPI Black Print, Barcelona

CROWNING HIS KIDNAPPED PRINCESS

MICHELLE SMART

MILLS & BOON

CHAPTER ONE

CLARA SINCLAIR PACED her prison cell. If she was feeling charitable she'd admit her cell, which easily measured thirty by thirty feet and came with its own four-poster bed, an adjoining private bathroom and had three high bay windows with views straight onto the palace's private harbour, was the kind of prison cell most incarcerated criminals would kill for. In some cases, again. Her current prison outfit was rather flashier than what an inmate would expect to wear too, being made of white silk with an overlay of white lace. If she hadn't been forcibly straitjacketed into it, she might think it beautiful.

She almost wished her female guards were still in the cell with her. Then she could have the satisfaction of calling them every nasty name she could dredge up and watch their faces turn puce. But no, they'd all gone off to get themselves dolled up for the Monte Cleure event of the decade—Clara's marriage to King Dominic of the House of Fernandez. Her other prison guards, two beefy men, were stationed on the other side of the door as they'd been since the first time she'd tried to escape. Still, she hadn't shouted at them in at least twenty minutes, so she hammered on the door, and yelled, 'May your bedsheets be cursed with ginormous bloodsucking bedbugs, you *pigs*!'

As with every other insult and curse she'd aimed at them these past two weeks, she was rewarded with silence.

The clock on her wall chimed the quarter hour. Goody. Only fifteen minutes to go before she was married off to the biggest pig of them all, the King himself. And she couldn't even make a scene in the royal chapel, not with the threat to Bob's life. Dominic would do it too. And probably take great pleasure from it.

What kind of evil bastard gave a woman a puppy and then used it as a weapon to threaten her with? The man she was marrying in fifteen minutes, that's who. For now, Bob was safe and fast asleep in his basket. He would remain safe only if she said, 'I do,' without punching the groom. Or the priest. Or any of the guests.

Until she'd arrived in Monte Cleure and found herself held against her will, Clara had never hit anyone in her life, nor felt the urge to, not even her half-brother, who'd treated her like doggy-do since their father died and who was equally responsible for her predicament as the King himself.

What kind of evil bastard sold his own sister? Her brother, the Honourable Andrew Sinclair, that's who.

She banged her fist on the door again. 'You're going to burn in hell for this, do you know that?' she shouted before dramatically flinging herself onto the floor.

Bob woke up and padded over to curl onto her lap.

Stroking his soft head, she felt no compulsion to cry. She was too angry for tears and, in any case, tears solved nothing. Clara had learned that as a small child when her tears had failed to bring her mother back to life. She'd also learned that moaning and bewailing your bad fortune solved nothing either.

If she was going to escape, she needed to get a move on.

What had she missed? She had ten minutes left before they dragged her to the chapel.

Think!

The fireplace had been bricked up within minutes of them finding her wriggling up it. The air vent covers had been superglued in place as a precaution. Opening a window and screaming for help had resulted in Bob being dangled out of the window with the threat to drop him in the private harbour forty feet below.

She would make Dominic's life a living hell. She would be the wife from Hades. If he thought he could bully her into compliance then he had another…

A tapping sound jolted her out of her furious musings and she raised her head sharply. There was a face at the window.

Certain she was imagining it, she blinked then blinked again. The face was still there.

It was a handsome face, the mouth curved into a wide grin, the tilting head indicating for her to hurry and open the window.

Scrambling to her feet, Clara almost tripped over the train of her wedding dress in her haste to reach the handsome stranger.

As she tugged at the sash window, she thought vaguely that there was something familiar about the handsome stranger but the joy of imminent rescue overrode it, as did the difficulty she was experiencing in opening the ruddy thing.

Dominic hadn't had it glued stuck, had he? She couldn't think when, not when she'd been confined to the room for two whole weeks, half of which had been spent with her head stuck out of this very window wondering if it was possible to make herself a rope out of her bedsheets and escape that way. She would have done it too if her female guards, or 'companions,' as Dominic called them, had left her for longer than twenty minutes at a time.

Just as she was thinking she'd have to smash the glass, there was some give. A bit more muscle and up the window rose.

Yes!

'Hello,' she said, grinning broadly, placing where she knew the handsome face from. 'Are you the cavalry?'

Ice-blue eyes sparkled. Straight white teeth flashed. '*Ciao, bella.* Would you like a ride in my helicopter?'

Marcelo Berruti swung himself into the room and took stock of the beautiful young woman smiling at him like he was Father Christmas. Adrenaline pumped hard through him, an excitement he hadn't experienced since his military days. As a child he'd often scaled the walls of the castle he called home imagining himself a knight in shining armour rescuing a damsel in distress. Who'd have known he'd reach the age of thirty and do it for real?

This particular damsel didn't look in the least distressed. If anything, she looked like she was about to burst out laughing and he instinctively placed a finger to her lips.

'Shh,' he whispered, and pointed at the door.

Large dark brown eyes brimming with glee widened like a naughty schoolgirl caught smoking by an indulgent teacher, and he remembered how Alessia had admiringly described Clara Sinclair as the naughty girl of their exclusive boarding school. Alessia had failed to mention Clara's beauty, and he allowed himself a moment to sweep his eyes over the heart-shaped face with the high cheekbones, the soft plump lips his finger was currently pressed against and the perfectly straight nose, and down to the curvy body with the full breasts wrapped in a wedding dress.

The picture-perfect sight was finished with her dark blond hair swept up in an elegant knot.

Slender fingers suddenly grabbed his hand and moved his finger from her mouth.

'Are you here to ogle me or rescue me?' she asked in an exaggerated whisper.

'Can't a man do both?'

'Not when I'm about to be dragged out of this room and frogmarched down the aisle in five minutes.'

'That is a very good point.' Stepping away from her, Marcelo carried the chair from her dressing table to the door and quietly but securely placed it under the handle before looking at his watch and turning back to her. 'We have two minutes. Do you have anything you can change into?'

'In two minutes?'

'One minute and fifty seconds.'

She held her palms out and shrugged. 'It took an hour for them to pin me into this stupid thing.'

'Scissors?'

'Not allowed them in case I stab someone,' she explained cheerfully.

He dropped to his knees in front of her and took hold of the lace at the hem of the dress. 'Stay still.'

'What are you doing?'

'This…' Looking up at her beautiful face, he tore the lace.

She pulled a mock shocked face. 'But, sir, we've only just met.'

He grinned, put a hand to her hip and spun her around to help the lace rip until it was removed all the way to her hips.

In the distance came the telltale sound of his helicopter nearing them. Now for the silk of the dress. This proved harder to tear into than the lace.

'Use your teeth?' she suggested.

He pulled his own mock shocked face. 'But, madam, we've only just met.' And then he proceeded to do exactly as she'd suggested.

With thirty seconds to go, all that remained of the skirt of the wedding dress was ragged scraps of silk falling to mid-thigh on the most fabulous pair of golden legs Marcelo had ever seen. His hands fisted on the material he still had hold of as the compulsion to grip the curvy hips and press his face into the cleavage on display where the silk and lace of the dress dipped like a heart surged through him.

Never in his wildest dreams had he imagined his damsel in distress would be so damn sexy.

'Eyes to face, Berruti,' she scolded, holding her fore and index fingers like claws to her eyes.

He gazed up at the beautiful face. 'You know who I am?'

She rolled her eyes. 'I don't let any old riff-raff rescue me, you know.'

Dio, he wanted to kiss that smart, perfectly plump mouth but, with time pressing, he resisted, instead jumping to his feet and taking hold of her hand.

'How are you with heights?' he asked. The helicopter now hovered over them, its rotors so loud whispering was no longer an option.

'I guess we're about to find out?'

A rope appeared in front of the window at the same moment the handle of the door rattled.

'Time's up,' he said. 'Let's go.'

'Hold on a sec.' She yanked her hand from his and knelt down to scoop up a small chocolate-brown furry thing Marcelo hadn't noticed before.

'You can't take that,' he said as loud shouting and hammering penetrated through the door.

'I can't leave him. Dominic will kill him.'

Marcelo pointed at the dangling rope. 'We can't escape on that with a dog.'

Utterly unperturbed, Clara looked down at her cleavage. 'Rip this. Quickly.'

'What?'

There was a loud crash against the door.

'Quickly,' she said with the first hint of impatience. 'Rip it. Just a few inches.'

Realising what she intended, Marcelo put his hand on the top of the dress and tore it apart so it opened to reveal ample breasts hidden behind an ugly plain white bra.

Seeing he'd noticed, Clara smiled wickedly. 'You should see my knickers.' Then she carefully put the puppy down her dress in the space he'd just made.

'Lucky puppy,' he drawled. 'Can we go now?'

'Go on then.'

There was yet another loud smash against the door as he jumped onto the windowsill. Marcelo grabbed the rope. Clara seemed not to need instruction, nimbly climbing up beside him and wrapping her arms around his neck.

'Pleased to meet you,' she said, gazing up at his face with a grin.

He couldn't help grinning back as he wound the rope securely around them. 'Hold tight.'

'No, *you* hold tight.'

Laughing, he hooked an arm around her waist, stuck a thumb up at the helicopter, then held her tightly as they were lifted into the air.

Clara's stomach dipped and then she was weightless, flying, warm air rushing through and around her. She kept her fear locked tightly away, as tightly as she held to her old school friend's macho brother, and kept her stare firmly fixed on his face, feeding off the supreme confidence written on it that said they would be lifted to safety. She would not allow herself to think that, should his knot-making skills be sub-par, they were both liable to plummet to certain death... Oh, dear. She'd just thought it.

Think of poor Bob nestled between her breasts, she told herself. Judging by the way his sharp little claws were digging into her skin, the poor mite was terrified.

A jolt on the rope made her stomach dip again, and she squeezed her eyes shut and leaned her forehead into Marcelo's hard chest and prayed their pressed bodies was barrier enough to stop Bob scrambling out and, conversely, not too smothering that they suffocated him.

Before guilt that she'd done the wrong thing in bringing the puppy with them could set too deeply, hands grabbed hold of her and she was being roughly manhandled onto the helicopter.

Relief surged through her like a frothing tsunami, and she would have rolled onto her back from the sheer force of it if she wasn't bound to the hunk who'd taken it on himself to rescue her.

They'd made it! She was free.

The noise of the rotors wasn't loud enough to drown the thrash of her heartbeats ringing in her ears. She tried to catch a breath before opening her eyes. She had to blink a number of times before her vision cleared and she could attempt to get her bearings. The helicopter itself was huge and looked more military than civilian. Two men dressed in military fatigues were knelt beside them working to untie the knots binding her to Marcelo.

It came to Clara in a rush that she was trussed up on the floor of a helicopter with the Prince of Ceres and with a puppy scrambling frantically for release from the confines of her cleavage. The relief and absurdity of it all became too much and, unable to control it, Clara burst into peals of laughter. She was still laughing when the rope slackened, still laughing when she managed to sit up, still laughing as she carefully pulled Bob out of her cleavage. But then Bob licked her cheek and her laughter merged into tears that she couldn't control either. Through the sobbing laughter was an awareness that three macho men were warily studying her, no doubt alarmed at this display of female hysteria, a notion that only made her laugh and cry harder.

Her eighteen days on Monte Cleure, sixteen spent as a captive, had put her through the emotional wringer but she'd refused to succumb to distress, focusing everything on the anger she'd need as fuel to escape even when escape had seemed hopeless, and she sobbed and laughed until everything she'd suppressed was purged.

It took so long for her to regain control of herself that they'd probably left Monte Cleure airspace before she'd wiped the last tear away. Needing a tissue, she looked at the ragged remnants of her wedding dress and ripped off another piece of silk to blow her nose.

Then she looked at Marcelo. He was sat on the cold metal helicopter floor beside her, an air of amusement mingling with the concern on his face. During her bout of hysteria, Bob had plonked himself onto his lap, and a hand that was practically the same size as the puppy gently stroked his head.

Scrunching the makeshift hankie into a ball, Clara stuffed it into her bra. 'That has to be the world's most expensive handkerchief,' she said.

Thick black eyebrows drew in together.

'This dress cost Dominic a hundred thousand euros,' she explained before another short burst of laughter flew from her lips. Her purge of emotions had been cathartic. Now she felt as emotionally high as she was physically in this military grade helicopter. 'I might send it to him as a keepsake of our time together.'

Marcelo had seen feminine tears many times in his life. His sister, Alessia, could turn them on like taps. Most girlfriends had proven themselves excellent at summoning tears to get their own way—one lover, Gianna, had thrown herself at his feet weeping and wailing when he'd ended their relationship, something he always reflected on with bemusement considering they were only together a couple of months. Bemusement was his default emotion with female tears along with a certain amount of bracing himself for the sad eyes and woebegone expression that always followed. There was none of that with Clara Sinclair.

Her tears had been spectacular. The chokes of laughter the sobs had been interspersed with had only added to the spectacle. And then it was done, and now she was sat cross-legged on the helicopter floor, dark brown eyes puffy, her face streaked with mascara but with the expression of someone who'd already put the tears behind her. The adventure from the palace into the helicopter had made her hair come loose, windswept long dark blond hair splayed all around her.

'Better?' he asked, already knowing what the answer would be.

'Much, thank you. And thank you for rescuing me.' She blew a strand of hair off her mouth and grinned. 'I owe you one.'

'It was my pleasure.' And the knowledge of this incredibly sexy creature being in his debt only heightened the pleasure. She was fascinating.

She stretched her glorious legs out and hooked her ankles together. She had pretty feet, he noted. The puppy jumped off his lap and onto hers.

She fussed over the puppy then turned her attention

sharply back to him. 'I've only just noticed—you're wearing a tuxedo.'

'I am,' he agreed.

Her plump lips puckered and wriggled. 'I thought superheroes were supposed to wear spandex or something? And their pants over their tights?'

Laughing at the imagery, he shook his head. 'I'm wearing a tuxedo because I dressed for a wedding.'

Her eyes widened and she gave a bark of laughter. 'You were a guest?'

'I accepted as a representative of the Berruti royal family.'

'Amazing. And so sneaky!'

He shrugged as if the effort of rescuing her was nothing at all. 'The invitation came three days after my sister showed me your message.' The message had been as forthright as the woman who'd written it:

The King of Monte Cleure has imprisoned me and is forcing me to marry him. SEND HELP!!!

Marcelo had assumed it was a joke. Even Alessia had been unconvinced of its truthfulness—it was well known publicly that Dominic was searching for a royal bride, and Clara Sinclair's reputation preceded her—but when Alessia's reply went unanswered, doubt had set in and his sister had proceeded to give him earache about rescuing her old wayward friend. And then the wedding invitation had arrived by courier and Marcelo suddenly found a way to get one up on a man he loathed and who treated women like dirt and who gave royal families a bad name, *and* appease his sister all in one shot. Also, he'd been bored. An injection of excitement in a life that had been mind-numbingly predictable since his military career had come to a premature end had proved irresistible.

The initial plan for his old army friends to undertake the rescue mission while he sat in the royal chapel with his credentials as a bona-fide guest his alibi, a last-minute vision of himself sweeping in like a heroic knight in shining armour and the surge of adrenaline the thought had sent through him had also proved irresistible.

Marcelo hadn't had a rush like that in three years. He could still feel the after-effects buzzing in his veins.

'I wasn't sure if the message went out,' Clara said, thrilled that this one action had been successful. All her other efforts to escape King Pig had been abject failures. 'Dominic caught me writing it and stole my phone while I was pressing send.'

'Who did you send it to?'

'Everyone in my contacts.' All ten of them. Alessia, her only friend from her school days, had been her biggest hope. The other contacts had been her aunt in Australia, who no doubt would have called Andrew and been fobbed off by him, some work colleagues and an old lady who'd adopted one of the dogs from the animal shelter Clara worked at and who would call if her arthritis got too bad and she needed Clara to walk Buster for her.

'Clever.'

'Was there an international outcry?' she asked, more in hope than expectation.

'I'm afraid not.'

Her face scrunched in disappointment, making Marcelo laugh again. 'Going to tell me how you got yourself into this predicament?'

Her expression changed to indignant. 'Got *myself* into it? Nice bit of victim blaming there.'

'Clumsy wording,' he said by way of an apology. 'Go on, tell me. I'm curious.'

'Hmm…' Her lips puckered and wriggled again and then she sat up straighter and inched herself back so her back rested against the hard bench running along the helicopter's far side. 'Well, my brother asked me to go to Monte Cleure on his behalf to sell the amazing properties of the sparkling English wine he's producing on the family estate to the King of Monte Cleure. With me so far?'

'Indeed.'

'Great.' She flashed a smile. 'So I agreed to his request and off I popped to Monte Cleure and I was welcomed like a princess. *Amazing* hospitality. Honestly. Amazing. I was put up in the palace and dined on the *best* food, I had access to the spa and swimming pools, everything. Still with me?'

'Yes,' he agreed drily, although it was rather difficult concentrating on the words she was saying when the lips forming the words were so succulent.

'Good. Because this is where it gets interesting. On my second night, the king proposed to me.'

He arched a brow.

She nodded sagely in response. 'That was my reaction too. I only just stopped myself from laughing in his face, but I told him the truth, that I don't want to get married. I was quite pleased with myself for not insulting him with my refusal.'

'You weren't tempted?'

'Have you seen him? The man's a pig.'

'He's also a king,' he pointed out.

She gave a short rise of her shoulders. 'So what? Doesn't stop him being a pig. He even eats like a pig. It's disgusting.'

Having suffered a number of functions where Dominic

had been in attendance, Marcelo could only agree with this assessment of the man's eating habits. 'What was his reaction to your refusal?'

'He was very understanding. All piggy sweetness and light.' Her face darkened. 'The next morning, he joined me for breakfast and referred to me as his fiancée. I told him again that I didn't want to get married and he just laughed. When I went to collect my stuff to leave, my suitcase had been ransacked and my passport and purse stolen, and then King Pig came to my room and told me I was going to marry him whether I liked it or not and that I'd better get used to the idea or there would be consequences. The next day he brought Bob to my room and told me he was the first of many gifts I would receive if I was a *good girl.*' Distaste dripped in every syllable.

'Bob?'

She nodded at the puppy curled on her lap. 'He knew how much I love animals and thought a dog would make me want to marry him. Seriously, the man's on another planet.'

'Why you? Did he ever say?'

'Oh, yes,' she said matter-of-factly. 'He wants to marry me because I have royal blood in my veins—that it's heavily diluted doesn't matter apparently—and because I'm a virgin.'

CHAPTER TWO

FOR THE FIRST time since he'd appeared at her window, Marcelo looked nonplussed. 'I beg your pardon?' he said. 'You're a virgin?'

'Yep,' she answered cheerfully. Clara was not in the least embarrassed about her virgin state. 'Apparently a virgin is more of a guarantee that any child will be his. Because, obviously, once a woman's experienced sex she turns into a raging nymphomaniac and has to have it with any man within a ten-mile radius and is so overtaken by lust she forgets to use contraception, especially when she's out there having her wicked way with all those men who aren't her husband.'

Marcelo just stared at her. She became aware that the men who'd hauled them onto the helicopter were staring at her from their seats on the bench too. They all appeared dumbfounded.

'What's wrong?' she asked, looking from one to the other. 'You're not married and now worried your wives are out there shacking up with your nearest neighbour, are you? Honestly, that was just Dominic's tiny, paranoid mind coming into play. I mean, I don't know, maybe your wives *are* having affairs but if they are, I assure you, it's not because they're nymphomaniacs but because they're unhappy in your marriage so my advice would be to fix any unhappiness. Women like to feel loved and appreciated. And wanted. Flowers are always appreciated too but I wouldn't recommend using them as a form of apology— if you need to apologise and show how remorseful you are, a grovelling apology on bended knee works a treat.'

'Does it?' Marcelo asked faintly.

Her face scrunched as she shrugged. 'Well, that's what I'd prefer if my husband upset me but I don't suppose I can speak for other women, and it's all a bit moot because I'm never going to get married. I'd quite like a man to get on bended knee and produce a grovelling apology though.'

'For what?'

Clara considered the question. 'My father for not protecting me? My brother for selling me to a pig? Yes. Those things warrant grovelling apologies. But it's not quite the same thing, is it?' She considered it some more. 'No, on second thoughts, grovelling on bended knee to your daughter or sister feels a bit wrong. Those kind of grovels should be left for lovers to do. And my father's dead so I'm going to have to wait until I join him in hell before I get any apology off him, and Andrew wouldn't know an apology if it slapped him in the face.'

The stupid thing was that until she'd received her brother's beautifully written letter—Andrew was a traditionalist—inviting her to dinner, Clara hadn't cared that she was estranged from him…or, more truthfully, that he was estranged from her. Older than her by two decades, Andrew had always treated her with disdain, like she was a nuisance to be tolerated, even when he'd been her legal guardian. He'd resented her as a child for being the catalyst of his parents' divorce, their father leaving his mother for Clara's mother, and as she'd grown older she'd grown into an embarrassment to him. Before that dinner invitation arrived, she hadn't seen him in the four years since he'd turned up at her flat on her eighteenth birthday, not with a present for her but with details of a savings account her mother had set up for her when she'd been born. The last deposit had been made when Clara was four. There was enough in it for her to replace her sagging fourth-hand sofa with a less sagging second-hand one, little enough money for Clara to know her father had kept his second wife's spending tightly controlled.

She hadn't realised until she'd received Andrew's letter and her heart had felt fit to burst that she'd nestled a secret hope her pompous brother could look past the circumstances of her birth and the personality traits he found so insufferable, and want a relationship with her. She guessed that's why it hadn't occurred to her that what she'd taken to be his attempt at a reproachment between them had a malevolent ulterior motive.

Andrew's loathing of her ran deeper than she'd known.

Something flickered in Marcelo's ice-blue eyes. 'You think your brother sold you to Dominic?'

'I don't know in what form he was paid for it—he doesn't need the money as he's loaded, so probably wants the cachet of being brother-in-law to a king—but yes, he sold me to him.' Andrew had tricked her and sold her to a monster. Feeling her belly roil and churn, she squashed the pointless pain down and gave her attention to something much worthier: Marcelo's hair, which he was currently running his fingers through.

It was nice hair, Clara decided. And much nicer to focus on than allowing her brain to think about her brother. It hurt much less too. Almost black in contrast to those ice-blue eyes—mind you, the ring around the iris was as black as the pupils, adding a different dimension to them—Marcelo's hair was long at the front and currently flopping over his forehead thanks to being ravaged by the wind. Marcelo

Berruti had the look of someone who took great pride in his personal grooming, the black beard covering the square jaw just the right side of designer stubble. She wondered if it was soft to the touch or bristly and then thought that that was a thought she'd never pondered before. Interesting...

Marcelo Berruti was interesting. Physically. If interesting was a substitute for drop-dead gorgeous. Because that's what he was. Drop-dead gorgeous. Even his mouth was sexy, all full yet firm. And wide. She wondered what those lips would feel like against hers, which was also interesting as Clara had never wondered that about any man before. Now that the shock of being airlifted onto a helicopter had abated, she could admit that it had felt very nice being held against his solid body.

'Have you got a girlfriend?' she asked on impulse.

The kissable lips parted then closed. He blinked then gave a short shake of his head. 'Are you for real?'

'Of course.' She held an arm out to him. 'See? Touch me. I'm as real as you are.'

He looked from her extended arm to her face and gave another short shake of his head. 'Do you have a filter for your mouth?'

'No, but I probably need one. Dominic did threaten to gag me a number of times.'

'What stopped him?'

'He was scared I would bite him.'

If Marcelo shook his head again he would give himself whiplash. This woman though...

He'd known she was a handful. Alessia had told him that much, how the teachers at their strict school had grown so exasperated at having to continually sanction her that Clara had been placed in a bedroom with Alessia in the hope his sister, a year older than her, would be a good influence. That arrangement had lasted until Clara's expulsion. Alessia had confided in him, 'There were so many rumours flying around about the expulsion being to do with a fire alarm going off in an exam but that didn't make sense to me and nothing was confirmed. Whatever it was, she was a complete handful and drove the teachers nuts but, for me, there was something inherently loveable about her that made you want to protect her from herself.'

He didn't think he'd met a woman in less need of protection in his life. She might have the looks of someone who'd just stepped out of a Botticelli painting but that runaway mouth would drive a saint to losing its patience. And he'd only known her an hour!

'He would never have controlled you,' he murmured.

She sighed and rubbed her fingers through Bob's fur. 'He would have used this little one to control me. He really had done his homework on me, but between you and me... and them...' She indicated his two paratrooper friends who'd come along to help and were clearly listening, agog, to their conversation. 'I think he'd run out of options. He took the throne a couple of years ago and needed to start breeding, but every eligible princess or duchess or whatever in Europe turned him down. I personally think he was a bit desperate when he decided I was the perfect woman to be his queen.'

Marcelo's own sister had been one of the eligible princesses to turn the King down. The refusal had come from their mother, who, earlier that year, received an official request from Dominic for a meeting about Princess Alessia. Knowing exactly what the meeting would be about, she'd diplomatically refused. Like the rest of the Berrutis, the Queen abhorred the King of Monte Cleure. Not only would she never take it on herself to arrange her children's marriages, she would rather lose her throne than sanction her daughter's marriage to a man who had absolute power in his principality and treated women as playthings and those of his family as second-class citizens. There had been many unconfirmed rumours that he used to hit his own sister before she fled to America.

If Clara was speaking the truth, and judging from the blunt, unfiltered way she spoke he had no reason to doubt her, her brother had sold her to that very man. He didn't know what was more disturbing—the idea that a man could treat his own sister in such a cruel manner or the way she relayed it so matter-of-factly and then moved straight on to another subject as if her brother selling her wasn't something that needed to be dwelt on.

'Anyway, you didn't answer my question,' she said, cutting through his disturbed thoughts. 'Do you have a girlfriend?'

He rubbed the back of his neck. 'Not at the moment.'

'Cool.'

'Cool?' he repeated.

She smiled brightly. 'I'm in your debt, remember?'

His mouth dropped open. How many shocks could one woman throw in such a short space of time? 'I thought you were a virgin?'

Now she pulled a face of disgust. 'Your mind! It's filthy! I was going to offer to buy you dinner as a thank you for rescuing me, not offer my body to you.'

He almost laughed with his relief. Clara might be the sexiest woman he'd ever met in his life but as soon as she'd mentioned the word 'virgin' he'd taken an automatic mental step back. 'I'm glad to hear it.'

'Good. I mean, you're a sexy man... Has anyone ever told you that?'

Taken aback at her nonchalant delivery, Marcelo could only answer honestly. 'Yes.'

Her expression turned to one of admiration. 'No false

modesty, even better. But you are a very sexy man and very handsome so I thought it best to check that you don't have a girlfriend before making the offer of dinner because I would be miffed if you were my boyfriend and you went out for dinner with another woman. So what do you think about dinner? It might have to wait until I get back to the UK and can sort out my bank accounts—King Pig has my purse. Oh, and my passport. Where are we flying to?'

'Ceres.'

'Your island?'

'Yes.'

'Is there a British embassy?'

'Of course.'

'Good. Can you drop me there please? I'll need to get a new passport issued. Do you know how long that'll take?'

'I'm afraid not.'

She shrugged. 'Never mind. It'll take as long as it takes. Do you think they'll let me take Bob in with me?'

'I have no idea.'

She pouted and blew her cheeks out. 'Okay, I'm going to have to improvise. But that's okay.' She blew her cheeks again then fixed her sparkling eyes back on him. 'I'll blag it.'

'What does *blag it* mean?' Educated in England though he'd been and as fluent in the language as he was in his own tongue, *blag it* was a term he'd never heard before.

'I'll just walk in with him and see what happens.' She nodded vigorously. 'Okay, that's the plan sorted. I'll get my passport sorted, beg for help for a flight home if they can't sort my banking out on Ceres—if I ask nicely, they might let me give them an IOU, sort Bob out—does your island have animal shelters?' Her face clouded. 'Will they let me keep him there while I arrange everything to bring him home with me?'

'I'm sure arrangements can be made for Bob,' he assured her, barely keeping up with the thread of her thoughts. Her mind must work at supersonic speed, jumping from thread to thread in the time it took a mere mortal to think about one thing.

She brightened like a switched-on light. 'Brilliant. So, once I've got access to my bank account, can I take you out for dinner as a thank you?'

Let Clara take him out to dinner…? Now that was a decision that did not come easily. On the one hand she was ravishing and sexy and, he had to admit, entertaining. On the other hand she was a virgin. That was a big warning klaxon in his head telling him to not touch, but then it occurred to him that he was a grown man fully capable of accepting a dinner date as a means of gratitude and not as a date-date, and that sharing a meal did not have to mean the inevitability of sharing a bed afterwards.

'On one condition,' he told her.

She looked at him expectantly.

'That you occasionally give your mouth a rest and my ears a break.'

She beamed. 'Deal.'

The first Clara knew that they'd reached their destination after what felt like hours flying over the Mediterranean was when the helicopter made its descent. They'd made one refuelling stop in which she'd given Bob a quick walk—Marcelo made a makeshift lead for him—and borrowed Marcelo's phone to call her colleague Liza in England who was looking after Samson and Delilah for her and make sure they were okay and reassure Liza that she wasn't dead and would be home soon to take them off her hands.

Holding onto Bob tightly, she jumped out. They'd landed in a field, the grass of which was a bit scratchy under her bare feet, but she wasn't going to complain. Rather scratchy feet than be married to King Pig! And the sun was hot and shining on her, which was nice. It felt like an age had passed since she'd last been out in the sun, and she spent a moment enjoying the warm rays on her face.

'Right, which way's the embassy?' she asked Marcelo after she'd profusely thanked his men and pilots for rescuing her.

A look of bemusement came over his handsome face. 'You're planning to walk?'

'I'm very fit. I walk with the dogs for miles every day at home.'

He smiled. 'It's already taken care of.' He pointed to the two cars waiting by the hangar. 'The second one will take you to the embassy.'

'Oh, you are fabulous, thank you.'

'You're welcome.'

Practically bouncing on her toes to reach his face, she planted a kiss on his cheek. The bristles were soft!

Allowing herself one final stare at the gorgeous face and fabulous ice-blue eyes, Clara debated whether or not to plant a kiss to his firm mouth, just to see what that felt like too, but decided against it. She didn't want him getting the wrong idea and thinking she'd changed her mind about offering her body to him.

Instead, she reached for his hand—oh, wow, it was huge compared to hers—and squeezed the fingers. 'I know I'm going to take you out to dinner once I've sorted the mess that is my life out, but I also know it in no way repays the debt I owe you. You can call it in any time or any place and I will fulfil it. I'm not exaggerating to say you've saved my life, and probably Bob's too.'

The lines around his eyes crinkled and he squeezed her fingers in return. 'It has been…an experience.'

She cackled with laughter, knowing exactly what he meant. Clara was well aware she'd been born without a filter but situations of heightened emotions always made her motormouth tendencies worse. She thought Marcelo had done very well not to at least threaten to gag her, so kudos to him.

'It certainly has,' she agreed. 'Thanks again.'

Flipping a final wave at him, she set off to the cars, keeping her focus on the one he'd designated as hers to stop herself from looking back at him.

She'd never wanted to look back at a man before. Another first.

This really was a day of firsts. She supposed it was because Marcelo was so ruddy attractive. If she was a girl who enjoyed sexual pleasure she would have had no hesitation in offering herself to him, but Clara preferred sensory pleasure of a more inanimate kind. Beautiful clothes and stylish furniture—even second-hand ones like she had—couldn't hurt you or lie to you or abuse your trust the way humans did. Lies really were the worst because it was lies that destroyed trust. Too many, especially when they came from the very people you were programmed by birth to trust, destroyed something fundamental inside you, making it impossible to believe in anyone. The only person who'd never abused Clara's trust was her mother.

Marcelo watched her walk away, as bedraggled, truculent and sexy a sight as he had ever seen even from the rear. Even Clara's walk was sexy. She wasn't trying to be sexy. She just was.

Look at those legs. Smears of grime from the helicopter streaked her calves, scraps of what had started the day as a beautiful and expensive wedding dress clung to the toned golden thighs. Her feet were bare, long untamed hair strewn…

'Wait,' he called.

She stopped walking and turned around.

Damn it. He couldn't let her walk into the embassy like that. Sure, they would help her but there was something so wonderfully uncaring about the way she carried her dishevelment that his heart twisted on itself.

Why didn't she care?

'Come back to my place,' he said before he could change his mind. 'Have a shower and some food. I'll get Alessia to bring some clothes for you…and then I'll take you to the embassy.'

Clara's lips swirled while her eyes narrowed with thought. Then her features loosened and she grinned. 'Do you promise not to lock me in a room and threaten to kill my dog if I don't marry you? Because I'm very keen to get home to my English dogs and my job.'

Marcelo laughed at the very idea. He had nothing against marriage. He would marry one day, but not for a long time. Civilian life was so unutterably boring that the thought of settling down any time soon and losing the only excitement to be found in this royal life was, for the moment, anathema. Mind-numbing tedium was his life. The agreement with his family when he joined the army was that once his military life was over, he'd become a working member of the Berruti royal family. That his military life had come to a premature end was irrelevant. The deal stood. The adventures he'd enjoyed in his army days were memories that would have to sustain his impulsive, thrill-seeking tendencies for the rest of his life because royal life consisted of duty and decorum.

It was a shame, he mused, that Clara was a virgin, and a proud one at that. If she wasn't, he'd have no hesitation in taking the seduction path with her. A very short-lived seduction. Never minding his aversion to settling down, he had a strong feeling that wherever Clara went, chaos followed. If there was one thing incompatible with royal life, it was chaos.

She was the least virginal woman he'd ever met. In fairness, he didn't think he'd known any virgins since his school days, unless he counted his sister, who he assumed was a virgin considering she never dated, but he would rather swim in an algae-ridden pool than bring the subject up and find out. It brought him out in hives just to think it. To his mind, virgins were decorous and shy. He doubted Clara had a shy bone in her delicious body.

And she *was* delicious. There was not an inch of that body he wasn't attracted to. He could still feel the softness of her plump mouth on his cheek and the pad of his finger from when he'd pressed against it to quieten her. His finger had sunk into it.

She was hot and delicious and the least virginal of virgins in the history of virgins. A conundrum to be figured out by a better, more patient man than him.

Or a woman? Was that why she was a virgin? Did she prefer her own sex?

But he'd seen interest in her eyes. He was certain of it. Marcelo knew when a woman was attracted to him and Clara didn't have the guile to try to hide it.

But that didn't mean anything. She'd blatantly told him he was handsome and sexy. She'd also told him she had no intention of sharing her body with him and there had been nothing in those honest brown eyes to contradict that.

But as the good lady herself would say, this was all moot. He'd feed her and give her the privacy to clean herself up, and then he would send her off to the embassy and never think of her again.

Folding his arms across his chest, he raised a brow. 'I promise.'

She gambolled back to him like a spring lamb. 'Then I accept. I'm starving!'

CHAPTER THREE

'THIS IS LIKE something from a fairy tale,' Clara enthused. She opened the window and stuck her face out so she could see more clearly the ancient amphitheatre nestled alongside the castle perched high in the rolling Ceres hills. As the car rounded a bend, she saw the amphitheatre separated the castle into two distinct complex stone buildings that were a mishmash of shapes and architecture that was impressively theatrical. Here was classic medieval and renaissance and surrealist architecture blended into something fantastical, and it was huge, both the castle and the grounds. 'And I thought the house I grew up in was big! Has your family always lived here?'

'For five hundred years,' Marcelo answered.

'I bet you had some amazing games of hide-and-seek.'

'I've never played.'

The car came to a stop as she twisted to face him. 'Really? Is that because your family is all royal and stuffy?'

His lips twitched. 'Not at all. We just played different games when I was a child.'

She nudged him with her elbow. 'Alessia invited me here for the Easter holidays once but I got expelled before it could happen and my brother wouldn't let me come as punishment. I would have got you all playing hide-and-seek.'

Her door was opened and she jumped out, already itching to explore the place. It would take weeks to explore it all. Months! Bob was just as enamoured, racing in big circles around the lawn that edged the section of the castle they were parked in front of.

Marcelo joined her. 'I never knew that.'

'What?'

'That you were going to stay with us.'

'Stay with Alessia,' she corrected, then added kindly, 'But I'm sure we would have let you play with us. But probably not your brother—Alessia said he was a right bossy-boots.'

'I would suggest you don't mention that to him,' he advised drily.

'I doubt I'll be here long enough to meet him but if I do…' She mimed zipping her lips.

The wide, full lips pulled into a grin. 'Come on, Clara Chaos, let's get some food inside you.'

Marcelo couldn't stop himself from soaking Clara's reaction to the castle interior. From the private reception room they entered and all the way down the wide corridor that led to his private quarters, her head craned this way and that, and she kept stopping to admire the artwork and, in some cases, pull a face of distaste.

When they reached his door, he unlocked it and indicated for her to enter.

'Whoa…' Her eyes were bright as she did a full circle to take everything in. 'This is yours?'

'My private quarters, yes.'

'Has it always been yours?'

'No, I lived with my siblings in my parents' quarters until I joined the army. These quarters were given to me when I turned twenty-one to use as a base when I was on leave.'

She grinned knowingly. 'Was that so you could bring women back and guarantee some privacy?'

Her cheery bluntness took him aback again.

'I bet women have always chased after you,' she said, kneeling to put Bob on the floor. Marcelo tried not to wince to see the puppy immediately roll over the thousand-year-old Persian rug.

'Haven't they?'

Not realising her comment had required an answer, Marcelo found himself at a loss at what to say. Clara was just too disarming in both her physical presence and her unnerving habit of uttering whatever came into her head.

In the end she gave a nonchalant shrug. 'You're a prince, you're rich and you're handsome. Stands to reason women would chase after you.' There was a slight narrowing of her eyes. 'But I bet you're a man who prefers to do the chasing himself. Do you ever pretend to be a commoner?'

'For what purpose?'

'To see if they still want you without all the trappings. I would. I mean, let's face it, King Pig only wanted me for my blood—that the future King of England is something like my thirteenth cousin apparently makes me a catch. And I'm poor! Anyway, is it okay for me to take a shower? I feel really grubby.'

Feeling like he'd just let a tornado into his quarters, Marcelo led her up the stairs to his guest room, which had its own bathroom attached to it. 'Help yourself to whatever you need,' he said. 'I'll get Alessia to drop some clothes over and get the chef to rustle something up for you to eat. Any dietary requirements?'

'I hate broad beans if that counts?'

'I will be sure to tell Chef that. Enjoy your shower, or you can have a bath if you prefer.' An image flashed in his mind of her reclining naked in the bath. He pushed it firmly aside and added, 'Please, take your time. There is no rush.'

She beamed. 'Thank you. Can you make sure Bob gets something to eat soon? He's only got a small belly and needs to be fed regularly.'

'I remember,' he assured her. At their earlier fuel stop Clara had managed to charm—or, more likely, bamboozle—one of the pilots into giving up his beef sandwich so she could feed it in small chunks to the puppy. She hadn't taken a scrap of it for herself. 'I will sort it as a priority.'

'You are clearly taking the path straight to heaven, thank you.'

Still smiling, she closed the bathroom door. The distinct sound of it locking echoed through the oak.

Marcelo gazed down at the fluffball at his feet and sighed before lifting him into his arms. 'I don't know about you, Bob,' he said in his native tongue, 'but your owner is a unique force of nature.'

Bob licked his face in agreement.

This was one amazing bathroom in one amazing set of private quarters in one amazing castle. The House of Fernandez's palace in Monte Cleure was beautiful too and comparable in size, but the Berruti castle had character and intrigue seeped in its walls. Well, the walls she'd seen, which was only a teeny fraction of it all.

Soaking in the huge roll-top tub, Clara happily admired the frescoed ceiling high above her featuring naked cherubs and nymphs splashing and swimming in a natural pool in the middle of a wood. Very sensual. Very fitting for the man it belonged to. If this was Marcelo's guest bathroom, what kind of bathroom did he have for his own private use? If the rest of his private quarters were an indication, she'd guess something akin to a Roman bath.

When boredom kicked in, she washed her hair, scrubbed her body, grabbed the towel closest to hand and climbed out.

Marcelo's guest bathroom came equipped with a full array of toiletries and after drying herself, she brushed her teeth with a new brush but was disappointed not to find any cosmetics. Clara loved wearing make-up, felt naked without it. Maybe Alessia would let her borrow some. She looked forward to seeing her old friend. Alessia had been the only girl at their horrible boarding school Clara had liked.

Securing the towel around herself, she stepped into the adjoining room. It matched her prison cell for size and had the requisite four-poster bed, but it had far more personality and the most fabulous pale blue satin sofa that wasn't really a sofa, more a four-bottoms-wide padded chair with gold legs and arms. Plus, if she found herself imprisoned in it, she was only one floor off the ground and could easily jump to safety.

'Marcelo?' she called as she left the room. When there was no answer, she wandered down the stairs and into the living room. As she called his name a second time, French doors opened and he stepped in from his private garden with Bob at his heels.

'There you are,' she said, kneeling to scoop up Bob, who'd come tearing over to her. 'Did you manage to get any clean clothes for me?'

From the look of his damp hair and the fresh scent emanating from him, Clara guessed Marcelo had showered. He'd changed out of the tuxedo into a pair of tight-fitting blue jeans and white V-necked T-shirt that admirably displayed his sexy, muscular physique. Oh, he looked *good*. And that scent!

He turned his head away from her and spoke through

what were clearly clenched teeth. 'I put them on the guest bed for you. Didn't you hear me call out to you?'

'No. You should have shouted. Is something the matter?'

'No.'

'Are you sure? You seem very tense.'

His chest rose. The square jaw was definitely locked. 'Alessia isn't in so I've given you some of my own clothes to wear.'

'Ha! You're twice the size of me.'

'They're clean. Go and get changed.'

'Okay… You sure you're okay?'

He inclined his head curtly, still not looking at her. 'Food will be ready in a few minutes.'

'Cool.' She stepped to him, ready to hand the puppy over if the answer to her question was no. 'Is Bob allowed upstairs with me?'

'No… Yes. That's fine.'

Marcelo held his breath until she'd left the room and he heard her footsteps bounding up the stairs.

Sinking into the nearest chair, he pressed the palm of his hand to his forehead and tried to rid himself of the image of Clara dressed in nothing but a tiny towel. It was not a sight he'd been expecting and the effect had been immediate and potent. He'd had to hold his breath to stop the warm scent of freshly bathed Clara from dousing his senses and avert his eyes from the feast that was her knockout body wrapped in nothing but a small towel.

His evasions hadn't been quick enough. Both her scent and the image had burned into him. *Dio*, his heart was still thumping. His loins still throbbed.

She had been oblivious to the effect. If any other woman had paraded before him in a tiny towel he'd have assumed it was deliberate, but Clara had acted as if it were perfectly normal.

Couldn't she have wrapped herself in one of the over-sized towels? Did she have to select one that barely skimmed her buttocks?

He took some long breaths and reminded himself that in an hour or so he'd be able to send Clara to the embassy with his conscience clear. He'd make a call on her behalf, he decided. Smooth her path. He was a prince of the country, his word held sway. He'd put all his resources at Clara's and the embassy's disposal. Anything to get this danger-ously sexy but untouchable woman off his island and allow his equilibrium to return to its normal state.

But then she joined him in the dining room and his heart thumped hard again.

'I need your help,' she said, and lifted the navy polo shirt he'd given her to her waist. The belt he'd provided her with to hold his jeans up was too big even fastened at the tightest notch. 'These are going to fall down. Can you make another hole in the belt for me? I don't mind if you'd rather not ruin it doing that as the polo shirt is long enough for me to wear as a dress, but I haven't got any knickers on and if there's a gust of wind when I leave the castle I might frighten your fellow countrymen.'

He gritted his teeth to fight off the imagery and beck-oned the nearest servant to fetch him a sharp, pointed knife.

'Take the belt off,' he said in a curter tone than intended.

'Okay.' She pulled it off and, as she passed it to him, the jeans fell to her ankles. Stepping out of them, she picked them up and put them on the back of the chair next to hers and took her seat. 'What's for dinner?'

He filled his lungs with much needed air before answer-ing. 'Roast mushroom gnocchi.'

'It smells wonderful.'

Their bowls were filled for them and a knife for Marcelo to make a notch in the belt placed beside him.

'You've got that face again,' Clara observed after barely a minute of silence while they ate.

'What face?'

'*That* face. All tense, like you're sucking on a particularly sour lemon. Don't you like gnocchi?'

She was observant. That supersonic brain didn't miss anything.

How would she respond if he imitated her unfiltered bluntness and said, *If I'm tense, it's because you're the sexiest creature I've ever met and you've candidly declared that you're not wearing any knickers and I can clearly see you're not wearing a bra either and right now I can't stop my mind from imagining you naked and my taste buds are salivating to imagine the taste of your skin, and I feel as horny as the horniest of teenagers.*

'I have a headache,' he answered, hoping she would take the hint and keep quiet for a little longer.

It wasn't what she said that made him wish for her silence, he recognised. It was her voice. The more he listened to it, the more he wanted to listen. It had a musicality that was as alluring and entertaining as the rest of her.

Clara Sinclair aroused *all* his senses. And more.

'Have you taken any painkillers?' she asked.

'Not yet.'

She managed another minute of silence before piping up with, 'I put my dirty clothes in the laundry basket but if you get me a bag, I'll bin them. Unless you have an incinerator?'

He shook his head and helped himself to more parmesan. He didn't trust himself to look at her, not when his eyes itched to study her like a rare masterpiece. Many women stripped of their make-up looked washed out. Not

Clara. Her natural luminosity shone through and elevated her beauty.

When Marcelo had been a child, his father would drag him around the castle trying to pique his interest in the thousands of pieces of art in the royal collection. Occasionally—very occasionally—a painting or sculpture would capture his interest and then he would be captivated enough to return to it time and time again. Those particular items were now housed here in his private quarters.

He wanted to stare at Clara as he still often gazed at those masterpieces.

As soon as he finished eating, Marcelo set to work on the belt. Once he'd stabbed the hole in it, he handed it back to her.

Smiling her thanks, she snatched her jeans off the chair beside her, threaded the belt through then stuck her legs in them and hopped onto her feet. Twisting around so her back was to him, she pulled them up her thighs. Unprepared for the glimpse of peachy buttock as the denim was pulled over her bottom, Marcelo was unable to stop himself from snapping, 'Do you not have *any* modesty?'

She spun around. Startled brown eyes fixed on him. 'What are you talking about?'

He gritted his teeth. He didn't know whether to laugh or shout at her blitheness. 'I just saw your bottom.'

And coming so soon after she'd nonchalantly walked around in front of him in a teeny towel, an image he'd been doing his damned best to scrub from his retinas, had the effect of adding fuel to the fire he'd only just brought down to a moderate simmer.

She fastened the belt. 'So? It's only flesh. We all have it.'
Yes, but not everyone's flesh is as delectable as yours.
'Did you parade in front of Dominic in a towel?' he

asked tautly, not because he thought she would have done but to make a point.

Plonking herself back on her seat, she inched the chair back and began rolling the jeans up at the ankles. 'Dominic gave me the heebie-jeebies from the word go. You don't.'

'I'm still a man, Clara.'

'And?'

'You're a beautiful woman,' he told her stiffly. A very beautiful, incredibly sexy woman. A woman who, if she wasn't a virgin, he would seduce without a second thought.

'And?'

'I see you don't suffer from false modesty either.'

'I can't help how I look any more than you can help how you look,' she said with her usual bluntness.

He took hold of his glass of water and held it tightly as he brought it to his lips. 'It doesn't bother you, parading around half-naked in a towel and allowing a glimpse of your backside to a man?' Surely she must see the danger?

'I wasn't parading and I didn't allow you a glimpse. I turned my back to you so you wouldn't be embarrassed about seeing my vagina.'

He almost choked on the water he was about to swallow.

She covered her mouth, clearly suppressing a giggle. 'I would never have pegged you as prudish.'

That annoyed him. 'I am not prudish.'

'Then why are you acting prudish? I thought you'd seen plenty of female flesh in your adult life?'

'There is a time and a place.'

'We're in your private quarters. Who else is going to see me?' she asked with infuriating reasonableness.

'That is not the point.'

'But it's *my* point.'

'You're not worried I might be overtaken by lust?'

'Why? Are you?'

'Of course not.'

'Then what's your problem?'

The woman could turn a saint to drink. 'Your lack of self-preservation!'

She swirled her lips, a groove appearing on her forehead. 'It's very touching that you care but you don't need to worry about me. To me, human flesh is just flesh, the wrapping of the human body, but if you're worried about your own control then don't—if I thought you were in any way a monster, I wouldn't be sitting here, and if it makes you feel better, I've been taking self-defence classes for years.'

Spotting the contradiction in this, he said, 'Because of the threat men pose to you?'

But she dismissed his assumption with a, 'No, because of the threat they pose to my dogs.'

He was incredulous. 'Your dogs?'

'Dognapping has become increasingly common and I'm not going to let anyone take mine from me without a fight.' The serious hue of her eyes turned into a sparkle. 'I can show you my moves if you want?'

Now he'd heard everything. 'You think you could *fight* me?'

Her eyebrows waggled with mischief. 'Wanna try?'

'No!'

'Is that because you're so much bigger than me and think you would hurt me? Because I assure you, it's far more likely that I would hurt you.'

Surely she couldn't believe that, he thought incredulously. He was big enough and strong enough to snap her in two. 'Would you have been able to fight Dominic off when he tried to force himself on you?' he challenged. It was a challenge that sent nausea roiling violently in his stomach as, for the first time, he realised what the implications would have been if he hadn't rescued her that morning.

The sparkle faded to nothing and he knew Clara was thinking the exact same thing.

'I was prepared to,' she said, speaking quietly for the first time. 'I would have fought like hell. I tried to fight him when he first locked me up but he had his bodyguards flanking him and they stopped me. He always had them at his side when he dealt with me.'

Bile rose up his throat. 'Did he hurt you when he dealt with you?'

She shook her head and gave her first bitter smile. 'He didn't want my skin marred for the wedding photos.'

The bile flooded his mouth. It was the most rancid taste he'd ever experienced and, for the first time in his life, Marcelo wished to harm someone. Properly harm them. Maim them.

Before he could swallow the foul taste, his private secretary tapped on the door and slipped into the room.

What she whispered in his ear made his stomach pitch.

Maintaining his composure, he rose to his feet. 'Excuse me,' he said to Clara. 'My mother has requested a meeting with me. Have some dessert. I shouldn't be long.'

And then, on his return, he would see her into a car and wave goodbye to the sexiest, most infuriating woman he'd ever met in his life.

'You cannot be serious?'

The looks on the faces of Marcelo's parents and siblings on the other side of the table, all convened for this family emergency, told him they were.

He kneaded his temples in an effort to temper the forming headache. 'I can't marry her. Dear God, Clara Sinclair is completely unsuited to being a member of *any* royal family let alone this one.'

'Dominic thought she was good enough for him,' his mother pointed out.

'Dominic was, by Clara's own admission, desperate.'

'Our situation will become desperate if you don't,' Amadeo, his brother, said. 'As Mother said, it doesn't have to be for ever, only a year or two, just long enough to be convincing.'

'Even a day is too long. She has no decorum and no filter on her mouth.'

'Then you will have to teach her.'

'I am not a miracle worker.'

His mother put her hand flat on the table and leaned forward. 'What matters is the public's perception. This has the potential to destroy us. Marrying her is the only way to mitigate the trouble your actions, however noble they were, have brought on this family.'

Marcelo looked from face to face. Beneath the implacable facades lay compassion. They all knew he wasn't ready to marry.

But they knew—and he knew—that this mess was a situation of his own making and that it was his responsibility to fix it before the snowball he'd set off turned into an avalanche.

He threw his hands in the air. 'Okay, I'll ask her, but she won't agree to it. Clara doesn't want to get married. She wants to get back to England and resume her life.'

'Then it's up to you to convince her,' his father said. 'For all our sakes.'

CHAPTER FOUR

FOR WANT OF something to do in Marcelo's absence, Clara decided to clear the table, but no sooner had she started when two members of his staff bustled in and insisted she leave it to them.

Was there anything worse than boredom? she wondered. She'd been bored rigid in her Monte Cleure prison cell but at least she'd successfully kept her mind occupied thinking of escape routes and ways to torture Dominic, and dreaming up insults and cutting remarks to her women gaolers who so rarely left her side.

She had no idea why it had upset her when Marcelo challenged her about whether she'd have been able to fight Dominic off. It had got to the stage where she believed rescue would never come so she'd made her plans for it, and those plans were simply to fight until her last breath. It had amused her to imagine the public's reaction to her wedding night death. Better than the alternative of imagining her own corpse. The thought of her own death as a concept didn't particularly bother her. So long as her animals back home were taken care of then she was happy to go. It wasn't that she didn't enjoy life—she did, very much, even if at times it felt a little lonely—but more that she didn't fear the pain and grief for those she loved, mainly because there wasn't anyone left who loved her. It was a simple fact. She thought some of her colleagues might miss her, some might even shed a tear, but they wouldn't *grieve* her and would probably quickly forget her. Even Samson and Delilah, her dogs, would transfer their affection to Liza. Dogs lived in the moment. It was an ethos Clara tried hard to emulate.

Maybe Marcelo's challenge had upset her because she'd had a fleeting moment of wondering what if? As in, what if Marcelo hadn't rescued her?

Clara didn't deal with what ifs. They were pointless. When bad stuff happened the only way forward was to dust yourself down, put it behind you and carry on.

How funny, though, that he should be so prudish about flesh. It hadn't occurred to her that he'd be uncomfortable to see her in a towel. Marcelo had had lots of lovers.

She remembered catching a glimpse of him when she was fifteen and he'd turned up at her boarding school one Saturday to take Alessia out. Clara had been confined to her room that weekend for some misdemeanour or other, and she'd sat on her windowsill watching the bustle of activity unfolding in the grounds when the tall, gorgeous stranger had caught her eye. She'd guessed by Alessia's reaction that he was one of her brothers and when she'd been subsequently put in a room with the Ceresian princess some months later, she'd asked about him. And that had been that. Clara hadn't given him another thought in the following years, apart from the times when she flicked through social media and caught a glimpse of his name. She always followed the links, always hoping to find he'd settled down with one of the beautiful women he was often pictured with. Any man who went out of his way to take his little sister on jollies from boarding school was all right in Clara's book and deserved to find happiness. Andrew hadn't made a single visit in all her years there.

She supposed that's why it hadn't occurred to her that her flesh would make Marcelo uncomfortable because, to a degree, she trusted him so it hadn't occurred to her that it would be more appropriate—how she *hated* that word. She'd lost count of the times her teachers would say, 'That is not appropriate behaviour, Miss Sinclair.'—to leave the room before putting the jeans back on. The towel couldn't be helped as she genuinely hadn't seen the clothes on the bed, but even if she had, the same degree of trust in Marcelo applied. He would not lay an unwanted finger on her.

Trust, however limited, in a man? In *any* human? This really was a day of firsts.

Helping herself to a slice of the lemon mousse brought in for her, she stretched her legs out and wriggled her bare toes and contemplated that it was just as well she'd be leaving for the embassy soon. Marcelo made her feel all funny inside. More nervous energy than usual ran through her veins and she kept staring at the dining room door like she was waiting with bated breath for his return. This was curious and a touch disconcerting. But only a touch. Lots of women, she imagined, would have a fit of the vapours to be in his presence so in comparison the effect he had on her was minor.

All the same, she found herself straightening when he returned to the dining room.

He closed the door behind him.

One look at his face told her something terrible had happened.

She half rose from her chair. 'Has someone died?'

A look of amused but pained torture contorted his gorgeous features, and he shook his head, lowering himself into his seat and gripping at his hair.

He closed his eyes for a long moment and, when he

opened them, fixed them directly on her. 'There is no easy way to say this.'

'Then just say it,' she encouraged. 'Straight to the point is always best.'

The corners of his lips twitched for a moment before his shoulders rose and he took a deep breath. 'I need to convince you to marry me.'

Marcelo watched Clara carefully, bracing himself for whatever unpredictable reaction she would give.

The large eyes widened. The plump mouth sucked in so hard her cheeks sucked in with them, disappearing until her lips were the size and shape of a bird's beak.

And then she covered the bird's beak and half her face with her hand, and her shoulders began to shake. To his alarm, tears spilled over the hand smothering her mouth but the alarm barely had time to register for she whipped the hand away, slapped it on the table and threw her head back.

She wasn't crying. She was laughing. She was convulsed with it.

She slapped the table a number of times and must have swiped at the tears a dozen times before she regained control of herself, and even then her chest and shoulders continued to shake.

'Marry you?' she finally managed to splutter. 'I've heard everything now. And you're *serious*!' More laughter echoed around the room. 'You *are*. I can see it on your face. You want me to marry you! Is that what your mother wanted to see you for? Is this her idea? No way it's yours. She must be desperate!'

Marcelo had left his family feeling as if he had the weight of the entire castle on his shoulders, but now, with Clara's laughter ringing in his ears and her glee shining before his eyes, he felt that weight lift.

He'd imagined tantrums. He'd imagined her throwing things at him. He'd imagined curses. He'd imagined her making a running jump through one of the dining room windows and then continuing to run until she found the British embassy.

Knowing she preferred straight to the point honesty, he said, 'Yes. Unfortunately my rescuing you did not go undetected—your guards broke the door down and managed to get some pictures of us hanging from the helicopter. Dominic has launched a full diplomatic war and is making threats against our nation. To get public and political opinion on our side, not just here on Ceres but in Europe, my mother and the rest of my family think we should marry as soon as possible and spin things that you and I are a love match and that I stole you away from Dominic because I had been a stubborn fool who didn't realise until it was nearly too late how much I love you and couldn't bear to see you married to someone else.'

'That's what your family thinks?' There was a flash of astuteness. 'And what do *you* think?'

He sighed and pushed his chair back. Rising to his feet, he said, 'I think I need a drink. Want one?'

She stretched her legs out, hooked her ankles together and folded her arms across her ample breasts. 'Why not?'

He removed a full bottle of fifteen-year-old Scotch and two glasses from the cabinet at the far end of the room and carried them to the table. Pouring them both a hefty measure, he slid one to Clara and took a large drink from the other.

He let the welcome fire burn down his throat and said, 'I'm afraid that I agree with my family.'

Once his mother had spelled out how quickly and spectacularly the fallout of his rescue had spread, there had been no other conclusion to reach.

It was his mother's disappointment that smarted the most. That it was deserved disappointment only made it worse.

Marcelo had let his ego and need for excitement over-rule his good sense, and now Dominic had a clear photograph of Marcelo's face as he held tightly to Clara in her wedding dress hanging from a helicopter flying above the House of Fernandez palace. Marcelo was media savvy enough to know it was going to be press dynamite.

His family were right to be angry with him. He was furious with himself. Three years of duty and self-control thrown away in one impulsive action causing a diplomatic incident that could easily escalate. Unlike Ceres, which had a ruling government, Monte Cleure had a ruling monarchy, which meant Dominic was in charge. The Berruti royal family were mere figureheads of their great nation, an anachronistic relic of the past kept alive only because of the affection of its people. It had been drilled into Marcelo and his siblings since they first learned to talk how precarious their positions and titles were. Their castle was wholly owned by the family, its upkeep and maintenance paid for by the income from foreign tourists—they allowed Ceresians in for free—but everything else that came with their position was subject to keeping the public and politicians onside.

Ceres people were romantics at heart. They would forgive a tale of madness caused by love more easily than they would a tale of madness caused by ego, boredom and a loss of self-control.

'Have you got a copy of the photo of us?' she asked once she'd had a sip of her Scotch.

'On my phone.' He brought up the picture that had been forwarded to him and passed it to her.

She studied it with avid interest. 'You can't see my face to identify me but that's definitely you.'

The guard who'd taken the photo had captured Marcelo's face in its entirety.

'When I manage to get a new phone you'll have to send it to me,' she added, pushing the phone back to him. 'I might get it made into a poster and stick it on my bedroom wall…although I might have to photoshop my bum—it looks huge!'

If he wasn't so filled with anger at himself and the dangerous situation he'd put his family in, he would have laughed.

'If I refuse to marry you, what happens?' she asked. 'Do you lock me in a room and put armed guards outside my door to stop me escaping, then drag me up the aisle and threaten to kill my dog if I make a scene?'

Marcelo raised an incredulous eyebrow that she even had to ask that, then had another drink of his Scotch and rubbed his forehead. 'I can't force you to marry me. My family have much influence in this country but our power is limited. And if I could force you to marry me, I wouldn't—I didn't rescue you from that bastard to force you into an unwanted life with me.'

Curiosity danced in her eyes. 'Then why did you?'

'Boredom.'

'Boredom?'

Marcelo grunted and shook his head in self-recrimination. That's what his actions boiled down to. Boredom. Three years of unswerving, mind-numbing tedium dressed as duty had been smashed apart by one loss of tightly leashed self-control.

He must never let it happen again.

A slow grin spread over Clara's face. 'If I marry you, I guarantee you won't be bored.'

That pulled him up, and he studied her open face. 'You're not considering it?'

The grin didn't dim a jot as she downed her drink and pushed the glass back to him. 'Fill me up, big boy. And yourself. My demands don't come cheap.'

He couldn't believe she was even contemplating it. 'You are serious?'

'I'm in your debt, remember? I mean, you can't have forgotten. You only rescued me, what, ten hours ago?'

Was that all the time that had passed?

He refilled her glass. 'Marrying me goes far beyond any debt you owe me.'

'Not to my mind. You saved my life and Bob's life. I'm happy to be a princess for a while if you're certain it will help…' Her eyes narrowed slightly. 'We wouldn't have to share a bed, would we?'

'No.' His answer was emphatic but her question made him reel as sleeping arrangements were something he hadn't yet considered. There hadn't been time to consider anything other than his mother's forceful if sympathetic insistence that he fix the mess he'd created for their family and their people by marrying Clara.

'And we wouldn't be expected to stay married for ever, would we?' she asked before he could consider the other implications of marriage to this truculently sexy, wholly unsuitable creature.

But his body was already considering it, a tightening in his loins…

'I mean, would we be allowed to divorce?' she continued. 'It wouldn't bother me if we didn't but I assume you want to settle down in a real marriage at some point? By the way, are you okay? You've gone all face-sucking lemons again.'

Realising his fists were clenched, Marcelo loosened

them and tried to loosen his jaw too. Clara didn't miss a trick and, unlike him, didn't need time to consider things, her supersonic brain taking everything in and digesting it and moving straight to the tangents and implications of each one.

'Divorce is allowed here after two years of marriage,' he said. 'We would have to put on a show of being together for, say, a year, and then quietly go our separate ways—'

'We can let people believe I'm homesick for England!' she interrupted enthusiastically, his answer clearly having put her mind at ease.

'That would work, I'm sure, and then after a year of quiet separation, file for divorce.'

'Cool.'

'Cool?' he echoed in disbelief.

'It all sounds very reasonable. But I do have demands… well, requests. I'll marry you whether you agree to them or not.'

'Name them.'

She held her hand up and, as she listed her requests, ticked them off with her fingers. 'I want Samson and Delilah brought over to live here, preferably by car. And clothes. Lots of beautiful clothes. And cosmetics. The good stuff.' The good stuff like her mum used to have. Clara's memories of her mum had faded over time but the scent of expensive make-up could evoke her face as clearly as if she was standing right in front of her. It would evoke too the beautiful clothes her mother had worn with such panache. Much better to remember her looking and smelling wonderful than to remember how she'd been at the end. 'And I would like a donation made to the animal sanctuary I work at to cover all their costs for the next five years and a decent lump sum paid to my colleague Liza—she's the one I called earlier who's been looking after Samson and Delilah for me.'

'What else?'

'If it's not too selfish a request, when we separate, can you buy me a house in the English countryside? Nothing too big, two bedrooms will be ample, a big one for me and my dogs, and one for my clothes. And I would like a bit of land so I can open my own animal sanctuary. So maybe a house with an outbuilding?'

'Anything else?'

She thought hard before giving a decisive shake of her head. 'No. That's everything.'

If Marcelo's incredulity pulled any tighter it would snap. 'Do you know how much my family is worth?'

Her shoulders rose in a don't-care shrug.

'Billions.' Along with the castle that was their main home, the Berruti royal family had a portfolio of assets spread across their own island, neighbouring Sicily and mainland Italy that had been owned by them for centuries. Acutely aware that, though loved by their public, Ceresian society had evolved and that they could no longer justify any of their lifestyle being funded from the public purse, beginning with his grandfather, the family had actively monetised those assets and cannily added to them, and paid a crack team of people to run it all for them under the family's supervision. All that and the royal art collection too.

Not a flicker of being impressed crossed Clara's face. If anything, there was a flicker of distaste there.

'Money doesn't interest you?'

'I only care that I have enough of it to live on. Money turns people into monsters,' she replied in as flat a tone as he'd heard from those lips before.

'My family are not monsters.' If they'd been monsters

he wouldn't feel so rotten for imperilling them with his rash actions.

The grin returned. 'I know that. Maybe your family are the exceptions? I take it you've warned them what a nightmare I am and how utterly unsuited I am for the role of a princess?'

His mouth dropped open. Not only did she have a supersonic brain but she was a mind reader as well.

She sniggered and drank more of her Scotch. 'I'll take that as a yes. Doesn't that just prove how desperate King Pig was for a wife? You might need to gag me when we're out in public though. So, when are we getting married?'

Marcelo rubbed his aching head. 'You are sure you agree to this? It is a big thing I'm asking of you.'

He shouldn't be trying to talk her out of the sacrifice she was prepared to make when the alternative could mean the destruction of the Berruti royal family.

'You're not asking, I'm volunteering.' Her shoulders rose again. This time he wasn't quick enough to avert his eyes from seeing her unbound breasts move under the polo shirt with the motion, and he had to clench his teeth to counter the stab of lust that lanced him from it.

Dio, he needed sleep. A full eight hours would do the trick of restoring the connection between the brain in his head and the brain between his legs.

'It'll be fun,' she added.

'I can't guarantee that.' Fun was the last word he'd use to describe his life.

'I can,' she refuted brightly.

Despite everything, laughter burst out of him, and, finally accepting that this was the path he had to follow for the next year, he raised his glass. 'To a successful fake marriage.'

Eyes brimming with merriment, she clinked her glass to it. 'Long may it not continue.'

In unison, they tipped their drinks down their throats.

The deal was sealed.

God help him.

Clara tapped quietly on Marcelo's bedroom door; quietly in case he was asleep. She'd nearly fallen asleep herself when she'd remembered something and sat bolt upright.

To her relief, the handle turned and the door partially opened. Marcelo's face appeared in the gap. Straight away she saw he had no top on and found herself in the novel situation of trying to stop her stare from drifting down so she could get a good look at his naked chest.

Her eyes won and she dipped her stare to eye level and caught a glimpse of broad golden shoulders and defined pecs with a healthy smattering of dark hair whorled in the centre.

'Is something the matter?' he asked, and she quickly looked back at his face.

Probably it was having only the light from her bedroom illuminating the hallway causing it but he looked even more gorgeous than when she'd wished him a goodnight, so gorgeous that as she gazed into his eyes a warmth spread through her like a steadily creeping flush. Marcelo's voice sounded more gravelly too. Sexier. For the first time she noticed the hint of an accent in it.

'Clara? Is something the matter?' he repeated.

She cleared her throat. 'Yes,' she replied quickly, and castigated herself for being distracted by a man with no top on. How silly was that? All the same, with the faint scent of warm male now hitting her senses, she thought it prudent to step back before continuing. 'Well, it's something that matters to me. I know I said I didn't have any further requests but can I keep Bob?'

A faint smile appeared on his shadowed face. 'I assumed that was a given.'

She put her hand to her chest—Lord, her heart was thumping—and expelled her relief. 'Thank you. That's everything.' She sidestepped away from his door. 'Sorry for disturbing you.' Another sidestep nearer to her own door. 'Goodnight.'

'Goodnight, Clara.'

She threw herself back into what was no longer a guest room but *her* room and tried not to slam the door behind her in her haste.

What on earth had just happened?

What had possessed her body to act as if she'd never seen a topless man before? She'd seen plenty of naked male chests in magazines and on social media. Loads. And she was quite sure she'd seen her brother topless once, when she'd been around ten in an exceptionally hot summer, so hot that even Andrew had felt compelled to remove his stuffy tweed suit. Or she might have dreamt that last part. Dream or not, thanks to technology, the male body was no mystery to her, so why she should react in such a way was *bizarre*.

Climbing back under the sheets, she gazed at the canopy of her bed and breathed deeply. Hopefully lots of air in her lungs would settle her heartbeat. She let her arm drop over the side so Bob could nuzzle back into her hand as he liked to do before he fell asleep. She'd given him a couple of her pillows to use as a bed. Marcelo was taking her shopping tomorrow. She'd ask if he would buy Bob a proper bed.

Who'd have thought she'd end the day with a reminder to herself to ask Prince Marcelo Berruti to buy a dog bed?

What an extraordinary day it had been. She'd woken

feeling sick, certain the day was going to end with her death or something worse and here she was now, sleeping in a room every bit as sumptuous as her prison cell but with the door unlocked and no fear in her heart, and that was entirely down to Marcelo. He'd saved her life and the life of her defenceless puppy. He'd put his own life on the line for her—at the time she'd been too caught in the moment to appreciate the inherent danger of his rescue—and the more she thought about it, the more her heart swelled with gratitude that a stranger would go to such lengths for her.

Deep down she hadn't believed that anyone would care enough to attempt the rescue, and she didn't care that he'd done it because, by his own admittance, he was bored. She was alone in this bed, unharmed and whole because of him, and for that she would gladly pledge a year of her life to him. He was honest too, a trait Clara valued above everything. He could have spun her a tale about wanting to rescue a damsel in distress because *it was the right thing to do* or some other such nonsense, but he'd stuck with the truth. Kudos to him. But his rescue of her and failure to see the potential fallout of his actions signified another of his personality traits—impetuousness. She guessed that must be a nature thing because ten years in the military would have taught him to use his brain as well as his brawn.

Being practically twice her height and definitely twice her width, Marcelo had a *lot* of brawn. She hoped he continued wearing white T-shirts. They looked good on him and really flattered his physique—his pecs were *amazing*, and even better, as she now knew, in the flesh. The work that must go into maintaining them! There had been a time earlier that evening when they'd been discussing how they were going to handle things over the next few weeks and she'd noticed his nipples through his T-shirt. She'd felt a mad urge to tweak one of them. What was *that* all about?

Weird. Hopefully she wouldn't get too many mad urges like that in the future. Or that other weird moment when her fingers had tingled to touch the soft bristles of his stubbly beard again. Why that had happened she couldn't figure out. Her curiosity had already been sated on that score, so why want to touch it again?

When Bob left her hand to curl up on his makeshift bed, Clara lifted her now numb arm and did likewise. Burrowing under the sheets, she continued to think about Marcelo.

When sleep eventually enveloped her, Marcelo's face was the last thing her conscious mind saw.

CHAPTER FIVE

CLARA'S DELIGHT TO find Alessia in the living area when she came down the next morning was evident by the joy on her face even before she threw herself at her. 'It is so good to see you,' she enthused, embracing her tightly. 'Thank you, thank you for sending your brother to rescue me.'

'It was nothing,' Alessia laughed. 'Can you let me go now? I'm having trouble breathing.'

'Sorry.' Giggling, Clara unwound her arms but put her hands on Alessia's biceps so she could study her properly. 'You look fantastic.'

'Thank you. You're looking good too.'

'Ha! I look like I've been dragged through a hedge backwards. I haven't even brushed my hair yet.'

Marcelo watched the exchange with the strangest tightness in his chest. Clara was still wearing his polo shirt. It still fell to her knees. He was still unable to eradicate from his mind that beneath it she was naked. Hours he'd spent, lying in his bed, trying to switch his brain off, but the current running through his veins had been too strong for sleep to come easily. There had been too much running through his head too.

One impulsive act in three years had changed his life irrevocably.

If he'd stuck to the original plan, Clara would have still

been rescued but his presence in the wedding chapel would have been proof of his innocence in the matter. There would be no diplomatic or trade threat to his country.

He still couldn't wrap his head around how quickly she'd agreed to marry him. She could have refused and there would have been nothing he could do about it. But she'd had no hesitation in agreeing to it. To insisting.

What kind of woman did that?

A woman like Clara Sinclair.

As short as their time together had been, it had been more than enough for him to learn a great deal about her, more than he'd ever learned about anyone in such a short time. Clara was too open for there to be any ambiguity. She didn't *do* ambiguity. She did unfiltered honesty.

She'd processed the seriousness of the situation and, feeling she owed him her life, had pledged herself to him. It had been as simple as that.

The weight of responsibility lay heavily in him. Responsibility to Clara to make the next year as easy for her as he could while she navigated her way through the royal role she was to selflessly undertake. Responsibility to his family to ensure Clara made that navigation seamlessly without further damage to the monarchy.

The pitfalls, though, were obvious. A loose cannon was marrying into his family. A loose cannon who made his blood thicken just to look at her.

The only thing that had made him take a mental step back from his desire for Clara had been her virginity. It had been an easy step to take when he'd expected to spend no more than a few hours with her.

Gazing at her now, dishevelled from sleep and as sexy a sight as he'd ever seen, he couldn't work out if it was excitement or dread thrumming through his veins at what his immediate future held.

There shouldn't *be* any thrumming. Excitement had no place in his life. Adrenaline, mad rushes of blood to the head…those were the things that drove a man to act on impulse and do foolish, thoughtless things like personally rescue a distressed damsel from a cruel king.

'Can you believe we're going to be sisters?' Clara enthused to his sister as she bounded to the French doors to let Bob into the garden. 'How crazy is that?'

'Crazy,' Alessia agreed, although she was the only member of Marcelo's immediate family who hadn't been surprised at Clara's ready agreement to marry him, which he'd informed them about after his and Clara's talk. His parents and brother had all been dumbstruck. He was quite sure Clara would have found their expressions funny.

The amusement left Clara's face. 'But you know it isn't for ever?' she said, her tone serious.

'Marcelo explained everything.'

'Good.' The smile returned. 'It is always best to be honest. Your brother is a very sexy man but I like living on my own. I don't think I could cope if it was for ever. And I don't think Marcelo could cope with me for very long either.'

Alessia's face showed she was trying not to laugh. 'We're just grateful that you've agreed to marry him at all.'

'It's the least I can do. Just not for ever.'

Somehow her face managed to glow even brighter when Alessia showed her the dress she'd brought over from her own quarters for Clara to wear that day.

'It's a maxi-dress on me,' Alessia explained. 'But it's roomy so you should be able to fit in it okay.'

Compared to Marcelo's six-foot-three height, Clara was short. Compared to his diminutive sister who, like their mother, didn't even reach five foot and was as thin as a pencil, she was tall. Short or tall, Clara had curves in abundance, and he almost got a full view of her voluptuousness when she crossed her arms to grab the fabric of her polo shirt dress, clearly about to whip it off, but then her gaze landed on him and, after a moment's thought, stopped what she was doing.

Shooting him a cheeky look that quite clearly said, 'See, I can be modest,' she gathered Alessia's dress into her arms. 'I'll take a shower. I don't suppose you've got any make-up on you?' she added hopefully to his sister.

'Sorry. We can get you all the make-up you want when we go shopping.'

'You're coming with us?'

'Marcelo's asked me to take you.'

He was not prepared for the disappointed pout Clara threw at him. 'You're not coming?'

'No,' he said smoothly. 'There is much to organise for our wedding, and besides, Alessia will be a better shopping partner for you. I get bored easily.'

'So do I! But not when shopping for clothes. I can do that all day.' She turned back to Alessia. 'You can give me some pointers on princess stuff when we're out—I really don't want to embarrass you all once I'm thrown under the public gaze so I'll need strict instructions on how to behave.' Hardly drawing breath and not waiting for his sister to respond, she spoke again to Marcelo. 'Will you look after Bob while we're gone?' The puppy had come in from his trip to the garden and was currently trying to scramble onto a seventeenth-century armchair.

'No problem.'

She beamed. 'I'm going to get ready. Won't be long.'

The silence Clara left in her wake was like the aftermath of a tornado.

Marcelo found himself reluctant to meet his sister's stare. When he did, she gave a rueful smile. 'She likes you.'

'I like her too.' To his own amazement, he found this was true. Clara Sinclair was a force of nature—a *handful* as Alessia had described her—and honest to the point of rudeness, but he fully understood too what Alessia had meant about her being inherently loveable.

But what he didn't like was the way he responded to her, and it wasn't even his physical response to her that nagged at him. Clara Sinclair's spirit was so different from the people who littered his royal life that it tugged at him. Made him hanker for a life he could never have.

Marcelo didn't have a clue how Clara had managed to squeeze herself into Alessia's dress.

'Can you even breathe in that?' he asked, trying very hard not to stare at her breasts so clearly delineated beneath the red fabric. Thankfully Alessia had taken his warning of Clara's lack of underwear seriously and had chosen a material and colour that didn't have the slightest hint of transparency to it.

She sucked her cheeks in and widened her eyes, then laughed. 'Just.'

'You can borrow something of mine if it would be more comfortable?'

'Fashion isn't supposed to comfortable,' she dismissed.

'You have nothing on your feet.'

'Then we'll just have to go to a shoe shop.'

'Can't you borrow a pair of Alessia's?'

His sister coughed.

'My feet are two sizes bigger than Princess Twinkletoes,' Clara explained.

'Don't worry,' Alessia said. 'I've already called ahead to Bonitas. We'll go through the private entrance. She won't have to walk on the streets barefoot.'

'How much spending money do I get?' Clara asked.

Marcelo strode to the glass table in the corner where his private secretary had left the items he'd ordered before he went to bed. 'I've set you up with an unlimited credit card.'

'What does that mean?'

'That you can spend whatever you like. There is no limit.'

Doubt rang in her voice. 'But there has to be a limit.'

'Not with this card.' He passed it to her.

She studied it with suspicion before a hint of mischief came into her eyes. 'You realise that if it's true and this really is unlimited then I'm going to take advantage of it?'

'That's the whole point. I want you to go shopping and buy everything that catches your eye. Anything you want. Don't look at the prices.'

The smile she bestowed him with made him feel like he'd grown three feet.

Clara watched one of the guards who'd accompanied her and Alessia on their shopping trip load all her new possessions in the boot of the car. Soon, the other car that had accompanied them—Alessia was a princess and so needed protection—was being loaded too.

It had been the most fantastic shopping trip of her entire life. Even better, she'd had company for it, something she'd not had since she was an adolescent and her brother had made his housekeeper take her shopping when she needed new clothes and stuff. To go shopping with a friend had been wonderful and she very much hoped it was something they would do again in her year in Ceres.

They were welcomed back at the castle by a horde of reporters at the gate to the Berruti family's private entrance. Pressing her face to the window in fascination, Clara was almost blinded by the flash of cameras.

'They're here for you,' Alessia said.

'What for?'

'What do you think?'

'Oh, yes, I'm the girl hanging from the helicopter in the arms of her prince. I suppose that makes me newsworthy.'

She'd have to get Marcelo to send that picture to her as soon as she got the new phone she'd bought set up. It had been like looking at a picture from a movie still, with the suave Knight in Black Tuxedo securely holding the ragged woman he'd just saved. Clara's only disappointment—apart from her bum looking big—was that the photographer had failed to capture Bob in it.

When the cars came to a stop, three men descended on them and efficiently emptied Clara's purchases so all she was left to carry was her new swanky handbag, which had cost more than her monthly salary.

After hugging Alessia and thanking her for being such great company, Clara opened the door into Marcelo's quarters.

She found him in his private garden with Bob, catching the last of the day's sun on his terrace. He barely moved a muscle from his seat at the outdoor table when she made her grand entrance.

'Ta-da,' she said and did a twirl. 'What do you think?'

Bob told her what he thought before Marcelo did, dashing over to paw at her ankles.

'That's a nice dress,' Marcelo finally answered.

'Isn't it?' she agreed, delighted with her dress but less than delighted with Marcelo's guarded expression. She'd hoped for a bit more enthusiasm for a dress that she'd completely disregarded his advice for and looked at the price of. Even she in all her excitement had baulked at spending two months' salary on a dress but only for a few seconds. She'd never felt such soft silken material against her skin before or checked her reflection out at every mirror and window she subsequently passed. 'Between you and me, I needed to get out of Alessia's dress. At one point I lost all feeling in my boobs. How's your day been?'

There was the faintest twitch of his lips. 'Busy.'

'Booked a date for our wedding?'

'All set for four weeks yesterday.'

'I'll pop it in my diary so I don't forget,' she teased, and was rewarded with the expressionless gorgeous face breaking into a shaking head smile. That was better. She liked it when Marcelo smiled. It set off a warm glow in her belly. 'Anything you need me to do?'

'No.' He looked at his watch. 'Dinner will be ready in thirty minutes.'

'Oh, good, I'm starving, and it means we've got time for you to check out what I've bought.'

'Didn't Alessia check it all for you?'

'Yep. She was great, but it's your arm I'll be seen on and I don't want to embarrass you by wearing things you find unsuitable.' Clara was determined to be the best public wife she could be to this daring and generous man. Even though he'd failed to go shopping with her, he'd spent so much time in her head that day he might as well have been there. Every item she'd bought had been with Marcelo's face in mind hoping he'd like it as much as she did. 'Also, I have a surprise for you.'

He raised a questioning eyebrow and got to his feet.

Itching to dive through all her purchases, Clara skipped up the stairs.

All her new stuff had been laid neatly in her dressing room. Her mum had had a dressing room too, much smaller than this but, to little Clara, it had been the most fascinating place on earth. An old memory flashed through her of sitting at the dressing table and smearing red lipstick on and trying to use it as blush like she'd seen her mum do and then prancing into the bedroom to show it off. Her mum, who'd been in bed with another of her many headaches, had told her she looked like a beautiful clown.

'What are you thinking?' Marcelo asked, noticing how Clara had seemed to have retreated into her own world. Usually, she was so *present*. He supposed that's why his quarters had felt so still without her. Only one day in her company and her absence had been tangible.

She blinked and met his stare with a smile. 'About my mum.'

'Am I right thinking she's not with us any more?' he asked carefully.

'She's dead if that's what you mean?'

'I'm sorry.'

'People always say that,' she mused. 'That they're sorry. Why is that, do you think?'

Disarmed at the question, he shrugged and answered as honestly as he could. 'To be polite?'

'As a form of social nicety?'

'When you put it like that, yes.'

'That's what I thought. I mean, you didn't know my mum, so why would you be sorry that she died?'

'Sorry for *you*.' And sorry that she could ask such a question. 'How old were you when it happened?'

'Six.'

He winced. Younger than he'd guessed. 'And your father?'

'He died of a massive stroke when I was twelve, but you don't need to be sorry about that for me. I haven't cried for him since his funeral.'

It was a comment that momentarily dumbfounded him, reminding him of how she'd so blithely informed him that she'd have to wait until she joined her father in hell before getting an apology from him.

How could this woman of all people imagine she'd be going to hell? And what had her father done to make her think he was already there and stop her shedding any tears for him once he'd been laid to rest?

Before he could put any of these thoughts into words, Clara, who'd been unpacking boxes, waved an arm at the items she'd laid out like a fan on the dressing room sofa, and chewed on her bottom lip. 'So, what do you think? Tell me if you think I got carried away. I didn't mean to buy so much but the clothes were all so fabulous and having no spending restraints went to my head—honestly, I earn a pittance at home…but in fairness, I do get free accommodation, but my actual wages are tiny so I don't have much to spare on clothes and normally buy second-hand in charity shops—'

'Clara,' he interrupted.

'Hmm?'

'You don't have to explain yourself. The credit card is unlimited for a reason and is yours to keep. Go mad with it whenever you want. I've arranged for you to have your own driver so whenever you want to go shopping or leave the castle for any reason, all you have to do is summon him and he will take you.'

Her eyes widened. 'Are you serious?'

'Yes. There's a team of palace protection officers ready to accompany you too. I don't want you to feel trapped in any way.'

'You are the kindest, most thoughtful man. And after you let me spend all that money…' She shook her head in wonderment.

'I'm not doing it to be kind,' he felt compelled to tell her. 'You have to remember, in less than a month you are going to be my wife and will have the title of princess. All eyes will be on you.' They would be on her whether she was a princess or not. He didn't imagine Clara could walk down a street without turning heads.

She bit into her lip again then, almost shyly, said, 'So what *do* you think? Are these clothes suitable for a princess?'

Recognising that his opinion really did matter to her, he smiled. 'Yes, *bella*. They are as beautiful as the princess who will be wearing them.'

All as beautiful as the dress currently wrapped around her curvy body, a vibrant red-and-yellow-checked sixties vibe creation that suited her personality as much as it suited her looks, with a high neck, short sleeves and a hem that came to mid-thigh. When she'd appeared in his garden he'd had to stop himself from doing a double take, not just from how ravishing she looked but from the glow of happiness that had suffused her. It was a glow he'd longed to touch, and he'd had to root himself to his seat and force his features to remain neutral to counter it.

Colour spread over her cheeks and, for the first time, she flittered her stare away from him, only for a moment, but as her stare was normally so implacably bold, it was noticeable.

'When we're in public will we have to pretend to be in love?' she asked, lifting the lid of another box.

'Do you think you can?'

She caught his eye and, her cheeks back to their normal colour, grinned. 'I will give it my best shot.'

'Explain something to me,' he said, asking one of the many questions about his soon-to-be wife that had occupied his thoughts that day. 'How can you be okay going along with such a public lie when you're clearly honest to your bones?'

She considered the question a moment before reaching for another box. 'We're marrying for real so that isn't a lie. The end of our marriage won't be a lie either—I *am* homesick. And I won't be telling any lies, will I? Your palace press machine will be doing all that. I'll only be acting when we're in public together, and while I don't think I'll be able to act as if I'm in love with you, I'll definitely be able to act like I fancy you, which should look like the same thing because in case you haven't noticed, I find you remarkably attractive, so that won't be a lie either.'

Dio, her nonchalance in the way she admitted her attraction! That was a turn-on in itself, and the heat simmering in his veins, which he'd been doing his utmost to ignore, ramped up four notches.

Clenching his jaw, Marcelo dragged his stare away from Clara's face only to find it locked on the open box in her hands. It contained a set of lacy red underwear.

Following the movement of his stare, she grinned and put the box down without removing the garments. 'An improvement on the bra I wore yesterday, eh?'

He cleared his constricted throat and did everything in his power to stop himself thinking of Clara wearing those skimpy items but his willpower was no match for his rabid imagination and, to his horror, heat pooled in his groin and tightened his loins.

'Quite,' he said, having to speak through a jaw he didn't dare unclench. 'Come on, leave that. I'll get the staff to put it away for you.'

'Not a chance—I've been looking forward to doing it myself, thank you very much.' Lifting the lid of yet another box, she shot her happy stare back at him. 'Here it is.'

'What?'

'Your surprise.' She handed the box to him. 'A present for you.'

Now he really was dumbfounded. 'You've bought *me* a gift?'

'It's not much,' she said, and to his astonishment she looked shamefaced. 'I'm afraid I don't know you well enough to know what gifts you'd like and Alessia was no help whatsoever. She was useless.'

'You didn't have to buy me anything.'

'I wanted to. You've done so much for me…'

Marcelo forced his jaw to relax but he could still hear the tension in his voice. 'How many times do I have to tell you that you're the one doing me the favour here and that your agreement to marry me far outweighs any debt you feel you owe me?'

'We're going to have to agree to disagree there but even if I did agree with you I would still have wanted to get you something. When my mum used to go shopping she always brought me a present back with her and it always made me feel…'

Clara shook her head. How hard it was to vocalise something as simple as a gift received. The warm glow that would spread from her chest knowing she'd been thought of. It was a feeling so long ago and distant that remembering it sent a pang through her. She hadn't mattered enough to anyone for surprise gifts since her mother died. But that was okay, she told herself. She didn't need gifts. She had everything she needed. Life was good.

'What she made me feel was a nice feeling and I wanted you to have that feeling too,' she continued. 'Are you going to open it? I have receipts in case you hate them.'

He lifted the lid. In it was two smaller boxes. One contained a belt, the other a pair of cufflinks in the shape of a ball and chain.

'The belt is to replace the one you trashed last night trying to make it fit me,' she explained, standing close to him. She caught a whiff of his lovely warm scent. He really did smell wonderful. Too wonderful. So wonderful he was making her salivate.

Confused at the strange feelings rushing through her, she edged away a little and said, 'The other is a bit of a joke, but a joke meant with kindness.' She pulled a face, suddenly uncertain that he would get it. As a rule, people didn't get her or her jokes.

But then Marcelo's gaze lifted and met hers, and her heart swelled.

'I get it,' Marcelo said, unbelievably touched as well as amused.

'I thought you could wear them on our wedding day. I'll try not to be your ball and chain,' she assured him. 'I won't get in the way of your life.'

'Yes, you will,' he contradicted. 'Just as I'm going to be your ball and chain and get in the way of your life. It's going to be you and me for the next year, *bella.*'

Her eyes softened. 'I can think of worse men to be chained to.'

And he could think of worse women too...

For a long moment nothing was said between them, not until a burst of anxiety suddenly creased her face. 'Before I forget, I bought myself a music system for my room. Is that okay?'

'For the last time, you do not have to ask permission or justify your spending to me in any way, shape or form.' Straightening, he added, 'Spend whatever you like whenever you like.'

'Thank you. I'm glad you said that because I also bought myself a Ferrari.' She'd barely finished telling him that when she burst into a cackle of laughter. 'That was a joke. I can't drive.' She stood suddenly still and stared at him with widening eyes before her shoulders jiggled. 'Can you teach me?'

'To drive?'

'Yes.'

He had a vision of them tearing over Ceres' mountain range in one of his sports cars, the top down, Clara's long hair streaming behind her, laughter on her face, her hand on his lap, the new perfume she was wearing that he'd been doing his best to block from filling his senses, adrenaline pumping through them both…

He severed the image with a firm, 'No.'

'Why not? Can't you drive either?'

'I've been driving since I was sixteen.'

'Then why won't you teach me?'

'Because you would drive me nuts.' In too many ways.

She was not in the least perturbed at this. 'What if I promise to keep my mouth shut?'

'Are you capable of doing that?'

'There's only one way to find out…'

'Yes, and that's not when you're behind a wheel,' he told her firmly.

She laughed and skipped away from him to return to her purchases. 'And I thought you were a man who thrived on adventure.'

CHAPTER SIX

'WHEN DO YOUR parents get back?' Clara asked as she shared breakfast with Marcelo two days later on the garden terrace under the rising sun. Having lived in a flat above the animal shelter for six years, it was lovely to have a garden. Enclosed for complete privacy and beautifully maintained by the castle gardeners, she thought it wonderful.

She'd joined Marcelo ten minutes earlier and other than a quick glance at her appearance, a swift, 'Good morning,' and a pat on the head for Bob, he'd sipped at his *caffè latte* and picked at his pastry in silence whilst reading the news on his phone.

Her question didn't drag his gaze from his phone. 'A week on Friday.'

They'd flown to Australia on an official visit the day after Clara's arrival on Ceres. Seeing as she hadn't yet met them, she assumed the timing wasn't anything personal. 'When do you think I'll get to meet them?'

'I imagine a dinner will be arranged on their return. I know they're keen to meet you.'

She reached for a second chocolate brioche. She wondered how big her bum would get if she ate two chocolate brioches for breakfast every day for the next year. Marcelo, she'd noticed in her short time here, limited himself to only one. Marcelo, she also noticed, had so far conducted their conversation without looking at her. She didn't think he could be properly reading his phone as he was definitely listening to her with both ears. 'You'll have to teach me table etiquette.'

'Didn't they teach you that at school?'

'I skipped those lessons.'

That made him look from his phone to her.

She grinned mischievously. Clara liked it when she had Marcelo's full attention. It meant she could look at his gorgeous face. 'Those lessons were boring. What kind of conversation will they expect from me?'

His sensuous lips stretched into a smile. It amazed her how often she found her gaze drifting to them. When he'd taken her to the British embassy the day before to sort her passport out, there had been a moment when she'd been so caught up watching his mouth move as he spoke to the official that had speedily taken it upon himself to deal with her case—having a prince of the island at her side had certainly helped on that score—that she'd completely zoned out.

'Just normal, everyday conversation,' he said. 'Don't worry about it. In private they're pretty informal.'

'Only *pretty* informal?'

'They're from a generation where being royal meant formality. My mother was raised knowing she would be queen and was trained from birth for her role. She is modern in her outlook but that modernity sometimes clashes with the values and sensibilities she was raised with.'

'I hope I don't say or do anything to offend her. She's going to be my mother-in-law for a year so I imagine it would be a bit awkward if she decides she hates me. I mean, what if she's wearing a really horrible dress and asks me if I like it? Would she do something like that? Some people do and then when you tell them the truth, they get all huffy. I don't get it. Why ask for an opinion if you don't want a truthful answer? Isn't that dishonest? To ask the question in the first place, I mean.'

Marcelo smothered an inward sigh and put his phone down. He'd had a terrible night's sleep. It had taken him longer than normal to get off and then he'd pulled himself awake from a dream involving Clara and the red lace underwear he'd caught a glimpse of in her dressing room. Every time he'd closed his eyes after that, the dream had remained vivid, the knowledge she lay in a bed only a wall away feeding it. Lord knew when he'd drifted back off but the end result was he felt decidedly unrefreshed and then, within minutes of sitting down for some sustenance, the woman who'd prevented his sleep had appeared on the garden terrace all sleepy-eyed and tousle-haired and dressed in a pair of perfectly modest silk pyjamas that showed perfectly well her lack of underwear. He couldn't see anything he shouldn't but the way the silk caressed her curves meant it didn't need to be transparent. It had taken approximately one second for his loins to react.

However, ignoring Clara, even to get a grip on his increasing hunger for her, was not an option. He had a year of this to look forward to. He had to get used to it.

But damn, it was hard not to look at her and react, not when she was so damn sexy. Look at her now, her chair pushed back from the table, one knee pulled up to her chest, unashamedly devouring her brioche. What man's blood wouldn't burn at such a sight?

Pushing his plate to one side, he said, 'Do you ever tell white lies?'

She ripped off a piece of her brioche. 'No. A lie's a lie.' The brioche disappeared between the plump lips that had also featured heavily in his dream.

'Not even to spare someone's feelings? To make them feel good about themselves or better in themselves?'

She swallowed her bite with a shrug. 'I don't like to hurt people's feelings. I try very hard and not always successfully to live by the maxim of *If you've nothing good to say then don't say anything at all*, but I can't tell a lie. The consequences can be very bad.'

'The voice of experience?' he queried idly, taken with the tiny crumb lodged in the corner of that amazingly kissable mouth.

She nodded. 'My mother died of a brain tumour. Did you know that?'

Taken aback at her words, he blinked sharply to pull his focus away from her mouth. 'No.'

'She was ill for a long time. Everyone knew. But no one told me.' Clara compressed the pointless churn in her belly. There was no point getting upset about something that happened so long ago.

She rarely spoke about her mother's death, not because she didn't want to but because people so rarely asked. Of course, Marcelo hadn't asked but she figured this was a story he needed to know. She wanted him to know.

'She would spend days in bed with terrible headaches and I thought it was normal, and I thought it was normal for mummies to sometimes go to hospital for long spells for their headaches. I thought it was normal because that's what I was told. But I knew what death was because I remember visiting her once with my father and asking him if she was going to die and he said *no*. I distinctly remember him telling me that she'd be better soon, and I believed him. When she was home, I would get into bed with her every morning and cuddle her and, if her head wasn't hurting too much, we would watch cartoons together, and I had no idea that she would soon be taken from me because I believed my father's lies and all the other people who lied too. Right until the end they kept the lie going, even when she weighed little more than I did and was too weak to raise her head. I lived in a house with death hovering over us and I was the only one who couldn't see it because I believed their lies. I was the only one who didn't get the chance to say goodbye to her.'

To that day, Clara couldn't say why she'd never asked her mother but was glad she hadn't. She didn't think she'd be able to endure knowing her mother had lied too.

Marcelo's heart thumped painfully but so coldly into the ice that had filled the cavity of his chest.

All too clearly he could envisage Clara as a six-year-old child trying her best to be quiet and not make her mummy's head hurt any more than it already did. He could envisage it clearly because he remembered his sister at that age. Alessia was seven years younger than him and when she'd been six, Marcelo thirteen and Amadeo fifteen, their parents had gone on a state visit to New Zealand over the Easter period for a month while the boys had been home from school. Alessia had missed their mother so much she'd spent days inconsolable. Marcelo had seen it as his job to cheer his baby sister up. It was that time, he was sure, that had forged the closeness between the two of them.

He closed his eyes and tried to get air into his closed lungs. 'Do you think they lied because they were trying to protect you? You were very young.'

'I'm sure that's how they justified it to themselves,' she answered matter-of-factly. 'My brother said as much when I asked him about it once.'

That would be the same brother who'd sold her to a man rumoured to hit women. The same brother whose name Marcelo had searched two nights before when he couldn't sleep. What he'd discovered had enraged him. Andrew

Sinclair was worth fifty million pounds. He'd been the sole heir of their father's will. A few calls later and he'd learned that Terence Sinclair had made no financial provisions for his only daughter once she reached the age of eighteen. He'd left her fate entirely in the hands of the half-brother who hated her.

No wonder Clara believed her father had gone to hell.

Marcelo forced his focus to remain on the words Clara was saying rather than his rage at the men whose duty had been to care and protect her.

'But that doesn't change the outcome, does it?' she said. 'I went to her bedroom one morning for our cuddle, and her bed was empty. She'd died in the night. The undertakers collected her body while I was dreaming in my bed and I never saw her again.'

'Clara…' He shook his head, trying to clear it of the noise filling it. His breakfast churned violently in his stomach.

What she'd lived through would churn anyone's stomach.

She reached across the table and squeezed his fisted hand. Smiling kindly, she said, 'It's okay. You don't have to think of a platitude for me. I can see by your face that my story has upset you and I'm sorry for that. I didn't mean to ruin your breakfast.'

He loosened his hand and twisted it so he could squeeze her hand back. Gazing into her dark brown eyes that contained not a jot of self-pity, his guts cramped tightly.

Clearing his throat, he said, 'I am glad you told me.'

Her nose wrinkled. 'You don't look like you're glad about it.'

Any other time, he would have laughed at her astuteness and willingness to speak what she saw.

'Glad is the wrong word,' he conceded. 'But you are

going to be my wife and a member of the Berruti royal family, and it is my job to protect you for the time you and I are together. Understanding you will make it easier for me to do that.'

She stared at him with ringing eyes and a faintly disbelieving expression for the longest time. 'You want to *protect* me?'

He squeezed her hand again without thinking.

Yes, he realised, a growing part of him did want to protect her. He'd thought Clara the woman least in need of protection and he still did think that, but his sister had been right—there was something about Clara that made you *want* to protect her. He couldn't put his finger on what that vulnerability was but it was there.

'You are giving up a year of your life for my family's sake,' he said. 'Protecting you is the least I can do. Understanding you will help me do that.'

'I *can't* lie,' she said simply. 'Even the thought of telling a lie makes me want to be sick.' A hint of mischief flashed in her eyes. 'I can't begin to tell you the amount of trouble telling the truth has got me into over the years.'

'I can imagine,' he said drily. 'How on earth have you held a job down for so long?'

'Because I spend most of my time with the animals, I'm great at my job and they pay me such a pittance it'd be hard to get anyone else, which is why I asked you to make that donation to them as they really need the boost in funds.' Then the mischief faded and her voice slowed and quietened. 'It's not just that I can't tell a lie. I can't bear to hear them either.'

'Understandable.'

Her fingers tightened around his. An urgency came into her voice. 'Promise you will never lie to me.'

Marcelo's guts cramped again. He didn't like to think

of himself as a liar but, like most people, he told white lies to spare others' feelings and, sometimes, to spare his own. This might be the hardest promise to keep he'd ever made because Clara would view a white lie as seriously as any other lie. Taking a deep breath, he jerked a nod. 'I promise.'

Her shoulders and mouth loosened. 'Thank you. Trust is very hard for me but I want to go into our marriage giving you the benefit of the doubt, otherwise I think it would make life difficult for both of us. And, while we're discussing my many faults, if you hadn't already noticed, stress and heightened emotions tend to make my mouth run away with me even more than normal. I try to control it but I'm not always successful, so if we're on an official engagement and you notice me blabbing away like a roadrunner on speed, you might need to step in and shut me up.'

'Our first public engagement is planned for the weekend,' he informed her.

Alarm flashed. 'That soon?'

'The world needs to see us together. We're going to have a pre-wedding party the week before the wedding which will be a much more formal affair, so this will be a good primer for you. It's a closed, select event at the Agon embassy so a good way for you to get a taste of a royal engagement without overwhelming you.'

'But I'm not ready, even for a primer. I don't care if I embarrass myself but I don't want to embarrass you.'

'We have four days to make a start. Your tutors—experts in decorum and etiquette—start tomorrow so that will get the basics covered. We can come up with tactics to curb your roadrunner mouth and then we'll stay out of sight until the pre-wedding party and work in more detail with you.'

Her eyes gleamed and she giggled. 'That sounds like a lot of work. Sure you still want to marry me?'

Glad of the lightening of the mood, he went along with it. 'It's too late now—the press release announcing it went out yesterday. I think, though, we might have to take some preventative measures to make sure you're never on the receiving end of reporters' personal questions.'

'Very wise,' she agreed approvingly. 'And probably wise to warn your mum not to ask me if her bum looks big.'

Welcome laughter welled in him. Marcelo tugged her hand to his mouth and kissed the knuckles lightly. 'I will warn her.' And his father and siblings. He didn't think Alessia could know the details of Clara's mother's death.

'Thank you. Can I have my hand back now please? It feels very nice you holding it but I need to take a shower. Are you okay to watch Bob for me?'

Resisting the temptation to kiss her hand again, he released it. It disturbed him how much he wanted to keep hold of it. 'Sure.'

He was helpless to stop himself from watching her pad back inside. Helpless to stop his eyes fixing on the delectable bottom so vividly delineated beneath the silk.

When she stepped over the threshold, she paused and looked back at him.

Her shoulders rose sharply then dropped. A smile formed. And then she turned again and disappeared.

Marcelo cradled his head then covered his face and tried hard not to imagine Clara naked in the shower.

How was it possible for one woman, in the space of one conversation, to evoke so many feelings in him? Feelings that cut to the bone. Feelings that made him want to jump out of an aeroplane with her strapped to his back sharing the rush of adrenaline and then hold her tight and shield her from the dangers of the world, slay a dragon to protect her and then lay her on a bed and devour her.

The next year was going to be long.

It was going to be torture.

Clara was apprehensive about meeting the priest who'd be marrying them but, after three days of intense princess training, her brain was frazzled. There was so much to learn, from the little things like posture and not fidgeting to the bigger things like how to address dignitaries. On paper, she supposed it all looked slightly pointless and unnecessary, because seriously, who cared about decorum and etiquette in this day and age? But that was the point— it mattered to Marcelo and his family, and so it mattered to her. She was only a day away from being introduced to the world as an imminent member of the Berruti royal family and the last thing she wanted was to embarrass Marcelo by getting things wrong. She'd already had one vivid dream where she entered an embassy dressed to the nines but with her dress tucked into her knickers, so to give her brain a break from it all was welcome.

The chapel was tucked away behind the castle. To reach it, they passed the ancient amphitheatre, Marcelo pointing out numerous grottos and reflecting pools and, far in the distance, the ancient maze that still delighted visitors of all ages.

Up close, the chapel loomed taller than she'd expected, and she entered it with a thudding heart.

In three weeks and one day, she and Marcelo would make their marriage vows in here.

It was a thought that made her shiver but, oddly, not unpleasantly. So many odd feelings had enveloped her since her arrival here. They were all linked to Marcelo.

Somehow, in the course of a week, Clara had become

attuned to another human's presence. Become used to sharing her meals with a hunky two-legged creature rather than furry four-legged ones. Used to Marcelo's watchful presence in her princess lessons. Used to his supressed smiles when she said something her decorum teacher considered—that dreaded word—*inappropriate*. She'd even got used to him having had enough of her company by nightfall and retiring to bed as soon as their evening meal was finished.

She quite understood why he needed space from her. Clara had known since she was a little girl that she could be too much for most people.

She knew he didn't go straight to sleep as when she took herself to bed hours later each evening she'd see a glow of light under his door. Once, with her heart beating fast, she'd put her ear to his door and heard his television. And that was the one thing she was struggling to understand—why her heart beat so erratically around him. Before Marcelo had come into her life she'd never given her heart a second thought; it was just another organ in her body quietly getting on with its job of keeping her alive.

It was beating erratically now as she gazed up at the high, domed roof and the vast yet intricate stained-glass windows with Marcelo standing so close. Loud, echoing thuds against her ribs.

Wrapping her arms around her chest, she took a seat on a pew and broke the silence. 'I thought chapels were supposed to be small?'

'My ancestor who had it built was intensely religious,' he replied, sitting beside her. 'He would have been a monk if he hadn't been heir to the throne.'

'What would you have done if you hadn't been born a prince? Would you still have joined the army?'

He rubbed the back of his neck. 'I don't know. I joined

because I itched for adventure before taking up royal duties full-time and the military is considered a worthy job for a royal to take. Royal life is incredibly dull—be thankful you only have to put up with it for a year. Amadeo always wanted to be a racing driver but that was out of the question.'

'Too dangerous?'

'Yes.'

Was her awareness of Marcelo's muscular thigh only inches from hers dangerous? Was the temptation to place her hand on it dangerous?

Clara had never felt temptation of a sensual kind before she'd met Marcelo.

The look she often caught in his eyes before he blinked it away, like he wanted to devour her, felt dangerous too. Thrillingly, excitingly dangerous.

What would it feel like to be kissed by him? Would it be nice? Or would it repulse her? Or, worst of all, would she feel nothing?

If they did ever kiss, would he find it nice or repulsive or boring?

Probably it was best to never find out. As things stood, they had a great relationship—the best relationship she'd had with a human since Alessia. Why ruin it over something as tedious as desire? That's if what she even felt for him was desire. Maybe it was just curiosity brought about by being thrown together and their proximity. That he was so ruddy handsome and sexy only added to the mix.

'Did you enjoy your time in the army?' she asked, the first question to come into her head for distraction against the awareness licking her skin, an awareness that really was inappropriate in a house of God.

'I loved it. There's great camaraderie and adventure in the military. I'd hoped to stay until I was forty.'

'What happened?'

'Nothing dramatic. I got a chest infection that developed into pneumonia. Laid me up for months and weakened my body enough that I was no longer able to do my job effectively, so I was medically discharged.'

'That sounds dramatic to me.' Dramatic enough for her heart to make a strange icy swoop…

At the audible shock in Clara's voice, Marcelo faced her. 'I recovered so not dramatic,' he assured her, 'but it took a lot of work to rebuild my strength. I'm fighting fit now, but it took over a year before I was back to full health.'

How he'd hated those long months, rebuilding his strength for a life of duty and tedium, the career he'd loved gone, the life he'd loved over.

'Was your life in danger?'

'At one point, yes.'

'Then that's definitely dramatic. Why didn't the media report it? I mean, you're a prince so that would have been newsworthy, wouldn't it?'

'The life of a royal is a life of scrutiny.' That was another thing he'd loved about the military—the anonymity, that he could be himself without having to worry about anything he said or did being reported or scrutinised.

His discharge didn't just terminate his career but his freedom to be him, Marcelo the man rather than Marcelo the prince.

Sitting here, properly alone with Clara for the first time in days, close enough to feel the heat of her body and smell her sultry perfume, he was very much aware of his mortal side. The primitive side. Responding to her perfume and the heat of her skin…

Clenching his fists on his lap, he took a deep breath before continuing. 'The press can be rabid and as far as I was concerned my illness and recovery was a private matter. My family and colleagues knew my wish for discretion so…' A thought suddenly occurred to him and he twisted his face to her. 'How do you know the press didn't report it?'

'Because I would have read it. I've read all the reports that caught my eye about you since I was fifteen.' Her eyes gleamed with amusement as she explained. 'I saw you pick Alessia up from school once. I thought it was a really nice thing, you taking her out—my brother didn't visit me once when I was at school. She told me after that you often took her out when you were on leave. I've kept an eye out for your name ever since because I wanted to assure myself your life was going well. I like it when good things happen to good people. But don't worry, I wasn't cyber stalking you in particular. I did the same for Alessia too.'

'So that's how you recognised me?' he murmured, but whatever she said in answer was lost through the sudden rush of blood pounding in his head as he gazed into the dark brown eyes that did something to him.

Clara did something to him.

The tempo of his heart became a burr, thickening his blood to a heavy sludge.

Her eyes pulsed. Colour rose on her cheeks. Their faces were so close he could hear the raggedness of her breath.

She was so damned irresistible…

You're in a house of God.

Swallowing hard, he turned his gaze to the door that led into the priest's private domain. As if summoned by Marcelo's will, the door opened.

Marcelo finally released the breath he'd been holding.

It took a long time before he felt controlled enough to meet Clara's stare again.

Before she could answer, the priest emerged.

CHAPTER SEVEN

THERE WERE NO princess lessons the next day. Instead, Clara had to endure two hours of tedium with a world-famous designer who clearly thought she was God's gift to wedding dresses. An hour of that time was spent acting like a human mannequin while her measurements were taken.

It had been exactly a week since Marcelo had rescued her from her fate and whisked her to Ceres and this was the first time she'd been bored.

No, she admitted. Not bored. Restless.

She couldn't stop thinking about the moment she'd held her breath in anticipation of Marcelo kissing her. But it had been only a fleeting blink of a moment, passing so quickly she wasn't even sure whether or not she'd imagined it.

Wishful thinking?

She shivered.

'Can you keep still?' the designer scolded.

'Sorry.'

Focus, she told herself. Consider standing like a mannequin good practice for that evening's function when she'd have to put her new princess face on.

But no matter how hard she tried, she couldn't stop her mind lurching back to Marcelo. She wondered how he was getting on in Milan, where he'd flown to after breakfast to arrange his own wedding outfit.

When the measurements were done and the designer reached, again, for her bulging portfolio, inspiration to get rid of her struck.

'How many wedding dresses have you made, in total?' she asked.

'I have lost count. About one hundred and three.'

Clara wasn't quick enough to hide her cackle of laughter. 'Then you must have a good idea what suits individual women?'

'Of course.'

'Then why don't you let your imagination go wild on this dress for me? I definitely want the skirt of the dress to be like a meringue and I don't want the top part to be heart-shaped...' Not when she'd had a heart-shaped wedding dress for King Pig. 'And I'd like to look like a proper princess for the day—a bit like Cinderella when she goes to the ball—but those are my only stipulations. You're the expert. You must know what will and won't suit me. Use all your knowledge and experience and create something you think is fit for a princess for me.'

After a bit more cajoling and flattering, the designer finally agreed. By the time she left, she actually seemed excited to be given a free rein. Clara suspected most of the women she created wedding dresses for turned into Bridezilla.

Finally alone, Clara took Bob into the garden for some training, clutching her phone in case Marcelo called or messaged. He'd said he'd be back by lunch. It was almost three p.m.

Being here felt very strange without him. Very strange. And it was strange too how keenly she felt his absence, how her ears had pricked up at every external noise as if it could be him returning, how her stare kept gluing itself to the door waiting for him to throw it open.

There was no sign of him when she went back inside an hour later. Swallowing the icy feeling forming in her heart she went through her phone and selected the playlist she'd spent hours creating, pressed the button indicating the living room and then pressed shuffle. Seconds later, music piped out of the four corners of the room where the staff had rigged up speakers for her.

Where was he?

She'd give it another ten minutes and then call him. With the number of bodyguards who accompanied his every step out of the palace she was sure he was fine, but the icy feeling was spreading.

A song came on that she adored and she sang along, trying even harder to tamp down the icy worry in her chest. The palace beauty team would be here soon to turn her into a princess for the night but there was no sign of her prince.

Where was he?

She sang even louder.

'Having fun?'

Startled, she spun around and found Marcelo standing at the threshold of the living room wearing one of those snug T-shirts she liked so much matched with a pair of black jeans. His almost black hair was as perfectly coiffured and groomed as it had been when he'd left the castle and just to look at him made her heart bloom with pleasure as well as relief and delight. 'You're back!'

The smile on Clara's face was like no smile Marcelo had been on the receiving end of before. Not from his family. Not from any of his lovers.

No one had ever looked at him like that.

The smile still alight on her face, she added, 'I didn't hear you come in.'

He worked hard to keep his tone neutral over the thumping of his heart. 'Hardly surprising with all this noise.'

Marcelo had flown to Milan needing breathing space from Clara. Breathing space from the battle raging inside himself. Hours spent every day with a woman who made his blood burn, trapped in her zany orbit, hearing her frequent laughter, watching her face screw in concentration as she undertook what she called her princess lessons, retiring to bed early every night because the buzz in his veins deepened when night fell and they were left alone together, finding no solace in his bedroom, too alert for the tread of her steps and the creak of her bedroom door, eyes glued to the wall separating them...

His awareness of her was rapidly consuming him but it wasn't his growing hunger that had seen him escape his island for some respite. It was Clara's spirit, that unquantifiable something that sparkled from her and sang to the part of him prone to rushes of blood to his head and impulsive behaviour.

The part of him that had no place in his life any more.

Clara and this whole situation was his responsibility. Marcelo's impulsive actions had put the monarchy in its greatest peril in two centuries. He needed to keep his head and, to do that, he needed to keep Clara at arm's length. He needed to fight.

The problem was what he needed to do and what it was possible to do were two different things. How did you keep someone so full of life and joy, someone so *present*, at arm's length? Especially when you wanted them so much it hurt.

And especially when they smiled at you the way Clara smiled at him, with her whole, beautiful face.

'Sorry.' She turned the volume down with her phone. 'Better?'

'Yes. I can now hear myself think,' he said wryly, then

shook his head. 'I would never have had you down as someone who likes sentimental love songs.'

'Love songs are the *best*,' she enthused.

How long would it take before she ceased to amaze him? Clara had to be the least sentimental person he'd met in his life and he'd found her singing and swaying to a song about unrequited love. She'd been oblivious to his presence and so he'd had a few moments of private observation watching the movements of her body, her curves softly showing through her white fitted calf-length trousers and multi-coloured long-sleeved top, dark blond hair loose and spilling over her shoulders. In those unobserved moments there had been an inexplicable tightening in his chest that had been far more acute than the tightening in his loins.

His loins were far easier to control.

And then she'd spun around and the look on her face when she'd seen him…

'How did you get on with the designer?' he asked.

'Great! I managed to get rid of her by giving her free rein on it.'

He laughed. 'I thought you'd love being involved in the creation process.'

She pulled a face. 'Turns out I much prefer choosing from finished products. Did you get your outfit sorted?'

'I did. And while I was there…' Filling his lungs with air, Marcelo stepped over to her. 'I bought something for you.'

Her eyes lit up, which was something considering there was a permanent light in them. 'A present?'

'An engagement ring.'

Marcelo had left his favourite tailor with the details for his wedding suit efficiently sorted, enjoying his breathing space away from Clara. And then he'd noticed the adjoining jewellery shop. He already knew Clara's ring size from when it had been measured for her wedding ring. Choosing an engagement ring would take five minutes of his time. Well, it would have if his impulsive decision hadn't turned into an obsessive quest to find *the* perfect ring for her. He'd visited six exclusive jewellers before the perfect ring revealed itself.

She was practically bouncing on her toes. 'Can I see?'

Doubt over whether she'd like it kicked in. His heart thumped hard as he opened the lid for her.

After what felt like a whole era had passed, she tore her gaze from the ring to him.

'That's for me?' Clara whispered, struggling to work her vocal chords.

Throat moving, he nodded. 'If you don't like it, tell me. I can return it. We can go shopping together and choose one you like.'

'But I do like it.'

'You do?'

Her heart was fit to burst. 'It's the most beautiful thing I've ever seen. Is it really for me?'

'Do you see another woman here in need of an engagement ring?'

His attempt at a joke brought a smile to her face. And set an unbidden tear trickling down her cheek.

'I thought you liked it?' he said, brow crinkling with confusion.

She wiped the tear away and sniffed and laughed at the same time. 'I *do*. I love it. I just can't believe you've chosen something so beautiful for little old me.' No one had ever gifted her anything so beautiful before. She hadn't received a present in years, not a proper meaningful gift that wasn't part of her work's Secret Santa.

Not knowing why her eyes were leaking, she wiped another tear away.

'Are you going to try it on?' he asked.

She held her hand out to him. 'I want you to put it on me.'

She felt rather than saw his hesitation. 'Please?' she said. 'I'm never going to have this moment again.'

Clara would never marry for real. She wasn't capable of forming the kind of bond that marriage followed—how could she when all trust had been knocked out of her at such a young age? For real bonds to form, trust was needed. Trust that they would never lie to you and trust that they had your best interests in their heart, and only her mum had ever had her best interests at heart. In any case, she doubted there was a man alive who could put up with her! But here, in this moment, she wanted to experience the romance of a ring being slid on her finger. Just for the experience. Just for the moment. And just with Marcelo...

It was comments like that which had fed Marcelo's determination for the perfect ring. Her honesty. Her lack of guile. Her lack of self-pity. Her matter-of-factness that relationships, never mind marriage, were not for her.

How easy it would have been for her to become bitter at what life had thrown at her but Clara latched on to the good rather than focus on the bad. Look how she'd spent her time in Ceres focusing on training to be a princess rather than indulging in bitterness and recriminations at the heinous behaviour of her brother and the King of Monte Cleure.

Surely it must affect her? Her brother had sold her to a monster who would have forced her into a marriage from which she would have been lucky to escape with her life, but, other than the time she'd opened up about how she'd been prepared to fight to her last breath on her wedding night, you'd never know what she'd been through.

There had been myriad reasons for him to buy her the perfect ring but deeper than all of them had been the need to do something special for her.

He'd had a strong feeling that it had been a long time since anyone had done anything special for her.

He attempted another joke. 'Do you want me to get down on one knee too?'

She pulled a humorous face. 'Let's not go overboard.'

Chuckling, he carefully plucked the fifteen-carat oval diamond set on an elegant pavé band covered in sparkling diamonds from the box and took hold of her hand.

The thumping of his heart became a boom.

He put the ring to her slender wedding finger. He'd never noticed what pretty hands Clara had before. Was it his imagination or was there a tremor in it?

Slowly, he slid the ring over her knuckle until it nestled snugly on her finger. The diamond glittered.

He lifted his gaze from the ring to her eyes. They shone as brightly as the jewel on her hand but the expression in them was one he hadn't seen before.

'It's perfect,' she said. 'How did you guess I would like it?'

He rubbed his thumb over the main diamond. 'I was going to get something colourful and elaborate but when I saw this…' He took a deep breath. 'It's simple and solitary and sparkling and beautiful. Just like you.' And worth every cent of the money he'd splurged on it, which had cost more than he'd paid for his Bugatti. It was the single most expensive item he'd ever bought.

Clara's lungs practically closed from the rapid expansion of her heart.

'Are you calling me simple?' she tried to jest, but it came out too choked to be funny. In its box, the ring had been stunning. On her finger, its beauty overwhelmed. It was an engagement ring fit for a real princess.

But, just like she would never be a real wife, she knew she could never be a real princess. Gazing at the sparkling diamond on her finger only reinforced that feeling. She would try, though. Try her darnedest to be the best princess she could be and make Marcelo proud and make herself at least a little worthy of this ring.

He squeezed his fingers around hers and gave something that was almost a smile. 'I meant it as a compliment. You have no artifice.'

'And that's a good thing?'

'At least I won't have to spend our marriage wondering what you're thinking.'

The overwhelming feelings finally became too much to contain and, tugging her fingers from his hold, she flung her arms around his neck. 'Thank you. I promise to take good care of it.'

She felt him stiffen but the erupting emotions were too strong for her to let go. Her nose had landed right below his collarbone and as she breathed in her senses were filled with the scent of Marcelo. It was a glorious scent, potent, masculine, a scent that burrowed inside her...

She barely registered the loosening of his body until his strong arms wrapped around her waist and pulled her tighter to him.

In the beat of a second it wasn't just his scent seeping through her senses.

In that beat of a second every nerve ending in her body shot to attention and Clara found that she was the one now stiffening as the beats of her heart quickened and sent hot blood surging through her veins.

The music changed. Another of the love songs she adored.

She needed to let go of him.

She wanted to move even closer.

The tips of her breasts were pressed against the hardness of his chest. There was a sensitivity in them she'd never known before.

Everything felt so heightened, like her senses had taken a double shot of caffeine. She pressed her cheek tighter into the top of his chest, filled her lungs with more of his scent and listened to the heavy thuds of his heart. She tried to swallow back the moisture filling her mouth but her throat didn't seem to be working properly. Nothing seemed to be working as it should. Her body had gone off-piste.

A hand swept deliciously up her back and threaded through her hair to cradle her head.

Slowly, Clara lifted her chin to look at him.

What she found on Marcelo's face slammed her heart against her ribs.

His jaw was set tight, his lips a tight, rigid line. His eyes…they were a darker blue than she had ever seen them and bore into hers with a hooded intensity that burned right into her core.

Suddenly, she couldn't breathe, too intent on the mouth closing in on hers to draw breath.

She could feel his breath whispering against her skin.

He was going to kiss her…

Her eyes fluttered shut as warm, firm lips brushed like a feather against hers.

Something deep inside her melted.

A loud knock on the living room door cut through the spell with the effect of a bucket of ice being tipped over her.

One moment she was locked in Marcelo's arms, the next she was five paces apart with no recollection of actually moving her feet or jellified legs.

'My apologies for the terrible timing,' Alessia said from the living room door, clearly embarrassed at having walked in on them at such an intimate moment. 'I've come to get Bob.'

For a moment Clara wondered what she was talking about and then it came to her. Alessia was dog-sitting for the night.

Events unfolded before Marcelo like he was watching from behind a screen. Clara, more flustered than usual, dashing around in search of all the puppy's stuff. Alessia's promise to bring the puppy back in the morning. Clara seeing them out.

And then she returned to the living room and the screen cleared.

Closing the door, she rested her back against it.

Their eyes clashed and held.

The silence was so complete you could hear a feather fall.

Colour rose high on her cheeks. Her chest rose slowly too then fell jaggedly. Her teeth sank into the plump bottom lip that had felt so incredible brushed against his.

He cleared his throat. 'Are you okay?'

She gave an overt blink. Her shoulders rose, her chin jutted and something that could have been a laugh flew from her mouth. 'I can't work out if I'm relieved or disappointed that Alessia interrupted us.'

This was such a classic piece of Clara honesty and so similar to what he was feeling that laughter swelled. 'Same.' What else could he do? Say it was a mistake?

Mistakes, no matter how fleeting, did not taste that good.

'Really?' A wide smile lit her face. Resting her head back against the door, she said, 'I'm glad it's not just me. I mean, I knew I found you attractive but any woman with eyes would find you attractive so I didn't think that was strange in itself, even though you're the only man I've ever found attractive, but now I have all these feelings running through me and…' She rubbed her arms. 'I don't know what to do. I mean, I've never kissed a man before.'

Something warm and thick that had nothing to do with desire filled his chest. 'Why not?'

'I've never wanted to. I've never been interested in men or sex. Don't get me wrong, I don't dislike men as a species or anything. It's just that I'm happy in my own company with my dogs and, to be honest, I've always found the thought of sex itself rather boring—I fast-forward sex scenes on TV.' Her teeth sank again into her bottom lip and her voice dropped. 'But now I think I must have changed in some way because there is something about you my body reacts to, and it keeps getting stronger. It's scary but…exciting, I think. So what about you? How do you feel? Because I'm not imagining that my feelings aren't one-sided, am I?'

There was such vulnerability in the way she posed this final question that he could only answer with the truth. 'No, *bella*, you're not imagining it.'

There came a point when a man had to admit defeat.

He must have been mad to think he could keep Clara at arm's length when in the space of a week she'd infected every waking moment. Even his nights weren't safe from her. She'd slipped into his dreams as if she'd always been there, and now that he'd experienced the thrill of her soft, sexy curves pressed against him and felt the tremble of her desire, his personal Rubicon had been crossed.

There was no going back. Not for him.

His hunger for Clara was too great to be contained any longer.

He wanted her. Every inch of her. In his arms and in his bed.

She blew out a puff of air and laughed tremulously. 'Oh, good. It'd be really embarrassing if you found me as attractive as a warthog after I've just unloaded all that on you.' She swallowed but didn't drop her stare. 'So what do we do about it?'

His every sinew tightened.

How easy it would be to close the space between them and show her what they should do about it, but instinct told him that would be a huge mistake.

There was a reason she was still standing across the room from him.

Clearing his throat, he said, 'That's up to you.'

Those mesmerising eyes stayed fixed on him for the longest time before her face broke out in another wide smile. 'In that case, I'm going to take a shower before the beauty team arrives.'

It took a beat for him to remember that they had their first official joint royal engagement that evening.

This was what Clara did to him. Made him forget himself.

'That will give me the time I need to think about whether we should take this any further.' She shook her head and stepped away from the door, rolling her eyes self-deprecatingly. 'Sorry, I know I do want to take it further. I just need to figure out if it's something we *should* do. And you should think about it too.'

And with that, she left the living room leaving Marcelo to his wild, tortured thoughts of the perilous turn his life could be about to take.

CHAPTER EIGHT

CLARA ADJUSTED THE band of her dress one last time before deciding she was ready. She hoped the ambassador's reception would be more exciting than it sounded. She hoped her boobs didn't fall out of her dress. She hoped her princess lessons paid off and she didn't embarrass Marcelo. Somehow, she had to contain the excitement that had been careering through her since their kiss that hadn't been quite a full-blown kiss but still a kiss. Excitement always made her motormouth worse and dulled her impulse control, and she had never, in her entire life, felt anything like this before.

She'd relived the moment approximately once every minute. Sometimes twice.

If Alessia hadn't interrupted them, how far would they have gone? How far would she have let it go?

The more pertinent question was how far did she *want* it to go? She knew her attraction for Marcelo had exploded. She knew she adored his company. She knew she adored him, and not just because he'd saved her life or brought her the most beautiful piece of jewellery in the world.

The problem was her complete lack of experience with men. Just because she'd liked being held in his arms and had practically swooned with desire at their way too brief kiss did not mean she'd like anything else. Just because the mere thought of his hands roaming her body sent thrills racing through her did not mean the reality would be anything like it.

And what about *his* expectations? Clara would never second-guess another person's thoughts.

Luckily she'd put all her jumbled questions in order by writing them down, and she shoved the note into her clutch bag before taking one last deep breath and leaving her bedroom.

She laughed when Marcelo took one look at her in the living room where he was waiting for her and his eyes practically fell out of his head.

'Now *that* is a reaction I like!' she said, delighted at such a visceral reaction.

He rose from the sofa. '*Dio, bella*, you look amazing. That dress…' He smacked a kiss to his fingers.

Loving the compliment, she beamed. 'You look amazing too. I keep thinking you should only wear jeans and T-shirts because you look so sexy in them but you're just as sexy in a tuxedo.'

His laugh sounded very much like a groan. 'Clara, I've spent the last two hours trying my best not to think sexy thoughts of you and then you come out with that while wearing a dress like that? Are you trying to kill me?'

'Let's wait until we've been married a few months before I try that, eh?'

Marcelo rubbed the back of his neck and suppressed another groan. He didn't see how he would make it to their wedding day without losing his mind, never mind a few months into it. Especially when Clara wore dresses like this one, a red velvet toga-style dress with the thick straps constituting the top half skimming either side of her full breasts to the diamond-studded sash tied around her waist. Her hair had been left loose, one side tucked behind her ear showing off diamond waterfall earrings. Her only other jewellery was her engagement ring. It sparkled as brightly as she did.

He could hear voices beyond the walls of the living room. His team were gathering.

'Ready to meet your public?' he asked.

'As ready as I'll ever be. Do you have a gag ready if needed?'

Stepping before her, Marcelo gazed deeply into the, oh, so expressive dark brown eyes. *Dio*, he longed to kiss her. Instead, he satisfied himself with tracing the back of a finger lightly down her cheekbone, and was gratified when her lashes fluttered and she shivered.

'You've got this, *bella*,' he assured her quietly, praying that he was right. 'The press will be camped outside the embassy and will take pictures of us together, but that will be your only contact with them. For the function itself, if you feel at any point that things are getting too much and that you're losing control, take my hand and squeeze it hard.'

'That sounds like a plan but you might find I spend the whole function squeezing it.'

'You've got this,' he repeated.

Her eyes softened. 'I hope so. For your sake.' And then a flare of the mischief he was becoming so familiar with flashed. 'Sure you don't want to bring a gag as backup? Just in case?'

Bursting into laughter, he took her hand and kissed the knuckles.

A short while later, they climbed into the back of their car. As Clara arranged herself next to him to minimise creases to her dress, Marcelo reflected that, for once, he was attending a royal function without dread of the certain tedium.

Whatever happened when they got home, whether she took the plunge and joined him in his bed or not, having Clara on his arm guaranteed the event would not be boring.

For that alone, he was grateful to have Clara Chaos in his life.

The reception was far more gruelling than Clara had anticipated. Held in the ambassador's residence in what looked from the outside to be a magnificent town house, it was filled with glamorous women and dashing men.

Trying to remember everything that had been drilled into her, especially the need to think before speaking, was a nightmare and much harder in practice than in theory.

They all wanted to talk to her. Funnily enough, everyone seemed to want to know about her relationship to the British royal family. There were more than a few crestfallen faces when she told them she'd never met anyone more senior than a viscount, and that had been at a garden party when she was a child.

'Why has no one asked me about King Pig?' she whispered to Marcelo when they had a brief respite from the deluge of interested people.

'They've been warned not to,' he murmured.

'Why?'

'Officially, because you're too traumatised to discuss it.'

'And unofficially?'

'Because it will lead to other questions where you would be forced to lie and as you can't lie, it is better to avoid it altogether.'

'Very sensible.' She smiled at a waiter offering a tray of canapés to them and helped herself to another tiny mouthful of something that resembled a miniature Yorkshire pudding stuffed with crab meat. It didn't even fill her mouth and he'd moved on to another guest before she could take another one. 'Are they going to serve any real food any time soon?' She was getting hungrier by the minute.

'It doesn't appear so,' Marcelo said in an undertone. 'There's a good restaurant a few streets away we can go to when it's polite to escape.'

'I'll try not to faint from hunger in the meantime.'

Ice-blue eyes captured hers. Amusement gleamed in them.

A frisson raced up her spine and she quickly looked away. She needed to keep her focus and not be distracted by Marcelo's gorgeous face and the crazy feelings looking at him evoked in her. She needed to be Princess Perfect for him.

Over the next hour that passed, though, Clara's composure start to flag. Holding herself straight the whole time and watching every word that came out of her mouth was exhausting, and so she was delighted when Marcelo spoke into her ear. 'Time to make our exit. Follow my lead.'

After a flurry of goodbyes and thank-yous, they left through a different door than they'd arrived.

The convoy of cars that had driven and accompanied them there were waiting for them.

'Can we walk to the restaurant?' she asked impulsively. If felt like she'd been cooped up all week and she had a real urge to breathe the evening air and see a bit of Ceres that wasn't castle.

He raised an eyebrow. 'In those shoes? Aren't your feet hurting you yet?'

She laughed. Until six days ago, Clara hadn't even owned a pair of high heels. 'They're killing me!'

'And you still want to walk?'

'If it's not too much hassle.'

She detected a moment's hesitation before he grinned

and beckoned one of his guards over to relay the new instructions, and then they set off.

The Ceres capital's streets were how Clara had always pictured Rome, all narrow and lined with high renaissance buildings.

'How did I do?' she asked. 'I didn't insult anyone by mistake or embarrass you in any way, did I?'

'Not at all. They all thought you were charming.'

'Charming? Me? Ha! Still, that's good. I did try to behave like a princess.'

'Clara…' Marcelo shook his head. It had been an impressive effort on her part but it had pained him to see the effort she'd made, the fixed smile on her face. At times, her nails had dug into his palms but he doubted she'd even been aware of it. 'You did great, okay? You just need to relax a little and let the real you shine.'

'But people don't like the real me and I want your people to like me for your sake.'

There she went, in that matter-of-fact manner that took people aback at the first meeting of her, bluntly confiding that people didn't like her as if it were a simple fact of life.

'Of course people like you. *I* like you,' Marcelo told her, at a loss at what else he could say to refute her assertion. 'Alessia likes you.'

'It's okay, I wasn't fishing. Some people like me. Most don't. They find me too much. Oh, look, there's a caricaturist!'

They'd reached a piazza with a huge fountain in the centre, brimming with people eating and drinking the evening away in the plentiful restaurants and bars with outside seating. Following her gaze, Marcelo saw an artist speedily drawing a cartoonish portrait of a young woman striving to keep a straight face.

'You want one done?'

'I'd love to. But not right now. If I have to wait much longer for food I might start eating my own arm.'

'Then it's just as well we're nearly there.'

And just as well she'd refused, Marcelo thought with a stab of inward fury.

It was happening again, that impulse Clara brought out in him to say, 'To hell with decorum and duty.'

A prince of Ceres stopping at a caricaturist? Eschewing his carefully laid out security detail to walk the city streets? They were hardly things that could be described as thrill-seeking, not in the way that part of him had been sated in his army years, but there was something about Clara that pulled those old, suppressed feelings out and made him yearn to throw caution to the wind and feel alive again. He could lie to himself that Clara's eyes when she'd asked if they could walk, which had had the same pleading quality Bob's got when begging for a treat, had been the reason he'd agreed but spending all this time with someone as honest as Clara forced a man to be honest with himself and the truth was he'd wanted to throw the shackles of his position aside too, even if only for a short walk.

The restaurant, a favourite of his family for its discretion and privacy, was busy but, as expected, the owner quickly found a table for them and another close by for his bodyguards, welcoming Marcelo with the subtle fawning he remembered from his visits here before.

'This is cool,' Clara enthused once they were seated at a small table for two, wine poured and their order taken.

'It has excellent food.'

'You've brought lots of women here?'

'Enough,' he answered drily. Marcelo was getting used to his fiancée asking the questions most other people were too frightened, wary or inhibited to ask. He liked that she could ask something like that without a hint of jealousy too. He liked that he didn't have to second-guess her.

'There's lots of women looking at you,' she observed. 'And I don't think it's just because you're a prince.'

He let his eyes soak up the beauty before him. 'I imagine there's a lot of men looking at you too, and I don't think it's because you're about to become a princess.'

She pulled a don't-care face. 'All the women kept staring at you at the embassy. I was worried I'd have to hit them with my bag if they started groping you.'

He burst into laughter. 'That really would be most unbecoming of a princess.'

She grinned. 'Then it's just as well I resisted.'

'Indeed.'

Clara leaned forward. The table was so small that if Marcelo were to lean forward too they could kiss. Lowering her voice, she said, 'Can I take my shoes off or would that be unbecoming?'

His eyes crinkled with amusement. 'Go ahead.'

Using her toes to work the heels, she slipped them off and stretched her aching feet. Straight away her toes prodded into male legs.

'Sorry.'

He smiled slowly. 'I'm not.'

Another of those dizzying rushes of heat flushed through her and, for a long, long moment, Clara's brain went entirely blank.

Luckily food arrived. Bread rolls and a plate of olives and cold meats were laid before them. Her stomach growling, Clara dived straight in.

This really was an excellent restaurant, she decided, all moody and dark. In the other corner a female singer was crooning songs as dark and moody as the décor. As it was in Italian, she didn't have a clue what she was singing about and decided she'd rather not know in case it was something inane. Instead, she jiggled her shoulders to the beat and enjoyed the feel of Marcelo's legs brushing against hers. There was nothing accidental about it now, and she enjoyed the thick, swirling sensation that coursed through her because of it. She hoped to enjoy more of this sensation later. Hoped a lot. But, of course, that was all dependent on Marcelo.

She had to wait until they'd finished their first course before she could remove the list she'd written earlier from her clutch bag.

'What's that?' he asked.

'A list of questions for you.'

'Questions about what?'

'Sex.' She waited until he'd finished choking before elaborating. 'I did like I said I would and had a good think about whether I want us to take things further, and I really, really do, but there are things we need to discuss first, so I wrote it all down so I wouldn't forget anything.'

As he looked a little dazed and was blinking more than was normal, she thought it best to add, 'That's if you still want something physical to happen between us?'

He took one long last blink, straightened, drank half the wine in his glass then fixed his stare back on her. His lips curved into a half-smile. 'Yes, *bella*, I want that very much.'

'I like you calling me that.'

'*Bella?*'

She nodded. Every time he called her it, a warm glow fizzed inside her.

'It suits you.'

'Thank you. So, can we go through my list?'

He took a deep breath, obviously bracing himself, then inclined his head. 'Go ahead.'

'Does sex hurt the first time or is that an urban myth?'

There was a flickering in his eyes. 'It doesn't hurt men but it's different for women. I think it can be uncomfortable the first time but, from what I understand, so long as you're relaxed and ready, the discomfort is fleeting.'

'How will I know if I'm ready?'

'Your body will tell you.'

'How?'

'Trust me, you'll know.'

Unconvinced at this assertion, Clara looked at her list for the next question. 'What if we get naked and I decide I want to stop?'

'Then we stop.'

'Have you had sex with a virgin before?'

'No.'

She shot her stare back to him. 'But you're sure you'll know if I'm ready?'

'No, *bella*, *you* will know.'

Still unconvinced, she said, 'Do you promise?'

'I promise.'

Hmm. She supposed time would tell. If it got that far.

'What was your first time like?'

'Over much too quickly,' he deadpanned.

She sniggered. 'How do you know if it's over too quickly?'

'As a rule, if the man comes before the woman, then it's over too quickly.'

She opened her mouth to ask her next question but before she could speak, their waiter returned to the table.

Marcelo exhaled slowly, glad of the reprieve the arrival of their main course brought.

Never in his life had he had a conversation like it. Strangely, there was something erotic about the business-like manner Clara approached the subject.

And there was a lot erotic about the way she happily, unashamedly devoured her risotto. The stirrings he'd been battling in his loins refired. Idly, he wondered if she would have the same enthusiastic appetite in the bedroom.

As if she could read his mind, once she'd cleared most of her bowl she went straight back on topic. 'If I have sex with you and I don't like it, will you expect me to have sex with you again?'

'No.'

'What if we're actually having sex and I don't like it and ask you to stop?'

'Then I would stop.'

'Has that happened to you before?'

'No.'

'Would your ego be bruised?'

'Probably.'

'Would you hate me for it?'

'I would hope not.'

She considered this then nodded. 'I wouldn't hate you if you decided you didn't like having sex with me. If we have sex, will it change the dynamic of our relationship?'

'Probably.'

'For good or bad?'

'I don't know.'

'So it would be a risk? I'm just thinking that we're going to spend the next year living together so we have to weigh up whether having sex is worth the risk.'

'Every action we take in life involves a degree of risk.'

'But we have evolved to mitigate most risks. We wear seat belts in cars, helmets on motorbikes… Do you wear condoms?'

'Always.'

'Do you have condoms?'

'Yes.'

'Sensible. If we get as far as having sex you'll have to wear one because, for obvious reasons, I've never taken contraception.' She finished her wine then topped both their glasses up. 'So, what do you think? Do you still want to have sex with me after all that?'

He gazed into the dark brown eyes and thought a man could sink into them and never come back up for air. 'More than I have ever wanted anything. And you? Are you willing to take the risk too?'

'Oh, yes…so long as you accept that I might change my mind halfway through.' She shrugged apologetically. 'I don't know how I will feel when we're naked and doing stuff so I can't promise anything.'

'Everyone has a right to change their minds.'

'So you accept that I might change my mind?'

'I will accept whatever you're willing to give.'

'Then shall we go home and possibly have sex?'

He arched a brow. 'Now?'

She looked at their almost empty plates. 'Unless you want dessert?'

Marcelo laughed through the pain of desire firing through him. 'As much as I long to whisk you back to the castle right now, we need to wait a few minutes or my obvious arousal will be front-page news.'

Her beguiling eyes widened. 'You're aroused right now? *Really?*'

He covered her hand with his and brought it to his mouth. 'Did you really expect me to have an hour-long discussion about sex with the sexiest woman on the planet and for my body not to react?'

Her eyes gleamed. 'I have a lot to learn.'

Now that she'd made her mind up Clara was impatient to get home but the short drive back to the castle, her hand tightly entwined with Marcelo's, dragged interminably. She remembered going on a school trip to a theme park when she was ten. She'd never been to a theme park before and had longed to ride on a roller-coaster. The night before, she'd been far too excited to sleep and had almost thrown her breakfast up before she left. That was the closest she could remember to how she felt now.

The thuds of her heart accelerated when their driver entered the castle's grounds. So powerful were they that their ripples churned in her belly. But there was no fear that she would be sick from them.

How funny that she'd lived twenty-two years without even a flicker of desire for a man and then, virtually overnight, her mind had become consumed with thoughts of Marcelo and sex. Now it was like those thoughts had fed into her bloodstream and spread to every nerve ending. Anticipation thrummed so heavily in her that her only fear was that she wouldn't like it when he touched her. She hoped she would like it and that all these wonderful new sensations had some meaning, otherwise why would she have them? It would be a disappointing waste.

They'd reached their private carpark.

They were home.

Suddenly anxious, she tugged at his hand. 'Promise you won't be angry with me if I change my mind.'

Through the castle grounds night lights, she saw his features contort.

Brushing a thumb along her cheekbone, he quietly said, 'I will take whatever you're willing to give. Nothing more. You have my word.'

The driver opened the door.

Clara gazed into Marcelo's steadfast stare a moment longer then smiled her relief and twisted round to jump out.

While she waited for him to join her, she gazed up at the

stars and hugged herself. Whatever the outcome of what they were about to share together, she knew she was in safe hands and that when she got cold feet or found what they were doing too repulsive to continue, he would put his clothes back on and wish her a goodnight.

The odds were, it would be rubbish—how could reality live up to expectation, even if her expectations were low?—but at least when she eventually morphed into a white-haired spinster with a menagerie of pets, she'd be able to look back on this night and say she'd had a go at sex. She doubted they would go as far as full-blown sex because she had no idea how she was supposed to know when she'd be ready and just because excitement threaded her insides did not mean it would be the same on the outside. She might find his touch on her naked flesh repellent. She hoped not. She hoped she would like it enough that at some point her body would flash a neon sign at her that said, *You're ready!*

Once inside and the staff dismissed for the night, Clara kicked her heels off while Marcelo headed to the bar and removed a bottle of Scotch and two glasses with a raised eyebrow in question.

'Why not?' she murmured, thinking for the hundredth time how sexy he looked in a tuxedo. She hoped he looked as sexy naked. She hoped it got that far.

He poured them both a glass.

Eyes locked together, they drank.

'Another?'

She shook her head and pressed her palm to his cheek so she could feel the soft bristles of his beard on her skin. 'Let's go upstairs.'

He captured her hand before she could remove it. His stare bore into her with its intensity. 'Nothing more than you are willing to give.'

She smiled. 'And nothing more than *you're* willing to give.'

He laughed. It sounded pained to her ears.

At the top of the stairs, Marcelo opened his bedroom door and extended an arm in invitation. The expression on his face clearly told her he wouldn't argue if she changed her mind and locked herself in her own room.

She wasn't even close to changing her mind. At least, not yet...

CHAPTER NINE

Clara hadn't been in Marcelo's room before. Her first impression was that it was very big and very masculine. There was no second impression because her attention was completely captured by the humungous bed. She headed straight to it and lightly stroked the black sheets.

Not hearing any movement, she turned and found Marcelo propped against the closed door watching her.

She soaked him in, her prince of a man. Could he see the thuds of her heart through her skin or hear the beats raging so loudly in her head?

He straightened.

Her breath quickened.

For the better part of the evening Marcelo had been fighting arousal. Clara's presence alone was enough to turn him on but their long conversation about sex had pushed him over the edge and for the first time in his adult life he'd been visibly aroused in a public setting. The drive home had consisted of him staring straight ahead and trying to keep a lid on his consuming awareness of the woman attached to the hand that had gripped his so tightly, knowing that when they reached the castle, Clara was trusting him to back off if she gave the word.

But now he was here, in his bedroom, facing her, the moment his body had been aching for finally at hand, and he, the man who'd always enjoyed sex for sex's sake, found he had cold feet.

This was all too clinical, something he would likely have celebrated with all his other lovers as it meant a guarantee of no awkward morning-after conversations but here, now, with Clara... It felt wrong.

He didn't know what he wanted but he did know that he didn't want clinical. Not with her.

Grabbing his hair, he opened his mouth to tell her this was a mistake and that the risk they'd discussed earlier was too great when she did something that stole the words from his tongue and the breath from his lungs.

She put her hands to her shoulders, pinched her sleeves and pulled them down to her waist.

All evening he'd tuned out the fact she was unlikely to be wearing a bra. Now he had proof of those suspicions.

Swallowing hard, his breath now back in sharp, ragged inhalations, Marcelo fought with all his might to halt the burn of desire roaring back to life inside him.

Her unflinching stare glued to him, she worked the dress's sash loose then moved her hands behind her back.

Seconds later, the dress fell to the floor.

Beneath it she was naked.

The thumps of his heart were violent enough to send blood pounding in his head.

She was more beautiful and ravishingly sexy than even his deepest fantasies had conjured, a Botticelli and nineteen-fifties bombshell combined together and brought to spectacular life. That she stood there without a hint of shyness when he knew he was the first man to have seen her naked only added to the effect.

She gazed at him a moment longer then stepped out of the red velvet puddle of her dress and walked towards him. There was no hesitancy in her steps.

It was only when she stopped before him that he noticed the colour high on her cheeks and the staccato of her chest as she fought the same battle for breath he was fighting.

The hint of a smile formed. She reached for his hand and lifted it, placing the palm at the top of her breasts. 'Can you feel my heartbeat?' she whispered.

It pulsed rapid and strong.

'Clara…' His intended protest turned into a groan when she gently lowered his hand to cover one of her breasts. It felt so full and yet so soft that the arousal he'd been battling enflamed him and he squeezed gently, reflexively. When he felt the nipple harden against his palm he had to smother another groan.

Her eyes widened. Darkened. She put a hand on his shoulder, lifted herself onto her toes and brought her face up to his.

Push her away. Tell her to get dressed. Leave the room. Do whatever you have to do to end this before it goes any…

Her hot breath danced over his lips. 'You smell wonderful.'

This had to *stop*.

Finally doing what he should already have done, Marcelo removed his hand from her breast, cupped her cheeks and looked Clara square in the eye, filled with resolve to end this now before it went any further.

But looking her in the eye was his biggest mistake he could have made because everything contained in them, everything she was feeling, was there for the reading. Desire. Curiosity. Wonder.

But no fear.

His groan escaped his mouth before he could stop it and his hungry lips fused hard against hers.

Her response blew his mind, scorching him with a heat that melted the mental shackles binding him.

He couldn't fight a hunger this strong. Not when it felt this good, this primitive, this *essential*.

Clara sank into the hard, possessive kiss with a moan of pleasure, her lips parting as her senses were instantly overloaded with the dark, intoxicating taste and scent of Marcelo.

The sensations their earlier almost-kiss had evoked in her were *nothing* on this. Nothing.

Flames erupted inside her, licking her into a furnace and liquefying her, and it was all she could do to bite her fingers into his shoulders to hold herself upright and sink even deeper into the possessive demands of his mouth. Parting her lips in movement with his, she experienced an even greater shock of pleasure when his tongue swept against hers. Oh, heavens…

If Marcelo didn't have such a good hold of her, her knees would have given way.

'You're laughing?' he accused raggedly, rubbing his nose into her cheek as he speared his hands through her hair.

'You just made my knees go weak,' she scolded with a laugh that sounded like no laugh she'd ever made before.

She felt dizzy. Breathless. Unable to believe what was happening inside her, the pulsing ache at the apex of her thighs, the tightening of her skin to an almost unbearable sensitivity…

The pads of Marcelo's fingers pressed into her scalp before he gently fisted her hair to pull her head back. His eyes were as liquified as her bones, his voice a husky growl. 'Shall we lessen the danger by moving to the bed?'

'You've still got all your clothes on.'

He gave another of those laughs that sounded like it came from a place of pain. 'It might be safer to keep it that way.'

'But I want to see you.' It shocked her how badly she wanted to see him naked. That tantalising glimpse of his chest her first night there had plagued her thoughts ever since.

He kissed her again but this time there was none of that delicious movement…but it didn't matter, not when he inhaled so deeply, making her certain he was breathing in her scent.

Sliding his hands down her arms, sending the most incredible tingles racing through her, he threaded his fingers through hers and led her to the bed.

Clara was glad to lay down. It wasn't just her knees that felt weak. Her legs felt like they'd been injected with water and, struggling to catch her breath, she watched Marcelo rip off his black bow tie and undo the top button of his shirt before stretching out on the bed beside her.

Propping himself up on an elbow, he gazed down at her for the longest time, and smoothed a lock of her hair off her forehead.

A shiver of delight danced over quivering skin.

Her heart was racing so hard she could no longer feel the individual beats.

Marcelo placed the lightest of kisses to the succulent mouth.

The urge to rip his clothes off and lose himself in Clara's heavenliness was so strong that he was working harder than he'd ever done before at anything to keep his desire in check.

He'd never felt hunger like this before but, his promise to her lodged at the forefront of his mind, he vowed to control it. He must.

When she stroked the bristles of his beard, he closed his eyes. Her every touch sent darts of fire through him, and when she glided her hand down his throat, he clenched his jaw and breathed deeply.

How could a simple touch burn the way hers did?

One by one, she unbuttoned his shirt.

His eyes flew open when she pressed a hand flat against his naked chest.

She was still gazing at him with that same expression, the strangely touching combination of wonder and desire and curiosity.

Her lips curved. 'Your skin is so smooth.'

He traced a finger over her collarbone. 'Yours is soft.'

She trembled and took a long breath. Her breasts lifted with the motion. He yearned to taste them, to take those pale pink nipples in his mouth and…

The painful tightening in his loins sucked the air from him.

Clara lay back down, greedily watching Marcelo shrug his shirt off and revelling at the darkening of his eyes as he watched her stretch her body. She'd never imagined her skin could be so sensitive to a touch or that someone's touch could feed a need for more touches. She'd never imagined, either, that she could take such pleasure in looking at someone. If she were asked to select one man to be an example of masculine perfection, Marcelo would be top of a list of one.

His hands went to the band of his trousers and, his stare fixed tightly on her, undid it and pulled the zip down.

Jaw clenched, he pushed them along with his underwear down past his hips, releasing his erection. Clara's eyes widened.

That made him smile wryly and, divesting himself of the last of his clothes, he laid beside her and stroked her cheek.

'Remember, *bella*, you're in control here. We don't have to do anything you don't want. We can stop right now.'

'Marcelo…' For once it was a struggle to speak the

words in her head. 'You make me feel all…' She shook her head and palmed his cheek. 'I'm not ready to stop.'

'Anytime it gets too much for you, you tell me.'

'I will but right now I think that if you don't kiss me again I might have to kill you.'

Swallowing hard through his laughter, he bowed his head and kissed her.

Oh, but it was so hard and yet so tender and so, so addictive.

Wrapping her arms around his neck, Clara scratched her nails into the soft bristles at the nape of his neck and closed her eyes as the sensory pleasure of Marcelo's mouth and tongue winding with hers infused her.

She kept her eyes shut when his mouth moved from hers and gently kissed its way down her neck…heavens, that felt wonderful, and she would have cried her disappointment when he left her neck if he hadn't cupped her breast at that moment and sent another gasp flying from her lips.

The first time he'd touched her breast the effect had been a surprising pleasure. This time the pleasure was heightened, and she became aware of heat bubbling deep within her. It had been building all the way back since their embrace hours ago, but now it was no longer some distant squirmy feel between her legs but a pulse beating hard, and when Marcelo's mouth closed over the tip of her breast, the pulse tightened and she instinctively arched into his mouth and clasped his head.

She'd definitely found the door to heaven, she dimly thought as, kneeling between her legs, he lavished all his attention on the parts of her she'd been excited about when they'd first developed because she'd thought they automatically made her a woman but had then promptly became just another part of her with no more sensitivity than her little finger.

How wrong she had been. This was the headiest form of bliss she could have imagined.

What she loved as much as the wonderful things he was doing to her with his mouth and tongue and hands was the pleasure he was clearly taking from it too, and when he dipped down lower to kiss her belly, she thrilled at the scorch on her skin, thrilled at every little caress, until he kissed lower still and she suddenly realised where he was headed. Instinctively pressing the top of her thighs together, she gave a startled, 'What are you *doing*?'

Marcelo stilled and squeezed his eyes shut before resting his chin on Clara's beautifully rounded stomach.

She'd raised her head from the pillow. Her face was flushed and there was a dazed sheen he'd never seen in her eyes before.

'Do you want me to stop?' he asked huskily.

'Yes… No… Were you going to kiss me *there*?'

'Yes.'

'Why?'

Oh, his beautiful, confident, supersonically brained and yet utterly naïve fiancée.

'*Bella*, have you never brought yourself to orgasm before?'

Surprise flashed in her eyes. 'No.'

In that moment he felt such a wave of tenderness for her that it engulfed his heart. 'Then I want you to close your eyes and trust me when I say that kissing you there will give you nothing but pleasure.'

She still looked doubtful. 'Really?'

'Trust me. But you need to switch your brain off, close your eyes and feel. Don't think. Just feel.'

She stared at him a moment longer then rested her head back on the pillow. 'I trust you.'

Dio, that declaration engulfed his heart even stronger.

Clara took a deep breath and closed her eyes, and thought that maybe she shouldn't have skipped all the sex scenes on TV, and then she remembered that Marcelo had just told her not to think and—

She sucked in a breath as he gently parted her thighs and lowered himself further down the bed. The heat bubbling between her legs turned into a furnace as anticipation gripped her.

His tongue pressed into a spot that made her gasp and her eyes fly open.

What on earth…?

He pressed again at the same spot.

Oh…

Her thoughts turned into mush. And so did her body.

Closing her eyes, Clara sank into the unexpected but, oh, so incredible pleasure Marcelo was bestowing on her with his tongue, and when he moved a hand up to her waist, she grabbed hold of it and threaded her fingers tightly in his.

His tongue moved over and over the pulsating spot… and she moved with it, instinctively arching herself into his steadily rhythmic tongue to deepen the pleasure.

This was incredible. Oh, good heavens, she was on fire. The flames were suffusing her, throbbing and pulsing, building into something she could feel herself edging closer and closer to. Moans and gasps rang distantly in her ears… *Her* moans. Her gasps.

It was Marcelo's groan that sent her spiralling over the edge, and she cried out as spasms of unrelenting pleasure flooded her with a force that sent white light flickering behind her eyes and sent Clara soaring to paradise.

By the time the earth reclaimed her and she blinked her eyes open, Marcelo had climbed up her body. His gorgeous face hovered over hers. She'd never seen such wonder in his stare before. Or such unadulterated desire.

Her heart bloomed in gratitude for the unselfish pleasure he had just lavished on her, and she hooked an arm around his neck and lifted her head to kiss him, the shock of the musky taste on his tongue and the distant knowledge the taste was *her* diminishing as the flames deep inside her rekindled with fresh arousal. When she felt the stab of his erection against her inner thigh she was suddenly consumed with the need to feel him where the flames burned deepest. Inside her.

'Please,' she moaned, raining kisses over his face and wrapping her legs tightly around his waist and arching herself into him and trying to draw him into her. 'Please. I want this.'

Marcelo had no idea how he'd held on as long as he had.

Never in his life had he experienced as heady and erotic an experience as he had bringing Clara to orgasm with his tongue. Never had he known someone so responsive to his touch. And never had he been so responsive to another's touch. He was already close to coming himself and he'd had no gratification. Not of the physical kind.

There was a fever in his skin, his blood, his bones, all burning for her. The urge to give her what she was pleading for, to thrust himself into her slick heat…

In that moment he would gladly have a child with this woman if it meant he could be inside her bare and feel every single part of their lovemaking without barrier.

Cupping her face, he kissed her hard, then pulled at her plump bottom lip with his teeth.

'Protection,' was all he could growl, and groped for his bedside table and the condoms in his top drawer.

Snatching the closest to hand, he ripped into the foil

with his teeth and, still nestled between Clara's legs, twisted onto his side and deftly sheathed himself.

No sooner had he protected them than Clara's hungry, passionate mouth found his and she pulled him fully back on top of her, wrapping her arms around him as their tongues danced another heady duel and Marcelo positioned himself right where they both so desperately wanted him to be.

With Clara urging him on with her body and those soft moans that went straight to his loins, he gritted his teeth and inched his way slowly inside her, grasping at the last of his consciousness to remind himself that she was a virgin and...

She arched her bottom and thrust right back so they were fully fused together.

Wide, shocked eyes locked on his. A thump of dread that he'd hurt her spread through his chest.

Before he could get the breath to ask if she was hurt, a wide smile of wonder lit her face and then her hot mouth was back on his and she was pressing every inch of her flesh into his flesh as if trying to fuse their skin together too.

That was the moment Marcelo lost himself completely.

Clara had never imagined it could be like this. This, making love with Marcelo, the feel of him inside her, the fusion of their bodies, the heat of his damp skin moving over her as he thrust in and out of her wildly, hands scrambling for flesh to hold onto, mouths biting...it was the most heavenly, thrilling feeling on this entire earth.

She didn't want it to end. She wanted this moment and all these beautiful sensations to last for ever. But she could no more stop the swell of release from building than she could stop the tides from turning, and when the spasms flooded through her, she clung desperately to him, crying out his name, holding onto the ecstasy for as long as she could, holding onto the thrills wracking her as Marcelo shouted out her name and bucked into her one last glorious time.

CHAPTER TEN

MARCELO'S HEARTBEATS WERE the heaviest he'd ever known. They tremored through his bones and skin.

If the world had to end now he would leave it gladly.

He could feel the strength of Clara's heartbeats through their conjoined bodies. He could hear the raggedness of her breaths.

She held him as tightly as he held her and he knew in his bones she didn't want to break the spell binding them together any more than he did.

But no enchantment could hold for ever and, as deeply reluctant as he was to move, he knew his weight would soon crush her, and he gently eased his face out of the crook of her neck and lifted his weight from her.

Groins still locked together, he gazed down at her face and into the dark brown eyes filled with more of that wonder.

She swallowed hard. 'Well…that was something.'

He tried to speak, say something witty, but his brain couldn't conjure anything and, even if it had, his mouth wouldn't cooperate.

So he kissed those delectable lips instead.

Her fingers scraped through his hair and then she sighed. And then she gave a flash of that mischievous grin he was coming to adore. 'Can we do that again?'

Laughing, he kissed her again. 'Soon,' he promised. 'Excuse me a moment—there is something I have to dispose of.'

Carefully withdrawing from her, Marcelo got off the bed and moved on surprisingly weak legs to the bathroom.

When he returned to the bedroom his heart lurched to find Clara gathering her dress from the floor.

'What are you doing?' he asked.

She smiled. 'Going to my room.'

'Why?'

Confusion drew her brows together. 'That's where my bed is.'

A lump formed in his throat. 'You can sleep here with me. If you want.'

She breathed in deeply, her lips pulling in and tightening into a straight line. 'Is that what you want?'

And then he saw it. The latent vulnerability.

Clara was preparing to leave his bed because she assumed that's what he wanted. She assumed he wanted her to leave because that's what she was used to. Rejection. It's what she protected herself from in her solitary life...

How many times could a woman break a man's heart?

'Yes. I want you to stay.'

Her smile as she dropped her dress broke his heart all over again.

Back under the sheets together, he gathered her into his arms.

'I've never slept in a bed with anyone before,' she confided. 'Apart from my mum. She'd let me sleep with her if I wasn't feeling well.'

He kissed the top her head and rubbed his nose into her silky hair.

'How many women have you slept with in here?'

He knew she wasn't talking specifically about sex. 'It isn't a competition.'

'I know. I'm just being nosy.' At least, Clara thought she was just being nosy.

She felt strange. Really strange. The beats of her heart were still erratic and there was a lethargy in her bones countered by a buzzing in her veins. But there was something else too, as unexpected as it was frightening because it reminded her a little of how she'd felt when she was a child and possessive of her mother. She had a vague memory of her Australian cousins coming to stay and one of them, Beth, grazing her knee and Clara's mum kissing the knee better. Clara, unused to sharing her mother's affection, had made sure to remind Beth that she was *her* mummy, not Beth's.

What she was feeling now was similar to that feeling and yet different. It came from a different place but she was at a loss to explain where that place was, and as she was at a loss she decided to push it from her mind and simply enjoy being held in Marcelo's arms.

Just lying there, being held so tenderly, his fingers making circles in her lower back...

It felt wonderful.

'Is sex always that amazing?' she asked.

He breathed deeply. 'No.'

Unsure if he was telling her the truth—after all, Marcelo had had sex with lots of women—Clara tilted her head back so she could see into his eyes.

As if he guessed why she was looking at him, he brushed his lips to hers and weaved his fingers through her hair. 'What you and I just shared, *bella*, that is not normal.'

'Really?'

'Really. What you made me feel...' He took another

deep inhalation through his nose. 'I have never felt anything like that before.'

Well, that warmed her already impossibly warm insides up.

'I can't believe I was happy to go through life never experiencing that,' she said, fresh wonderment filling her. 'Do you think it would be like that with someone else for me? Or is it just because you're an amazing lover?'

He gave a choked laugh. 'I don't know. The chemistry between us is rare.'

'And you would know,' she agreed. 'And I suppose it's that chemistry that makes me want to do it all again.' Wriggling out of his hold, she raised herself up so she could study his face. 'What you did to me…is it nice if a woman does the same to you?'

He palmed one of her cheeks. 'Yes, but it's not something you should do because you feel you have to return a favour.'

'I think I would like giving you pleasure.' She encircled a brown nipple. 'I would definitely like to try.'

'You might like it more if I showered first.'

Her beaming smile shot straight into Marcelo's heart. 'Then let's take a shower together. I'm dying to see your bathroom.'

Deliciously spent from a second night of making love, Clara rested her chin on Marcelo's chest and tiptoed her fingers up and down his abdomen. 'Are you ever tempted to leave?' she asked idly.

There was a pause before he said, 'What, quit being royal?'

'It's been done before in other royal families.'

'What makes you ask?'

She laughed softly and pressed a kiss to his nipple. 'You

rescued me because you were bored out of your mind. You're a man who thrives on adventure. Let's face it, there's not much excitement to be had as a working royal, not for a man like you.'

Marcelo stretched an arm above his head and fixed his gaze to the ceiling. 'There are days when I would like nothing more than to turn my back on it all but the damage to my family would be immense. Besides, this is the deal we made—they would support my military career and in return, when that career was over, I would become a full-time working royal. I'm living the life that's been mapped out for me since my birth and I shouldn't complain because it's a great life.'

'So you suppress yourself for your family's sake.'

'For duty's sake,' he corrected.

'But in your case, duty and family go hand in hand.'

'Sure,' he agreed. 'We are figureheads for our country. There are expectations about our behaviour. I got enough excitement in the army to last me a lifetime.'

'Obviously not or you'd have let your army friends rescue me,' she teased.

'That was one moment of madness that will never be repeated,' he said seriously.

'So you *are* suppressing yourself.'

'I have to.'

Pulling gently at the dark hairs on his chest, she said, 'If you really intend to stick to this life for the long-term then you need to find a way to channel your boredom. Otherwise you're just a caged tiger.'

'Better a caged tiger than a wild tiger causing more damage to the institution I was born in and the family I love.'

'I get that, but you need to find a way to take the edge off your boredom and accept your life as it is rather than fight it, or you're going to make yourself miserable. Look at me—I've lived on my own for six years. Sometimes I get a little lonely so I've learned to stave it off at the head with loud music or adrenaline-filled films or comedy TV shows. Plus I always have my dogs to cuddle up to. *Et voilà*, my loneliness is banished!'

Dio, he hated to think of her being lonely. Hated to think of her taking steps to mitigate the loneliness. Clara was too vibrant to live such a solitary life.

Before he could get his thoughts in order, she sat up and, with a flexibility that astounded him, straddled him. A spark of mischief flickered in her eyes. 'I know what will bring some excitement into your life.'

'Oh, yes?' He covered a breast and squeezed gently. 'And what's that?'

'Driving lessons.'

He groaned. 'That, I fear, will be too much excitement. And of the wrong kind.'

She grinned wickedly. Writhing lower, she licked his navel. 'Then let's see if I can give you some excitement of the right kind.'

Clara couldn't stop checking her make-up for smudges. She was minutes away from meeting her imminent in-laws and wanted to make a good first impression. It really mattered to her, which was why she'd insisted on getting ready in her own room rather than Marcelo's, where she'd spent most of the past week holed up. It was for his sake that she wanted the evening to go well. She imagined it would be awkward for him and make for an uncomfortable atmosphere if his parents hated her.

A knock on her door cut through the music blasting out.

'Come in,' she yelled, grabbing her phone to turn the volume down.

Marcelo strode into the room, freshly showered and dressed in a white shirt, navy waistcoat and charcoal trousers. One look was enough for her heart to catch in her throat and her pulses to accelerate.

It made her laugh to think she'd scorned those men in Marcelo's helicopter for taking seriously her words about women becoming nymphomaniacs once they'd had sex as she was seriously wondering if *she'd* turned into a nymphomaniac. Because sex was literally all she could think of. Sex with Marcelo.

Who'd have thought that she, Clara Sinclair, would fall head first into lust? It was the most delicious feeling, but also quite scary because there was no rationale behind it... unless you considered that Marcelo was the sexiest man to walk the planet and then it became the most rational thing on earth.

Which was why she'd insisted on getting ready on her own. She simply didn't trust herself not to get distracted by his gorgeous face and fabulous body.

Tonight, if only for a few hours, she was determined not to think about sex.

But only for a few hours. Sex with Marcelo was far too joyous to willingly deprive herself of it. Once they were married they'd have to take on official royal duties and have much less private time together, so she figured she might as well make the most of it while she could. He was clearly of the same mind, and she relished that this hunk of a man couldn't keep his hands off her.

'How are you getting on?' he asked, stepping over to her. 'Nearly ready?'

'I think so. As ready as I'll ever be. How do I look?' She'd selected a pair of blowsy muted yellow trousers, pairing them with a cream silk blouse with black polka dots and a matching silk scarf, topping the outfit off with a pair of the highest, most fabulous red heels she'd ever worn. With no beauty team to work their magic on her that night, she'd spent an age on her hair, twisting it into a side knot, then an even greater age on her make-up. She'd completed the look with a pair of diamond drop earrings.

He put his hands on her hips and studied her with that sensuous intensity she so adored. 'You look beautiful.'

She hastily pushed his hands away and stepped back. 'Please don't touch me or you'll make me want to have sex, but thank you. Do I look presentable enough for your parents?'

He folded his arms across his powerful chest and fixed her with a lascivious stare. 'You look good enough to eat, but if you mention wanting to have sex again I can't guarantee you'll still look presentable.'

Even his words were enough to make her insides clench in a heated throb. She took another step back. 'Please, don't. This is important to me.'

His stance softened. 'You sound nervous.'

'I *am* nervous. What if your parents don't like me?' Then she shrugged and answered her own question. 'I don't suppose it matters, does it? It's not as if they're going to be stuck with me for long.'

He breathed in deeply, a strange look forming in his eyes. 'I don't know how anyone could find you anything but adorable.'

Her heart made a skip. 'That's kind of you to say.' She took her own deep breath. 'Well, there's only one way to find out…'

Marcelo's parents, like his siblings, had their private quarters in the same part of the castle as his, but Clara had never been inside their domains. Mainly because she and

Marcelo had barely left theirs. And also because, other than Alessia, they'd all been abroad.

The heels of her shoes clacked and echoed down the expansive corridors. Every person they met en route nodded politely—she could admit to feeling a little disappointed that commoners didn't have to curtsey or bow to family members; she'd have loved that!—and then they rounded a corner and were met with high double doors guarded by armed footmen.

The footmen nodded then stepped aside to admit them.

The moment they crossed the threshold, Clara's heart set off at a canter.

If the armed footmen hadn't been a giveaway that she was about to meet a monarch, what she walked into would have sang it loud and clear.

She'd thought Marcelo's quarters were rich and sumptuous?

They'd clearly entered a welcome room, and as she followed Marcelo through it, she craned her neck to take in the gold and cream papered walls, the gold wall lights, the gold and crystal chandeliers…and then they were walking through another vast area of deep blues and gold which in itself led to…

A much smaller room.

A much smaller, *cosier* room. But with the most extravagant furnishings she had ever seen…oh, how she coveted that yellow and gold chaise longue…and those gold and green drapes…ooh, and that bronze sculpture of the Madonna and Child…

And then they were in a dining room three times the size of Marcelo's, the table that could easily seat thirty people set for six in the centre; three either side…and the middle chair of the right-hand side wasn't a chair, it was a throne.

Terror grabbed her throat and, forgetting her vow not to touch him until the evening was over, Clara instinctively grabbed Marcelo's arm and strained her face to his. 'Your parents are the King and Queen,' she hissed.

Bemusement spread over his handsome face. 'Funnily enough, I am aware of that.'

'No, silly. I mean, they're *royalty*. Proper bona fide royalty.' Seeing the bemusement turn to alarm, she tried to explain her incoherent thoughts as coherently as she could. 'Yes, I know they're royalty. I know you're royalty. But it's always felt quite abstract to me, a concept without any meaning behind it because to me you're just the really sexy, gorgeous man I'm going to marry for a while, and now it feels real and I'm about to meet a real king and queen and not just the people who are less than two weeks away from being my in-laws and what if I make a complete fool of myself and get the etiquette wrong and—'

A finger placed gently to her lips cut her panicked words off.

'*Bella*, breathe,' Marcelo ordered.

The large dark brown eyes blinked slowly. The slender shoulders rose slowly then fell.

He waited until certain she had control of her emotions then rubbed the back of his fingers against her soft cheekbone and quietly said, 'You have nothing to worry about. This is an informal family dinner—'

'Informal? That's a throne!'

'Trust me,' he soothed, wishing he could kiss her fears away but suspecting that to do so would only increase her panic as he would likely smudge her perfectly applied red lipstick. Fearing everything she'd learned in the princess lessons she so diligently sat through had flown out of her head in her anxiety, he told her what he thought she most needed to hear. 'This is informal. They're all looking forward to meeting you. You will be sat opposite me during the meal. If at any time you feel anxious, just look at me, and please, remember to breathe.'

The large eyes didn't flicker as she soaked his words in but then she blinked and gave a laughing shake of her head. 'That's useless advice considering that looking at you makes me unable to breathe properly. Seriously, man, wear a mask or something. Living with you is making my blood pressure go through the roof.'

At that moment, the double doors on the other side of the room opened and his parents entered, followed by his brother and sister.

The well-trained, unobtrusive staff filed in behind them and poured glasses of wine while Marcelo made the introductions.

By the end of her first glass, when they were all seated, Clara was feeling much more settled. Marcelo's family were human. What a relief!

As he'd promised, she was sat opposite him. She would have liked to have sat beside Alessia but his father, King Julius, sat between them, opposite Queen Isabella, who was as tiny as her daughter. The Queen was flanked by her two sons. Despite the size and grandeur of the room, there was an intimacy to the setting that Clara relaxed into, helped by the very real effort to be jolly and welcoming she suspected all the Berrutis were making, even the slightly frightening Amadeo. As the eldest sibling, he was next in line to inherit his mother's throne. She quite understood why Alessia had always referred to him as bossy.

Her new family were keen to know about her and peppered her with questions throughout their meal. What surprised Clara the most about the food was how homely it was, and she said so, adding, 'I imagined you would eat that posh stuff you get in the Michelin-starred restaurants.'

King Julius, who'd attended the same Scottish boarding school his sons attended and spoke fluent English the same as they did, burst into laughter. 'We have to suffer enough of that during our official engagements.'

Queen Isabella smiled. As a born princess, she'd been raised in this castle and taught by governesses. Her English was good but much more hesitant. 'You like it?'

'Very much,' Clara enthused. 'I prefer this to the posh stuff too.'

'I don't,' Alessia chimed in. 'Give me the posh stuff any day.'

'Are you still haunted by those atrocious meals they served at school?' Clara wanted to know.

Alessia shuddered. 'I still get nightmares. Don't you?'

'I still can't eat cabbage.'

'Did you enjoy your school days?' Amadeo asked over the laughter.

Now it was Clara's turn to shudder. 'God, no.'

Julius turned slightly to her, eyes alive with curiosity. 'Alessia tells us you were expelled. If you don't mind me asking, what was the reason?'

'Oh, I don't mind at all, but I wasn't technically expelled—I was asked to leave for setting off a fire alarm while there was an A-level maths exam on.'

'That *was* you!' Alessia exclaimed.

'Yes, but I didn't mean to do it. A bunch of us were mucking around outside the science block and I put my finger to the alarm as a joke and Kerry Buchanan pushed me and my finger went through it and set the alarm off. The whole school was evacuated and it mucked the exam up.'

'That sounds an extreme punishment for an accident,' Marcelo commented with a furrowed brow.

'Ha! They just used it as an excuse to get rid of me,

and the alarm was only a small part of it, really—I think me calling Miss Wilson a lying old hag played a part too.'

Alessia cackled with laughter. 'You didn't!'

'Well, she *was* a liar. She saw the whole thing and then lied and said I did it deliberately, and Kerry lied too and so did the others. They all lied.'

Clara smothered the pointless swell of anger remembering this event evoked. It was history and everything had been so much better for her since. Here, in this room, was her future and sitting across from her was the one person she was starting to believe she could rely on. Someone she adored. Someone she would miss when their time together came to an end…

'Why would a teacher lie?' Amadeo asked. Clara could hear the doubt in his voice. She understood it. People always doubted her.

'Teachers are as capable of lies and deceit as all other humans,' Marcelo answered for her.

Beaming at him, delighted that he was sticking up for her, Clara explained, 'She never liked me. I think it might have been from when I yawned in class and she asked if I was tired and I told her the truth that her voice was sending me to sleep. She had it in for me after that, was always marking me down and giving me detentions for any little thing.' She shrugged. 'She lied about the fire alarm incident, I called her a lying old hag, the head insisted I apologise, I refused so my brother was called in and advised to withdraw my enrolment from the school so I didn't have a permanent exclusion on my record. And that was that. My education over.'

A long silence followed.

It was Alessia who broke it.

'I can't believe they treated you like that,' she said, now sounding distressed. 'And over a fire alarm when other girls did so much worse and got away with it. That's not fair.'

Clara leaned across the King to pat Alessia's arm. 'Don't upset yourself. I was glad to leave that place. I hated it there. I've been much happier since I left.'

Who wouldn't be happy surrounded by dogs and cats and gerbils and all the other pets deemed too troublesome for their owners to care for them any longer? To Clara, those unwanted animals were her kindred spirits. No one had wanted her since her mother died, but that was okay. It really was. She was happy on her own.

She had also, she had to admit, found happiness with Marcelo. A different kind of happiness, one that was thrilling and joyous, a period of her life she would look back on with real fondness. But a period that had an end date to it. No doubt, by then, he would be happy to see her go.

'I'm so sorry for not calling you after it happened,' Alessia said, sounding close to tears. 'I should have done. I was a terrible friend.'

Her distress was so obvious that Clara left her seat to embrace her. 'Don't be sorry. You were a vacuous, vain, self-centred teenager like the rest of the horrid girls who went to that school, but you were always kind to me. If they hadn't forced you into having me as your roommate I would have run away long before I was expelled. You made that last year bearable for me.'

Alessia disentangled herself from the hug to fix tear-filled eyes on her. 'Was that a compliment or an insult?'

'Definitely a compliment. You couldn't help being a product of your environment.'

'You managed not to be.'

'Yes, and that's why I only had one friend. Now stop crying—you're getting tears in your lovely food.'

CHAPTER ELEVEN

MARCELO COULD NO longer taste his food. Even if he could taste it, he'd lost his appetite. The conversation surrounding him rang distantly in his ears. Apart from when Clara spoke. He heard her every utterance with crystal-clear clarity.

And there she sat, happily eating her dessert and drinking her wine and conversing and laughing as if what she'd relayed had had no bearing on her life. As if that incident hadn't stolen her future from her. Because she'd never attended another school. Never undertaken any of the exams that hold the key to having a life without limitation. She'd described the flat she lived in that came with her job. It was half the size of this dining room.

How could she be happy about any of that? How could she not be filled with anger and bitterness at everything that had been stolen from her?

How could she sit there, erupting with laughter with Alessia as they tried to explain the funky chicken dance they used to do for fun in their boarding school bedroom to his bemused mother?

These were thoughts still going round and round in his head when they wished his family goodnight.

'Well?' Clara asked the moment the guarded doors closed behind them, slipping her hand in his. 'How did I do?'

He swallowed back the bile that had been lodged in his throat since her narration. 'Very well.'

'Did they like me?'

'Judging by their body language, yes.' But he'd seen the private looks exchanged between his parents. As he'd suspected, his family had all been taken with Clara and her fresh, unfiltered view of her world. But those same characteristics also gave them doubts. From the way Amadeo kept trying to catch his eye, his brother's doubts were grave.

Marcelo had warned them that marrying Clara into the family was a gamble, but when the alternative was a diplomatic war, they'd collectively agreed it was a gamble worth taking. They had no right to complain if it turned out to be a gamble they might be on the losing side of.

As far as Marcelo was concerned, their doubts were unfounded. They hadn't seen now hard Clara worked in her lessons. They didn't know how determined she was to get things right. As long as she performed like a princess in public they had no cause for complaint. Damn it, she was only taking the role as a favour to them.

Aware anger was rising in him over things that hadn't been said or even alluded to, aware that it was a deep protectiveness of Clara making him want to slay dragons on her behalf, Marcelo expelled a long breath and tried to expel the misplaced anger with it. The dragon he wanted to slay wasn't his family but her brother.

When they reached their private quarters, Bob set himself straight on them. After fuss from them both, he made himself comfortable on his favourite sleeping spot: Marcelo's seventeenth-century armchair.

And then Clara set herself on him.

Throwing her arms around his neck, she rose onto her toes. She would have kissed him if he hadn't moved his face out of the way.

Her face clouded. 'What's wrong?'

Removing her hands from his neck, Marcelo clenched his jaw and breathed in deeply. 'What you were saying about your expulsion...'

'What about it?'

'I keep thinking about your brother. He shouldn't have accepted it. He should have fought on your behalf.'

'You must be joking. He fully supported the school's decision.'

'Did he kick you out of your home because of it? Is that why you started working at the shelter at sixteen?'

'Not at all—I got the job off my own back. Legally, he was supposed to look after me until I was eighteen but I'd had enough of school and being surrounded by humans who hated me so I decided to get a job where I was surrounded by animals instead. They're much nicer creatures and they never tell lies. And I was so lucky that the job came with accommodation. Andrew was delighted to be rid of me, though I'm quite sure he'd been looking forward to me turning eighteen so he could help me pack my bags and see me out of the door.'

'Why didn't your father make provisions for you?' Marcelo was aware his voice had risen to match the anger rising back up in him.

'Because he was an idiot who thought the sun shone out of Andrew's backside. The family wealth has been passed down to the eldest child for generations and the unspoken deal has always been for that child to look out for their siblings but my father always refused to see how much Andrew hated me. I'd have much preferred to have been sent to Australia to live with my mum's sister, but hey ho, I was stuck with Andrew. He did what was legally required and that was it.'

'How can you be so calm about this? You could be discussing the weather!'

'Why are you so angry?' she asked.

'Why aren't *you* angry?'

'I have nothing to be angry about.'

'You have *everything* to be angry about. *Dio*, Clara, all your life, the people who should have protected you treated you—'

'Being angry doesn't change anything,' she interrupted. 'It's done. Andrew will join our father in hell for how he's treated me over the years plus he's not getting an invite to our wedding so the whole world will know we're estranged and that we've snubbed him—trust me, that's social death to him. I was always an embarrassment to that man. And I told you, I was happy to be expelled. I hated that place and that place hated me. No one wanted to be friends with me and I can't say I blame them,' she continued, barely pausing for breath. 'I was always getting the other girls into trouble. I didn't mean to but the teachers knew that if they asked me who'd been breaking whatever school rules had been broken and I knew who the culprit was then I'd tell them. I didn't want to and I never would have volunteered the information but if they asked me, what else could I do?'

'But I thought *you* were the troublemaker?'

'I was that too. Well, that's how they viewed me. I never meant any harm, unless you count bunking off the lessons I hated as harmful, but if a teacher saw me yawning and asked if I was bored when I was bored then what was I supposed to say other than yes? And why was organising a petition to employ people who can actually cook rather than serving cold food that's so overcooked the nutrients are long dead and buried considered troublemaking, or picketing for the heating to come on earlier in the mornings so we didn't turn into icicles when getting dressed? And why was pointing out to a maths teacher that there's a simpler way to formulate an equation considered troublemaking?'

Pulling her back to him and wrapping his arms tightly around her, he rested his cheek against her silky hair and tried to get a grip on the tempest of emotions flooding him.

'Teachers are never keen to have students challenge their authority,' he muttered.

With the strong beat of Marcelo's heart thumping beneath her ear, Clara sighed. For a moment her indignancy relating her hated school days had come close to bubbling into something darker.

It disturbed her how often she'd found herself squashing the darker emotions of her past since she'd been in Ceres. Maybe it was because she'd so stupidly allowed herself to believe that Andrew's request that she travel to Monte Cleure on his behalf meant he finally wanted to put the past behind them and let her be a sister to him. Or maybe it was because relating it all to Marcelo brought it all back and made it feel more present than it had in a long time.

'Thank you,' she said.

'For what?'

'Sticking up for me earlier. For being angry on my behalf even if it is pointless. It means a lot.' It meant more than she could ever express. No one had ever stuck up for her before. Not since her mother. Having someone on her side felt truly special, and she would hold onto it for as long as it lasted.

He gave a muted laugh and pressed his lips to the top of her head.

'Have you stopped being angry now?' she asked.

'I'm trying.'

'Try harder.'

He gave a muted laugh and kissed the top of her head for the longest time. 'I don't think I will ever stop feeling angry about this. Your life could have been so different.'

'But my life is *good*. It's a happy life. I know not many people understand me or get me but I'm cool with that. Like when I told Alessia she was a product of her environment, well, I'm a product of mine. Losing my mum was the single most traumatic moment of my life. I didn't speak for three months after she died and then when I found my voice again it was shutting up that became my issue. It was like a filter had been ripped away not just from my voice but from my eyes and my impulse controls, and I can't always control it but I do try and while you and I are married I will try as hard as I can to remember my lessons and not embarrass you.'

He held her even tighter. 'You could never be an embarrassment to me. You're uniquely you. Never lose that.'

She pulled her head back to look up at him. Her eyes were shining but Marcelo detected a faint hint of disbelief. 'Do you mean that?'

'Yes. And I mean this too…' He swallowed hard. '*Bella*, when we say our vows, I want them to be real.'

As Marcelo spoke, a rush of relief flushed through him to finally put into words the feeling that had been growing inside him.

'But they will be real,' she said. 'I'm never going to get married again so I won't be telling any lies when we say them.'

'That's not what I mean.' He pressed his forehead to hers. 'I don't want our marriage to last for only a year. I don't want any end date.' If he had to marry, why not the woman he was having the best sex of his life with? And it wasn't just sex. Clara was a breath of fresh air in the staleness of his life—why let that go over an arbitrary cut-off date when he knew damn well he'd never meet anyone like her again? She might not be the perfect princess he was supposed to settle down and breed with, but she was the perfect woman for him.

She pulled her head back again, her eyes wide. 'Are you saying you want to marry me for real?'

'Yes.'

'Why?'

'Because you're the only woman who can make the mundane fun and I will never meet another you.'

She just stared at him.

'What do you say?' he asked into the silence.

She blinked and grazed her bottom lip. 'Can I think about it?'

A week later, just as the beauticians finished working their magic on Clara for the pre-wedding party, she received notification that Samson and Delilah were cleared to travel to Ceres. After firing messages back and forth, she was delighted when it was confirmed their journey's end would coincide with her and Marcelo's return from their honeymoon in the Seychelles. She'd have her family back again!

How lucky was she? She'd have her smart, gorgeous husband and three dogs under the same roof as her.

Hurrying into Marcelo's room to share the good news, she found him fastening his ball and chain cufflinks. Inordinately pleased at this, she beamed before explaining everything.

'I'm getting my babies back!' she finished.

He raised an arched brow. 'Your babies?'

She hugged herself. 'That's how I think of them. I've known since I was a teenager that I won't have babies of my own, so my dogs take that baby space in my heart... Why are you looking at me like that?' There was the

strangest expression on his face but she couldn't quite de-
cipher it. 'Do you think I'm mad or something? I mean, it's
fine if you do, but you already know I'm bats about my—'

'You're not mad, *bella*,' he interrupted softly. 'I was just
thinking you will make a wonderful mother and wondering why you've never wanted any of your own.'

'Oh. Well, it's not that I don't want them but rather…
Sorry, do you really think I'd be a good mum?'

He smiled but there was still a lingering of that strange-
ness. 'You'd be loving and protective. What more would
a child need?'

'A father? I mean, that's why I never thought I'd have
them. You need sperm to make a baby and as I never
thought I'd have sex and the thought of using a turkey
baster doesn't appeal…' Her words tailed off at the stark-
ness of Marcelo's stare.

She swallowed, suddenly uncertain and suddenly a lot
breathless. 'What?' she whispered.

'We could have children.'

Her hands flew to her chest. The thuds of her heart
smashed against them. 'What?'

'You and me. You want children. I want children. If you
agree to marry me for real then why not?'

In the week since she'd asked for time to think about
his proposal, he hadn't mentioned it again. But it hung
between them.

Clara was in a genuine flux about it. Her feelings for
Marcelo ran deep but were those feelings only because of
the sex? How was a girl supposed to know? Her life had
been happy since she'd been expelled from that horrible
school and she'd left home. She and her pooches all lived
for the moment taking each day as it came.

She couldn't compare that happiness to what she had
with Marcelo because it was so different.

Her happiness with Marcelo was off the charts but she couldn't help the whispers in the back of her mind that these feelings shouldn't be trusted.

'Do you really want to have children with *me*?'

His gorgeous face was steadfast. 'There is no one else on this earth I would rather have children with.'

Thuds battered hard against her chest.

She could be a mum, she thought dazedly.

She could have children with him.

An image flashed in her mind. A fast forward of her life. Her and Marcelo with a small boy and girl, running through the castle vineyard, Samson, Delilah and Bob racing with them. Beaming smiles on the humans' faces. Wagging tails from the animals. Kisses. Hugs. Piggybacks.

Could that really be hers?

Could it?

Looming larger than life in the whole perfect picture was Marcelo. The man who'd brought the woman out of her.

He'd saved her life. That alone was enough for her to hold the deepest of affection for him. Marcelo would always have a piece of her heart and the whole of her gratitude.

She wanted to trust him with the rest of her heart, she realised as emotion swelled from deep inside her.

She wanted to trust the whole of herself to him.

Reaching for his hand, she threaded her fingers through his and stared into his piercing ice-blue eyes. His chest was barely moving. He was holding his breath, she realised.

She smiled. Looking at him always made her want to smile. 'If I was to have children with anyone, it would be you. Only you.'

His throat moved. After a long moment his mouth opened but a loud rap on the bedroom door interrupted the moment and in an instant the glow of emotion evaporated and was replaced by the same nerves she'd experienced just before she'd met Marcelo's parents.

Marcelo noticed the immediate change in Clara's demeanour. Fear rang large in her eyes and it crushed the urge to demand she put him out of his misery and tell him what she was thinking, about a real marriage and, now, about children. About having a family with him.

Now that he'd become accustomed to his own feelings on the matter, the thought of marriage and children: family, no longer made him want to run for the hills. Not when the wife and mother was Clara.

She'd kept him hanging for her answer for a week. Keenly aware of what she'd be giving up to be his wife for real, namely her future freedom, he'd vowed not to pressure her. He'd tried telling himself it would be no big deal if she turned him down—why would anyone voluntarily tie themselves to a royal institution in this day and age?—but the longer she'd kept him hanging, the tighter his guts had cramped.

But, he rued, even if they weren't about to be the star attractions at a party filled with nobles, politicians and a smattering of celebrities, he couldn't force her to commit to something she was still unsure of. He knew it. He'd seen it in her eyes before the fear had taken over.

'You look stunning,' he said gently, taking her other hand and bringing it to his chest. And she really did, wearing an elegant cream halter-neck dress that swished softly to her ankles, her hair swept off her face in an equally elegant chignon. 'Every inch the princess.'

Her chest rose and fell raggedly and then the wide smile he'd come to adore so much beamed into his heart.

Squeezing his fingers, she said, 'Come on, my prince. Take me to the ball.'

Hands clasped together, they left their quarters.

As they took the long walk through the maze of wide corridors to the stateroom the party was being held in, Marcelo wondered if Clara's honesty had changed him in some way. When they'd first agreed to marry, he'd had no problems at all with making vows he didn't intend to keep. Now, all he could think was that he needed those vows to be true. From both of them.

The enormous duck-egg-blue and gold-coloured stateroom had been decorated with an abundance of silver and gold balloons and decorations that glittered under the clever party lighting. Although this party was being hosted for diplomatic purposes, another way of reinforcing to the world that Marcelo had swept Clara from the Monte Cleure palace out of love, royal officials had gone to great lengths to create the illusion of a real engagement party. Clara hadn't even thought of it as an engagement party until she saw the pile of presents carefully displayed on an antique table in the corner. In a week, she supposed there would be more presents for their actual wedding.

An hour into the party and Clara relaxed a fraction. What she found helped was reminding herself that all the people here were human just like her. Even the President. Even the King and Queen of Agon. Even the business-man currently believed to be the richest person on earth.

One thing she was particularly grateful for was the Queen taking her under her wing. Arm in arm, they circulated amongst the two-hundred-strong guests, introducing Clara properly and exchanging a few words before moving on.

And, as always, she was grateful for Marcelo. When the buffet opened—and it was a buffet like no other she'd ever had with its vast array of creative and colourful platters—she remembered the training she'd been given and ate dainty portions which, mercifully, he kept adding to for her.

Marcelo was a prince in every way.

Her prince.

The most exciting, unselfish lover a girl could wish for. Her personal cheerleader.

Her protector.

The man who suppressed such an intrinsic part of himself for duty and family. The reason she was so determined to master decorum and etiquette.

How could she possibly be torn about accepting the life he was offering, which was a whole life with him? A true lover. Children. A family. All the things she'd never allowed herself to want simply because it was akin to wanting smaller feet. Pointless.

And now Marcelo and the chance to create their own family was being dangled before her and she realised she *did* want it. She wanted it badly.

So why hadn't she already snatched his hand off for it?

Another hour passed. Somehow she, Marcelo and Amadeo had been drawn into a group of people whose names she didn't remember. Clara was careful to look interested, smile a lot and adopt the listening pose when anything was addressed directly to her. One woman brought up the topic of artificial intelligence and the next thing she knew a rabid discussion about the benefits as opposed to the dangers was under way.

'What's your opinion on the matter?' the most vociferous of the antis asked her.

Remembering the one thing that had been drummed into her over and over, namely never give an opinion on anything, she replied, 'Oh, don't ask me! I was expelled from school at sixteen and left without any qualifications.'

The originator of the subject's eyes widened before laughter rang out around their small grouping. Even Amadeo was smiling, but when Clara met his stare, there was something—a coldness—that sent unpleasant prickles up her spine.

Had she said the wrong thing?

She tried telling herself she'd imagined it, for every time their eyes met thereafter, there was nothing but the same warmth he gave everyone else, but she thought it wise to keep all talk to the minimum, and spent the next hour exhausting herself with the strength of her concentration.

'Relax, *bella*,' Marcelo whispered in her ear when they found themselves alone for the first time since the party started.

'I'm trying but it's so hard. I'm terrified of saying the wrong thing again.'

Before he could answer, Alessia joined them and swiped two glasses of the free-flowing champagne from a passing waitress. She handed one to Clara, who sipped at it. No way was she going to overindulge that night, not when she was fighting her motormouth with everything she possessed. It really didn't need any stimulus, thank you very much.

As the evening had worn on, the music from the professional DJ—deliberately chosen to project a youthful image to the world—had steadily increased, tempting more and more people onto the dance floor. Clara kept experiencing nostalgia pangs, remembering school nights when Alessia would put her music on in their room and they would dance madly...

As if her nostalgia had conjured it by magic, a song came on that immediately made Clara and Alessia look at each other. It was their funky chicken song.

Excitement rushed through her, transporting her back

to that nostalgic time as if she were right there, right now, and, without thinking, Clara quickly knocked back her champagne, gave her empty glass to Marcelo with a cheeky grin, then dragged a protesting Alessia onto the dance floor.

'Come on, Princess Twinkletoes,' she laughed, 'You know what to do.'

CHAPTER TWELVE

'How did I do?' Clara asked nervously as she slipped her shoes off in the entrance hall of their quarters.

Marcelo removed his jacket and bow tie, taking in the flush of colour heightening her cheeks and the glow suffusing her. But there was uncertainty mingled in the happy glow.

He thought of her dancing with Alessia. The joy on her face as she'd flapped her arms and kicked her knees back and did that chicken thing with her neck, and encouraged Alessia to join in. How the whole dance floor had ended up joining in this spontaneous mad dance, the laughter on the dancers' and watchers' faces alike…with the exception of Amadeo. His brother had tried to hide it but he'd been angry at this lapse in decorum when there was a press corps in attendance.

He remembered too the flash of cold anger on his brother's face when Clara blithely brought up her expulsion.

Clara had seen that flash too. He was certain of it. He'd seen the way her features had crumpled in consternation before she'd picked herself back up again, but only to hold herself even more rigidly.

Knowing it would devastate her to think she might have caused embarrassment when she'd been so determined to be on her best behaviour for them, he put his hands on her hips and pulled her to him. 'To me, you're perfect.'

It might not be an answer to the question she'd asked but it was a truth. And it was a truth that smoothed away the uncertainty and made her chest rise sharply. A dreamy smile lit her beautiful face as she clasped his hands and tugged him into the living room.

Skipping away from him, she put her bag on a table and pulled out her phone. A moment later, music filled the room.

It was one of the love songs she so loved to listen to.

Her eyes locked back on his and the dreamy smile returned. Stepping to him, she put a hand to his chest. 'Dance with me.'

Putting his hands back to her hips, he slid them around her waist as her hands slid up his chest and around his neck.

Eyes locked together, they began to sway to the music.

The tune changed. Another love song came on. This one had a more sensuous vibe.

The dreamy smile had faded but its echoes rang vividly in her eyes. 'This song makes me think of you,' she whispered. Her thigh slipped between his.

Their lips brushed together. They continued to sway.

He untied the neck of her dress. Her hips continued to sway as he pulled the zipper down to her bottom. The dress swayed in time to the floor.

She arched her neck, inviting his kiss. And then he kissed the swell of her breasts before sliding a hand around her back to unclasp her strapless lacy bra. It was the red one he'd seen in its box when he'd still been foolish enough to think he could resist Clara's erotic chemistry.

Her fingers skimmed over his throat to the top button of his shirt. When she'd finished unbuttoning them, she spread the shirt apart and pressed the tips of her naked breasts to his chest. Her breaths were slowing and becoming more ragged against his mouth. Desire saturated her stare.

Working simultaneously, still swaying, lips still brushing together, they undid Marcelo's trousers and pushed them down with his remaining scraps of clothing. Clara's knickers followed. Not breaking the connection between them, they stepped out of the discarded items. His erection jutted into her abdomen. She moaned.

He clasped her bottom and kissed her deeply. Passionately. She wound her arms around his neck and raised a thigh, rubbing herself against him.

Groaning, Marcelo lifted her into his arms and carried her to the nearest wall. Lithely, she wrapped her legs around his waist and held herself tightly to him.

Dio, he wanted so badly to be inside her, but there was a growing whisper in his head reminding him he needed to get protection…

As if she could read his thoughts, she dug her fingers into his skull and looked him deep in the eyes.

'I want to feel everything,' she whispered.

He stilled. Breathing heavily, he tried to read the desire-saturated eyes.

'Make love to me, Marcelo. Be my husband for ever.'

As Clara uttered the words, a sense of rightness filled her that was as powerful as her hunger for Marcelo's possession, and then he thrust into her and his naked possession was so all-consuming that her thoughts spilled away and all she could do was lose herself in this most glorious and heady of rides as he drove into her over and over, taking her to a peak that convulsed her entire body until he slammed into her one last time, roaring her name.

Marcelo thought he must have died and gone to heaven.

Clara was riding him. Her hands were on his shoulders,

the tip of a breast in his mouth as he lavished it with the attention that always fed her arousal.

Dio, he loved her breathy moans. Loved the way she rode him with such abandon. Loved the exquisite feel of being bare inside her slick tightness… *Dio*, he didn't think he could ever get enough of that feeling.

And he loved her.

He'd known it since the impulse to punch his brother in the mouth for that flash of cold anger at Clara's mad dancing had found him clenching his fists and then avoiding him for the rest of the evening lest he give in to it.

Her moans deepened. Her fingers bit deeper into his flesh.

Dio, he loved her. He wanted her, wanted this, for the rest of his life.

She was his.

And he was hers.

Sensing Clara was nearing her peak, he gripped her hip as she threw her head back, her hair falling like a waterfall. She stiffened and ground down and then the spasms tightened around him and pulled him deeper inside her, so deep that Marcelo let himself go with the mindless abandonment he'd never allowed himself before.

Two days later, Marcelo waited until his family were seated before launching into the speech he'd mentally prepared. 'We need to delay Clara becoming a full-time working royal. I know this will add pressure to your workloads, but I need our engagements to be closed house for the immediate future.' His and Clara's royal diaries were already filling with engagements. They were due to hit the ground running as soon as they returned from their honeymoon. 'Clara and I have decided our marriage is going to be permanent, and that is why I've made this decision.

She's going to be a permanent member of our family and I need her to be comfortable and happy in the role she plays in it, and she's—'

Amadeo rose from his chair, his face taut with anger. 'Are you trying to ruin us? We can mask her inadequacies for a year but for *life*?'

'If you could see past your own snobbery you'd see Clara has the potential to be the greatest asset this family ever had.'

'Never.'

Marcelo spread his hands flat on the table and leaned forward. 'Did you not see everyone's reaction to her last night when she was dancing? How they responded to her? She's a breath of fresh air. Our people will love her, but for now she needs more time and space to adjust to this life, and to learn to relax into it. I will not have her feeling that she can't breathe when we're working, when this is going to be her life for the rest of her life. I will not have her feeling that she's not good enough when she *is* good enough. She just needs to believe it in herself.'

He was met with silence.

'Let me make this clear. Clara is going to be one of us for good and you all need to learn to accept this if you want me to stay a part of this family.'

'Don't say such things,' his mother said, visibly upset.

'Then give me your support. Give Clara your support.'

'Of course we'll support—'

'How can you ask us to support you in a marriage that might see you taking a back seat from most of your duties indefinitely?' Amadeo demanded, interrupting their mother.

'If the doctors hadn't saved my life, I would have taken a back seat from all of my duties permanently,' he reminded him icily. 'Clara is determined to be an asset to this family.

With help and support she can do it, but, and I reiterate this, it will take time. She is the only woman who will make marriage tolerable for me so if you want me to live up to your expectations and breed the next generation it will be with her or no one. Now, do I have your blessing or not?'

'You have mine,' Alessia said with a rueful smile. 'And I agree with your reasoning. Anything I can do to help, just let me know. Congratulations by the way.'

One by one, the others, even a reluctant Amadeo, gave their blessings too.

'Thank you,' Marcelo said. 'One last thing—I would appreciate if this discussion stays within these walls until after our honeymoon. Clara doesn't need to know about this meeting or the reduced number of engagements. She's had no involvement in setting them up. I will not have her hurt for anything.'

Clara couldn't stop smiling. So utterly delicious did she feel that for the first time in possibly her whole life she wished she had a friend she could share these feelings with. Alessia couldn't count because she didn't think Alessia would appreciate Clara raving about what a wonderful lover her brother was and how making love to him without protection had brought a whole new closeness to them. Of course, it wasn't the act itself as the meaning behind it, but it all merged together and represented the same thing. They'd committed themselves to each other. Their marriage would be real. They would have a family.

Oh, she could hug herself.

A real family? *Her?*

And soon she would have Samson and Delilah with her too. Her life really would be complete!

Needing to let the joy out, she did three cartwheels in a row. Bob, who she was currently training to walk off-lead in the field off the back of their private garden, found this very exciting and ran around in circles to show his admiration. She wondered if she should bow for the castle's security team, who would no doubt be observing her from their monitors. Their private quarters were private and that included their garden. Everything else was under surveillance.

Marcelo was worth the intrusion she one day hoped to become used to.

Her phone beeped. Indicating first for Bob to sit, she pulled it out of her back pocket. Her good mood plummeted.

It was her brother. How he had her new number she didn't know and figured it was probably best she never did know as she might have to kill the person who'd given it to him.

Gritting her teeth, she read:

Hope the wedding preparations are going well. Wondering if you can check with the organisers as my invitation seems to have got lost in the post. Alison and Johan have received theirs and are en route to Europe.

Oh, that cheered her right up. Alison was her mother's sister, the aunt who lived in Australia. She imagined Alison and Johan's delight in confirming to Andrew that they'd received the golden ticket he so obviously craved.

What an arrogant plonker that man was. To think she'd once longed for his approval! She didn't need his approval any more. She didn't need or want anything from him. If she didn't have Marcelo and his family's reputation to think of, she'd sell her story to the press and shame Andrew to the whole world. Still, this was just as good a shaming incident. No way the British press would let Andrew Sinclair's failure to attend the wedding of the year go unreported.

Striding back to the castle, eager to share the message with Marcelo, she fired a message back that lifted her mood even more.

Oh, dear, that is a shame. Why don't you ask your good friend King Pig if you can be his plus one as I hear he's struggling to find a victim to take with him? Actually, no, scrap that as I think his invitation got lost in the post as well. Amazing how karma strikes, isn't it? Hope Florence and the kids are all well. Please tell her that if she ever sees sense and dumps your sorry ass, she'll be welcome here with open arms.

She pressed send as she stepped into the boot room and then blocked her brother's number so she never had to deal with him again.

Feeling lighter in her heart than she'd done in years, Clara removed her boots and wandered through their utility room. She gave a cheery good morning to one of the maids, and was about to head to Marcelo's offices, where he was tied up in meetings, when she spotted the tall man sat reading a newspaper at the round corner table in the living room.

'Hello,' she said, surprised to see Amadeo. 'Are you waiting for Marcelo? He's in meetings with—'

'I have just left him,' he said, cutting her off and rising to his feet with stiff awkwardness. 'I am here to see you. Please, take a seat.'

The maid poured them both a coffee before Amadeo dismissed her with an imperious flick of his head.

'Clara…' Amadeo sighed. 'It will make it easier for both of us if I can speak freely.'

'I appreciate honesty, so go ahead.'

He nodded. 'I thought as much. Before I go any further, I want you to know that none of this is personal. I have no wish to hurt your feelings, but I am concerned your behaviour could bring harm to my family.'

An icy shard sliced through her chest. 'Is this about my dancing?'

'You didn't just dance the funky chicken or whatever it's called the other night,' he continued with a touch of disdain. 'You told the world that you were expelled from school.'

'I didn't tell the world. I told the people in our group.'

'All of whom have few scruples when it comes to sharing gossip. Which is what your expulsion now is. Gossip. It won't be long until the press hear about it. They might already know—enough of them were in attendance that night.'

'Photojournalists,' she felt compelled to remind him.

'The clue is in the journalist part. Have no illusions, they will hear about it and when they do it will be open season. We have no control over what the press chooses to print or what our people think. What concerns me is that you're a loose cannon who will unwittingly give the press even more fodder.'

She lifted her chin defiantly. 'I have nothing to hide.'

'We all have things we wish to keep private.'

'I don't. In any case, they would have heard about the expulsion at some point.'

'Possibly. The fact is, we'll never know because you kindly fed it to them yourself.'

'Do you want to cancel the wedding?' she asked bluntly over the ice now infecting her entire body.

'It's too late for that,' he replied with equal bluntness. 'And as it is going to be very difficult for everyone if we have to spend the next year doing damage limitation whenever you're incapable of knowing when not to speak, we've agreed that all your future engagements will be of the closed-house kind like the one you attended at the embassy, and all other scheduled engagements are to be given to other members of the family. This will leave you with very few engagements and so greatly reduce the potential risks for embarrassment.'

Cheeks burning with humiliation, Clara looked him straight in the eye. 'This doesn't just concern me, it concerns Marcelo. Have you spoken to him about this?'

'These measures are his idea.'

Her stomach plunged like she'd fallen through a trapdoor. 'You what?'

'He called a family conference about it earlier.'

Bile filled her throat again and smothered her taste buds. She had no idea how she was able to talk through it. 'And did he agree to you being the one to tell me?'

'No. He requested you not be told.'

'So why *are* you telling me?'

'Upon reflection, I decided you deserved to know. Walls have ears, even castle walls—I didn't want you to hear about it through exaggerated whispers. I thought it best to talk directly to you so you understand why we are taking these measures and to reiterate that this isn't personal.'

She jutted her chin. 'It feels personal.'

He raised a shoulder in apology. 'We are indebted to you for agreeing to marry Marcelo and sparing us a diplomatic war with Monte Cleure, but you yourself observed early on that you're not princess material.'

Taking a deep breath, she looked him straight in the eye. 'Then you must be relieved I'm only going to be a part of your family for a year.'

It was the flicker in his eye that gave him away and, in one fell swoop, everything became clear.

Amadeo had sought her out not to chastise her but to warn her off his brother. He didn't want her to be a permanent member of his family. This was his way of telling her she had to stick to the one year of marriage as had been originally agreed.

Rising to his feet, he said, 'We *are* indebted to you, Clara, and we want your year with us to be as happy and as comfortable as it can.'

'As long as it's far from the public eye and only for one year?'

He gave a faint smile. 'Marcelo said you had a quick brain. I thank you for your understanding.'

She waited until he was about to leave the room before calling his name. 'Amadeo?'

He turned back to her.

She summoned her brightest smile. 'Has anyone ever told you that you're a pompous ass?'

Marcelo swam harder than he'd ever swum before. Length after length he drove his body, determined to work the guilt out before he returned to his quarters.

By the time he'd exhausted himself, his mind was clearer.

There was no need for guilt.

He wasn't lying to Clara by keeping the family conference from her. Their wedding was five days away and she was fizzing with excitement for it and their subsequent honeymoon. Why dampen her spirits and hurt her feelings? She'd put in so much hard work that he didn't want her feeling like she'd failed.

He found her in the garden training Bob to walk to heel under the shade of the cherry blossom trees.

'I thought you were going to do that earlier?' he said, striding to her.

She smiled then looked down at the growing puppy. 'We *did* do it earlier, didn't we, Bob, but we got distracted.'

'By what?'

'A text message from my brother. He asked where his invitation to our wedding was. In far more many words, I told him to do one. How's your morning been?'

'Boring. How did your brother get your number?'

'Who knows?' She tapped her thigh and Bob stopped at her ankle. Feeding him a tiny piece of a treat, she casually said, 'So, what boring things did you discuss at your meetings?'

'Nothing important. Just the usual staff meetings.'

As soon as the words were out of his mouth, Marcelo knew he'd made a mistake.

CHAPTER THIRTEEN

CLARA TURNED HER face to him with an expression Marcelo had never seen before.

Contempt.

'So you don't think scheming to keep me out of public life is important?'

So many curses flew through his head accompanied by such a wave of nausea that for a moment he was incapable of speech.

Since Amadeo had left, Clara had been holding herself together by the skin of her teeth and reminding herself not to jump to conclusions. Just because someone said something was true did not make it so. That was a life lesson she'd learned at far too young an age.

Marcelo's face told her perfectly well that Amadeo had been telling the truth.

'Come on, Bob,' she said. 'Time to go.'

Then, with her only friend in this whole horrid island by her side, she marched into the house and raced up the stairs to her bedroom. She'd barely passed the threshold before Marcelo followed her in.

She wished she hadn't been looking at his face when he caught sight of her suitcases, bought for their intended honeymoon and now open on her bed, one half closed, the other open, both rammed with clothes, or she wouldn't have seen him visibly blanch.

'You're not planning to leave?' he said hoarsely. 'We're getting married on Saturday.'

'*Were* getting married,' she corrected, 'and yes, I am leaving. I gave you a chance to tell me the truth and you blew it.'

But he was still staring with horror at her packed cases. 'You *can't* leave!'

'Watch me.'

Squeezing his eyes tightly shut, he took a long, deep breath. '*Bella*, I understand why you're upset—'

'Do you?'

'You feel lied to.'

'No, I don't *feel* lied to, I *was* lied to. By you. A subtle but distinct difference.'

'*Bella*—'

'You no longer have the right to call me that any more. You can address me as Clara if you feel the need to address me as anything.'

'I want to address you as my wife. *Dio*, Clara, I wasn't scheming—'

'Don't bother trying to defend yourself. I won't believe a word of it and whatever you say to me, I can't stay and I certainly can't marry you. You lied to me when you promised—*promised*—to always tell me the truth. You told me I was perfect as I am when it turns out you doubt my ability to fit in with your family and my ability to carry off the role of Princess and want to limit my royal engagements because of it. You told me you were having meetings with your staff when it was a family conference to discuss *me*.'

He threw his head back and closed his eyes. 'I assume it was Amadeo who fed you this poison?'

'At least he doesn't shy from the truth.'

'A version of the truth twisted to suit his own purposes. I have no doubts at all about your ability to carry off the role of Princess and I told him that, just as I told him that I will not put you through official outside functions until you've learned to relax into the role.'

'That's not how he put it across to me.'

'That's because he doesn't want our marriage to be permanent,' he said with a dose of Clara's own bluntness even though it made his heart rip to say it. 'For Amadeo, duty isn't something to be endured, it's something to live and breathe. You threaten his sense of what being a royal is. The rest of us can see you're too special for us to allow your spirit to be crushed under the weight of pure proto-col. I saw what it cost you the other night before you found yourself on the dance floor and lit the place up, and I will not watch you put yourself through that again. I want you to thrive and that can only happen if you're allowed to be yourself, an alchemy of Clara and the Princess.'

'Actually, the only way I can thrive is far away from liars like you.'

Something cold and sharp was scratching at Marcelo's throat. It had risen from his chest, a strengthening cloud of ice shards penetrating through him. He was losing her, and all he could do was scramble for words to make her stay.

'Goddammit, Clara, you talk about breaking trust— what about the promise you made to me? You gave your word that you would marry me. You can't just change your mind.'

'Don't you get it? I *can't* marry you now.'

'Because of one mistake? Because you believe Amad-eo's twisted poison over me?'

'No, because I've lost all trust in you. Did you know, when my father died, Andrew sat me down and very calmly explained that our father was dead. No bluster or beating around the bush. Just sat there and told me, and told me that he was now my legal guardian and that I would be going to boarding school and not to bother whining about it. I hated him but I respected him for his honesty. At least I knew where I stood with him, and maybe I should have paid more attention to his honesty because then I would never have fallen for the only lie he ever told me which was when he tricked me into going to Monte Cleure. I *wanted* to trust him and believe in him… And I wanted to trust and believe in you. I *did* trust and believe in you and that makes it all so much worse because now I will never be able to trust another word you say or trust that anything you've ever said to me was truthful, and I can't say the vows I'd prepared to give my whole heart for because they would be a lie.'

The scratching at his throat suddenly subsided. The icy shards cleared, the jumble of thoughts he'd held about Clara, built in their time together, finally putting themselves in order.

'Or are you just using this one mistake as an excuse to run away from happiness?' he mused thoughtfully, dropping onto her armchair.

Her head reared like she'd been jolted.

For a long time they just stared at each other, and the longer he gazed into the suddenly frightened brown eyes, the more convinced he was in the sense of his thoughts.

He shook his head slowly. When he finally opened his mouth, his tone was low but steady. 'You wear your emotions like no one I've ever met, but you suppress the real stuff, don't you?'

'Don't talk rubbish,' she scorned.

'You only wear the superficial happiness, because that's all you allow yourself to feel. Everything else terrifies you.'

Clara suddenly felt a violent urge to cover her ears.

Backing against the wall to steady herself, she opened her mouth to tell him to shut up *right now* but no words came out.

It was the way he was looking at her that frightened her. Like he was seeing right into the heart of her in the place where no one was allowed.

Not even herself.

'All this time we've been together I've never understood how you're so able to compartmentalise everything. You refuse to get angry about things, not even your brother for selling you to a pig—you just told me how he relayed your father's death with all the calm of a weather lady, and now I know why you relay the awful things that have happened to you in that tone and it's because you don't dare even let the emotion out in your voice.'

Clara's heart was thumping so hard the beats were making her nauseous. She didn't want to hear this. She couldn't find the words to tell him to stop.

For the first time since she was a little girl, her mouth had stopped co-operating with her brain.

Frightened, she hugged her arms tightly around her chest.

'You say you're happy living on your own but fill your evenings with noise to drown the silence. You fast-forward sex scenes because you say you find them boring but I wonder if it's because you're too frightened to watch real, human connection and have to confront everything you're hiding from.'

Shut up!

Her plea stayed stuck in her throat.

'Your entire playlist is made up of sentimental love songs, but that's all the romance you allow yourself. Anything else requires risk and you haven't evolved a mechanism to mitigate the risk to your own heart, have you, so you shut it down completely. You were far too young when you lost the one person who loved you with all their heart, and everyone who should have been there to help you navigate your grief rejected you. You had to deal with it alone in a silent scream.'

Shut up!

But her scream stayed stuck in her throat. Just as it had sixteen years ago.

'You crave human connection but you're so convinced that people won't like you and will reject you that you shy away from it, and if I'd been paying better attention I would have realised this day would come the minute we became lovers because real emotion terrifies you, doesn't it, whichever way it falls. And real happiness is an emotion. And what you and I have shared is real happiness, don't ever doubt that. But you don't believe in it. You don't believe in me, and you don't believe in yourself, and so you only allow yourself to exist and not truly live.'

Frustration and sadness leached into the steadiness of his voice. 'I understand why. Everyone you've ever loved and trusted has abused your trust.'

How desperately she wanted to cover her ears but now her body felt as paralysed as her voice.

Marcelo took a step towards her. That one step was enough to make her flinch.

Close enough to stretch out an arm and stroke her face, he took in the ashen pallor of Clara's cheeks. Took in her muteness.

His words were distressing her. He could see it clearly. But if they had any chance of a future, they were words that needed to be said. They were words she needed to hear.

'You're not the only one who's been existing and not living, *bella*,' he said hoarsely.

She flinched again. Her eyes were darting everywhere

but him, but she was listening. He knew it. He knew her. He loved her. And she loved him. He was certain of it. She was just too scared to admit it, not even to herself.

'I told you about the time I nearly died with pneumonia but what I didn't tell you—something I have never told anyone—is that dying didn't scare me. I was aware that I could die and I *didn't care*. I've never cared about death. My time in the military is the closest I have ever felt to happiness…until you, that is. In many respects it was a perverse happiness because much of it came from knowing my time could end at any time. Accidents happen all the time. Don't get me wrong, I didn't want to die—I didn't actively seek death—just that I was drawn to the things that could end it prematurely. I always have been. My mother always said I was born without fear.'

He paused for a breath and gazed at the bowed head of the woman who'd wound her way around his heart and then burrowed a permanent niche into it.

'You've said many times that I saved you but…' A shard of his heart broke off. 'Clara, you're the one who saved *me*.'

He heard a sharp intake of breath.

'You're the one who taught me that I could have a fulfilling life without having to throw myself off buildings or indulge in rescue missions. You're the one who taught me that I needed to accept my life and find ways to counter the boredom, to tame the tiger without stifling the essence of him. What I didn't tell you is that since you've come into my life, *you've* filled that hole in me. I can endure any amount of tedium in my life if you're by my side because you banish the tedium. You've brought sunshine into these stuffy castle walls and made it feel like a home and not a prison to me.

'I know you're scared, *bella*. I'm scared too. I'm scared I've lost you.' He faltered as another shard of his heart broke away and he had to swallow hard to get his throat working again. 'I'm going to leave you alone now. I will not try to stop you leaving if that's what you still want, but I will ask this question of you—and I beg you to look into your heart for the answer… Why do you listen to those sentimental love songs so much if there's not a part of you yearning for some of that love for yourself?'

Her shoulders juddered but still she made no move to look at him.

'I ask that because you can have that love with me, because *I* love you. I love you more than I ever believed it was possible to love someone.' His heart swollen enough to burst, he stroked a lock of her hair and took the one sliver of encouragement he could that her flinch was less than when he'd stepped closer to her. 'I love you, Clara,' he whispered, 'and I will not give up on us. I will wait the whole of my life for you. You just need to reach into your heart and believe it.'

An hour later Marcelo was the one to flinch when he heard the main door close quietly.

Holding his face in his hands, he gave in to the pain that had been steadily bleeding inside him and wept.

Clara had gone.

Clara's hotel room was the most depressing space she'd ever stayed in. Worse than school. But it was the only hotel in the whole of Ceres's capital that allowed dogs and had vacancies. Still, she cheered herself up—or tried to—by taking Bob for lots of walks, often carrying him so his little puppy legs didn't get worn out. She'd explored so much of the capital that many of the streets were becoming familiar. The only place she'd done a U-turn from was the huge piazza with the central water fountain. The memories that had hit her at the sight of it had hurt her bruised heart. It reminded her too acutely of the night she'd been brimming with excitement at the step she'd been about to take of becoming Marcelo's lover.

It made her inordinately sad that they'd never had the chance to return and get a caricature portrait done.

But other than those walks, she seemed to have lost all her energy. She didn't even have the vim to rip at the peeling hotel wallpaper by her bed. She'd lost her appetite too, something that had never happened to her before. Not just that, she should have started the process of getting Bob's passport sorted but had failed to muster the energy to do that most important thing. The ache in her heart seemed to have sucked all the life from her, and what didn't hurt just felt empty. Hollow.

When she dragged herself out of the hotel bed on her fourth day there, she realised she hadn't had a shower since she'd checked in. Or changed her clothes.

Oh, this was ridiculous! She needed to step out of this funk.

The problem was, no matter how hard she tried, squashing the pain in her heart and moving on with her usual positive attitude was proving impossible, not when the image of Marcelo was lodged so securely in her mind's eye and the words he'd said to her playing like a stuck record in her head. Not when she missed him so much it hurt to breathe.

Not even the sun on her face could lift her spirits.

She just needed to try harder, she decided. Much harder. This pain would pass. It always did. She would smother it and move on with her life.

After taking Bob for a quick run in the hotel garden, she stepped under the trickling showerhead and determinedly washed every inch of herself, then put on a clean pair of jeans and a top.

A knock on her door cut through the all-pervading silence of her hotel room.

She looked through the spyhole and jumped back in shock to see Amadeo there.

He knocked again.

She opened the door a crack and used her body as a barrier to stop Bob escaping to greet him. 'How did you know I was here?' she rudely asked as a greeting.

'I asked around all the hotels that admit dogs. May I come in?'

'If you must,' she muttered.

As the room only had one small seat, Clara perched herself on the windowsill and folded her arms. 'What do you want?'

'To apologise.'

Well, that was unexpected.

'I've treated you abominably.'

'Yes.' When he didn't fill the silence, she said, 'Well…?'

'Well?'

'Your apology?'

'I thought I had…'

She shook her head.

He nodded as if to himself then met her stare. 'I'm sorry for how I treated you. It was cruel and I behaved as you rightly called me, as a pompous ass. I make no excuses. I didn't think you were right for Marcelo or for our family.'

The mention of Marcelo's name made her bruised heart flutter. 'Does he know you're here?'

'No. I thought it best not to tell him. He's not in a good place. He still hasn't cancelled the wedding. He can't let go of the hope that you'll come back to him.' His eyes narrowed and his speech slowed. 'I thought he was in denial, but now I see you, I think I'm the one who's wrong. You look terrible.'

Her heart was fluttering madly now.

'Thank you,' she croaked.

A faint glimmer of a smile appeared. 'He looks terrible too. You have matching eye bags.'

'Have you finished doling out the compliments?'

She almost caught a glimpse of white teeth.

'Yes, I am done, but I do have one more thing to say. Against my best advice, which did result in him punching me in the stomach, Marcelo will be at the altar tomorrow, waiting for you. If you come to your senses and decide to marry him, you will find no objection from me. I will welcome you into our family as I should have done from the start.'

Clara kicked the bedsheets off for the hundredth time that night. The sun filtering through the cheap curtains told her it was now morning. She didn't know why she'd bothered going to bed at all. Far from feeling any better, she felt decidedly worse.

Bleary-eyed, she threw some clothes on, took Bob, who'd been just as unsettled throughout the night, outside, then went into the restaurant for a cup of strong coffee. She couldn't stomach the thought of food, but Bob needed to eat and the hotel was good enough to provide meals for dogs. Once he'd wolfed his food down and she'd downed another coffee, she took him for his walk and tried to muster some of her old enthusiasm.

Heading towards the sprawling woodland park that all the local dog walkers seemed to favour, she was passing one of Ceres's many churches when it turned ten a.m. Each peel of the bell made her heart shudder and her brain leap to the person whose face had kept her from sleeping.

He would, at this moment, be getting ready for their wedding.

It was a thought that made her feel wretched.

The church clocks struck eleven as she headed back to the dreary hotel.

One hour.

When would he arrive at the chapel? How long would he stand there before he gave up and understood in his heart that she wasn't coming?

It was the thought of Marcelo standing at the altar waiting for the bride that would never come that filled her head as she trudged up the hotel stairs to her room. It made her heart hurt, made it *bleed*, and as she opened her door she stepped into a pool of strong sunlight filtering through the window.

Her life before Marcelo had been *happy*. She'd been relentless in her happiness, a state of mind she'd forced herself to inhabit. She'd had her job and her dogs. She'd been content with a future that consisted of being a grey-haired spinster. She hadn't felt that she'd been missing out on anything.

She'd been in denial.

Sinking onto the bed, she lifted Bob onto her lap and ran her fingers through his soft fur.

Like her canine friends, Clara had lived for the moment.

Many of the dogs at her sanctuary had been mistreated and, while they too lived for the moment, thinking no further than their immediate needs, the mental scars of their mistreatment would show themselves whenever they felt threatened. One Labrador's owner had worn black boots whenever he kicked him. That Labrador was the sweetest creature but the sight of a pair of black boots would make him cower.

Isn't that what she'd been doing? Hiding herself from all the emotional blows, cowering from anything that could truly hurt her again because Marcelo was right; she'd had to navigate the grief of her mother on her own and, not having the tools to deal with it, she'd swallowed it down deep inside her and smothered it, and then dealt with every blow and rejection that came after in the same way.

Her happiness had been a façade even to herself.

And then she'd met Marcelo.

A tear rolled down her cheek.

Marcelo…

She hadn't been looking for him but he'd found her.

The joy and happiness she'd shared with him had blown everything else away. Happiness with him hadn't been a state of mind or a decision. It had just been. That taste of real happiness…

The way he held her. The way he danced with her. The way he looked at her. The way he made love to her.

He did love her.

He'd been the one to knock down the wall she'd built to stop her from feeling true human emotions, to *smash* it down.

He loved her.

She couldn't hide from her feelings any more, she realised as another tear fell. She couldn't compartmentalise this pain. Couldn't compartmentalise Marcelo.

And it wasn't just that she was no longer capable of smothering pain. She no longer wanted to. If this was the price to pay for the joy she'd experienced with Marcelo then it was worth it. Worth every ounce of it.

And it was worth risking her whole future for… No. Not risking. There was no risk. There was no need to be scared. Not with him.

Marcelo loved her. She *did* trust that. She did trust him.

He loved her and would never, ever do anything to hurt her. Not intentionally.

With a wide smile forming on her face, Clara closed

her eyes and let the streaming sun drench her skin with its light and a different form of light fill the emptiness inside her to the brim.

The light of love.

She loved Marcelo. The emptiness she'd carried inside her since leaving the castle was his absence.

She loved him and she believed in him. She believed in *them*.

A jolt of electricity blasted through her veins and she whipped her phone out of her back pocket. It was now eleven-thirty.

She made the call.

Alessia answered on the first ring.

Marcelo stood at the altar not looking at anyone. He'd not uttered a word since he'd entered the chapel. He'd refused to look Amadeo, his 'best man,' in the eye since their arrival. He'd hardly looked at him since the punch to the stomach Amadeo had invited when he'd realised the depth of Marcelo's despair. Punching him had made him feel better for about a second.

His family thought he'd lost his mind. He suspected they were right.

He understood more fully now why Clara had hidden away from her pain. The five days without her had been a pit of agony. The time had passed so, so slowly. He couldn't begin to imagine going through this torture for the rest of his life. He *had* to believe she would come.

He had to.

But as the minutes ticked by and the chapel rang the half hour, the dread rose.

'Marcelo,' his brother reluctantly whispered, 'we need to face facts—'

He silenced him with a look. He would not give up. He couldn't.

Aware that the packed congregation were restless and whispering amongst themselves, Marcelo turned his back on them, bowed his head and prayed.

God, if you bring Clara back to me, I'll be a better man. I'll open bereavement centres for children. I'll open animal sanctuaries. I'll—

A blast of music jolted him from his prayers. What jolted him even more was the recognition. It was the song he'd danced with Clara to...

He spun around.

His mouth dropped open.

Walking up the aisle in a white dress any princess in the world would be proud to wear was Clara. She was looking straight at him, beaming. At her side, with an identical grin and in a deep green bridesmaid dress, and carrying Bob, was his sister.

He blinked vigorously, hardly daring to believe what his eyes were telling him.

She got closer.

It wasn't until she was a couple of feet from him that he saw she wasn't wearing a scrap of make-up. Her hair had been swept into a loose bun, the tiara was skewed.

She had never looked more beautiful.

For a long moment, they did nothing more than stare at each other in wonderment.

And then the beaming smile returned. 'Ready to get married then, my prince?'

He couldn't help himself. Forgetting tradition and propriety, he pulled her into a tight embrace and kissed her passionately, his senses filling with the taste and scent of the woman he'd deep-down believed he'd lost for ever.

When they came up for air, he gazed in awe at the beautiful face he loved so much. 'You came.'

Her eyes shone up at him. 'I love you.' She sighed. 'I love you so much. I'm so sorry for—'

He put a finger to her lips. 'No. You are here. That is all that matters, and you, my princess, have just made me the happiest man in the world.'

Tears welled in her eyes, but then she blinked and a flash of the old mischief suddenly crossed over her face. Marcelo thought he might just burst from the happiness that bloomed at the sight of it.

'You might want to check my feet out before you call me your princess again.'

Holding her hand tightly, he stepped back to drop his gaze to her feet.

She pulled the skirt of her dress up a couple of inches so only he could see. Instead of the traditional cream or white heels a bride usually wore, Clara had donned a pair of trainers.

'Princess Twinkletoes forgot to bring the shoes,' she explained with a giggle. 'I would have run back to our quarters for them but thought you were probably on the verge of a heart attack as it was.'

Laughing loudly, he hugged her tightly again then took her hand firmly in his and faced the bemused priest.

Without an ounce of hesitation, they both pledged their lives together.

It was the best day of both their lives.

EPILOGUE

'Now put your foot on the accelerator until you hear the bite.'

Something deep below Clara rumbled and roared.

'I said *until* you hear the bite,' Marcelo said with barely concealed impatience.

'But you didn't say I had to stop,' she countered, although she didn't really blame him. This was their second driving lesson in as many days, and everything he'd shown her and told her to do seemed to go through one ear and out the other.

'Not stop, hold your foot exactly where it is.'

'You should have said. I'll try again.'

This time, when she heard the bite, she smiled and said, 'What now?'

'Take your foot—slowly—off the clutch. The car will…'

The car lurched forward, cutting his instructions from his tongue.

She looked at him and grinned. 'Oops.'

He just stared at her before his face creased into a grin. And then his eyes narrowed in that expression he got when a thought occurred to him. 'Do you have any paper on you?'

'Of course not. You're lucky I'm wearing any knickers.'

That made him kiss her. Which was what she'd wanted. He pulled back, still grinning, opened his window and shouted out at one of his protection officers. As they were at the Ceres national racetrack, a full complement of their protection were there to witness Clara's driving ineptitude.

In no time at all, a notebook and pen were being handed to him.

Curious, Clara watched as he wrote a list, admiring his penmanship. Her writing was atrocious.

Then he handed the notebook to her. 'Written instructions for you.'

She read what he'd written. A step-by-step guide to driving a car.

'Why didn't you explain it like this?' she asked.

'I did.'

'Didn't.'

He fixed her with a look. She scowled then read the instructions a couple more times before handing the notebook back to him.

Two minutes later she was happily cruising at twenty miles an hour, well aware of the smug smile on Marcelo's face.

When she'd brought the car to a stop she turned to him. 'How did you know?'

'It was a guess. I just thought you might take instructions visually better than you do verbally.'

Amazed, she found she'd lost her ability to speak.

It constantly surprised her how well her husband knew her, so well that he sensed things about her that even she didn't know.

He knew her. And, far from repelling him, he loved her.

Just as she loved him.

'I'm two days late,' she blurted out, unable to hug the secret to herself any longer.

The smug expression turned blank.

'My period. I'm two days late.'

He stared at her with that same blankness but she could see behind his ice-blue eyes to the ticking brain and knew he was making the same calculations. Clara's cycle was as regular as clockwork. In the three months of their marriage she'd never been even a day late.

The biggest smile broke out on the handsome face she loved so much and in the blink of a moment her mouth was being crushed by his.

Wrapping her arms tightly around his neck, she kissed him back and gladly welcomed the fresh wave of happiness filling the well inside her.

Eight months later, Marcelo and Clara welcomed their first child, a daughter they named Marianne Isabella after their mothers. She was a princess in every way. Apart from her motormouth speech which developed very quickly.

* * * * *

MAID FOR THE GREEK'S RING

LOUISE FULLER

MILLS & BOON

CHAPTER ONE

THE HONEYMOON SUITE at the legendary Stanmore Hotel in London's Mayfair was quite possibly the most beautiful room Effie Price had ever seen. It was certainly one of the most expensive, although not as expensive as the Royal Suite upstairs, where one night alone would cost more than half her annual salary.

As a maid.

She glanced down at her neat black uniform dress and white apron. And right now, she was being paid to clean the room, not gawp at it.

But it was hard not to just stand and admire the cream-coloured living room. It was big enough to land a small plane in, and as well as the glittering chandeliers and bespoke handcrafted furniture the suite was a technophile's dream, with remote-controlled everything.

Was it worth it?

Running her hand across the marble swags on the feature fireplace, she sighed. It was a rhetorical question. Aside from not having the money, she was twenty-two years old and had never had a boyfriend. This might be the closest she was ever going to get to a honeymoon suite.

'There you are. I've been looking for you—'

Picking up a pile of used towels, Effie glanced over her shoulder as Janine and Emily, her friends and fellow chambermaids, put their heads round the door. Actually, according to her job description, they were 'accommodation assistants', but nobody except management ever referred to any of them as anything but maids.

Reaching out, Janine grabbed the pile of towels and dumped them firmly in the laundry basket. 'Shoo!' She pointed at the door. 'We can finish up.'

Effie shook her head. 'It's okay. I'm nearly done.'

Mentally she ticked off her to-do list.

In the bedroom, the Icelandic down duvet sat plumply on the Christian Liaigre four-poster bed, with the pillowcase folds facing away from the door so the guests didn't see them when they walked in. All the woodwork was buffed, the mini bar and desk were both restocked, the bath and sink had been cleaned, toiletries replenished, towels and robes replaced, mirrors polished—

'I just need to vacuum.'

'I can do that.' Eyes narrowing, Emily jerked the handle of the vacuum out of reach. 'Come on, Effie. We've got this. You have somewhere to be, remember? This is the big day.'

Effie felt her stomach flip over. *The big day.*

It sounded like one of those essay-writing prompts you got at school. She breathed out unsteadily. She had loved making up stories in her head, but her dyslexia had made writing them down so hard. Often, she'd chosen to use words she could spell rather than embarrass herself.

Only this big day was not in her head. It was happening in just over an hour.

A wave of part panic, part excitement crested inside her. Ever since she was a little girl, she had dreamed about owning her own perfumery business. Her mother, Sam, had worked from home as a beautician, and every day women would arrive to have a facial or their make-up done.

To Effie, watching the lines around their eyes soften, it had seemed to her almost as if her mother was weaving a spell.

And, for her, making perfume had that same transformative magic. Not just the process of turning the raw ingredients into a unique scent, but the alchemy that scent performed on the person wearing it. The people smelling it. Perfume could change your mood…make you feel happy or sexy or strong.

But she didn't just want to change the lives of strangers. She wanted to get her mother out of a situation where she had to constantly worry about money.

Today, finally, she would be able to make that happen.

She felt her skin prickle with nerves and excitement. She still couldn't quite believe it, but if this meeting went well, and the bank agreed to the loan, the money would be in her account in forty-eight hours. And then her life would change too. Finally, she would stop living in a minor key.

That was her dream—her promise to herself.

And if she kept that promise then all of this—emptying bins, picking up other people's dirty laundry—would be over. She looked over at her friends, her throat tightening. There were some plus points to her job, though.

Two minutes later she was making her way along the corridor.

Her glasses were hurting a little, and she had just slipped them off and was rubbing the place on her face where they had made a small indentation when a man stepped out of the lift, a woman tottering beside him, clutching his arm as if it were a lifebelt. Her footsteps faltered. The guests in this part of the hotel were either wealthy, famous, or wealthy *and* famous, but either way eye contact and conversation were discouraged and, lowering her gaze, she edged closer to the wall as she walked.

'This doesn't look right.'

The man's voice made her head jerk up. More than that: it made goosebumps break out on her arms.

She didn't usually notice voices, mainly because she experienced the world through other senses—how things smelled and tasted. But this man's voice was impossible to ignore. It was rich and deep, with a teasing, shifting accent.

If it was a scent, she thought, it would be a mix of lavender and sun-warmed tobacco, with just a hint of tonka bean.

Make that burnt caramel, she thought, as her eyes fluttered upwards to his face and took in thick, dark hair that gleamed like polished jet beneath the recessed downlights. Sculpted bones beneath smooth gold skin. A dangerous, curving mouth and blue eyes—the bluest eyes she had ever seen. Blue eyes she wanted to high-dive into.

Even though in reality she couldn't actually swim.

He was the most astonishingly, conspicuously beautiful man she had ever seen.

Her throat felt dry and tight, and suddenly it was difficult to catch her breath. She reached out, touching the wall to steady herself. It was that or fall over.

The man was looking down at the woman beside him, and for that she couldn't blame him. Whoever she was, she was his equal in beauty. All long limbs and a mane of glossy blonde hair. Like the horses her father used to watch on the television, walking around the paddock before the race started.

The memory pounded through her like their thundering hooves and suddenly she was shaking inside. She didn't want to think about her father. Thinking about him would just make her feel crushed and powerless, and right now she needed to be strong. Or at least to appear strong.

Only that was hard to do if, like her, you were small and ordinary. And forgettable.

'This is the wrong floor.'

The man stepped backwards, pulling the woman into the lift with him. Turning to hit the button, his eyes met Effie's and she blinked as his blue gaze slammed into hers with the force of a wave.

She felt her feet slide sideways. Around her the walls shuddered and fell and everything she knew or thought she knew was swept away. She was standing in a place she didn't recognise, her body quivering with a wild, dizzying, nameless yearning for—

The lift doors closed.

For what?

Slipping her glasses back on, she stared at her reflection in the polished steel doors, panic and confusion banging inside her. She had no idea how to answer that question. How could she? She had nothing to compare the feeling to.

Not that she minded being a virgin. In fact, when her friends wept over their latest break-up she felt relieved. Her parents' unhappy, lopsided marriage had made her nervous about trusting in big things like love and devotion. As for sex—she simply hadn't met the right person.

Or even the wrong one.

It wasn't just that she was quiet and reserved. Being her mother's carer had meant there was little opportunity for a normal teenage social life. Sex, intimacy and relationships had bypassed her completely, so that aside from a few clumsy kisses on New Year's Eve she had never touched a man or been touched. And this man—this stranger—hadn't touched her, only his gaze had felt like a touch. It had felt real, *intimate*.

Shaking her head, Effie backed away from the lift and hurried along the corridor.

It made no sense. *She* was making no sense. Obviously

she was nervous about the meeting. That was why her head was spinning. And why her body felt taut and jittery.

On the ground floor, she checked her watch. She had left plenty of time to get changed, but as usual when she walked through the main part of the hotel in her uniform several people stopped her to ask for directions to the restaurant or the lift and it took another twenty minutes before she finally got downstairs.

She needed to get a move on. Sidestepping the clusters of guests, she headed towards one of the side entrances, undoing her apron as she walked and pulling her hair out of its bun into a ponytail.

It was too late to get changed now, although it didn't really matter. The bank knew what she did and she wasn't ashamed of her job. But there were still some people who couldn't see past the uniform, and she didn't want to be defined by any prejudice that might provoke.

Her pulse twitched.

What would be wonderful would be to look like the woman from the lift. Smooth and glossily sophisticated. Instead, she was thin, with boring brown hair and boring brown eyes beneath boring brown-rimmed glasses.

But maybe if she'd been smooth and sophisticated, she would have been too enchanted by her own appearance to think about making perfume. And she loved making perfume. For her, scent was so much more than just a finishing touch to an outfit. It was a ticket to a life far beyond the four walls of her tiny bedsit.

She felt a rush of excitement as exhilarating and potent as any of the perfumes she created, and a faint smile pulled at her mouth as she stepped into the bright spring morning. She should definitely add that into her proposal. Maybe she should just put a note on her phone—

Her phone!

She stumbled forward, her foot catching on the thought as if it was a crack in the pavement and, yanking open her bag, fumbled inside. But her phone wasn't there. It was sitting in her locker. Without it she would never be able to find her way to the bank. She had no sense of direction, and it was a waste of time asking people for help in London. They almost always turned out to be tourists.

She was just going to have to go back and get it.

Spinning round, she began swiftly retracing her steps, her skin prickling with anxiety.

It would be all right, she told herself. It was only two stops on the underground plus a short walk, and she still had twenty minutes until her appointment.

She hurried down the street to the side entrance of the hotel, jumping out of her skin as a huge black SUV glided past her noiselessly and slid to a stop beside the kerb. It would be okay. All she had to do was go to her locker—

The door to the hotel swung open and a man erupted into the daylight, flanked by two heavily built men in black suits. His eyes were hidden behind a pair of sleek sunglasses, his attention fixed on the phone in his hand. But she didn't need to see them to know they were blue.

It was the man from the lift, and he was heading straight for her.

For a few half-seconds she hesitated, one foot hovering above the step, her brain telling her to move, her body frozen. Finally, she made a last-minute attempt to sidestep him, but it was too late. She had a fleeting impression of a broad, masculine chest in a blue shirt, topped by a dark-stubbled scowl, and then her bag tumbled from her shoulder and she let out a gasp as her body collided with a solid wall of muscle.

'Oh, I'm so sorry!' she apologised automatically—guests were always right. But her words were cut off as the man from the lift reached out and caught her elbow to steady them both. His grip didn't hurt, but his beauty did. Her heartbeat stumbled. Up close, his face was arresting, extraordinary. But it wasn't just his face making her head feel light.

Beneath that impeccable dark suit there was a barely concealed animal vitality, a power and a ferocity that filled her with a prickling kind of panic, so that she was suddenly and acutely conscious of the rise and fall of her breath beneath her too-tight skin.

'You wouldn't need to be sorry if you'd been looking where you're going,' he said curtly, staring down at her in a way that made her body feel taut and loose at the same time. He took a step closer and tapped the lens of her glasses. 'Maybe these need replacing.'

Effie stared up at him, her cheeks colouring—not just at the injustice of his remark but at the intimacy of his action.

She slipped her arm free. 'Actually, you walked into me, Mr…' She hesitated, waiting for him to provide his name.

'Kane,' he said finally. 'Achileas Kane.'

The name hovered between them like one of the glittering dragonflies she sometimes saw by the Serpentine when she went to Hyde Park after work. She shivered inside. Achileas…from Achilles, the greatest warrior of Ancient Greece, legendary hero of Troy. Formidable. Ruthless. Remorseless.

And the current occupant of the Stanmore Hotel's Royal Suite.

'And you are…?'

His voice was soft, but there was a hard undercurrent in it that made her shake inside.

'Effie Price.' Feeling the shimmering, dismissive never-heard-of-you sweep of his blue gaze, she said quickly,

'And, like I was saying, you walked into me, Mr Kane. So maybe I'm not the only one who needs glasses.'

She felt her breath catch, and something stirred inside her as his pupils flared like twin lighthouse beams across a darkening sea. Behind her the noise from the main road seemed to fade and she was aware of nothing beyond the beating of her heart.

Skin prickling, needing to escape from his penetrating blue gaze, she reached down to pick up her bag. But he beat her to it, and as they straightened up he held it just out of her grasp. Stray beams of sunlight added tiger stripes to the mitred planes of his mesmerising face.

'Is that right?' he said smoothly.

She felt a rush of irritation. The sun might seek him out, burnishing him with celestial golden light like a mythical hero, but nothing could gild his arrogance.

'Yes, it is. Oh, and while we're on the subject I'm taking back my apology,' she added, when she could breathe again. Just because he looked like a Greek god, didn't mean he could act like one. Throwing down thunderbolts with his eyes and looming over her in his dark suit so that he took over the entire world—or at least the bit she was standing in.

'Excuse me?'

Now he was looking at her as if seeing her for the first time.

Probably he was. She had spent most of her life being ignored and side-lined—why should this moment be any different? Or perhaps he was just stunned that anyone, particularly someone like her, should question his world view.

'Taking it back?' His voice had dropped another notch, but it was his mouth that caught her attention, curling up at the corner into a sensual question mark that seemed to tug her upwards like a fish on a hook.

Suddenly, instead of feeling side-lined, she felt side-swiped by the fierce intensity of his focus, but she just about managed to hold his gaze. 'I'm not sorry,' she said shakily. 'How can I be sorry for something I didn't do? I was just being polite,' she said quickly, answering her own question as his eyes narrowed on her face. 'In fact, you should be apologising to me.'

Seriously?

Achileas Kane gazed down at the woman tapping one small foot in front of him, his fury vying with wordless disbelief.

To say that he was in a bad mood would be something of an understatement. The day had started on a wrong note when they had finally left the party at Nico's house this morning.

They. His jaw tightened. He hadn't arrived with Tamara, and he certainly hadn't been planning on leaving with her. Their nine-week relationship had been a purely physical and mutually satisfying affair that he had brought to a close a good six months ago.

But for some reason last night Tamara had decided that, far from being over, their relationship needed rekindling, and on a more serious footing. She'd got horribly drunk and then been horribly sick. Afterwards she'd refused to let go of his arm, clinging on to him as tenaciously as the ivy on Nico's Georgian mansion, so that in the end it had been easier just to bring her back to his hotel room and let her sleep it off.

Only when he'd told her he was leaving she'd gone nuclear, screaming abuse not just in English but Russian too, and threatening him with all manner of violent and painful acts of retribution.

And when that had failed to change his mind, she'd told him she was going to call her father.

Oleg Ivanov was a Russian oligarch. Immensely wealthy in his own right, he had recently married off one daughter to a tech billionaire and was now actively looking for suitable grooms for her two younger sisters.

Achileas's spine tensed. And he was going to have to keep on looking. Matrimony was not on his agenda and, given that one in two marriages ended in divorce, he wasn't exactly sure why it was on anyone else's.

You could make countless vows in front of an endless stream of witnesses and it wouldn't change the facts. Fidelity was a social construct, not a biological imperative, and as the unwanted, unacknowledged bastard son of shipping tycoon Andreas Alexios he was living proof of that.

A familiar ache pushed against his ribs. Sometimes it felt like a hollowed-out space inside his chest—an agonisingly silent, still vacuum that nothing could ever quite fill. Other times it throbbed like a bruise. But it was always there, and he'd learned to live with that sense of being incomplete, of being on the outside looking in, surplus to requirements.

Only now he had a chance to change that.

Despite his matrimonial lapse, Andreas was a traditional Greek man. A patriarch from one of Greece's oldest shipping families. He was also ill and, faced with his own mortality, was looking at his legacy.

A legacy that didn't include a legitimate male heir with his bloodline.

Which was why he was now ready to welcome his illegitimate son into the Alexios clan.

After thirty-two years, four months and ten days, Andreas had decided he wanted his only son in whatever was left of his life.

The thought rang a single jarring note in his head. As a child he had always known that Richard Kane wasn't his father, and he had fantasised endlessly about meeting the man who was. Of course, when it had happened, nothing had gone as he'd imagined. It had been like meeting a stranger. A cool-eyed, patrician stranger.

Only now that same stranger was promising him legitimacy and acceptance.

On one condition.

He wanted his only son to settle down and marry. And, although it had been more hinted at than formally discussed, to produce the heirs that would ensure the patrilineal continuation of the house of Alexios.

Achileas felt his breathing stall. If only it was that easy.

He thought back to Tamara's histrionics.

Maybe it could be. She was wealthy, beautiful, and good in bed. Plus, she wanted things to get more serious. Well, it didn't get more serious than marriage. If he asked her to be his wife, he knew she would say yes in a heartbeat.

But the truth was he didn't want to marry Tamara. As for having children… That wasn't an option. How could a man who had never known his own father possibly know how to be a father himself?

Either way, he was sick and tired of relationships in general, and more specifically relationships with women who thought they could get their own way by yelling and crying and stamping their feet.

His eyes dropped to the woman looking up at him now. Not that this one was yelling or crying.

But apparently Effie Price was expecting him to apologise.

Aware of his bodyguards' carefully averted gazes, he felt a pulse of anger beat across his skin as he stared down at her.

Just who did she think she was talking to? More importantly, who was she to talk to him in this way?

I mean, look at her, he thought dismissively, his gaze skimming her flat shoes and cheap bag. *And as for that dress... It looks like something favoured by early nineteenth-century missionaries.*

If she hadn't walked into him, he would have walked straight past her. His eyes drifted over her small oval face. And yet she seemed familiar for some reason...

The frustration of the last few hours reverberated inside him and he felt something snap. He was tired and hungry and in a hurry. The last thing he needed right now was to be lectured by Little Miss Nobody.

'That's not going to happen,' he said softly.

She blinked owlishly behind the thick lenses of her glasses and there was a moment of silence. Then she lifted her chin, and he felt a sudden, wholly unexpected stirring of lust as his gaze slid down the soft curve of her throat.

'Then you and I have nothing more to say to one another,' she said primly. 'So, if you could just give me back my bag, I have somewhere to be.'

Achileas gritted his teeth. *She* was dismissing *him.*

He stared down at her, too stunned to speak, his pulse juddering like a needle across a record. *Nothing more to say?* No, that wasn't how this worked. He always had the last word.

'Excuse me, sir?'

It was Crawford, the head of his security detail.

'What is it?' he snarled, without turning.

'We have a situation, Mr Kane. Apparently, Ms Ivanov has called her brother and he's heading this way.'

Achileas swore under his breath.

Of course he was.

And, knowing Roman as he did, no doubt he would make a monumental scene.

His mouth thinned. No way: not now and not here.

Normally it wouldn't bother him in the slightest. He thrived on conflict and confrontation. It was one of the reasons he'd gone from business school graduate to hedge fund billionaire before the age of thirty.

But Andreas Alexios was pathologically averse to scandal. That was, after all, why he, his bastard son, had grown up with another man's name.

He felt the ache in his chest spread like an oil spill. It had all been sorted out long before he was born. Pretty much about the time his mother had found out she was pregnant a team of lawyers had arrived with an NDA, and in return for her silence she had received a generous financial settlement.

Of course, he knew now that that amount could have been multiplied tenfold and still not made a dent in the Alexios fortune. But what stung more than that was the fact that his father had sat down with his lawyers and carefully and precisely calculated the cost of abandoning his child. Just enough to ensure his son would always be comfortably provided for, to make him socially acceptable. But not enough so that he could stand on an equal footing with his half-sisters and cousins.

Or course that had changed. He had changed it through hard work and determination. And pushing his ambition, obsessively driving that hunger to succeed, to win, had been an unspoken need to best Andreas so that he no longer needed his father's wealth.

Nor did he want a relationship with Andreas. The years when he had wanted and needed a father were long gone.

What he wanted was revenge. Retribution for being ignored for so long. A reckoning, in fact. Taking what was his by right. Taking back what he was owed. Besides, the Alexios name would be good for business. *His* business. And that was all that mattered to him.

Losing his temper with Roman was a luxury he would have to forgo right now. He couldn't risk giving his father a reason to back off, and if that meant walking away from a fight, then so be it.

But it was galling not to have the last word.

He frowned at the thought, and then Effie Price looked up at him and he saw himself reflected in her glasses. Saw himself as she was seeing him. A narrow-eyed, unshaven surly stranger, looming over her.

Except that he wasn't in the wrong here.

'As it happens, I have plenty to say,' he said, focusing his temper and frustration on the woman in front of him.

There was a beat of silence and then her mouth pulled into a frown. 'Then perhaps it's your hearing that needs testing, Mr Kane,' she said, giving him another glimpse of her throat as her face tilted up to meet his. 'Because I just told you I have somewhere to be.'

The flush to her cheeks made her look almost pretty, and he gazed down at her, momentarily startled by both that thought and by the ripple of heat that skimmed across his skin in response to it.

'There's nothing wrong with my sight or my hearing, Ms Price. In fact, there's nothing wrong with any part of me.'

'Apart from your ego.' One delicate eyebrow arched upwards. 'That seems a little swollen…bloated, even. You might want to go and see a doctor about it.'

In comparison to the insults and accusations Tamara had flung at him earlier, it was nothing. So why did it sting so much? Why did he feel the need not just to deny her accusation but to prove her wrong?

Not knowing or wanting to know the answer to either question, he glanced away to where his bodyguards stood, waiting at a respectful distance.

This was ridiculous.

Roman could show up at any moment, and if that happened the fallout could easily derail his potential rapprochement with his father. And yet, for some reason he couldn't explain, he was still reluctant to end the conversation.

From inside the hotel, he heard the thunder of footsteps, and his shoulders tensed as he saw his bodyguards' heads snap as one towards the doors.

'Sir—'

Crawford stepped forward again. His head of security was a professional. Ex-Special Forces. His face was smooth and unreadable, but there was no mistaking the note of urgency in his voice now.

'We need to move.'

He glanced down at Effie Price.

In the dappled London light, she looked soft and small and young. Imagining Roman's explosive temper ricocheting around her in this quiet side street, Achileas felt a stab of irritation. He couldn't leave her to face that alone. But if he didn't leave now, who knew what she would see and hear? And the last thing he needed was a witness.

So, take her with you...

Later he would wonder what had possessed him to follow through on that entirely random thought, but in the heat of the moment it seemed not only rational but imperative that she go with him.

'You heard the man.' He turned towards her. 'We need to move.'

Her eyes flew to his, but she didn't move. In fact, to

his immense irritation, she seemed to dig her small feet into the pavement.

'Move…?' Staring up at him, Effie Price repeated the word slowly, almost as if she needed to say it out loud to confirm what she'd heard. 'What are you talking about?'

Behind him, raised male voices filtered into the street, indistinct but unmistakably Russian, and the footsteps were closer now—purposeful, unwavering.

It was crunch time.

He took a step forward. 'It's really quite simple. I need to leave. And you're coming with me,' he said firmly.

Her eyes widened cartoonishly and she opened her mouth to protest, but it was too late. He had already tossed her bag onto the back seat and, ignoring her soft gasp of surprise, he ushered her into the car and slid smoothly in beside her.

CHAPTER TWO

EFFIE FELT HER HEART leap into her throat as the car door slammed shut. Seconds later the huge black SUV began to move.

She couldn't believe what was happening.

One moment she'd been standing on the pavement… the next Achileas Kane had been propelling her into the car and she had obeyed, driven not by the hand guiding her but by the sheer force of his personality.

And now she was lying across the back seat of his car, his body wedged alongside hers, muscular legs a hair's breadth away from her thighs, his right arm resting lightly across her waist.

Just as if they were in bed together.

Thinking about her neatly made bed with its faded quilt, she felt her cheeks burn hot against the cool leather seat. As if a man like him would share *her* bed. Only Jasper had ever done that. And he was a cat.

Her breath caught.

This couldn't be real. Things like this happened to other people—not her. Her life had always been so small and contained. But none of that changed the fact that this was happening. To her. *Now.*

She swallowed against the mix of emotions rising in her throat and finally, when she got her breathing under control again, she said quietly, 'What exactly do you think you're doing?'

'I believe it's called an extraction.'

His voice was close, and deep, and she felt it move through her. Maybe if it had just been the nearness of his body she could have stayed remote—after all, she couldn't actually see him. But this close she couldn't block out the scent of him, and she had been right. There was lavender and caramel. But there was also the scent of his skin— clean, warm…

Closing her eyes, she breathed in shakily.

Male.

'Keep your head down.'

Her eyes snapped open. No *please*, she noted. Then again, it wasn't a request but an order, given by a man who had never had to ask for anything. Probably he'd never thanked anyone either. Why would he? No doubt he had been raised from birth believing he was entitled to the life he led. Who would he feel the need to thank?

She couldn't see much through the tinted glass window, but she heard the hotel doors burst open and then a man's voice, bellowing like a maddened bull.

'Where the hell is he?' he roared. *'Achileas! Achileas!'*

There was a quivering silence like the hush before the start of a play, and then he bellowed again—a furious, tumbling tirade of words in a foreign language… Russian maybe. It sounded like either a curse or a challenge. Amplified by his anger and frustration, the man's howls reverberated down the street, and even though the car was moving, Effie couldn't stop herself from shivering.

'You don't need to be frightened. Trust me, his bark is worse than his bite.'

Achileas's deep voice cut through the pounding of her

heartbeat, and she felt the scratch of his stubble against the shoulder of her dress as he adjusted his position.

'I'm not frightened,' she said quietly, and she was surprised to find that she was telling the truth.

Only that didn't make much sense, because surely, she should be frightened. After all, she had just been bundled into a car by a complete stranger. But—and this made no sense at all—*he* was the reason she wasn't scared.

Stunned, surprised, but not scared.

She cleared her throat and edged away from him—away from the hypnotic, destabilising pull of his scent. 'But nor am I particularly inclined to trust anything you say, Mr Kane. Given that you just dragged me off the street in broad daylight.'

'A necessary precaution,' he said, batting away her accusation with the expert dexterity of a lion flicking away flies with his tail. 'My head of security had information that a situation was developing. I didn't want you to get caught in the crossfire.'

His arm shifted against her and every nerve in her body went haywire, her skin pulling so tightly around her bones it felt like she had been shrink wrapped.

'I thought you said his bark was worse than his bite?'

She felt him hesitate. His irritation buffeted the car's interior. 'I did say that, and I was telling the truth. Roman Ivanov isn't violent, but he is volatile, and right now he's a little upset.'

As if to prove the point, another barrage of invective rippled down the street.

'With you, apparently.'

The muscles in his forearm bunched beneath his jacket. 'Yes, Miss Marple, with me. But it's not a big deal.'

'It sounds like it's a big deal to him.'

Abruptly he shifted away from her. She sat up, smoothing her hair away from her face. He watched her in silence, his blue gaze cool and assessing. His mouth—that beautiful, sensual curve—flattened into a line, and then he shrugged.

'He makes a lot of noise, but I've dealt with far worse. It comes with the territory.' His lips curved again, but he wasn't smiling. 'Home invasion. Kidnapping. Carjacking. I've had people threaten to burn down my house. *While I'm in it.* Not that I'd expect you to know what that feels like.'

Which, roughly translated, meant that he was rich and important; and she was not.

She stared at him for a long moment. 'I don't have to know,' she said quietly. 'I don't make a habit of upsetting people.'

He leaned back against the leather upholstery and stared at her steadily, a muscle pulsing in his cheek. 'It was nothing,' he said finally. 'Just a misunderstanding.'

There was a gritty silence. Effie thought back to the beautiful blonde-haired woman in the lift.

She might be inexperienced when it came to men but being a virgin didn't mean she was stupid. And you couldn't work as a chambermaid in a hotel like the Stanmore and not have your eyes opened. Or recognise a mess when you saw one.

Achileas's mess just happened to be a tall, leggy blonde instead of a pile of discarded towels.

At a guess, the woman was most likely the angry Russian's girlfriend. Or wife. Hence his bellowing fury. Not that it was any of her business.

She lifted her chin. 'Did he not look where he was going either?'

For a moment he didn't reply, and she held her breath as the silence in the car swallowed up her words. He did this, she thought. He was like a black hole, so intense and powerful that everything around him just buckled to his will.

'When you said you weren't frightened, I didn't believe you...'

His voice was soft with a huskiness that made her shiver.

'But you're not, are you?'

As his eyes arrowed into hers Effie felt her toes curl up in her shoes. Their intensity made her skin sting. Nobody had ever looked at her like that before—properly, intently, as if he was peeling off not just her uniform but her skin. As if he was *seeing* her.

Her heart thudded beneath her uniform. Her stomach was trembling with panic—far more panic than she'd felt when he jostled her into the car. Not because of his question, but because for the first time in her entire life she wasn't just a daughter or a maid or even a wannabe entrepreneur.

She was a woman.

An unfamiliar heat tiptoed across her skin, and she stared up at him, giddy with the utter newness of the sensations she was feeling. She had lied to him. He did scare her a little. But only like a deer caught in the dazzling beam of headlights. He was just too perfect. Too real. Too solid. Too close.

Too much.

Mostly, though, she was scared of herself.

This morning she had woken up and got dressed and come to work and she had known exactly who she was. Now she was struggling to remember. It was as if she was losing shape, growing soft, melting...

Moments earlier she had thought it was panic. But she knew panic, and it wasn't that pounding through her like a dizzying roll of thunder. This was something else. Something she had never felt or expected to feel. A kind of life-changing fire in her blood that consumed everything in its flames.

Her heart froze mid-beat.

Including the most important meeting of her life.

She gazed past him blindly, a flood tide of shock and dismay sweeping through her. The appointment at the bank had been centre stage and at the front of her mind for so long, and yet in just a few unsettling minutes this man—this stranger—had erased it.

And she had helped him. Like a child seeing something shiny and out of reach, in thrall to the wildfire of yearning he had provoked, she'd let herself be distracted, jeopardising her hopes, her plans, her future.

Abruptly she shook her head. 'Why would I be frightened, Mr Kane? You don't strike me as dangerous or depraved.' She took a breath. 'Just arrogant and thoughtless.'

He was staring down at her, eyes narrowed, his forehead creasing as if he couldn't believe what she was saying. Which was understandable, as she couldn't quite believe it either.

There was a tense, electric pause and then he said softly, 'I didn't ask your opinion of me, Ms Price.'

'And I didn't ask for this, Mr Kane.' She gestured around the SUV's luxurious interior. 'You just took me along for the ride.'

He leaned forward now, his blue eyes darkening like the sea before a storm. 'Along for the ride?' he repeated slowly. 'You heard Ivanov. I was doing you a favour,' he said, with all the sensitivity and self-awareness of a man unaccustomed to being either. 'What would you rather? That I'd left you there?'

She swallowed, her throat suddenly scratchy. *No.* And not because she had felt the warmth of his muscle-hard body next to hers or breathed in the to-die-for scent of his skin.

Her stomach flipped over and she remembered her appointment with the bank manager. She thought about all the beds she'd stripped. The bins she had emptied and the toilets she'd scrubbed. Then she pictured the empty chair where she should be sitting. She clenched her teeth.

'Yes, I would have preferred that. I was supposed to be meeting someone at the bank. It was important.'

His face hardened. It was like watching molten bronze cool.

'*You* have an important meeting?'

She felt her cheeks flush.

'*Had* an important meeting.' She pressed her hand against the door to steady herself. It wasn't strictly true, but it would be by the time she got back to the hotel and retrieved her phone. 'Thanks to you, I've missed it.'

He made a gesture of impatience. 'If it was so important, why didn't you mention it before?'

'I did mention it,' she protested, the unfairness of his remark making her breath judder against her ribs. 'I told you I had to be somewhere, but you didn't listen to me.'

His face was hard. 'You're a grown woman, Ms Price. If you want to be listened to then maybe you should make more of an effort to be heard.'

'In that case,' she said, squaring her shoulders, 'I'd like you to take me back to the hotel. No—on second thoughts, you can just drop me here. That way you won't have to worry about running into Mr Ivanov.'

He straightened then, and as his gaze narrowed on her face she saw the flame in his eyes, the smouldering male pride.

'As you wish,' he said, staring down at her, suddenly ferociously cold and hard and hostile.

She felt the hair on her nape rise as he snapped out something in Greek, and within seconds the huge car slid to a stop.

As the bodyguard in the passenger seat got out to open her door, she picked up her bag.

'Take care, Ms Price.'

His deep voice pulled her back into the cool interior, and she turned, her eyes locking with his.

'I'm not the one hiding, Mr Kane,' she said quietly.

His face changed. He looked startled—*no*, actually, what he looked was winded, as if instead of speaking she had landed a punch to his gut.

But then the door opened, and she was on the pavement, walking and then running, pushing through the lunchtime shoppers, moving as fast and as far as she could from his furious sapphire gaze.

I'm not the one hiding.

Jaw clenching, Achileas lifted the glass of whisky— his second—and threw back the contents, a pulse of anger beating erratically across his skin. Tension was part of his life. His work both generated and required it. But he had never been this tense—ever.

After Effie had got out of the car, he had been so incensed that he hadn't been able to speak. When finally, his voice had returned, he had curtly told his driver to take him to his apartment—one of the four homes he owned at strategic points around the globe.

His lip curled. Properties, not homes.

He didn't have a home. Not now, not ever.

His stepfather, Richard Kane, had been in the US military, and as a consequence the family had moved around a lot. Until the marriage had ended. And then shortly afterwards he'd been sent to boarding school in England.

The tension in his shoulders spread down his spine, knotting at the base of his back, new pain mingling with the old.

Boarding school had finished what his stepfather had started, effectively turning him into a nomad, a citizen of nowhere. A small boy with a suitcase that for a long time had been bigger than he was.

Returning to the States at the end of the first term, he'd found that as well as another new home he had a new stepfather—Mike. But by the time he'd left school, Mike was long gone. His mother was never alone for long. *Unlike him.*

Thinking back to the men who had come and gone over the years, he felt the ache in his chest press against his ribs. As it turned out, they had all been pretty interchangeable. After an opening flurry of dad-like activities none of them had bothered pretending they wanted to be a father—not a father to him, anyway.

Then again, why should they? He hadn't belonged to them. Hadn't belonged anywhere. He was like the cat in that Rudyard Kipling story. He walked by himself, and all places were alike to him.

He glanced around the apartment.

Like all his properties, it was real estate gold. Tall ceilings, big windows, plenty of open space, all decorated in largely neutral shades. There were no distinguishing features, no familial photos.

His fingers tightened around the smooth glass tumbler. He would have preferred to go back to the Stanmore, but there was a chance that Roman—or, worse, Tamara—might still be at the hotel and he didn't trust himself to be either calm or kind.

And that incensed him more, for it seemed to validate Effie Price's accusation. Maybe that was why he had been sitting on this sofa for over an hour now. Sitting and stewing over her parting shot.

He gazed morosely out of the penthouse's panoramic window, his eyes tracking across the skyline, leapfrogging between London's iconic landmarks. There was no reason that he should still be thinking about what Effie had said. She was nothing to him. Aside from her name, he knew nothing about her. And yet he felt as though she was here, sitting beside him, staring at him gravely.

Leaning back against the sofa cushions, his body tense, nostrils flaring, he suddenly knew why he was feeling that way. It was because she *was* here. Or at least her scent was, and it was filling his senses.

He felt his pulse accelerate.

Mostly he wasn't a big fan of women's perfumes, but this one…

Lowering his face, he breathed in the smell of her, heat creeping over his skin. It wasn't overtly seductive or cloyingly floral, like a lot of the perfumes women wore. But then it wasn't really a perfume. Perfume was manmade, stoppered in a bottle in a factory and sold to the masses.

Effie's scent was something more subtle…both delicate and tantalising, like a promise hovering over her skin.

His pulse slowed a little as he remembered the moment when he'd pulled her down onto the seat beside him. Their bodies had barely touched, but her scent had travelled over his skin like the softest caress, so that for a moment he'd had to fight against the urge to pull her close and keep inhaling her scent.

Infuriated by the memory of how near he'd come to losing control, he stood up and stalked across the room and out onto the balcony that wrapped around two sides of his apartment. In the early afternoon sunlight London looked oddly peaceful, with a warm, golden glow gilding the steel-framed skyscrapers and softening the sharp brick edges.

His mouth twisted. If only his father's edict could be similarly softened into something more appealing.

Had this been a business negotiation it would be easy to bat away Andreas's demands. But he couldn't take that chance—couldn't risk his father turning his back on him, couldn't risk losing the chance to get what he was owed.

For weeks now he'd been trying to find a solution. Only, thanks to Effie, instead of focusing on a reconciled future with his father he'd spent the best part of the day brooding over a past he couldn't change.

'Excuse me, Mr Kane.'

Achileas turned. It was Beatrice, his housekeeper.

'What is it?' he snapped.

'I'm sorry to bother you, sir. Crawford found this in the car, and he wondered if you would like him to dispose of it or return it.'

She held out a folder.

He stared at it for a moment, and then took it.

It was cheap-looking, made of plastic. The kind a child might use at school for handing in an essay. Flipping it open, he felt his breath snag on the name at the top of the first page: *Effie Price*.

It was a business proposal for a perfumery. Suddenly he was conscious of the hammering of his heart.

'No,' he said slowly. 'No, leave it with me.'

Walking back into the apartment, he sat on the sofa, put down his glass and started to read, skimming down the page with practised speed.

She was a maid at the Stanmore. That at least explained the dress.

His pulse twitched as he remembered that moment outside the hotel when she had seemed so familiar. He had seen her at work—by the lift. When Tamara had insisted on getting out on the wrong floor. Only she hadn't been wearing glasses then.

Ten minutes later, he shut the folder. It was a pity her missing her meeting because it was an interesting proposition. And she was clearly passionate about perfume and talented to boot, he thought, breathing in the last lingering traces of her scent.

But then again, he would stake his business reputation on her being refused any loan.

Yes, by his standards, the amount she wanted to borrow was tiny. Unfortunately, however, she had next to no security, and he could see problems with both her cost to revenue ratio and her customer acquisition strategy.

Tipping his head back, he stretched out his neck and shoulders.

None of which mattered to him, of course. He was just procrastinating, avoiding the moment of truth. That after weeks of thinking, deliberating, weighing up the alternatives and generally attempting to resolve the dilemma created by his father's stipulation, he was still no closer to knowing what to do.

And he was running out of time.

Andreas wouldn't—couldn't—wait for ever.

His hand beat out an impatient rhythm against the arm of the sofa. He knew he didn't want to get married, but he needed a wife. And, whoever she was, he needed her to understand that, while legal, their marriage would be just for show. Yet it would have to appear indisputably real to his father.

Only that was the problem.

All of the women he knew would not be willing to just act the part of his wife. They would want it to be real.

The obvious solution was to pay someone. But he could

hardly advertise the position on the Arete Equity website. His shoulders slumped. Surely there had to be an answer. Something he'd missed. But after months of fruitless rumination and circular arguments maybe it was time to face facts. Perhaps she didn't exist. This woman who needed money and yet would not be fazed by such an outlandish suggestion.

Or maybe she was right under his nose. He sat forward abruptly and picked up Effie's proposal, a charge of electricity snapping across his skin.

There it was: her address. Praed Gardens. His mind whirred as out of the unsatisfactory and messy randomness of his day so far, an idea slid into diamond-sharp focus inside his head, clean and pure like a drop of rain.

'Beatrice?' He got to his feet as the housekeeper appeared.

'Yes, Mr Kane?'

'Tell Crawford to bring the car round to the front of the building. I have a meeting with someone.'

His fingers flexed against the folder. He could talk to his lawyer en route…

Yanking open her fridge, Effie peered inside. Not that she needed to look. She already knew what was in there. Half a pint of milk, a bag of ready-washed lettuce, some yoghurts that were well past their sell-by date and a jar of tamarind paste.

Her throat tightened. She had been planning on ordering a takeaway for tonight—to celebrate. Only now there was nothing to eat. Or celebrate.

She probably should go to the supermarket, but honestly, she couldn't face it right now. She basically wanted today to be over. That was why she was already in her pyjamas. Because the biggest day of her life had turned into the worst.

By the time she got back to the Stanmore, found her phone and called the bank, she was an hour late. All she'd been able to do was apologise. She hadn't told them what had happened—just that she had forgotten the appointment. She could hardly tell them the truth. Who would believe her?

Oh, I forgot my phone, and when I went back to get it one of the guests at the hotel forced me into his car and drove off with me.

She shut the fridge door. Thank goodness she hadn't told her mum that today was the day. Knowing how much it would mean to Sam, she had been badly tempted to do so, but maybe she'd had a sixth sense about how everything would work out. What she should have done was book another appointment, but she was too exhausted.

And she couldn't help thinking that maybe it was fate... that maybe her dreams were just meant to stay dreams.

She swallowed past the lump in her throat. She hadn't cried. She rarely did. In her experience crying rarely changed anything, and there were worse things than missing an appointment with your bank manager.

A lot worse.

She'd seen more than enough of them first-hand. Lived with them and through them.

When she was a child, her father's gambling had always been there in the background. Sometimes he'd stopped for weeks, even months, but then he would come home, his face flushed with triumph, and it would all start up again. The lying, the stealing, the broken promises...

And then her mum had the stroke, her first. Even now she could remember the shock of going to the hospital and seeing the IV drip in her mother's arm.

That day Sam's life had changed for ever. She had never fully recovered. But neither had she given up. She might not be able to tint eyelashes anymore, but she had taught herself to paint—first still-life, then people. Her friends, her carers…

And her daughter.

Glancing over at the portrait her mother had done of her, Effie felt her legs tremble as the misery she had been fighting all afternoon threatened to take her feet out from under her. Despite her frailty, Sam was still her biggest supporter, and getting the loan, getting the business up and running, would have made her mum so happy.

If only she hadn't forgotten her phone. She never had before, but she had been distracted.

Distracted…

Her skin felt suddenly too tight, and as she pictured Achileas's fierce blue gaze a shiver of heat prickled over her.

Would she have forgotten her phone if she hadn't locked eyes with him in the corridor? Probably not. Only then she would never have come back to the hotel. Never bumped into him. Never felt his hand on her waist or breathed in the tantalising scent of his hard, muscular body.

She stared at her portrait. Unlike her, Achileas Kane was unequivocally beautiful, and it was okay to think that. Like admiring a beautiful painting in a gallery. But that didn't take away from how rude and arrogant and full of himself he was.

And yet if she could bottle how he made her feel in those few dizzying moments when he pulled her onto the seat beside him that perfume would be an instant bestseller.

There was a knock at the door.

Oh, no.

She turned and gazed across the room, her heart not just

sinking but plummeting like a stone down a well. There was only one person who ever knocked on her door at this time of the day.

Mark worked at the Stanmore too, as a porter. He had an unrequited crush on Emily and wanted to cross-examine Effie about her at every opportunity. To that end, he had taken to dropping in on his way home from work. Normally she just made him a cup of tea and let him talk, but she couldn't face him tonight.

She would just have to pretend she was going out.

Picking up her coat, she pulled it on quickly and unlocked the door.

'Good evening.'

Effie blinked.

It wasn't Mark. It was Achileas Kane, his big body filling the doorframe, his blue eyes fixed intently on her face. For a moment she couldn't breathe, much less speak. How had he managed to find her? More importantly, why was he here?

As if he could read her mind, he held out a folder... *her* folder.

'You left it in my car.' He frowned. 'Are you going out? Or going to bed?'

Her heart fluttering like a moth inside a glass, she stared at him, still lost for words. 'Neither,' she said at last.

His gaze swept assessingly over her in silence. 'In that case, perhaps you could invite me in.'

In where? Into her flat?

She stared at him in shock and confusion, then shook her head. 'I don't let strangers into my flat, Mr Kane. Just my friends. And people I have to let in. To read the meter or fix the boiler.'

'I see.' He shifted against the frame. 'Well, we might not be friends, but I wouldn't say we were strangers. And if it helps, I could always pretend to read the meter.' There was a beat of silence and then he said quietly, 'Please, Effie.'

It wasn't a big deal. He'd just called her by her name. But something about the way he put the emphasis on the second syllable made her head feel light, and she let the gap between the door and the frame widen.

'Okay, you can come in—but you can't stay long. I have work tomorrow.'

'At the Stanmore.'

'How do you know that? And how did you find out where I live?'

He gave a leisurely shrug as he strolled through the door. 'I read your proposal.'

She stared after him, stunned, almost hating him. 'You had no right. It's private.'

'Which is why I am returning it to you. Did you get to your meeting?'

His intensely blue eyes seemed to pierce her skin, seeing more than she wanted him to—seeing too much. 'No, I didn't.'

'That's a shame. It is a good proposal. A little amateurish, and not nearly ambitious enough, but it is well-argued.'

As he turned slowly on the spot she followed his gaze, trying to imagine what her small, neat flat must look like to him.

'Did you paint this?'

His eyes had stopped on her portrait, and as he leaned forward her body felt taut and achy…almost as if he was leaning into her.

She shook her head. 'No, my—' She was about to say *my mother*, but he already knew enough about her life from her proposal. She didn't need to reveal anything more to this stunning, arrogant man. 'No, Sam painted it.'

'Sam?' His face stilled. 'Are you in a relationship?'

'No, I'm not.' She shook her head again, turning away to pull off her coat so that he wouldn't see the lie in her eyes. Although it was more just letting him assume something than actually lying. 'Not that it's any of your business.'

'True enough.'

Straightening up, he turned to face her, and she felt goosebumps explode over her skin as his eyes found hers.

'But that could be about to change.'

She stared at him, trying to make sense of his words. 'I'm sorry, Mr Kane—'

'Achileas,' he corrected her. 'I think we've moved past any need for formalities.'

Had they?

Her heart thudded hard, his words accelerating her already racing pulse. 'Maybe…but either way I'm not sure I understand what it is you're trying to say.'

The shifting evening sunlight was licking the miraculous curves of his cheekbones, but his gaze on her face was as dark and powerful and impossible to ignore as a supernova.

'Then let me explain.' He sat down on the sofa and gestured towards the armchair opposite, as if this was his flat, not hers. 'I have a proposition for you. You know the kind of thing—I scratch your back, you scratch mine.'

The small living space seemed to shrink and grow airless as his words swept through her like a forest fire. *Scratch. Back. Yours. Mine.*

'No, I don't think I do know,' she said, trying desperately not to sound as panicked as she felt.

'It's quite simple. I will give you five times what you were asking from the bank. Only it won't be a loan. You won't have to pay a penny of it back.'

Effie blinked. 'You're going to give me five times what I asked for? For nothing?'

'No, not for nothing,' he said, his gaze narrowing in on hers in a way that made her breathing go shallow. 'I need something in return. Something a little, shall we say, unorthodox.'

She stared at him, startled by the word and the flurry of unsettling thoughts it prompted. 'So, what is it that you need?' she said after a moment.

He stretched out his legs and his mouth twisted into a smile that managed to be both mocking and dangerous.

'I need a wife.'

CHAPTER THREE

A WIFE!

Effie stared up at Achileas in stunned silence. She must have misheard him…misunderstood what he was saying. Or was he pranking her?

But as she searched his face, she saw that his expression was no longer mocking but cool and calculating. As if she was some small animal that had blundered into the trap he'd set.

'And you want to marry *me*?'

He frowned, and then, shaking his head, he laughed. Not the nice, warm kind of laughter that accompanied an amusing joke, but the humourless sort that people used when something wasn't funny.

Just wildly implausible to the point of being ludicrous.

Her fingers bit into the folder as she felt it ripple through her.

'Of course I don't want to marry you, Effie. But don't take it personally. I don't want to marry anyone.'

He shifted against the sofa, one muscular arm extending along the cushions. 'I do, however, *need* a wife.'

Now he was making even less sense.

'Need is a strong word, Mr Kane,' she said slowly.

'Achileas,' he corrected her again. 'And maybe you're

right. Need *is* too strong a word. Perhaps it would be more accurate to say that I *require* a wife.'

He stretched out his legs, making himself comfortable.

'My father, Andreas, is elderly and very old-fashioned. He has certain expectations, ambitions…' he hesitated '…certain *wishes* for his life, and for his son. And as his son I want to honour those wishes.'

The fog of confusion inside her head suddenly cleared.

'He wants you to get married?'

His dark eyebrows formed a solid line as he nodded. 'Correct. Like I said, he's very old-fashioned. His values are traditional, maybe even a little archaic. But, as someone who's been married for forty years, he believes matrimony is a cornerstone of life.'

Forty years of marriage. That was a good thing, wasn't it? It was a testament to his parents' commitment and love. And yet there was an edge to his voice as if the longevity of their marriage was not a matter of pride or delight, but inconvenience.

She felt suddenly closer to tears than she had all day. Didn't he know how lucky he was? How privileged? To have seen love given and received by two people who had chosen one another. It was as rare and elusive as orris, the precious oil produced from an iris bulb.

She couldn't imagine ever taking that for granted. Being like him. He was so pampered, so entitled…

Except that made him sound like a child—a sulky little boy—and there was nothing boyish about Achileas Kane. He was a man…the physical embodiment of unapologetic masculinity.

'But you don't believe that?' she said.

He shrugged almost lazily, but she could sense a tension that hadn't been there a moment earlier.

'Why would I? Why would anyone? Humans and their

ancestors have been walking the planet for about six million years, and for all but a thousand of those years they weren't monogamous. But, as I have explained, matrimony matters to my father. And as he grows older it matters more.'

Her heart thudded as he looked up, his clear blue gaze sharpening against hers. 'And he is getting frailer. That's why I require a wife. Just in the short term,' he added smoothly, as if this somehow made his bizarre request understandable.

Which it didn't.

But why should she care if it was understandable or not? She thought back to his short, derisive bark of laughter, then back further, to when he had told her that she needed to make more effort to be heard if she wanted to be listened to.

Then make him listen, she told herself.

'You might require a wife, Mr Kane, but I don't require a husband. Nor do I want one. Not even in the short term.'

Watching his dark brows snap together, she felt her pulse judder. Was that true? It was certainly true that she had never imagined getting married, but then she hadn't even had a boyfriend yet.

Remembering how she'd let him think Sam had been an ex, she felt her skin burn beneath her pyjamas. The truth was that she only knew a handful of men, and out of those only one husband: her father. And, much as she couldn't stop loving her dad, she would never want to be married to a man like Bill Price. A man who was so addicted to the high of winning that he ended up losing everything. His home. His family. His sanity.

Only that was a whole lot more truth that she was prepared to share with this man now sitting on her sofa. Achileas had bulldozed his way into her life, not once but twice today, and she was still reeling from their last encounter.

Glancing up, she found him looking at her in silence. From where she was standing, he looked relaxed, but she knew that if she got closer, she would see a muscle throbbing in the hard curve of his jaw.

'A wise woman,' he said softly. 'Marriage is for monarchs and fools. It's a plot device in a soap opera. But I'm not offering you a typical marriage, Effie. Our arrangement would be something more pragmatic. Think of it as a mutually beneficial merger of interests.'

A merger of interests.

She stared at him, panic beating in her belly as a cluster of feverishly inappropriate images chased through her head. Damp bodies moving together seamlessly on a tangle of sheets... Bodies peeled naked, hot skin rippling beneath a hand, a tongue—

No.

That wasn't what he meant—and anyway that wasn't who she was. She felt awkward and self-conscious about undressing in front of other women. The idea that she would ever be naked with a man like Achileas made her feel singed inside, and it took every ounce of strength she had not to turn and run to the door.

'We don't share any interests,' she said quickly.

There was a long, uneven silence. Then, 'You think?' He raised one dark eyebrow, considering her.

Claiming her.

She breathed in sharply as every nerve-ending in her body exploded.

That was nonsense. Of course he wasn't claiming her. He wanted to use her to pacify his father and in exchange he was offering her money.

It was a Faustian pact with a blue-eyed devil.

'I thought you wanted to start a business, Effie. I thought it was important to you,' he said now.

The dare in his voice danced over her skin, making her body twitch with fear and fascination.

Her hands clenched. 'It is.'

He stared at her steadily, his blue gaze no longer a sapphire gleam but the glint of tempered steel. 'How important? How badly do you want it? I mean, how far are you prepared to go? Because I can make it happen just like that.'

He snapped his fingers and she blinked.

He could. She glanced down to where he lounged on the sofa. His will was not like hers. It wasn't just an intangible concept. It was a hungry, living thing with a fiercely beating heart.

'Trust me, it will be a lot easier and less painful than dealing with a bank. If you even get that far. Banks are cautious about lending their money. Particularly to new businesses.'

Pulse jumping, she glanced down at his legs, noticing without intending to how the fabric pulled tight around the muscles of his thighs. Thighs that had been inches from hers just a few hours earlier...

'I know that,' she said quietly, hugging the folder protectively against her stomach.

She had read the statistics and they were daunting. Twenty percent of new businesses failed within a year. That went up to a terrifying fifty percent in five years.

'Then you'll also know that they're going to hold your proposal up to the light, and that if they see anything they don't like they will turn you down.'

Effie felt her stomach twist painfully. He was right. Banks weren't charities. And even when she was writing her proposal she had been horribly aware of her lack of experience and security. All she had to offer was an unquantifiable passion and a dream.

What if that wasn't enough?

At least if she agreed to what Achileas was suggesting she would have the money, no questions asked. Questions she might not be able to answer.

But marrying someone you barely knew even in the short term—whatever that meant—wasn't just unorthodox, it was crazy. She would have to be crazy even to consider it.

'Maybe they will,' she said quietly. 'But that's not a reason to marry a man I don't know.'

There was a small, stifling pause.

'So let's get to know each other,' he said softly, and then, more softly still, 'Tell me about yourself, Effie Price. Who are you?'

Staring up at Effie's small, pale face, Achileas felt his breathing jolt.

Why had he asked her that?

It wasn't a question he had ever asked anyone— certainly not a woman. Then again, he had never wanted to know the answer before, and if he did now, it was only for the obvious reason that he needed a wife.

His jaw tightened. *Need.* That word again.

He could play semantics, call it a requirement, but that didn't change the facts. If he wanted the key to his father's kingdom, he needed a wife.

Correction: he needed Effie to be his wife.

Back at his apartment, when the idea had appeared fully formed in his head, he had known there and then that she would be perfect. Why else would fate have thrown them together like that?

Unfortunately, Effie was not coming up with the same answer as he was.

A spasm of tension in his back—the same spasm that had been plaguing him for weeks now—made his shoulders tense against the misshapen fabric-covered lump that was masquerading as her sofa.

He was honest and arrogant enough to admit that he hadn't anticipated her being so resistant to the idea of him as a husband. Obviously, he had known she would be surprised, stunned, speechless... But he was Achileas Kane, founder and CEO of Arete Equity. He was rich, powerful and handsome. And she—well, she just was a chambermaid...a real-life Cinderella to his hedge fund prince. So, after her initial shock had worn off, of course he'd assumed that she would react like any normal woman.

His eyes narrowed on the way Effie was standing, her thin arms clutching the cheap plastic folder in front of her chest like some kind of shield, and he wondered why he had made that assumption.

What was the matter with her? Didn't she know how lucky she was? He was offering to *give* her five times what she was asking from the bank, and instead of being grateful and excited she was staring at him with that same, grave expression on her face as before.

And now she was shaking her head.

'You know who I am.' Her brown eyes hovered on his face. 'You know where I work, how much I earn. You know where I live...how I live,' she said, in that delicate, precise way of hers. 'But if you're serious about this "arrangement", then the question I need answering is, who are *you*?'

For a moment he was stunned, then outraged.

No, that's not how this works, he thought for the second time that day. She didn't get to question him, make him jump through hoops, *judge* him.

Nobody did.

Nobody except one man—the only man he could neither vanquish nor reject because, in spite of everything
Andreas had done and not done, it was the saw-toothed
ache of his absence that drove Achileas through each day.
An ache that was not yet rubbed smooth even though he
had turned it over and over endlessly, like an angry sea
throwing pebbles against the shore.

He hated how it made him feel so powerless. And now
this woman was wanting to know who he was. As if he
would ever tell *her*—tell anyone.

It was ludicrous, unthinkable, and he remained stubbornly silent. Having been on the receiving end of his
father's silence for so long, he knew first-hand just how
effective a weapon it was. But if he didn't answer her,
then what?

He glanced over at the tilt of her chin. Incredibly, it
seemed that she would refuse his offer and there would
be nothing he could do about it.

She might bend, but she wouldn't break.

Like one of those small, thin-stemmed flowers with
pale petals that seemed to grow everywhere in England. A
wildflower that looked as if one good gust of wind would
snap it in two.

But there was strength in those fragile stems. At school,
he'd had to endure cross-country runs through the grounds,
and after a storm, when everything else had been pulled
up by its roots or flattened, those delicate-stemmed flowers had still been upright.

'What do you want to know?' he said slowly.

'I'm not sure…'

She hesitated, and he felt something pinch inside him.
Outside the Stanmore, even in the car, she had been so
composed, so calm. Now, though, here in her home, with

her hair in a plait, and her taut, unblinking gaze, she reminded him of one of those Margaret Keane paintings of huge-eyed waifs. She seemed smaller, younger, wary... And he didn't like how that made him feel.

It was probably just the lighting in her flat.

Or her pyjamas. He had never seen a grown woman wear something so determinedly asexual. His gaze hovered momentarily on where the small, fine bones disappeared beneath her grey top, and he felt his body tighten.

Blanking his mind to what was surely just the consequence of six months of virtual celibacy, he gritted his teeth.

What Effie Price wore in bed was irrelevant to this negotiation.

Effie was an adult, and this was a business deal. And it was a good deal for her. Money aside, she would have access to his world. She would learn how to talk and dress and live like the woman she was pretending to be—and most important of all, after it was all over, she would have her own perfumery business.

He leaned forward slightly, breathing in. Her scent was in no way overpowering. On the contrary, it was elusive. And yet he could feel it tugging at his senses.

'I suppose I'd like to know why me?'

Her voice made his pulse jump and, looking up, he found her brown eyes watching him.

'Why not some other woman? Like the woman you were with at the Stanmore? She's very beautiful.'

'Tamara?' He shook his head, his body tensing automatically at the idea. Tensing in a way that it didn't when he thought of Effie. 'She's beautiful enough, but she's too highly strung.' *Exhaustingly so.* 'That's why I broke up with her. Not today,' he added, although he wasn't quite sure why. 'It was six months ago.'

'But surely there must be other women?'

There were.

A long unbroken stream of glossy-haired socialites like Tamara, or leggy models with bee-stung lips. None had lasted more than three months. Most had lasted a lot less, averaging about a week.

'You have certain qualities they lack,' he said, choosing his words carefully.

Effie was emphatically not his type. Too thin. Too plain. Too quiet. But that was a good thing. He didn't need any distractions. As for sex— This was essentially a business arrangement. He couldn't imagine her offering anything that would make it worthwhile adding *that* extra layer of complication.

'You mean because I'm poor?'

The directness of her words surprised him. But it was true. Her current account balance was pitiful, and her savings amounted to loose change. He glanced around the small living room, seeing the cheapness of everything. And yet that hadn't been his first consideration.

'Partly… But earlier, in the car, you kept your head. I don't know many women—or many men—who would have done that.'

Her clear brown eyes rested on his face. 'And that's what you need. Someone who can keep her head.'

It was a statement, not a question, but he answered it anyway. 'Yes, I do. This has to look real.'

'And what about you?'

She was looking at him, her gaze straight and unblinking. 'What about me?'

'Can you do this? Can you lie to your father and keep your head?'

He felt as if he'd been kicked by a horse.

Lie to his father? Yes, he could easily do that, he thought

bitterly. Given that officially Andreas had no son, he was a walking, talking, living lie. His jaw clenched. That was one of the things his father's money had paid for: the Alexios name to be kept off his birth certificate.

But Effie didn't need to know that he was a bastard, and that his future legitimacy was dependent on him marrying. Or that lying to his father was payback for the lie about his birth.

'It won't be a problem,' he said coolly, his blue eyes finding hers. 'All that matters to me is that my father believes I'm happily married.' He tipped back his head. 'So, do we have an agreement?'

The air was suddenly electric, quivering expectantly like a held breath.

Effie looked across to where the man sat, waiting for her to answer. She had chosen that particular sofa because it had been the smallest she could find, the only one that fitted into her flat, and his muscular body made it look like a piece of dolls' house furniture.

Her pulse scampered.

Actually, it wasn't a sofa…it was a loveseat—presumably because couples who were in love were happy to cosy up to one another. But Achileas wasn't in love with her, and she wasn't in love with him—thankfully.

Her heart gave a little shiver of pity for the woman who actually fell in love with Achileas Kane. Not because he was prepared to lie to his father in this way. Sometimes white lies were necessary. They were even forgivable if it meant that they prevented pain or additional suffering. No, what scared her was the ruthlessness and determination that simmered beneath that superbly tailored suit. The relentlessness that was almost elemental. Like a river of molten lava or a hurricane tearing up a city.

He was a man who was used to winning, to getting his own way. A man who didn't understand the concept of no. Her breath trembled in her throat. He made it sound so simple. Marriage for money. And she could see how it might work in theory. But in practice…?

She glanced across the room, her stomach clenching as her gaze settled on the portrait. *Who are you?* Achileas had asked her that question and there was the answer. Small regular features. Straight brown hair. Serious brown eyes. Fresh-faced. Forgettable. Utterly unremarkable.

In other words, not the kind of woman a man like Achileas Kane would ever notice, much less marry.

She bit into her lip. Anybody looking at them would have that exact same thought. That had been true when he'd cannoned into her outside the Stanmore, and it would stay true. This whole idea was crazy. She didn't even know why they were discussing it.

So why was the conversation still going on? Why had she even let him into her flat? Her insides tightened, blooming with a heat that was unfamiliar and seductive. Discomforting.

'Effie?'

Her name on his lips pulled her in and she turned to face him, the heat spreading to her cheeks.

He was why.

He affected her. He was like the most delicious, irresistible scent teasing her senses, and just for a moment she closed her eyes and breathed him in, let herself be swept away to a Mediterranean island—

But it was time to put the stopper back in the bottle.

Achileas Kane might be a man who didn't understand the meaning of no, but he was going to have to learn. Because he was wrong about her. She couldn't do this even if he could.

She took a breath to steady her nerves. 'Thank you for bringing back my folder, but I think I'll take my chances with the bank.'

He stared at her, his gaze rolling over her like an ocean wave. 'I think that would be a mistake.'

She shook her head. 'No, what would be a mistake would be trying to make this work.'

'It will work,' he said stubbornly, as she had known he would.

And then he pushed up from the sofa and rose, the simple movement carrying with it such an extraordinary impression of power that she took a step backwards. As he stopped in front of her, she felt breathless and off-balance. She had never been confronted by anyone with such a sense of purpose.

'It will work because my father will see what he wants to see.'

'And what if he guesses the truth?' she asked quietly.

'He won't,' he said, looking down at her, his fierce certainty buffeting her so that she had to dig her heels into the carpet to stop herself from stumbling backwards. 'How could he?'

'Easily,' she said quietly, heat breaking out on her skin as his eyes locked onto hers.

Did she need to spell it out?

'You can't really think that anyone will believe we're a couple? Especially your father—the man who raised you.' She cleared her throat. 'I'm not exactly your type, am I?'

There was a short, jangling pause, and then his gaze darkened and narrowed in on hers. 'Not historically, no. But I wasn't looking for a wife before.'

He wasn't looking for one now. Not a real one. Only at some point, if she agreed to this, she would have to act like a wife. They would have to look as if they were in love.

Not in private, but in public, they would have to look and talk and touch like lovers.

But how could she do that when she had never been in love? Never been intimate with a man.

Her breath frayed in her throat. 'We can't just tell people we love each other. We'll have to show them. And—'

His gaze narrowed fractionally. 'And what?' he prompted.

She swallowed, shifted. 'I'm not sure I can do that.'

Actually, she was certain she couldn't. Her only experience of kissing a man had been brief and botched and bumbling.

He stared at her for a long moment, then took a step closer—close enough that even in the fading light she could see the stubble forming on his jaw, the flecks of green and gold in his eyes.

'In that case we have a problem. For this to work we both need to feel sure…'

There was a shimmering beat of silence.

'But maybe I could help,' he said softly.

Something was happening. The room was changing, shrinking, growing darker. She was changing too. Her body was humming. She could feel tremors of heat pulsing through her, swirling up inside her like flames drawn up a chimney.

What did he mean? How could he help—?

Her brain stalled, her heart stopped as his lips brushed against hers. And then his hand slid over her jaw to cup her cheek, and he lowered his head and fitted his mouth to hers.

It was like a thousand stars exploding. She felt all breath leave her body. Around her the air grew thick and heavy. Inside, everything started to melt.

Her eyelashes fluttered shut. This was nothing like

any kiss she had experienced or could have imagined. His mouth was hot and hard, and the touch of his lips sent a fierce tingling heat straight to her belly. She arched helplessly against him, her hips meeting his, her fingers scrabbling against his arm, blindly, greedily kissing him back.

He made a rough sound in his throat, wrapping his hand around her waist and pulling her closer. The hard press of his body made flames roar through her, burning everything in their path, her hopes, the failure of her day, all logical thought so that there was nothing except Achileas and this devastating, demanding fire of need and longing…

'Effie—'

He pulled her closer, then moved back, pushing her away as if in some strange, one-sided tug-of-war. Opening her eyes, she looked up at him dazedly. His hand was still cupping her face, but the blue of his eyes was rolling back like a tide turning.

Stunned, made mute by what had just happened and by its abrupt ending, she glanced past him, trying to steady herself, to get her bearings. In the early evening sunlight, her flat looked both familiar and yet strange and new, almost as if she was in a dream.

But her grip on his arm was real. And so was that kiss.

A few tendrils of her hair had escaped to curl loosely against her collarbone, and she watched, mesmerised, as he reached out and wound one round his finger.

'Problem solved,' he said softly. 'All we have to do is agree to the terms of our arrangement and then we sign a contract, you sign an NDA, and we're good to go.'

She stared up at him, fighting to keep her tremulous, lambent reaction to him to herself. Because of course it hadn't been real for him. He had simply wanted to prove a point—and he had.

Unequivocally.

'So, do we have an agreement?'

His voice was rough, impatient, and she felt her stomach clench. But it would be different next time. *She* would be different. She would know what to expect. Besides, when they were alone and behind closed doors there would be no need to kiss at all, and they wouldn't kiss like that in public.

They weren't going to kiss like that ever again.

This deal was not about kissing. It was about easing an old man's mind, and it was about money, and afterwards she would have money. Real money. Enough to set up her business and give her mum the kind of care and comfort she deserved.

And okay, it was 'unorthodox', perhaps even a little crazy but it wouldn't be like her parents' marriage, and that was what she dreaded the most. Ending up in a relationship where nothing was as it seemed. Where trust and truth were vague, treacherous, shifting sands. At least this marriage to Achileas would have clear boundaries. Strict rules of engagement. There would be no secrets or lies between them.

Inside her head she heard a tiny click, like the hands of a clock stopping, and she let her gaze wander round the room, seeing it as if she had never looked at it before. This morning she had woken up thinking today would be the first day of her new life. It was what she'd hoped and planned for so long.

And now there was this. There was *him*. Achileas.

He hadn't been part of that plan…

But he could be.

'Yes. We have an agreement,' she said quietly, and she

felt a sharp rush of adrenaline and an eager anticipation that startled her with its intensity.

A flicker of triumph darkened his eyes to black. 'I'll have the paperwork sent over.'

CHAPTER FOUR

THIS WAS EXACTLY what he needed, Achileas thought, stepping onto the balcony that led off his bedroom and into the warm, fluttering air. After the fast-food and exhaust-fume-filled grey air of London there was something cleansing about the bright beat of the sun.

Greek sunlight was laser-white and hot—so hot that even wearing loose linen trousers and a T-shirt he felt overdressed.

He squinted through the light to where the sapphire sparkle of the sea met the cloudless blue sky, letting his eyes adjust, and then he caught a movement down on the sleek stone terrace. He tensed as a small, slight figure in a pale ankle-skimming dress and a cartwheel-sized straw hat stepped into view.

Effie.

He felt his breath catch.

It was just over a week since he had knocked on the door to her Lilliputian flat and asked her to be his wife. It had taken eight days to extricate her from her job, and get the legal documents written up and signed before flying first to Athens on his private jet and then by helicopter to the island.

His island.

He stared out across the terrace, his gaze leapfrogging

over the low stone wall that edged the pool area to the untouched landscape of wind-tangled cedar and feathery grasses, and further still to the smooth, wide strip of never-ending blue.

It was nearly seven years since he'd bought this tiny outcrop of rock at the edge of the Cyclades, and he still wasn't tired of the view. Truthfully, it was the only place on the planet where he stopped to notice the view. Perhaps that was why he came closest here to feeling at home.

It wasn't just the view. There was a serenity and a simplicity that both soothed and invigorated him. And, of course, privacy. His mouth twisted. Maybe it was a hangover from shared dormitories at school, but he liked to have his own space.

Except now it wasn't just his space.

Out on the terrace, Effie was making her way around the edge of the gleaming turquoise infinity pool. He watched her, his eyes narrowing on the sway of her hips as she moved. But his body was remembering the feel of those hips when he'd kissed her and she had kissed him back, arching against him, her body curving like a bow in his hands.

His fingers tightened against the rail. He had kissed her to prove her wrong. Instead, *he* had been proved wrong.

Tracking her progress across the smooth slabs, he felt his pulse speed up. She had tasted sweet like honey, and she had been so responsive. That was what had shocked him most—what shocked him now. He had thought she would be prim and proper, and there had been a kind of hesitancy at first, but then she had melted into him, against him.

He could feel it now. *Still.*

And he hadn't been able to hold back. Hadn't wanted to stop. It had taken a massive effort of will to pull away from her body, to tear his mouth from hers, and even then, he had struggled to hide the truth of things.

He jammed his hands in his pockets. It was his own fault. The self-inflicted consequence of six months of celibacy. And it wouldn't happen again. She wasn't his type.

But she was going to be his wife.

Only for that to work they needed to get comfortable with one another. Comfortable enough for him to be able to confidently introduce Effie to his father. The corners of his mouth curved into a small, satisfied smile.

Then, finally, he would be rightfully, publicly and legally acknowledged for what and who he already was. *An Alexios.*

It couldn't happen soon enough, he thought with a flicker of impatience. Now that he had a wife waiting in the wings, he just wanted it done. So, there would be no diving into the pool and swimming a few leisurely lengths as he would normally. He had told Effie to meet him for breakfast. He wanted to go over the story of how they'd first met.

His gaze dropped to the woman who would be joining him—only Effie wasn't there. His smile stiffened as he caught sight of her hat, disappearing out of view. Apparently, she had somewhere else to be. Somewhere he wasn't.

Blue.

Blue everywhere as far as the eye could see.

Effie turned slowly on the spot, blinking in the sunlight. Without her glasses it was almost like being underwater.

She had never experienced such an intensity or variety of one colour. It was as if after waking this morning she'd found her world had switched from monochrome to colour. The sky was a sweep of harebell-blue, darkening to navy where it merged with the sea. And the sea—

Holding her breath, she took a hesitant step towards the edge of the path and gazed down over the edge of the rockface. Up until this moment, the only sea she had ever seen in person had been on a rare holiday to Great Yarmouth. The North Sea had been wet and salty and vast, but that was where any resemblance to the expanse of water in front of her ended.

She stared in silence at the miracle of the Aegean, almost unbelieving. There was so much light, and even though the sea didn't seem to be moving every time she looked it was different, each rippling wave catching the sun's rays and making it shimmer like a gemstone so that there wasn't just blue but silver and gold.

And then there was the air.

Back in England, she'd never thought about breathing, and she knew that the air she was breathing here must be the same mix of oxygen and nitrogen. Only how could that be? Had it been washed in the sea? Was that why it was as soft and clean as freshly laundered sheets? There was salt and thyme and rosemary… It was as if the island itself was breathing—

Her head was spinning. It was too much.

But then should she be surprised, given who owned the island?

A shiver, not of cold but of heat, that had nothing to do with the quivering white sun, ran down her spine. *Too much.* That was what she had thought about Achileas in the car when he had looked over at her and everything had stopped. Then dissolved.

Her bones, her breath.

Her sense of self-preservation.

But locking eyes with him had been a warm-up act. His kiss had knocked the world off its axis and sent it spinning into space and she was still scrabbling to get back on her feet. And now she was here with him on this island—*his private island*—surrounded in every direction by a sea as mesmerizingly blue as his gaze.

She stared fixedly at the horizon, using it as a spirit level to steady herself.

Over the last few days, she had refused to let herself think about that moment in the flat, concentrating instead on practicalities. Like packing and getting a passport.

She hadn't told anyone what she was doing. Not the official version and certainly not the truth.

At work, it had been easy to let Emily and Janine and Mark believe that she was leaving to start her business. Which was sort of true. But when it had come to her mum, she had said nothing about that. As far as Sam was concerned, she was taking a well-deserved holiday.

Her hands curled at her sides. She didn't tell lies, and lying to people she cared about—to her mum in particular—was horrible. More horrible still was knowing that she could do it with such ease. Remembering how effortlessly the lies had spilled from her father's mouth, she felt her stomach knot. She didn't want to be a chip off that particular block.

But in spite of the lies, and the quivering, slippery panic she felt whenever she thought about being alone with Achileas, it would be worth it in the end. Picturing the rows of bottles in her yet to be opened flagship store, she felt a sudden, unfiltered upswing of happiness. It was going to be all right.

First, though, she had to get to know her husband-to-be.

In fact, she was supposed to be doing that now, she thought, a prickling panic darting over her skin as she realised the time.

Turning, she began to walk back along the path, quickly at first, and then more hesitantly. Distracted by the light and the sea and the air, she hadn't been paying much attention to where she was, and now she wondered if she had gone the wrong way.

She was on the verge of retracing her steps when a breeze from the sea whipped at her hat. Reaching up, she snatched at it, laughing, feeling a rush of exhilaration rising inside her at the absurdity and newness of it all.

And then suddenly, just as her fingers curled around the rim, he was there.

Blue-eyed, dark-jawed, even darker scowl.

Achileas.

They almost collided again. Just in time she took a hurried step sideways and—

She gasped, her eyes widening, her exhilaration switching to fear as the ground seemed to be cut away beneath her and she felt herself starting to fall.

And she would have kept on falling if Achileas hadn't caught her arm, clamping his hand painfully around her elbow to jerk her to safety.

Although safety was relative where he was concerned, she thought a moment later, her pulse twitching out of time.

Looming over her, his face was starkly furious in the daylight. And he was swearing more than she had ever heard anyone swear in her life. Not that she understood what he was saying as she didn't speak Greek, but she didn't need to.

Only it wasn't his anger that was making her pulse stumble. It was the jewelled brilliance of his eyes and the hard heat of his very male body. It felt so intimate, even though there had been no intimacy between them.

Except for that kiss, she thought, remembering his hard, insistent mouth and the surge of devastating, irrational hunger that had swept through her body to pool deep in her core. She felt goosebumps rise along her arms as his gaze locked on hers, eyes narrowing as if he too was re-living those frantic, feverish moments—

Abruptly, he let go of her arm.

'Do you ever look where you're going?' he demanded, swapping to English with a fluency that, despite her pan-icky heartbeat, she found herself envying.

'Do you?' she countered.

His eyebrows snapped together. 'I was looking where I was going. More importantly, I was also on time for our meeting this morning. Unlike you.'

He stared down at her, a muscle pulsing in his cheek. Beside them, the sea kept on being the sea, and she won-dered if he was regretting bringing her. Or just contem-plating throwing her in.

'I need you to pay attention, Effie, because I'm only going to say this once,' he said at last, his voice gratingly harsh in the whispering breeze. 'This is not some holiday. We made a deal. I am investing in your business and in return you will be my wife. But for that to be believable we need to spend some time together. So, when I say I'll see you at breakfast, I'm not asking you.' His blue gaze locked onto hers. 'I'm paying you. Is that clear?'

To be fair, it had been clear before. Only, stupidly, she had thought that there was an equality of sorts in their ar-rangement. But to him she was only a cog in the wheel of a machine, brought here to serve a purpose.

His purpose.

Because, of course, Achileas was the machine.

She gazed up at him, her heart beating in her throat. Sunlight was caressing his cheekbones and the line of his jaw reverently, like an adoring lover. But no amount of sun could disguise the hard, uncompromising set of his features.

'Perfectly.'

Her response was automatic, her voice as quiet and placating as it would have been if she was at work and he was a dissatisfied guest, but she felt a flicker of defiance as she spoke. As a maid she was truly just a cog, a tiny moving part. But wasn't a wife—even a fake one—by definition a partner?

'Good.' His brooding gaze held hers momentarily. 'Then let's get back to the villa. We've wasted enough time this morning already.'

It was on the tip of her tongue to point out that they could use the time it would take to walk back to the villa to get to know one another, but he had already turned and stalked off down the path. And, as it turned out, it took considerably less time to get back than it had taken her to reach the sea.

Achileas walked swiftly and with the same intensity of purpose with which he seemed to do everything else, eating the ground with his long, fluid strides, only pausing occasionally and impatiently for her to catch up.

It was as if he was in a race. But where was the finishing line? More importantly, what was the prize? Surely there were only so many houses and private jets and islands you could buy, she thought.

Back at the villa, breakfast was waiting for them on the beautiful stone terrace.

Effie sat down at the table and, like a member of an orchestra tuning up for a performance, her stomach started to rumble.

It was nothing like the breakfast she ate at home, she thought, gazing down at the array of plain white bowls and platters, filled with soft, billowing peaks of yogurt, freshly sliced fruit and delicious pastries dusted with icing sugar.

But, despite her hunger, it was the house that drew her gaze. She had seen it last night, when they'd arrived on the island, but she had been too tired—not just from the journey but from the days leading up to it—to register much about the exterior except that it wasn't quite what she had imagined.

To her, Greek architecture was either a ruined temple with lots of columns or those postcard-pretty white houses with blue doors and domed roofs. But the Villa Elytis was neither a ruin nor white. It was a soft shell-pink and it was beautiful. The most beautiful house she had ever seen.

Strangely, though, there was nothing about it to connect it to the man sitting opposite her. Inside everything was perfect but impersonal—like a stage set. Surely his whole life couldn't be a performance? Not in his home?

'Why aren't you eating? Do you want something else?'

Achileas frowned at her across the table. He was dressed casually, in linen trousers and a T-shirt, but somehow that only seemed to emphasise his innate unadorned authority.

'The kitchen can make you whatever you want.'

By 'the kitchen', he meant Yiannis and Anna. Feeling a swirling rush of solidarity with the nameless behind-the-scenes staff, she immediately helped herself to yogurt. 'No, thank you, this is wonderful.'

And it was. Rich and gloriously creamy, with a hint of lemon. The tiny custard-filled pastries were delicious too.

Achileas watched her while she ate. He didn't eat, but maybe he had eaten earlier. Or maybe masters of the universe didn't eat breakfast.

As she put down her spoon he shifted back in his chair, his blue eyes calmer now.

'We might have to adjust the timeline a little, but I think it's best if we stick as closely to the truth as possible.' He took a sip of his coffee. 'That way it will all flow quite naturally between us.'

She knew he was talking about the story they would

tell people—about how they'd met and fallen in love—but something in his darkly handsome face made her pulse pick up and her stomach knot as she remembered what had happened the last time it had all flowed 'naturally' between them.

'Actually, I think we should probably keep as far away from the truth as we can,' she said quietly. 'Being forced into a car by a stranger isn't usually a prelude to marriage.'

He stared at her steadily. 'Depends on the stranger.'

She felt the knot in her belly twist.

It was easier to be around him when he was angry. Safer. Cleaner. There wasn't any muddying of emotion. Her chest tightened as he leaned forward to pour some more coffee. It was even safer when he wasn't sitting so close. Because he smelled so good it made her want to breathe him in, to bottle him…

'Perhaps we could say you were rescuing me from a difficult guest,' she said, inching back in her chair.

The corners of his mouth curved very slightly. 'Like I said, we should stick as closely to the truth as possible. Maybe play around with a *Cinderella*-style narrative.'

That was a good idea. Perfect in every way, Effie thought. Except, of course, Prince Charming and Cinderella's marriage was based on love, not lies.

It took another hour before Achileas was satisfied with the start they'd made. 'Obviously we'll go over it again.' He finished his coffee. 'But we don't want to sound too scripted.'

She nodded. It was easy to see why he was so successful. He was meticulous and focused, but he also had an ability to take a step back and see the big picture. In other words, he was more than just a pretty face. And that face was more than pretty. 'Pretty' was slight and ephemeral.

Achileas Kane was beautiful. Unequivocally. In a way that transcended human limitations.

'Is there a problem?'

Looking up, she found herself impaled by his disturbingly intense gaze and, horrified that he might read her thoughts—that last thought in particular—she shook her head. 'No, I was just wondering how you ended up owning this island?'

He shifted back in his chair, his fingers tapping against the handle of his coffee cup. 'The usual way,' he said finally. 'I saw it. I wanted it. I bought it.'

Her stomach clenched. Was that what had happened outside the Stanmore too?

In a way, yes. And yet at the hotel he had simply seen the maid's uniform and not the woman inside. And afterwards he had only registered the details that mattered to him. Her lack of money. Her ability to keep her head. That was the Effie he'd seen and wanted. The Effie he had bought.

Everything else was of no interest to him.

Her pulse jerked as his phone began to vibrate against the table. He snatched it up, his lip curling like a wolf protecting its kill.

'*Wait!*' he snapped into the mouthpiece as he got to his feet. 'I have to take this, and then I have some other calls to make, so I won't be joining you for lunch, but we can finish up later.' His eyes found hers. 'Stay away from the cliffs. In fact, don't go wandering off again,' he said, in that imperious way that was as much a part of him as breathing. 'If you want to swim, use the pool.'

'I can't swim,' she said quickly. Not really…not out of her depth anyway.

He stared at her blankly, as if she had suddenly admitted to sleeping upside down in a tree. 'In that case, stay away from the pool too.' He glanced down at her face; his brow creased. 'It'll get hot this afternoon—much hotter than this—so keep out of the sun. Can't have you overheating.'

He leaned forward and she felt a wave of heat wash over her skin as he caught the brim of her hat and straightened it.

'After all, you'll be no use to me if you get sunstroke,' he added softly.

She watched him leave, her heart beating heavily in her chest, feeling stupid. Just for a few half-seconds she had thought he cared about her as a person. But he'd just been thinking about his own agenda. And now he had upped and gone.

Only what had she expected?

That he would stay and spend time with her because…? Because what? *Because of that kiss?*

The memory rose up inside her…more than a memory. It was tactile, scorching a path through her as if it had just happened. And then she remembered that look of dark impatience on his face and she shivered inside.

Stupid, stupid Effie.

It hadn't been real. She knew that. Knew, too, that it didn't matter that she was no longer wearing a uniform. When Achileas looked at her he still saw a chambermaid. Somebody paid to make everything look perfect.

Only instead of rearranging the contents of his mini bar or turning down the sheets on his bed, she was here to turn his life into a storybook romance.

She felt a spark of defiance. This was her life too, and maybe he *was* investing in her business, but he was wrong if he thought that made her *just* an investment.

He was right about the temperature, though.

It was getting hotter. And hotter.

The house, though, was cool. There was a beautiful light

breeze that fluttered through the villa, and with each tentative breath of air came that same intoxicating blend of sea spray and sunshine and herbs. So many fragrant herbs she felt almost drunk.

Did they grow wild on the island? Or was there a garden attached to the villa? Maybe later, when it got cooler, she might venture out to see, but until then…

Pulse quickening, she hurried to her room and retrieved her olfactive kit. Her fingers trembled against the wooden case. Other people had paintings or jewellery, but this was her most precious possession. It was like a genie in a lamp and a magic carpet rolled into one.

She might never have left England until yesterday, but in her tiny flat at Praed Gardens she could open this vial of cardamom and be transported to Jemaa el-Fnaa, Marrakech's main square. Un-stopper the petitgrain and she was in Provence.

Only this time would be different. This time, for the first time, she wouldn't be conjuring up a fantasy but attempting to capture a real-time experience. A moment of hope and possibility.

Fresh citrus, then—to create dynamism—starting with neroli. She leaned forward, forgetting Achileas and her doubts, feeling a rush of excitement pulsing down to her fingertips.

'What's the stock trading at?'

Shifting back in his seat, Achileas stared out of the window. Never a good sign. But then, he already knew the answer to the question. He always knew the answer to any question he asked.

All except one.

Who are you?

He'd asked Effie Price that question a week ago and he

was still no closer to really knowing the answer, and now it was starting to bug him.

Normally he took pride in his ability to read people.

Take the man on the other end of the phone. Dan Ryan. His newest portfolio manager. In five years' time Dan would have upgraded his suit to a more expensive design, and as well as his college sweetheart wife he would have a mistress. There would be a couple of children. Then another affair, this time more serious, followed by a divorce and another couple of children.

It was all so predictable, but avoidable if you accepted that biology and love were essentially incompatible.

'Sixty-five dollars. When we close the deal, we could be looking at a nineteen percent bump. It's your call, of course, but I'd like to size up.' Dan's voice was quivering with testosterone.

Something pale fluttered at the edge of Achileas's vision and his gaze narrowed. It was stupid, but some part of his brain kept expecting to see Effie in that hat drifting out of view, but it was just a bird—a gull. A flicker of irritation beat a path around his body, and he frowned, his patience and interest at an end.

'Find out who's being floated as the new CEO,' he said tersely. 'Then come back to me.'

He hung up.

Dan was smart, hungry, and desperate to prove himself. But desperation made you take stupid risks. Made you fly too close to the sun.

He was suddenly gripping the phone so tightly his palms hurt. The ache in his chest felt as if he'd swallowed a boulder. Was that what was happening here? Was he flying too close to the sun? Effie was so young and untested. Could she really pull this off? And what would happen if she couldn't?

Not wanting to dwell on exactly how that made him feel, he slammed his laptop shut. He was just tense for the very obvious reason that he had put this plan together almost on a whim, and now it was in play it was hard not to look for weaknesses.

Then try harder, he told himself firmly.

Standing up, he twisted his neck from side to side, rolling his shoulders. Maybe he would take that swim now. Or, better still, he could work off his tension on the punchbag.

As he walked through the cool interior of the villa, he remembered Effie asking him how he had ended up buying the island. He had condensed his answer into three short sentences, but it had actually been a long and conflicted process.

His mouth twisted. An internally conflicted process. The same old push-me-pull-you battle that always happened whenever he confronted his Greek heritage.

But there had been something about the location of the island—near the mainland, but not so close that he had to acknowledge his father's proximity—and he had felt a curious affinity with the incongruously pink neoclassical house with a chequered past.

What the—?

He came to an abrupt halt. He was supposed to be heading towards the gym. But apparently that particular memo hadn't reached his legs. Why else would he be standing in the doorway to the sitting room, staring as though hypnotised by the sight of Effie Price's downturned and hatless head?

The waft of her scent made his chest feel suddenly too tight for his ribcage and he gritted his teeth. She was leaning over one of the low coffee tables. Beside her was a hinged wooden box, a bit like a paintbox. It was open.

But instead of paints it held rows of glass vials filled with clear liquid.

'What are you doing?'

He knew his voice was unnecessarily harsh from the way her face jerked up to meet his, but he didn't care. In fact, he hoped it would encourage her to keep her distance. And remind her who was in charge.

'I was just playing around with some oils.'

His eyes dropped to the neat wooden case and despite himself he realised he was interested. A lot more interested than he had been earlier, talking to Dan Ryan.

'Playing to what end?' he found himself asking.

There was a tiny fluttering pause as her brown eyes rested on his face, composed but wary. 'I'm trying to create a fragrance.'

Of course she was. Probably another wicked concoction that would make his head spin like a carousel.

'And how do you do that?'

This time the pause that followed his question seemed to stretch through the open French windows to the horizon.

'It's a process,' she said at last. 'I start with an idea of the end scent, and then I have to think about what raw materials might produce that effect. In this case, I want to create something that is not too heavy. I want it to come and go like the lightest of breezes. But I still want it to stop you in your tracks.'

Effie was speaking quietly but he could hear her excitement, her passion. Glancing down, he noted both her flushed cheeks and the press of her nipples against the fabric of her dress, and he felt his body tighten with a different excitement as he remembered how she had turned to flame in his arms.

Had that been a one-off? Did making perfume normally absorb all her passion? What if some of that passion escaped again?

It was only then that he realised Effie was staring up at him, and that he had no idea how much time had passed since she'd started speaking.

'…that's the plan…' Her voice trailed off and she began to pick up the vials and slot them back in the case. 'Anyway, did you want to go over what we talked about this morning?'

He shook his head. 'No, I want to know how you make a fragrance that comes and goes but stops you in your tracks.' Actually, it was simpler even than that. He just wanted her to keep talking. 'I need to know,' he added quickly. 'I mean, I would know something about your job if this was a real relationship.'

She stared at him as if considering the logic of his words. 'I suppose that's true.' Her small white teeth chewed at her lip. 'Well, I started with neroli…but it wasn't vivacious enough.' Picking up one of the vials, she squeezed a drop of oil onto one of the thin strips of card and waved it in front of her face. 'This works better. It's bergamot. It's one of my favourites because it's the most multi-faceted of all the citrus materials.'

Leaning forward, he took the blotting paper from her hand. Her fingers brushed against his and he felt that phosphorus flare of desire as her eyes jerked up to his face at the whisper of contact.

He breathed in cautiously. 'Oranges? But spicier?'

She nodded. 'There's a woody aspect which will work well with the base notes I have in mind.'

He watched her run her hand over the vials.

'Now, because bergamot can be a little warm, I want to add clarity and brightness with pink pepper.'

It was oddly relaxing, watching her open the bottles

and add tiny drops of pepper, then lime and lavender. In fact, he felt calmer than he had in weeks.

'Is that it?' he asked.

'I wish.'

She shook her head, and then suddenly he forgot all about the perfume and the deal he'd made with her, and even about the ache in his chest, because she smiled a smile of such sweetness that everything he'd thought he knew and cared about was erased. It was a smile that changed her face, added light and colour and something indefinable, so that he found himself smiling back at her.

'This is just the starting point,' she said. 'Like the rough sketch of a dress you want to make. From here, I'll have to keep playing with different oils to build the composition, and then I'll have to add the alcohol.'

He held her gaze. 'How do you remember it all?'

She lifted up a notebook—the cheap kind with a cardboard cover. 'I take notes. Why don't you try some of the samples while I get this down on paper? See if you can work out what they are. Then maybe you can try mixing some oils.'

In other words, he should play quietly.

Watching her pick up a pen, he felt an odd mix of outrage and admiration. He hadn't been told what to do since he was a child. In business, most people fell over themselves to attract his attention and hold it. It was the same with women.

But not this woman. She had that same purity of focus that he'd had at her age.

Unnerved by the idea that he and Effie had something in common other than the deal they had made, he picked up one of the vials at random and opened it. It was numbered, not named, but he knew immediately that it was lemon.

Feeling pleased, he picked another. That was harder.

It was spicy. Like Christmas. Cinnamon? Cloves? He frowned and held up a third to his nose, breathed—

His heartbeat stumbled, then stopped. He felt his face dissolve with shock.

He was back in England. It was a cold, wet day, and he was cold, and his clothes were wet, and he ached everywhere—but especially in his chest. He felt desperate and wretched and lonely, winded by loneliness…

With an effort, he pulled his face from the black velvet gravity inside the open bottle and placed it down with extravagant care. 'What is this?'

Effie glanced sideways at the bottle. 'That's a synthetic for oakmoss. The original was—'

She looked up and frowned. She was talking to herself. Achileas was gone.

CHAPTER FIVE

'LET'S TAKE COFFEE out on the deck.'

Pushing back his chair, Achileas got to his feet and strode away from the terrace to where a group of cream linen sofas sat at elegant right angles. Behind them the Aegean was dark and shiny like spilt ink, except where the feathery evening sunlight danced across the surface like falling stars.

Effie watched him drop down onto the furthest sofa. It had been a long, disconcerting, and exhausting day, and she wasn't sure that she wanted to be out here alone with this baffling, mercurial man who made her say and feel stupid things.

Not that she could decline his invitation because he hadn't actually invited her. Although no doubt his autocratic suggestion passed for an invitation among men of his power and wealth.

After he'd absented himself from lunch, she had half wondered if he would bother dining with her, but when she'd stepped outside into the warm evening air at exactly eight o'clock, he'd been standing at the edge of the terrace, his gaze fixed on something in the distance. Even when he had joined her at the table his gaze had returned often to the endless sea.

He was either distracted or bored or both. And, despite

the meal being a masterclass of flavour combinations, he'd barely eaten. Just pushed the food around the plate as if that bored him too.

'Thank you, that was delicious,' she said now, as Demy the housekeeper appeared and began to quietly clear the table. 'Could you thank Yiannis for me?'

Achileas's staff had been lined up outside the house when they'd arrived, but she had been too tired to take in his terse rollcall of names and she had asked Demy to introduce her. There were some things she was willing to fake, but for this arrangement to work she needed to be true to herself—and that meant treating people with respect.

Even if it made things bumpy between her and Achileas.

A current of unease snaked across her skin. So far each time she had been herself things had got more than 'bumpy' between them.

She thought back to his abrupt exit earlier.

Bumpy and baffling.

And probably that wasn't going to change any time soon, given that they had nothing in common aside from an upcoming marriage of convenience. They were just two strangers who had met a little over a week ago, living under the same roof.

Effie glanced over to where Achileas was sitting, her breathing suddenly unsteady.

Except he wasn't a complete stranger to her. In fact, the more she spent time with him, the more he reminded her of her father.

Bill had moods too.

Sometimes he'd been great company. As a child she could remember watching him at a wedding. People were gathered around him and bursts of laughter had erupted as he'd told a joke or a funny story, and she had been proud of him, her handsome, charming dad.

Other days he was sullen and monosyllabic. He threw things at the wall when the bets he'd made at the book-ies that day had gone sideways. And sometimes he'd just get up from eating or watching TV and disappear with-out a word or a backward glance. Often, he would be gone for days.

In those moments she had wanted to cry. Wanted a different father. One who didn't stay up all night playing poker in the back room of some pub. One who knew when to stop. But Bill hadn't wanted to stop. He hadn't been able to. Gambling had been his life. Everything else—every-one else—had bored him.

Including her.

So why should Achilleas find her any less boring? She had seen the calibre of woman he usually dated and dis-carded. Even if she had been his type why would he be interested in her? He barely knew her.

And yet earlier today, when they had talked about the process of making a perfume, she had felt as if they had known one another not for days but for the whole of her life.

In those few moments he had seemed to change before her eyes. For the first time since they'd met the tension and the impatience that were as much a part of him as the stubble shadowing the curve of his jaw had seemed to lift. In those few moments she had glimpsed a different man.

A less guarded man.

A man not moving purposefully forward but happy to wait, to listen, to watch, to share.

A man with a smile that could make the sun melt. A smile that was almost as devastating as his kiss.

She blanked her mind. Or that was what she thought she was doing. But, heart thumping, she replayed that moment when he'd put the vial of oakmoss on the table and left without a word.

Oakmoss, or *mousse de chêne* as it was also known, belonged to the chypre family. It was actually a lichen which grew on oaks throughout Europe and North Africa. It had a unique scent. Both earthy and woody, with hints of musk, it was really not like anything else in the perfumer's 'palette'.

The one snag was that it had been blacklisted as a potential irritant, so its use had been restricted, forcing perfumers to play around with other ingredients like patchouli, or synthetic imitations of oakmoss.

It had been a long and frustrating process, she knew, to blend a synthetic that matched the original. But it needed to be done. Not only did oakmoss give a scent a longer life on the skin, but it was also widely used to anchor volatile notes in a fragrance.

She shivered. If only there was a scent that could anchor Achileas's volatile notes. But even with around two hundred essential oils and one thousand five hundred synthetic materials to choose from, she wasn't confident she could do that.

Getting to her feet, she made her way over to where he was sitting just as Demy arrived with a tray of coffee and petit fours.

'Just leave it,' he said tersely, flicking the housekeeper away with his hand. Effie gave Demy a small, tight smile and sat down on the sofa opposite him.

'I was thinking,' he said, stretching out his legs, 'about how to explain our getting from that first meeting to me asking you out…'

Effie frowned. 'But you wouldn't have asked me out.'

There was a short pulsing silence as the distance between them seemed to shrink and fill with a familiar dark impatience—the same dark impatience with which he'd dismissed Demy. It was always there, as if something was constantly chafing him. Only how could that be? He was wealthy and powerful. If that were true, he would simply snap his fingers and make it go away.

'You're not suggesting you would have asked me?' Eyes narrowing, he held her gaze as she shook her head slowly. 'Then what? Because I thought we agreed this would be a Cinderella story.' His lip curled. 'Surely you know how that works? It is, after all, a tale as old as time.'

'That's the wrong fairy tale,' she corrected him quietly.

Now the corners of his mouth twisted in what would probably be the beginning of a smile with anyone else. But this was Achileas, and it could just as easily be a scowl or a frown.

It was a scowl.

'Is there a difference? It's all happy ever after in the end.'

He shifted back against the sofa cushion, and when he spoke again, she could hear the harnessed tension in his voice. 'My point is that Cinderella is asked out by the Prince. In case you're having trouble following the conversation, in this scenario that's me.'

She felt her own flicker of impatience. 'He thinks she's a princess when he dances with her at the ball. In this scenario, obviously I'm not a princess. I'm Housekeeping,' she said pointedly.

There was another silence, longer this time, and thickly solid like the blanketing silence that followed a heavy fall of snow, expanding and thickening around her so that she could no longer hear the sound of the waves.

He shrugged. 'So, I saw past the uniform.'

His blue gaze hurt where it rested on her face.

'Isn't that love?'

The cynicism in his voice hurt even more than his gaze. How could he be so jaded? So dismissive?

She thought about her mum, always hopeful, always wanting to believe that this time would be different. And her father too, tearfully begging for another chance. Both of them buying into the dream of love over and over again, even though theirs was damaged beyond repair.

Yet here was Achileas, the product of a forty-year happy marriage, with a sneer in his voice.

'I thought we'd agreed to stick as closely to the truth as possible,' she said quietly. 'In that case, we should say you dropped off my folder and that should be the end of it. After that we can get creative, but wherever we say we met next has to be somewhere away from the hotel. Somewhere random. Somewhere nobody would know either of us. Where I'm not a maid and you're not...' she hesitated, her eyes drifting over his astonishingly beautiful, unforgettable face '...you're not you.'

She blinked as Achileas leaned forward, his muscular shoulders bunching beneath his T-shirt. For a moment she thought that he would dismiss her with one of those careless gestures he seemed to have at his fingertips. Instead, he picked up the coffee pot and poured out two cups.

Jaw tightening, Achileas watched Effie take her cup with a hand that trembled ever so slightly.

But that was Effie Price all over. She didn't scream or shout or throw things, only somehow that only made her quiver of resistance more seismic.

She had no reason to be angry, he thought irritably.

Okay, he was brusque with his staff, and maybe that touched a nerve with her, but it wasn't as if he was expecting *her* to lift a finger. All she had to do was learn her lines and lie in the sun. And if she thought he was about to modify his behaviour, then she could think again. She'd known who he was before she signed on the dotted line, and he had been straight with her.

Well, to a point.

Clearly, he couldn't tell her the whole truth, and nor did he want to. There was no need for Effie, of all people, to know that Andreas had only recently reached out to him. Or that his father's acceptance came with conditions. That was between him and Andreas and way over Effie's paygrade.

But some truths would have to be shared. She was going to find out that his mother and father were not a couple who had been married for forty years, and he was planning on telling her when he was ready.

So, yes, he had been and would be straight with her. But Effie—

He let out a breath he hadn't realised he was holding and felt his temper rise. This was her doing. She was the reason he couldn't breathe. It was bad enough that her teasing scent seemed to mark every surface...then she had to go and start mixing her potions in his sitting room.

The memory of holding that vial up to his nose pulsed in his head, bright like a neon sign, hurting the insides of his eyes.

He'd had to leave. He hadn't been able to stand there with that awful, raging thing scrabbling inside him and he still wasn't sure what had happened. One minute he had been inhaling the scent of oranges in an oasis of calm, the next—

His stomach clenched. Maybe that was why he had reacted so strongly. It was rare for him to feel so at peace, so at one with himself. In fact, he couldn't recall ever feeling like that.

Not even when he was a child.

Particularly not when he was a child.

Then again, while Effie might be the very definition of ordinary, with her brown hair and brown eyes and sensible clothes, this situation was exceptional. How could it not be? He was a man who didn't believe in love or matrimony, pretending to be in love with a woman he had met a week ago. A woman he was planning to marry, all so that he could punish one man. The father who had walked out of his life before he was even born.

He was turning himself inside out. Turning into a stranger.

Surely that, not this woman or some random scent, was the reason he was so on edge. But now was not the time to analyse that.

'Doesn't sound too hard,' he said, watching the sun's slow burnished descent into the sea. 'My free time is limited but it happens. I'm sure if we "get creative" we can come up with a solution.'

Her light brown eyes fixed on his face. 'I think you and I have very different definitions of that word.'

'Which one? Creative?' Leaning forward, he nudged the coffee cup towards her. 'Hard?'

Watching the pulse twitch at the base of her throat, he shifted back in his seat, conscious suddenly of the hammering of his heart.

She lifted her chin, held his gaze. 'It's complicated. You and I would never normally cross paths so it needs to be somewhere we could have met by chance, and yet it needs not to have been by chance at all, because it was a place we had in common all the time only without realising. Does that make sense?'

It did. He couldn't have put it better himself. In fact, he hadn't.

He held her gaze, torn between curiosity and admiration. 'Where do you have in mind?'

She sat up a little straighter, tilting her face the better to look at him. He knew there was no logical reason for it, and yet he still couldn't stop the tiny lick of flame as he caught sight of the pale underside of her throat.

'I was thinking of a garden or a gallery, depending on what you like doing in your free time.'

As she leaned forward to pick up her coffee her scent whipped at his senses, so that he had to press his body back into the seat to stop himself from climbing over the small glass-topped table and pulling her against him as he had in the car.

Taking a shallow breath, he let his gaze cruise casually over her small, tense body. 'I'm not sure either would be entirely suitable for what I like doing in my free time.'

She stared at him, the faintest flush of pink colouring her cheeks. 'How about a funfair, then?'

His pulse stumbled. He had wanted to get under her skin as her scent was getting under his, but instead he felt the slight hoarseness in her voice in all the wrong places. 'Why a funfair?'

'We could have gone on the dodgems. Bumped into one another intentionally for once.'

He laughed. Because it was funny. *She* was funny. And he was surprised to find that his anger and resentment of moments earlier was, like the sun, fading fast.

'We might just have done that,' he said slowly.

He couldn't remember the last time he had gone to a funfair. In fact, he couldn't remember 'fun' ever being part of his vocabulary. When he was a child, he'd worked and eaten and slept. As an adult, that list had lengthened to include working out and hooking up with women for a different kind of workout. But somehow fun—easy, lazy, meandering fun—had never played a part in his life.

There was always something driving him forward, a restlessness that haunted him, snapped at his heels. Even now, when he didn't need to work, when he could arguably just kick back and relax, he couldn't stop.

Glancing over at Effie's small, pale face, he felt his pulse slow. He couldn't remember the last time he had laughed with a woman either. Perhaps he never had. Laughter meant having the kind of intimacy that slowed things down, and he had never wanted to take things slowly. If he did that he might have to stop and think about who he was. And, more importantly, who he wasn't.

He cleared his throat. 'Practically speaking, though, a garden or gallery would be more believable. And I'm not really into gardens so...'

A memory, long buried, shuffled from the wings into the spotlight. A school trip, and then later, when he'd been old enough to go alone, furtive visits by himself.

'What about the British Museum?'

They both spoke at once.

Effie frowned up at him, her brown eyes tangling with his for a second, and then the corners of her mouth fluttered upwards into another of those mesmerizingly sweet smiles that made his heart beat faster.

No, they weren't brown, he thought with a twitch of surprise. They were amber...like the colour of iced tea. Her hair wasn't just brown either. There were strands of gold and red too, like autumn leaves spinning through pale sunlight.

'You like the British Museum?' he asked.

'It's one of my favourite places in the world. Not that I've seen much of the world.' Her eyelashes fluttered like moths around a lamp. 'I used to go there when I had a split shift. They have the most amazing glass perfume bottles from Ancient Egypt and Greece. Some of them are shaped like animals and others are incredibly simple, but beautiful, like a teardrop.'

Suddenly he couldn't quite catch his breath. She was moved by the memory. He could feel how important it was to her. Her excitement caught fire in him, too, and then out of nowhere he had the strangest feeling…almost like regret.

Regret that this wasn't real—that it never could be real for him. That he would never be able to make it real for her.

He shook off the thought. 'The British Museum it is, then.'

The look on her face altered, the smile flattening as if she realised that she had revealed more than she had intended.

'I think that would work, but…' she hesitated '…if you've changed your mind about all this, then it's not too late to say so.'

The sun had moved lower now, and the light was starting to fade. He felt a momentary chill. 'I haven't changed my mind.'

Straightening up, he drew back his legs as if to distance himself from that possibility. Effie didn't speak for a moment, and he frowned, impatient suddenly, again.

'Are you saying you have? Because—'

'I'm not saying that.' She shook her head, her brown eyes finding his. 'It's just that it's all happened very quickly, and earlier I thought you seemed…it seemed…'

He watched it all going through her head: those few moments of unscripted easiness between them, his abrupt departure, her struggle to understand. But for her to understand he would need to explain everything that had happened, and he couldn't put that into words. He didn't have the words.

He shrugged. 'It's just strange, sharing my space. I don't do that.'

The doubt faded a little from her face. 'It is strange,' she said at last. 'I haven't shared my space either, since—'

She stumbled over the word, and he felt a sting against his skin—fine, like a paper cut. *Since Sam.* That was what she had been about to say…only she couldn't say it.

'When did he move out?' he asked.

Now her gaze was on him again, wide-eyed, bewildered.

'Who?'

'Your boyfriend. Sam.' For some reason, that sentence was a lot harder to say out loud than it had been in his head. 'The one who painted you.'

The one you're still in love with, he almost added.

For a moment she didn't reply. She just stared at him as if she was trying to put into words what she was feeling. Then, 'Sam's not my boyfriend. She's not even a boy.'

Now it was his turn to stare. His eyes locked with hers as he replayed that moment in her flat when she had melted into him, the soft touch of her mouth and that shimmering charged heat that danced over his skin. Had that been an illusion on his part? An experiment on hers?

'Are you saying—?'

'No.' She was shaking her head. 'No. Sam's my mum.'

But of course she was. And the relief he was feeling was completely understandable. The situation was already complicated enough as it was. 'Why didn't you say that at the time?'

'I panicked. I suppose I thought it wouldn't matter, because you were just returning my folder, but now it does matter.' Her pupils flared. 'I don't like telling lies. It's wrong and it always ends up hurting someone.'

Stung by the unspoken accusation in that sentence, he said nothing, just let the silence stretch out and swallow up the memory of her words. 'In that case,' he said at last, 'I wonder why you've agreed to this. Actually, you don't need to explain.' His body tensed as he realised he already knew and irrationally hated the answer. 'I'm guessing the money has helped overcome your normal scruples.'

'It isn't like that.' Effie stared at Achileas, feeling the ripple of his anger move through her and beyond to the darkening sky, feeling her own anger rising in her throat. 'You're trying to make me feel guilty about a situation that *you* engineered,' she said, as calmly as she could.

Except she did feel a kind of shame for the lies she had already told and the lies she was going to have to keep telling.

'Is that so?' he said, mildly enough, but there was a dark gleam in his blue eyes like a shark's fin cutting through the surface of the waves.

She felt her breath catch. 'Yes, it is. I do feel bad about lying to people. And, yes, I am marrying you for the money, because that's what we agreed. But it's not the only reason. If you were just performing this charade out of self-interest I wouldn't have agreed for any amount of money.'

Was that true? She quickly searched her soul, panicked suddenly that she had become by stealth the kind of person she most feared becoming. Someone who lied not just to other people but to themselves.

But it was true. She couldn't have agreed to lie to Achileas's father for some scurrilous, self-serving motive any more than she could have burgled his home.

'You're lying to make your father happy. You're trying to give him what he wants the only way you can. That's why I'm here. Because you're trying to be a good son.'

And she understood that impulse. She would have done anything for her father. She still would. Not that any kind of intervention would work now. And maybe that was why, deep down, she had agreed to this crazy fake marriage. She might not be able to help Bill, but she could help Achileas make his father happy.

'It's all I've ever wanted.' His blue gaze rested on her face, dark now in the fading light. 'But I can see that might not have been immediately obvious at our first meeting.'

Their first meeting. A shocking point of contact like a fork of lightning. His iron grip on her arm. Her caught breath and that uncontrollable shiver of longing that had left her dizzy and aching.

Pushing away the memory, she nodded. The movement seemed to unlock her rigid body and gratefully she stood up. 'It's been a long day, so I think I might turn in—'

She spun round, intending to walk away.

'Why did you panic?'

Her feet stuttered to a halt, her head spinning madly at the sudden shift in conversation. Turning, she felt her stomach knot as she saw that Achileas had got to his feet and was staring at her, his gaze boring into her so that suddenly she wanted to turn and run. But her body was rooted to the stone terrace as if she was part of it.

'Earlier? You said that was why you lied about who Sam was.' He took a step closer. 'You said you panicked.'

Looking up into his beautiful face, she felt a jolt. The skin over his cheeks was pulled taut, like a fitted sheet over a too-big mattress. Only it was not with anger or impatience, but some other emotion that she couldn't name.

'You said you weren't scared of me.'

'I'm not.' She spoke without hesitation. She wasn't. Not in the way he meant, anyway, she thought a moment later. Only how could she put into words what she had felt? Why she had felt it.

'Then why panic?'

She stared at his lush mouth, feeling utterly off balance, as if she was a pendulum, swinging between a need to keep her personal life hidden from him and a need to lay it bare.

'I wasn't expecting you. You just turned up on my doorstep uninvited. And, in case you've forgotten, the last time we'd met you'd bundled me off the street into your car.'

'So you were scared.'

The knot in her stomach tightened. His voice had a way of demanding, *commanding* answers, and she knew he wouldn't stop until his questions were satisfied.

Inching backwards, away from the force field intensity of his will, she shook her head. 'Not scared. I just didn't want to give anything of myself away. I suppose I didn't want you to know that I'd never had a boyfriend. Never done anything…'

Her voice trailed off, but she didn't need to finish the sentence.

A muscle worked in his jaw. 'By "never done anything", you mean you're a virgin?'

Suddenly the silence was thick enough to slice. He was staring at her as if she had announced she was a mermaid. Was it that unusual? Surely she couldn't be the only virgin he had met in his life?

She lifted her chin. 'Yes, that is what I mean. And I'm perfectly fine with that,' she said, trying desperately not to sound as breathless as she felt.

Achileas didn't move a muscle, but something shifted. A slight movement in the air. A change to the light as if she had inadvertently touched a dimmer switch.

'So why did you kiss me, then?'

Her pulse darted like a startled bird. She had been pretending all day that it didn't exist. Now, though the silken, shimmering thread that was between them pulled taut with an audible snap. His eyes were fixed on her face, and she knew that he could see the faint tremor beneath her skin. The flush across her cheeks.

'I didn't kiss you,' she managed at last. 'You kissed me.'

The last rays of sun glimmered around his face like flames.

'I kissed you first,' he said softly.

His gaze narrowed in on hers in a way that made her breath go shallow.

'But you still kissed me.'

She had bundled that moment into the suitcase with all her clothes, relieved not to have to think about it. Only no secret ever stayed secret for long. As the daughter of a gambler, she should know that better than anyone.

She swallowed. Every single nerve in her body was quivering on high alert. 'I didn't know it could feel like that. That's why I panicked. I wasn't expecting to feel, to want—'

His beautiful, astonishing mouth curved into a question. 'To want what, Effie?'

At some point they had drifted closer—too close. Close enough to touch. Heart hammering, she looked past him at the dark blue sea. But that was a mistake because it was like looking straight into Achileas's eyes, and suddenly they were there, back at the edge of the cliffs, only this time he wasn't stopping her falling.

'This...' she said hoarsely. And, standing on tiptoe, she tilted her mouth and kissed him.

There was a moment when he tensed, and panic of a different kind fluttered in her throat. Perhaps her memories of that first kiss had been wrong—a feverish dream conjured up by the shock of his beauty and the scent of his skin. But then his hand wrapped around her waist, and he took her kiss as if he had been waiting for it his whole life. As if she was already his.

And it was nothing like that first kiss. That had been a sensual exploration, a deliberate provocation designed to stir her, to make her unravel. This was rawer, hungrier, as if he was as out of control as she was.

Heat rolled through her. Pinpricks of light exploded behind her eyes as his mouth moved over hers. And then his tongue parted her lips, and she tasted the dark bite of coffee and desire. Knotting her fists into his shirt, she pulled him closer, kissing him back.

Breathing unsteadily, he pulled her against him. She felt the hard muscles of his body and, harder still, the press of his erection against the soft flesh of her thighs. Hunger flooded through her veins like a levee breaking as he groaned against her mouth, and then he was kissing her neck, licking a path to the bare skin of her shoulder, and her legs were shaking so badly that she couldn't stand.

They stumbled backwards together onto the sofa, her hands clutching at his shoulders as he pulled her hair free of its band, sliding his fingers through her hair, holding her captive. Her body was softening. The heat of his mouth, his hands, moulding her, changing her, making her want to know more, to feel more—to be his.

With a small sound she arched into him, her fingers pulling clumsily at his shirt. He shifted above her, the hard planes of his chest crushing her breasts, making them ache, making the nipples tighten painfully, and she gasped.

He jerked backwards as if stung and she reached up to him, stung herself by the abrupt withdrawal of his body.

'Stop.' His hands dropped to her waist, and he held her down. 'Effie, stop.'

His breath was hot and uneven, just as hers was. She gazed up at him, her heart pounding, her body twitching with longing, need flickering over her skin like flames across an oil slick.

'What is it?'

'You should go.'

Her face felt as if it was burning. 'I thought—'

'Then you thought wrong. Your first time should be with someone who cares about you. Not someone who's paying you.' He stared down at her, his face hard, hostile. 'You need to go to bed. On your own.'

He took a step backwards, as if he was fighting for control. Or expecting her to drag him with her.

'I said go,' he snapped as she stared up at him dazedly.

And, cheeks burning, she got to her feet and went.

CHAPTER SIX

IT WAS EARLY.

Walking swiftly, Effie glanced sideways across the smooth water, lavender-coloured in the dawn light, to where the sun was inching up past the horizon. It was pale yellow and tinged on the underside with blue.

Calm, unshakeable, untroubled.

Turning away from the sea, she trembled. If only she could change places with the sun.

She had watched the sky lighten from her window and finally, when she'd been able to bear it no more, she got up and dressed and walked away from the silent villa.

She had no idea where she was going. No pre-set destination in mind. She just needed to move and keep moving.

Her sandalled feet slipped sideways and, reaching out, she rested her hand against an outcrop of lead-coloured rock.

She felt as if she hadn't slept at all. She'd stared into the darkness, her body rigid like a block of wood, her eyes dry and scratchy. Of course, she had fallen asleep, but it had been a short respite from her tumultuous thoughts. Now she was awake, and if anything, she felt worse now than last night, when she'd fled from the terrace and Achileas's single-word rejection.

Her pulse beat in time to the distant ebb and flow of

the waves. In the darkness, her shock and shame had been her own, but now, with the sun rising, she was going to have to face him. It was nearly seven hours since she had made a complete and utter fool of herself by kissing Achileas beneath the setting sun, but it might as well have been seven seconds.

She could remember it exactly. Not just a frame-by-frame replay of what had happened but of how it had felt. The heaviness of her breasts and that flower of heat blossoming between her thighs. Soft, quivering, insistent...

Her fingers shook as they had when she had touched the hard muscles of his chest and arms, and she breathed out shakily. Leaning forward, she pressed her hot forehead against the coolness of the rock. But it couldn't douse the heat beneath her skin.

She swallowed past the lump in her throat, unsure if the tears she was holding back were down to panic at what she had done or shame at her stupidity. Both, probably, although shame might have it in a photo finish.

Thinking back to the moment when Achileas had broken away from her, she rested her hand on the place in her stomach where she had felt that treacherous melting. Why had she done it? She had known that kiss they'd shared in her flat hadn't been anything more than a means to prove a point, only for some reason she had forgotten that fact. She had forgotten everything. Not just where they were and why they were there, but who they were.

Who she was.

Until Achileas had reminded her.

At the unguarded memory her eyes began to sting.

He had been blunt at first, but not unkind. Only her head had still been spinning with the drugging intensity of his hard mouth on hers and so she had just stood there. And then he'd snapped at her. Like an impatient grown-up dispatching a child who had tried to stay up after her bedtime.

Her cheeks burned at the memory. As if a man of Achileas's experience would be remotely interested in *her*. She had seen the women he dated—or one of them, anyway—and Tamara was sexy and sophisticated, not some clueless virgin.

And just because she was ready to be changed, it didn't mean he felt the same way.

Her one and only consolation out of the whole horrific mess was that Achileas was unlikely to bring it up so she wouldn't have to either. But she needed to keep replaying it inside her head until she could think about it calmly. And without her hands shaking.

It was getting sandier underfoot. Soaring dunes rose on either side of her and the path curved to the right.

She stopped short.

In front of her was a beach—a lagoon.

A perfect crescent of white ribbed sand curving in an arc around the clearest blue water she had ever seen.

It was empty, the air magically still, the sound of the waves gentle. Like a sigh, almost, or the soft intake of breath. She stared down at it, her mind emptied, all her disquiet and discomfort miraculously soothed. If she closed her eyes, it would be like when she was little, when she would climb into bed with her mum and listen to her sleep…

There was a splash and she breathed in sharply—only her eyes didn't shut. In fact, they almost popped out of her head.

She had been wrong. The beach wasn't empty.

A man was swimming, his muscular shoulders cutting through the waves with smooth, strong, rhythmic strokes like the prow of a ship.

She watched enviously, wishing she could swim with the same effortless grace. Abruptly he stopped moving beneath the water, juddering to a halt, and her breathing jerked as a head broke the surface and Achileas smoothed a hand over his face.

A ripple of panic washed over her, and then another of guilt. She shouldn't be here, spying on him. It was wrong on so many levels. Only she didn't dare move in case he spotted her. Panic replaced guilt. The thought of him emerging from the water and striding towards her like some Greek sea god, only in swim-shorts instead of some artfully draped robe, made it suddenly impossible for her to take a breath.

Hopefully he would start swimming again in a moment, and then she could retreat unobserved.

But he didn't start swimming. Instead, he just trod water with his face tilted up towards the lightening sky, as if he was communing with a higher power.

Was that why he was here?

She felt something stir inside her. There was certainly something different about him. He looked exhilarated. Freer. Lighter. Only not in the sense of being weightless— more as if a burden had been lifted from those muscular shoulders.

But before she had a chance to pursue that train of thought Achileas stood up and began wading towards the beach. She caught the gleam of light on wet skin, and then her heartbeat began stampeding like a herd of wild horses. She had been wrong again. Achileas wasn't wearing swim-shorts: he was naked. And whatever his body had felt like through his clothes, it looked a thousand times better, she thought on a rush of air.

Her skin was suddenly on fire. Now she really shouldn't

be looking. But she couldn't tear her gaze away. Instead, she stared down at him, open-mouthed.

He was, hands-down, the most shockingly perfect specimen of maleness she had ever seen. A mesmerising mix of flawless sleek skin and golden muscle. She watched, hypnotised, as drops of sea water trickled down his contoured chest, over the light smattering of dark hair that arrowed down to the line that bisected his abs, then lower still to…to—

The word seemed to fill her mouth, so that suddenly it was impossible to swallow, and she dragged her gaze upwards, shock fluttering in her throat—and something else. Something sharp and persistent like thirst. Only not thirst.

As if sensing her gaze, Achileas turned, and she felt the blue of his eyes like twin gas rings. Naked flame burned her skin and she stumbled backwards. Had he seen her? *Possibly.* Should she show herself? Her pulse catapulted. *Absolutely not.*

She inched her way back up the path and then, once she was sure there was no chance of him catching sight of her, she turned towards the villa and ran.

Her bedroom would be quiet and still. *Safe.*

Closing the door behind her, she sat down on the bed. This had to stop. And it would. She was just adjusting to living with someone again. Living with Achileas. That was all it was. That and the fact that only a short time ago she had woken every morning in her small flat with nothing more than a clumsy kiss at a party to fuel her imagination.

Her nipples tightened and she felt a thread of heat cutting through her like a freshly forged blade. She'd always had a vivid imagination. Now she had plenty of fuel for it. Too much, in fact. And none of it relevant to her arrangement with Achileas.

She glanced over at her phone. It was where she had

left it on the bedside table. Picking it up, she saw that there
was a message from her mum.

Have the most wonderful holiday. I can't wait to see the
photos.

Picturing Sam carefully selecting each letter as she
typed out her message, Effie felt her eyes burn. She loved
her mum every bit as much as Achileas loved his father,
and that was the reason she was here. *Not sex*—and particularly not sex with him. After all, as he'd said, her first
time should be with someone who cared about her.

As she'd expected, Achileas made no mention of the
night before when they met at breakfast. In fact, he behaved exactly as he had done the previous morning. As if
it hadn't happened. Or he had forgotten it.

She knew she should be grateful, and she was. But it
still hurt, knowing he could do that.

She made herself concentrate on spooning yoghurt into
her mouth.

'I thought we might go out to lunch today.'

She glanced up, her heart lurching. 'What do you
mean?' Surely he wasn't suggesting that they go public
yet? It was too soon.

Not taking his eyes off her face, he raised a dark eyebrow. 'It's a meal in the middle of the day. It comes between breakfast and dinner. And by "out" I mean at a
restaurant,' he said, his voice dropping a notch in a way
that made her skin prickle with warning.

It wasn't a suggestion.

Her body tensed. She was already feeling fragile after
last night, and she was guessing Achileas's choice of restaurant wouldn't be some small, discreet side-street taverna.

'Don't you think we should wait a little?' she said stiffly. 'I mean, we haven't really got our story straight.'

She felt a flutter of vertigo as he shifted forward, and there was a moment when it would have been so, so easy to tip herself into his clear blue eyes, but then he shrugged, dismissing her remark with a careless lift of his broad shoulders.

'Oh, I think we both know where we stand on the essential details.'

He sat back in his chair, motioning with his hand in that imperious way of his, and she watched in silence as Demy instantly appeared at his elbow with a fresh pot of coffee.

'Besides,' he said when finally, the housekeeper left them alone, 'what we do here, when we're alone, is of no consequence.'

Her spoon scraped against her empty bowl, and she quickly put it down. That told her, she thought, fighting a betraying flush of colour as he let his gaze drift dismissively past her to the Aegean.

'It can't be validated. For that to happen we need to be seen together. As a couple. Help people leap to the right conclusion.'

A couple.

Shaken by his words, she stared at him mutely. So, this was it: this was the reality of what she had agreed to back in London. Only she wasn't sure she was ready. Wasn't sure she would ever be ready.

'And how do we do that?' she asked.

His gaze narrowed across the table. 'The usual way.'

Remembering the last time he had used those words, she turned her head slightly. But she could only look away for so long and, folding her hands out of sight under the table in case they trembled, she met his gaze.

He stared back at her steadily, and she couldn't stop

herself from devouring his hard, arrogant beauty. The high sweep of his cheekbones, his straight nose…and that mouth. His beautiful sensual mouth that she knew could curl into a smile no mortal woman could resist…

But he wasn't smiling now. 'We'll take the launch over to one of the other islands. We can have a look at some temples…do some shopping. Then grab some lunch.'

He made it sound so easy. Probably it would be for him. But for her…?

She felt her pulse pick up. She knew how couples behaved. London was full of them, walking hand in hand, their eyes meshed, their bodies no more than a hair's breadth apart. Would Achileas hold her hand? Would he pull her against him as they walked? Press his mouth against hers, claiming her for all to see?

Her mind shrank back from the idea even as her body responded with a burst of shimmering electric heat that she was terrified he might sense.

She squared her shoulders. 'I don't think I have anything to wear.'

Now he smiled. It pressed against her skin like hot metal.

'I thought you might say that.' He leaned back in his seat, his astonishing blue eyes locking onto hers so forcefully that she felt as if a tide had rushed in and rolled over her, taking her out to sea.

'That's why I've arranged for a stylist to drop by with some suitable outfits. All you have to do is pick one and be ready to leave at eleven,' he added, picking up his phone and punching in a number, his focus already on something else.

It was not a request but a demand, she thought as she walked slowly back to her room. Like every other word that came out of his mouth.

Part of her couldn't help but admire the absolute conviction with which he lived every moment of his life. He simply didn't acknowledge the possibility of refusal or rejection. But then why would he? From birth he had been surrounded by immutable certainties. His family's wealth. His parents' love. They, and his father in particular, had given him the confidence to expect, to demand what he wanted.

Chest tightening, she thought back to her own childhood, to how every single thing, every day, had seemed like a battle. Nothing had ever been easy or permanent. Always there had been that sense of sand shifting beneath her feet. The fear that if she closed her eyes when she opened them again everything would be gone.

Like when she'd come home from school that time and the sofa and television had disappeared—taken by Bill to clear a debt or cover a bet.

The sofa's feet had left four neat circular indentations in the carpet, like miniature crop circles. No matter how often she had vacuumed over them they hadn't faded.

Maybe they never would. Maybe they would stay there for ever. Like the scars inside her.

The scars that had kept her hiding in the shadows—scars that made it hard to trust other people, to trust herself.

Except when she made perfume. Then she was confident in her judgement.

She sighed. It was too late to worry about scars and trust. Now there was this.

There was Achileas.

And there was a 'them'…an 'us'. Only, unlike other couples, their relationship required a burden of proof. They needed to be seen. And so, for the first time in her life she would have to step out from the shadows and into the sunlight.

Two hours later, Effie tottered out onto the terrace, feeling like an underprepared understudy walking onstage.

It wasn't Virginie the stylist's fault. The dress was indisputably lovely. It was also nothing like any dress she'd ever worn before or would ever have chosen to wear. Skin-coloured, with short sleeves, and a pleated hemline that hovered above her knees. Virginie had paired it with wedge-heeled sandals.

She looked—she *felt*—naked.

She felt like someone had burrowed beneath her skin and taken over her body.

Achileas, who had been scrolling down the messages on his phone, turned. There was a moment of silence as the ripple of his gaze moved through her, and even though she tried to stop it her stomach knotted fiercely.

If their relationship had been real, he would have told her she looked beautiful and kissed her, but he just nodded and said, 'Good, you're here.'

Stretched taut between fantasy and reality, she could only manage a nod in reply. He had changed, too, into a linen suit. On some men, linen could look cheap and crumpled. But Achileas was not like most men. It didn't matter what he wore. Nothing could disguise the authority that was as much a part of him as those dazzling sapphire-blue eyes.

'Good,' he said again, and then he frowned. 'I almost forgot…' Reaching into his jacket, he pulled out a small square box. 'You'll need to put this on.'

A muscle was working in his jaw, as if he wanted to say something more, but instead he opened the box. She stared down at the engagement ring, her heart thumping so loudly she was surprised the villa's staff didn't come out to investigate the noise.

Feeling all thumbs beneath his scrutiny, she slid it clumsily onto her finger. Surely the ring wouldn't fit.

Astonishingly, it did, and she felt a sudden wild desire to laugh. Because it didn't feel real. It was as if she was dressing up in someone else's clothes like she had when she was a child. Only then it had been her mum's nightie—not a designer dress and a diamond that was probably worth more than her entire block of flats.

'Ready?'

He stared down at her, the slow burn of his gaze making her skin tingle. *No*, she thought.

'Yes,' she said quietly.

Picking up his napkin, Achileas glanced across the table to where Effie sat gazing down at the menu.

After arriving at Mykonos, they had wandered around the upmarket waterfront boutiques hand in hand, and now they were here having lunch at I Karydiá, a restaurant that was currently creating a big buzz among foodies in that part of the world.

Everything was going according to plan—*his* plan. So, by rights he should be feeling good. Only for some reason nothing felt as it should.

But perhaps he shouldn't be surprised.

The day had started badly. He had woken early, in darkness, his body twitching like a sleeping dog chasing rabbits. But it was Effie who had been running in his dreams. Effie just out of reach, the pale soles of her delicate feet always one step ahead, as she darted through a landscape that was both familiar and alien. And he'd wanted to catch her, just as he had wanted to keep kissing her last night.

More than kiss her, he had wanted to strip her, to stretch her out beneath him and open her body to his—

He gritted his teeth as his groin hardened painfully.

He had stopped himself—stopped both of them going further…going all the way. He'd had to. Sleeping with Effie would complicate an already fraught situation. But taking her virginity—

He felt a beat of frustration skim over his skin.

Dreaming about Effie had been unsettling enough, and lying there alone in bed, with lust tugging at his night-heightened senses, had been like an exquisite form of torture. In the end, he'd given up and got up. Without even bothering to get dressed, he had gone down to the lagoon, stripped off his pyjama shorts and swum until his muscles burned.

But the pain had been worth it.

Emerging from the water, he had felt everything suddenly become clear to him. He had been trying too hard, thinking he needed to treat her differently because she was going to be his wife. But in public, where it mattered, Effie was no different from any other woman.

There and then, he'd made up his mind to start over. Act as he always did. And if that meant hopscotching around the neighbouring islands on a boat or idling over a meal in the best restaurant in town then so be it.

This day out together was supposed to have pressed the reset button—only thanks to Effie he felt tenser than he had at the villa.

He scowled at a passing waiter. He'd seen how she lived. She should be excited by all this. Grateful, even. Okay, on the surface she was making all the right noises, looking up at him with those huge saucer eyes, but he knew she was faking it and that annoyed him.

Women didn't fake it with him.

Only it didn't make any sense for him to feel that way, because everything about the two of them *was* fake, and that annoyed him even more.

His eyes dropped to the graceful line of her throat, then lower, to a beauty spot the size of a pinhead at the top of her cleavage.

It didn't help seeing her dressed like that.

He'd thought it would. He'd assumed that if she dressed like his previous girlfriends then it would be business as usual. He would feel attached rather than interdependent. But maybe because he was fighting to keep from touching her, he felt as if Effie was surrounded by some invisible glass barrier.

He thought back to the moment when she had walked out onto the terrace. With her huge brown eyes and those spindly legs, she had looked like a doe, picking her way through a forest. It was the first time she had worn something that didn't hang off her body, and *his* body had reacted viscerally—was still reacting—to the flare of her breasts and the sudden magician's reveal of all that flawlessly smooth bare skin.

'Are you ready to order, sir?'

The waiter had materialised by his elbow, but Effie chose that moment to shift in her seat, and as her legs brushed against his he momentarily lost the power of speech. Heart pounding, he braced his hand against the table, trying to clear his head.

'Yes,' he snapped, without looking at the waiter. 'We'll have the scallops and then the lamb. And a bottle of the Malagouzia.'

Her eyes darted to his face. She had, he knew, expected to choose her own food, but he'd done her yet another favour. It wasn't as if Michelin-starred restaurants were her stomping ground.

Their starters arrived promptly, followed by the main course, both of which were delicious. Only he was too on edge to really enjoy either.

'Was everything to your satisfaction?' the waiter said as he took their plates.

'It was delicious, thank you.'

Effie looked up at the waiter and, watching her smile, Achileas felt the muscles in his arms bunch tightly. Her smile was gentle and miraculous...pure. It was like catching sight of a harvest moon.

The waiter clearly agreed with him, he thought irritably, his jaw hardening. It made him feel territorial in a way that seemed both shocking and justified.

He reached over and caught her hand. She blinked, and his gaze sharpened. She'd done something different to her hair. The sides were pulled back but the rest was loose. She had caught the sun a little too. It suited her...brought out the colour of her eyes. Less iced tea, more single malt whisky, he thought with a jolt, wondering how he had ever thought they were boring.

'I think we'll skip dessert, *agápi mou*.'

'And do what?'

As he opened his mouth to reply, the memory of how she'd kissed him yesterday rushed into his head like an unruly wave and his fingers tightened around hers. Sunlight was bouncing off the sea outside into the restaurant, making the waves appear to ripple over the walls, and now he felt almost as if they were underwater. Around them, the other diners seemed blurred and indistinct.

'Whatever you want.'

Her pupils flared and suddenly he forgot his frustration. He forgot to be angry with his father. He even forgot that they were pretending to be a couple. Suddenly all that mattered was that molten light in her eyes.

Everything was soft and simple and—

There was a clatter of cutlery and then a crash, and Effie's eyes jerked sideways.

He frowned.

'*Syngnómi*, sir.' Glancing over with an agonised expression on his face, the waiter ducked down to pick up the plates he'd dropped.

Achileas stared at him irritably, and then his irritation increased tenfold as Effie pulled her hand free and bent down to help pick up the knives and forks.

'Leave it,' he snapped, catching her arm. 'It's his job. Although maybe it shouldn't be.'

She stared at him, a flood of colour spilling across her cheeks. 'It was an accident,' she said.

'It's incompetence,' he retorted, irritated on all kinds of levels by her defensive remark. 'And if I was paying his wages he'd be fired. I don't pay people to be incompetent.'

Her chin jerked up. 'No, just compliant. Excuse me.'

Astonishingly, that last exchange and the accompanying small smile had been addressed not to him but the waiter, and before he even had a chance to react Effie had pushed back her chair. He watched incredulously as she wove swiftly through the restaurant. Judging by the sudden stillness in the room, he wasn't the only one struggling with incredulity at this development and, fuming, he tossed some notes onto the table and strode between the rigid diners to the door.

Outside in the street the sun was hot and bright—but not nearly as hot and bright as his temper. Grabbing her hand, he pulled her down a deserted side-street. 'Don't ever speak to me like that again.'

She turned towards him, her eyes flashing almost gold in the light. 'That won't be a problem,' she said quietly.

'Good.'

'Because I don't plan on speaking to you again.' She stepped past him.

What? He spun round, staring after her. Stunned. Speechless. Cut off at the knees. What was she talking about? His jaw clenched. And where was she going?

He caught up with her by the quay. And that was a first. Never in his life had he chased after a woman. 'What the hell do you think you're doing?'

'I'm going back to the villa.'

'I'm not ready to go back yet.'

Her eyes flashed fire again, and despite his fury there was something glorious in her anger. 'It suits me fine to go alone.'

It was just like in London. Behind him, he could sense his bodyguards, studiously staring anywhere but at their boss. He swore under his breath. Only this time—incredibly—she really was leaving. With or without him.

The trip back to the villa was conducted in total silence. Back at the island, she stepped off the boat as it nudged up against the jetty, and once again he found himself in the extraordinary position of having to chase after her.

He stalked through the villa, blood pounding through his veins. 'What is wrong with you?' he demanded.

They were standing in her bedroom. She had kicked off her shoes and with her bare feet and flushed cheeks she looked young and defiant, like some student revolutionary.

'Me? Oh, I'm naive and stupid. But you already know that.'

'No, what you are is ungrateful,' he snarled. 'I take you out to lunch. I buy you a dress. I give you a ring. Do you know how many women would change places with you?'

'Yes.' Her eyes flared. *'None.* That's why I'm here. And you didn't buy *me* a dress or a ring. You bought those for your imaginary wife-to-be.'

'Not imaginary. We have a deal.' He bit out the words.

'And there was nothing in that deal that said I have to stand by and watch you treat people like dirt.'

He stared at her in shock, more shocked than if she had hurled her shoes at his head. And for a short, tense pause it almost felt like she had.

'That's what this is about?' His eyes narrowed. 'He's a *waiter*.'

The look of disgust on her face was not one he'd ever experienced or was likely to forget. 'He's a person. With a name. He's not just "the kitchen" or "Housekeeping". And I'm a person too, Achileas.'

He stared at her, jolted. It was the first time she had called him by his name. 'I know that.'

'Do you?' Her mouth trembled. 'If that's true then I don't know why you made me get all dressed up.'

'You had nothing to wear. Nothing appropriate, that is.' He made no attempt to soften his tone.

She shook her head, her eyes huge and bright—too bright. 'You're wrong. I do have something to wear. I wear it every day at work. I have a dress and an apron.'

The tightness was back in his chest.

'You're not making any sense, Effie.'

'Then let me explain. You talked to me in that restaurant like I was a maid. So why didn't you just let me dress like one?'

'That's not what happened—'

'It's exactly what happened. When I'm in my uniform I can deal with people like you, being rude and dismissive and treating me like I'm nothing. But you—you took that away from me.'

Something in her voice pressed against the ache in his chest. 'Effie—'

He reached out but she took a step backwards, holding up her hand as if that could stop him.

Except it did.

'I know I'm not beautiful or clever or rich. I know I don't matter very much in the scheme of things. But nobody's ever made me feel that worthless.'

He stared at her in silence, feeling emotions he hardly recognised. 'That's not what… I didn't mean for that to happen… What are you doing?'

She had turned away and was picking up things: a book, some pyjamas.

'I'm going to pack.'

'No.' He crossed the room in two strides. 'You can't do that.'

'Oh, yes, I can.'

Her mouth was trembling, but he could see in her eyes that she was serious.

'I mean, what are you going to do? Fire me? Give me a bad reference? I know you haven't quite got your head around this, Achileas, but I'm not your employee.'

'I know that,' he said again. 'But we have a deal.'

Her eyes found his, and if her anger had shocked him her pain felt like an actual blow.

'You know what? I've been poor all my life, but some things are more important than money.'

He blocked her path. 'Please, don't go. I don't want you to go.'

'And this is all about what you want—'

'That's not what I meant. You're putting words into my mouth.'

She stared up at him. 'In that case your next line is, *I'll leave you to pack*.'

He frowned. 'Effie, please… I don't know how to—'

There was a note he didn't recognise in his voice. 'Look, I'm sorry. I'm sorry for what I said, and for hurting you.'

'You probably always are.'

Her voice had changed too. The anger had faded, and in its place was a bruise that made him forget his own feelings.

'But this isn't just about you. It's about me.' She shook her head. 'And I can't do this. I thought I could, but I can't lie to myself as well as everyone else. I'll wear any dress, I'll put my hair up or down, but I can't, and I won't behave in a way that I know is wrong and pretend that it's okay. I promised myself I would never do that…that I would never be like him—'

He didn't understand what she was talking about, but he understood the pain in her eyes.

'Be like who?' With shock, he realised that he wanted to know. He wanted to know who had hurt her.

And then he wanted to hurt them.

'It doesn't matter.' She wrapped her arms around her stomach as if it ached.

'It does to me. I know you probably don't believe me, and I understand why you would feel like that, but if you could just give me a chance.' He took a breath. 'Please, Effie…'

Silence.

He made himself wait, although he couldn't remember ever doing so before—for anyone. To wait was to be powerless. But he would wait an eternity if that was what it took to make that terrible rigidity melt from her body.

The silence lengthened, and then, in a voice so low he could hardly hear it, she said, 'My father Bill.'

Her father.

He felt his chest tighten. He had been so wrapped up in

battling his own paternal demons he had never imagined she would have any of her own.

'Why don't you want to be like him?'

'He's a gambler.' Her mouth twisted as if she might smile, but she didn't smile. 'It sounds reckless and exciting, doesn't it? Like being a highwayman or a pirate. But it's not like that when you're living with one. It's terrifying. Every morning you wake up knowing that anything can happen. One day he spent a month's wages in a couple of minutes.'

'What did he gamble on?'

She stared past him, her elbows locked tight against her body. 'In the beginning it was horses, but then it was online roulette. He won occasionally. But mostly he lost. Because that's how it works. And he lied. All the time. To my mum. To me. To himself.'

The knuckles of her hands were white now.

'Are they still together?' he asked.

She shook her head. 'He left when I was fourteen. He used to come back sometimes. Let himself in and take whatever he could find. Pawn it or sell it…'

Her voice faded, but he didn't need to hear more to hear the deeper truth: that her father had robbed her of more than just possessions. He'd taken her trust.

Anger raged inside him—an anger that was separate from and yet mixed in with his own. Anger at the bad fathers of the world and the lies they told…the lies they forced others to tell. And with himself too, for making her lie. For pressing against the bruise.

'Every time he made the same promise. "This is the last time." But it never was. He can't help himself. He doesn't want to help himself. And he won't let anyone else help him either.'

He stared down at her, stricken, understanding that

sense of powerlessness, and then without any kind of conscious intent to do so, he reached out and took her hands. 'You were a child.'

She shook her head again. 'I didn't do enough. Look at what you're doing for *your* father.'

His chest tightened as she looked up at him, her face quivering.

'I should have tried harder...' she said. 'Tried to make him listen—'

It was on the tip of his tongue to tell her the truth. To tell her that he wasn't who she thought he was. That he was lying to Andreas not out of love but in revenge. To get back at the father who had disowned him. The father he had met only twice in his life.

Only he couldn't do it.

He felt his cowardice in the pit of his stomach as his hands tightened around hers.

'I doubt he would have listened,' he said, gentling his voice so that she wouldn't hear his bitterness and pain. 'He didn't listen to anything your mother had to say.'

There was a small silence. 'She didn't say anything.' Her shoulders flexed beneath a weight he hadn't known she was carrying. 'She couldn't. She had a stroke when I was thirteen and it affected her speech.'

Shock blotted out his own painful memories. But if her father had left when she was fourteen—

'Who took care of her?'

But even before she spoke, he knew the answer.

'I did,' she whispered. 'We had some help, but then I left school when I was sixteen and we managed just fine.' Her eyes were shining now, with unshed tears not of pity but of pride. 'Only then she had another stroke, a year ago, and now she's in a home because she needs specialist care. And I need her to be safe.'

And that was why she was here. With him.

The muscles of his face contracted. 'She'll always be safe. Because she's got you.'

He tried to smile, but the brightness in her eyes made it suddenly impossible to do anything but pull her against him as the tears she had been holding back started to fall.

She was so young—too young to have gone through all of that—and he hated it that it had happened. Once again, he found himself hating all bad fathers. Hating himself most of all.

His arms tightened around her. 'And you've got me.'

'But that's the point. I don't have you.' She tilted her tear-stained face up to meet his. 'You want this to work. You want us to look like a couple, but that's not going to be enough. We have to *be* a couple. Maybe not a "for ever" couple, who love each other and want to spend their lives together, but this has to be more than just playing dress-up.'

'I get that—'

But she was shaking her head.

'No, you don't. You think you can just give me clothes and a ring and that's your part done. Then it's on me to convince people. All you have to do is get the bill. And you can't forget even for a moment that you're paying, because deep down you think having money makes you a better person. But if you can't forget it, if you don't see me as your equal, then everyone—including your father—is going to know we're faking it.'

Achileas stared down at her dazedly. At work he was used to bragging hyperbole and brash rhetoric. Outside of work the people he mixed with had a swaggering language that mirrored their splashy lifestyle. And yet somehow Effie's quiet manner reinforced rather than reduced the truth of her words.

She really was one of a kind.

'You're not my equal, Effie,' he said slowly. 'You're way smarter than me.' Pulling her closer, he stroked her hair gently. 'I'm sorry. I'm an idiot. I thought this would be easy. I thought I could just slot you into my life. That's why I took you to lunch. Why I made you get dressed up.'

He hesitated, not wanting to admit to that rush of jealousy, but then he thought about her honesty and all the truths he was holding back. Surely, he could admit this.

'Only then you came onto the terrace in that dress, and I didn't like it.'

Effie frowned. 'I thought you wanted me to get dressed up.'

'I did. But only for me.'

Her eyes fluttered to his face, but she didn't react.

'And I didn't like it when you smiled at the waiter. I wanted you to smile at me. I wanted you to like me.'

There was another silence, and her voice was scratchy when she answered. 'I do like you. You know I like you. But you said—'

'I know what I said.'

He had wanted it to be true. Wanted to be free of that fierce, unforeseen hunger that made no sense. Only having pushed Effie away, he had been left with an emptiness that had filled his lungs, crowding out the air so it had felt as if he was drowning. And he had panicked. It was no excuse, but that was why he'd behaved as he had.

'I was lying. To you. To myself.' He swallowed, hard. 'The truth is, I do care. And you were right about the money. My job, my life makes things binary. You're either a have or a have-not. But a wise woman once told me there was more to life than money and she was right. I can't do this on my own. I need you, Effie. And I want you. I want you so badly that I can't think about anything else.'

He could see the faint tremor beneath her skin, the flush across her cheeks. 'But if you've changed your mind…'

There was a long, pulsing silence, and then she let out a long, slow breath, as if she was letting go of more than just air. She shook her head. 'I haven't,' she said quietly.

CHAPTER SEVEN

STARING DOWN AT EFFIE, Achileas felt the blood roaring in his ears. There was still time to stop this, to turn away. But he didn't want to turn away or stop. He couldn't.

And the truth of that swelled up, washing over him as he leaned forward and kissed her gently, his hands caressing, his fingers sliding over the smooth bones of her ribs, down to her hips, tilting her pelvis towards him, feeling the heat of her skin through the fabric of her dress.

He moved his lips across hers, tracing their shape, taking his time, more time than he ever normally would, and not just because she was a virgin. He wanted to taste her... to lick the heat from her mouth into his. And she tasted so good. Sweet like sun-warmed honey and more intoxicating than wine.

Her lower lip quivered, and he felt her breathe out shakily and he kissed her more deeply, kissed her until she was shivering against him, her skin, her limbs, her body trembling uncontrollably.

Everything about her was soft and pliant, and the need to touch more of her was pounding through his body. He wanted her. Only it was more than just wanting. His body ached with a hunger he had never felt before.

Hs hands rose up to cup her breasts, his groin hardening as her nipples stiffened against the palms of his hands.

She moaned softly, her fingers digging into the flesh of his arms. 'Should I take off my dress now?'

Her question, delivered in that quiet, precise way of hers, almost sent him over the edge. His face burning with shock and desire, he drew her against him, trying to slow his pulse, to calm the tangle of heat and hunger churning deep inside him.

'Would you like to?'

Effie stared up at Achileas, her heart pounding. 'Yes...' she whispered, although she wasn't sure that it would be enough.

She felt as if she'd spent too long in the sun—as if the heat had burrowed through her clothes into her body...if only she could unzip her skin.

Her pulse twitched as he kissed her neck, the bristles of his stubble sending a flood of hot sensation through her limbs and she shivered inside, drinking in the smell of him—part skin, part sunlight, all male.

'I'd like it too,' he said hoarsely.

His fingers moved to the front of her dress, and she felt the fabric tug as he pulled the buttons through the tiny holes. He was breathing unsteadily. As the last button popped free, he slid his hand slowly along her collarbone. Slipping the dress off her shoulders, he let it fall to her feet.

The air felt cool against her skin. She was wearing simple white underwear. Cotton, not silk. No lace. Reaching behind her back, she unhooked her bra, letting it drop beside her dress. Now she was naked except for her panties. She hooked her fingers into the fabric—

'Stop.'

His voice scraped across her skin, and she stared up at him dazedly.

'Let down your hair.'

The words, so stark, so direct, sent flickers of feeling everywhere. Hands trembling, she slid her fingers through her hair, jerking it free of the band at the nape of her neck.

'Now shake your head,' he ordered.

Dry-mouthed, she did as he commanded, staring up at him, her throat swollen with something that didn't have a name as her hair tumbled to her shoulders. No one had ever made her feel like this…so hungry and so helpless at the same time.

His gaze was dark and steady and unblinking. She could feel the intensity of his concentration, see the pulse beating in his neck, beating out the same rhythm as her heart, as if they were flamenco dancers stamping out a *zapateado*.

He muttered something in Greek, and then he reached out and caressed her cheek. The heat of his fingers blossomed deep inside her and her skin ached for his touch. Every cell, every single centimetre of skin, was humming.

She wanted to touch him too. Wanted to lean in closer, to explore him.

Even as she thought it, she moved her hand to the buttons on his shirt. With fingers that shook slightly, she pushed the shirt off his shoulders. The cuffs caught at his wrists, and he swore softly, jerking his hands free before drawing her closer.

Staring down at his bare chest, she swallowed. She was nervous, but mostly she was turned on. Her fingers touched the waistband of his trousers and the muscles of his stomach twitched, as if touched by some invisible current. And then he was leaning forward, kissing her hungrily, parting her lips, sliding his hand up her back to the nape of her neck.

The ridge of his erection was pushing into her stomach. Without breaking the kiss, he lifted her slightly so that it pressed against her pelvic bone, and a sharp heat she had never felt before flared between her thighs.

Head spinning, melting on the inside, she moaned, shuddering as his fingers brushed lightly over her taut nipples. His tongue was in her mouth, making her stomach clench and ache. It made her think of his hard body on hers. Inside her.

She reached for the zip of his trousers. Grunting, he jerked backwards, his hands catching her wrists. He was breathing deeply, and there was a dark flush along his cheekbones. For a moment he stared down at her intently, so intently that her skin tingled wherever his gaze touched.

'Let's go to bed,' he said softly, and he pulled her backwards, leading her by the wrists.

She let him. It was what she wanted. It was all she wanted. He was all she wanted. And he wanted her. Here and now. Everything else might be a lie, but this was their truth.

She watched dizzily as he stripped off first his trousers and then his boxer shorts.

Now he was as naked as he had been that morning.

Only this time he was bigger, harder…

Suddenly she could hardly breathe. Tiny waves of panic were rippling through her, colliding with the frantic beat of her heart.

'Don't be scared,' he said.

'I'm not.' She hesitated. 'Well, maybe I am a little bit.'

'You don't need to be. I won't hurt you. I won't let anyone hurt you.' His eyes were suddenly dark blue and fierce, his face granite-hard like his warrior namesake's.

He dipped his head and kissed her gently, his hands firm, compelling, sliding slowly over her body, pulling her onto the bed beneath him.

She drew in a sharp breath as his lips found the hollow

beneath her ear, and then she dragged in another as his lips trailed down her neck slowly, to her collarbone, and then lower still to her breast.

As his mouth closed around her nipple, her fingers bit into the thick muscles of his arm. She felt him tense.

'Is that okay?' he asked.

'Yes,' she whispered. *'Yes...'* she said again.

It was more than okay—only she didn't have the words or thoughts. Everything was dissolving except this fierce, insatiable hunger. Helplessly, she arched against him, pressing closer, wanting more, needing to satisfy the ache inside her.

Whimpering, she grabbed his hand, flattening the palm against the staccato pulse beating between her legs.

'Effie...' He groaned her name and she felt him shift against her.

'I want you,' she said.

He stared down at her, his eyes dark with passion. 'You have me,' he said hoarsely.

'No. Inside me.'

His dense black lashes fluttered at her words and her heart pounded. It might hurt, but she wanted to feel him. To feel his heat and strength.

Her hand flexed against him as he started to stroke her through the damp cotton. The tip of his finger slipped beneath the fabric and her hand balled into a fist as he brushed against her clitoris. She arched upwards, legs shaking. Heat was swamping her.

'Is that okay?' he said again.

Nodding, she clasped his face, pressing a desperate kiss to his mouth, her breath catching as his fingers caressed her. She felt him move, his body pushing forward, and her own body tensed in sudden panic. How could this work? He would be too big...

'Don't be scared,' he whispered again. His lips brushed against her mouth, her shoulder, her collarbone. 'It if hurts, or if you change your mind, we can stop any time—'

'I don't want to stop.'

He leaned over her, kissed her, and then his hands slid slowly under her bottom, and he pulled her panties down over her thighs, lifting her further up the bed, stretching out over her, parting her legs.

'I'll just get a condom.'

She watched as he reached onto the floor for his trousers, shivering with nerves and anticipation as he rolled on the condom.

Breathing out unsteadily, he rubbed the tip of his erection between her thighs, pushing into the slick heat a little deeper each time, and she responded instinctively, opening her body to his, moving her hands to his hips.

'That's it…' he murmured. 'Like that.'

His face was taut with concentration, his eyes burning into hers, and then he lifted her hips and slid into her.

Her breath caught. He felt hot and sleek and big, too big and for a moment she concentrated on absorbing the size of him. Then it stung a little, stretched a little more and her hands braced against his chest.

Instantly, he stilled. 'It's okay,' he said softly. 'Take all the time you need. Your body is just getting used to how it feels.'

She nodded. He was right, she thought a moment later as the muscles in her thighs loosened.

He shifted, taking more of his weight on his elbows, and looked down at her as if he was trying to commit her face to memory. 'Now move with me.'

Her pulse quickened as his mouth found hers, his kiss taking her with him so that soon her head was spinning, and her muscles were relaxed. Her hips lifted to accept him, her body stretching, opening, the pulse between her thighs getting faster and more insistent.

She reached for him blindly, wrapping her arms around his shoulders, chasing the pulse as he drove into her. Her skin felt white-hot. Her blood was like lava. She was melting inside, dissolving with need, and now her muscles were tightening again, tightening around him, trying to hold on to him, gripping tighter and tighter—

Her mouth opened and she made a sort of keening, one-syllable noise that swelled inside her unbidden. And then her body tensed, and she arched, a barb of sharp pleasure jerking her hips against his, flames rippling through her as she shuddered helplessly beneath him.

She felt Achileas thrust deeper. He buried his hands in her hair and his mouth covered hers as he reared forward, taking her with him, his body surging inside hers.

He grunted, limbs twitching, and she felt him ease down against her, his skin hot and damp.

Heart pounding, Effie stared dazedly across the room, half expecting to see the beautiful dressing table on fire. Or on its side, drawers emptied. Or the curtains ripped from the windows. Anything that would reflect the immensity of what had just happened inside the room.

But it was all exactly the same.

For a moment she listened to the sound of their fractured breathing, resting her fingers limply against his shoulders. Her lips were soft and puffy from all their kissing, and she felt like a piece of clay that Achileas had shaped with his hands into something new and beautiful.

Was that how she was supposed to feel? Was that what everyone's first time was like? So powerful and sensual? She hoped it was.

It had been just so beautiful…so utterly beyond anything she could have imagined. She'd had no idea that hands could stir and torment to such a pitch of pleasure. Or that skin could be so sensitive. Even now everything felt magnified and sensual—the shudder of his breath against her shoulder, the weight of his hand in her hair.

Achileas's breath.

Achileas's hand.

She felt her chest tighten. Everything about him was so perfect, and it had felt so good, so right, when he'd moved against her, inside her...

He was still inside her now, and nobody ever told you about that part. How good, how right, how perfect it felt. To lie there as one, bodies fused.

Her heart squeezed. He had made her want so much and now it was over.

'I didn't hurt you, did I?'

Achileas was looking down at her intently.

'No.' She shook her head, wanting to tell him the truth. But how could she? He had told her that she could change her mind and that he would stop. But she hadn't wanted him to stop, and it had changed everything. He had changed everything. Changed her from the inside out. Changed her understanding of the world and herself. He had made her want things, and she had asked and taken what she wanted in ways she had never done before.

His eyes held hers for a moment and then he shifted backwards, lifting his body carefully off hers.

Still floating on clouds, she reached for him.

'No, you stay here,' he said, and she felt a sharp pang like an actual physical loss as he rolled off the bed and disappeared into the bathroom.

But what had she expected him to do? He was hardly going to keep holding her against him afterwards, like a lover. And although they hadn't discussed it, it was obvious now that there was a reason for that.

Her first time with Achileas would also be her only time with him. The logical part of her brain had accepted that. But the other part—the part that had surrendered to him completely—couldn't seem to let go.

Her breath was trapped in her throat as she watched him walk back into the bedroom, carelessly, casually naked, and a riot of sensations and emotions stormed through her body. His eyes were unreadable, his face set into an expression she couldn't even begin to fathom. And then her heart skipped a beat as he climbed back into bed, and she realised that he had just been getting rid of the condom.

Gazing down at his muscular body, she felt her skin grow warm. She was not quite embarrassed, but a little shy at her naivety. And at his nudity. He was just so big and masculine and naked.

And still aroused.

She felt her body ripple back to life.

'What are you thinking about?' Achileas asked.

He was looking down at her, his blue eyes intent on her face. She tried to smile, to distance herself from the ache in her breasts and the flare of heat between her thighs.

'I was just thinking that now I understand what all the fuss is about.' They were lying close together. Close enough that she could feel the furnace heat of his skin, and better still breathe in his delicious maleness. 'I didn't before.'

He tipped his head back, his mouth curling into a question mark. 'Fuss about what?'

'Sex.' She bit her lip. 'I didn't get what people meant. But now I can see why they say it makes the world go round.'

The corners of his mouth tugged upwards. 'I think you'll find that's money.'

She pulled in a breath, lost in his smile. He was right,

it was money, but her brain didn't seem to be working properly.

Fighting to keep her voice casual, she said, 'So what do they say about sex?'

He reached out and brushed her hair away from her breast, letting his hand graze against the nipple until it hardened.

'I don't know and I don't care what they say. I only care about what you say. What you want.' His teasing smile faded and slowly he trailed his fingertips from her aching breast down over the curve of her hip to the triangle of hair between her thighs. 'What you like.'

She stared up at him in silence. That was easy: she liked him.

A lot.

Too much.

But this was just how people talked about sex, wasn't it?

He wasn't being serious.

Was he?

Suddenly she wished she knew more…had experienced more. Like Tamara and all those other women from his world. She knew so little about how sex worked, so little about this kind of intimate moment.

Her shoulders shifted. But she did know that there had already been too many lies in her life, too many hidden truths. She knew, too, that she wanted his hand to keep sliding over her skin.

So why not take a risk tinier than the last?

She cleared her throat. 'I like it when you touch me.'

His eyes on hers were dark and unreadable and she felt a wildness inside her, both hope and panic, as the silence stretched between them. And then he moved closer and kissed her softly…so softly that his lips barely whispered against hers. And yet she could feel the heat beneath, and the power. Always the power.

'I like it too.' His voice was rough sounding, as if it was an effort to admit it even to himself, and then his hands moved to her back, and he drew her closer. 'And I'd like to keep touching you, and for you to keep touching me.'

She stared at him mutely, shaking his words like a gold prospector, turning them over, sifting them, sieving them inside her head.

A short time ago she had been living on her own, living half a life in her tiny London flat. Now she was on an island, a private island in the middle of the Aegean, sharing a bed with a man. And not just a bed; she knew what Achileas's hard body felt like inside hers and the speed of change made her feel dizzy.

Her eyes skimmed back and forth over the smooth, contours of his chest and stomach, dipping lower with each pass. Years of living with the unknown had made her fear uncertainty, and she knew that to keep touching him would have unknowable consequences.

But right now, here in this moment, not touching him again was unthinkable.

She met his gaze, her pulse quivering. 'Do you mean like this?' Reaching up, she touched his face lightly.

'Yes, like that.'

He didn't move a muscle, but something flickered in his eyes like a flame, and she felt an answering flutter of heat low in her stomach. Impossible to ignore.

Now she touched his chest. His skin was warm and damp, and she could feel his heart beating through her fingertips. 'And like this?'

He nodded.

She hesitated, and then her hand moved from his chest to his groin. She felt his sudden stillness, heard his sharp intake of breath like the backdraught in a burning building. 'And what about this? Do you like that?'

He didn't answer. Instead, he leaned into her, lifting her face to his, and kissed her—kissed her until she couldn't speak or think or breathe, opening her mouth to his, giving her his answer. Her belly clenched, tight and hot and aching, as he rolled her under his body, and everything she wanted in the world was there with him.

CHAPTER EIGHT

NAKED, ACHILEAS STEPPED onto the balcony. He hesitated a moment, glancing back at the bed where Effie was sleeping. She had fallen asleep in his arms, her soft body curled around his, and he wanted to sleep too. But everything kept replaying in his head.

Starting with what had just happened.

His heart was suddenly speeding.

Even now it blew his mind, and a part of him couldn't quite accept what they had done. But the facts were clear and irrefutable. Effie had been a virgin when they'd walked back into the villa this afternoon and now, she wasn't.

Now she was his.

He glanced back to the woman on the bed again.

Her hair was spilling over the pillow like warm buckwheat honey. Thinking about how he'd tangled his hands through it as she clung to him, and the noises she had made, turned his breathing inside out, so that he felt almost faint.

She had been sweet and pliable, like spun sugar, and her body had been a revelation. Small, firm breasts, a waist he could fit his hands around, and that throat...

Her first time: not his.

Although in some ways it had felt as if it was. There had been a newness and a nervousness in him he had never felt before, even when he'd lost his own virginity. The desire to give pleasure, to take care of her was not unique—for him, good sex was always about mutual satisfaction. But Effie had been his first time with a virgin, and he had found it impossible to keep his usual distance.

Touching her, watching her face soften, feeling her body open to his, had made him feel—

What?

He didn't know. Other than anger, he shied away from emotions. More than one of his former girlfriends had accused him of lacking emotional intelligence. Maybe that was why he was finding it so hard to explain away these feelings now—feelings he couldn't even name, much less process.

But his confusion was probably down to it being completely unplanned. Truthfully, he thought he'd blown the whole damn thing back in the restaurant. He had been so tense, had behaved so unreasonably, and Effie—well, she had been furious.

And his fury had matched hers.

He felt his spine stiffen as he remembered his blind, ungovernable rage.

Nobody had ever talked to him as she had. From an early age, his temper, and his implacable determination to win at any cost had meant that everyone—including grown men twice her size—had backed down, placated him, or simply turned a blind eye to his worst behaviour.

Not Effie.

She had called him out. Told him the truth. She had held a mirror to his face; and he hadn't liked what he saw.

His chest felt tight against his ribs.

Confronting his failings had been hard, painful, *shocking*. But what had snuffed out his fury...the dark, impenetrable, all-consuming rage that clung to him like a shadow even on a cloudy day…was something else entirely. It was what Effie had told him about her father and her mother.

His fingers tightened around the rail.

When he was being rational, reasonable, he knew gambling was a sickness, and that therefore blame was inappropriate, but picturing Effie living in that situation made him want to rage at a higher authority.

Or punch something.

No wonder lying was such an anathema to her.

He stared out to sea, watching the waves break the surface, thinking back to their first meeting outside the Stanmore. Little Miss Nobody: that was what he'd called her then. And he'd been so sure of who she was. Small. Unimportant. A means to an end.

And, yes, she was small. But she was also talented and smart. Strong.

What she had done for her mother was nothing short of remarkable. Like him, she had turned her life around. His mouth thinned. The difference was, Effie had done it out of love—not anger and a desire for revenge.

He was glad. Grateful. So much of his life had been spent trying to push back the darkness he carried inside, and her strength, her purity of motive, was a tiny, flickering candle. It was making him question the man he had become. She was making him question the man he had become. The man he wanted to be after all this was over. On that basis Effie was way more than a means to an end.

And yet he was still lying to her.

He turned away from the restless sea.

Even after she had revealed so much of herself to him, he hadn't told her the truth about Andreas. He lacked her courage, and he hated that. But he couldn't tell her that his father had never wanted him. Or that even now Andreas's love and acceptance came with a condition.

How could he do that when she was the condition?

Later. He would tell her later, when everything between them was more settled, and after that they would face his father together. Then, when it was all over, she would leave, and he would get on with his life. A life without his dark burden.

His eyes narrowed. In the bedroom Effie was awake, and right now there was a new item at the top of his agenda. In fact, there was only one item, *one agenda...* and he walked towards her.

'What are you doing out here? Apart from wearing too much clothing.'

Effie jumped. A pair of warm hands slid around her waist and Achileas's stubbled jaw grazed her throat as he kissed her softly.

'I was just watching the boats. There's so many of them today.'

His fingers tiptoed beneath her shirt—*his* shirt, technically—and instantly she could feel herself sliding into that yielding place between the warmth of his hands and the sudden pounding of her heart.

'It's that time of year,' he murmured. 'It's the Galanólefki Ball this weekend.'

'What's that?'

He moved closer, and she felt more of that same mix of weakness and wonder as his body fitted around hers, hard where she was soft.

'It's an annual fundraising ball in aid of a selection of children's charities, hosted at the Hipparchus Observatory in Athens. A glitzy gala night attended by local luminaries and global celebrities. Or that's what it says in the papers.'

His mouth had found the sensitive hollow just below her ear and she felt her pulse leap beneath his lips. Resisting the urge to let him explore further, she turned in the circle of his arms.

'What is Gala…? Gala—?' She stumbled over the word, distracted by the miraculous contours of his bare chest.

'Gal-an-ó-lefki,' he said slowly. 'It's what the Greeks call their flag. Like you have the Union Jack. It means blue and white. That's the dress code. It's a big deal. Wall-to-wall billionaires, and it does a lot of good. The ticket price alone raises millions.'

His eyes tracked the flotilla of white yachts slicing through the blue waves and she sensed that he was debating something.

'Actually, Arete is one of the sponsors.'

'It is?'

They were talking easily. Like a couple, in fact. She was still coming to terms with that. With how much things had changed between them over the last few days. Three days, in fact. Three days since she had told Achileas the truth about her father's gambling and her mum's illness.

He had been angry. Of course. He was Achileas. But he had put his anger aside and he had held her against him, his arms tight around her body, as if he wanted to keep her safe. Wanted her to know he would keep her safe.

And she wanted that too. But most of all she wanted him.

Her throat was suddenly so dry it hurt to swallow. It was three days since she had lost her virginity, and her knowledge of sex and bodies—both her own and his—had grown exponentially hour by hour. Three days in which the half-formed fantasies she'd had about sex had been swept away by a man who had initiated her into an A to Z of positions and techniques that she was pretty sure few people even knew existed.

Her stomach cartwheeled. Somehow, he made sex feel

like the most natural thing in the world, and intensely, mind-meltingly erotic. She simply couldn't imagine a better first lover.

A better lover.

Her ribs were suddenly too tight. Not that they were *making love*. She might be new to all this, but she understood enough to know that even though it felt like a wildness in her blood this was just sex.

'You sound surprised.' He was staring at her intently, an eyebrow raised, the blue of his eyes rivalling the spring sky above their heads.

She shook her head. 'I'm not surprised. I know you can be a good person.'

In bed, he was gentle, teasing, sometimes fierce and demanding. But he was always patient and generous and focused on every beat of her blood.

'You do?' He raised an eyebrow, as if he was reading her mind—which, to be fair, he probably was.

'You were kind to me when I told you about my father,' she said, as evenly as she could.

'You were upset.' His voice was cool. 'I did what any normal person would do.'

She stared at him, confused. There was a tension around his mouth that hadn't been there before, but why? It was almost as if she had accused him of something bad.

'What about this…us?' she said quietly. 'There's not many sons who would do what you're doing for their father?'

'And you think that makes me a good person?'

Before she could reply he shifted against her, his mouth curling into something that was not quite a smile. 'I'm flattered I've gone up in your estimation. But as far as the ball goes our sponsorship is good for business. Good for the charities. It's a fun evening. Everyone's happy.'

Except he didn't sound happy. The tension had transferred to his voice. Was it something to do with the ball? Did his father expect him to attend? Was he not going because of her?

'It sounds amazing. A once-in-a-lifetime experience.'

His gaze sharpened on her face. 'Are you saying you want to go?'

Was she? Three days ago, the idea would have terrified her. But now it didn't seem so scary. There was a truth to their relationship now...even if it wasn't the whole truth and nothing but the truth. And she wanted to take that tension from Achileas's body.

'Maybe,' she said, trying to keep her voice light.

'Really? It's just that the other day you said we should wait a little. Get our story straight.'

'That was then. Things are different now. We know each other better.'

His pupils flared. 'Yes, we do,' he said softly, and the dark shimmer in his voice reached inside her and prised her open.

Trying to ignore the maddening heat storming through her body, she said, 'And it would be a good place to be seen together in public.'

He nodded, and then his eyes narrowed, fixing on something past her shoulder. She shifted in his arms. Out at sea, yet another ship had appeared. It was moving slowly, like some oversized prehistoric monster, and beside it even the huge superyachts looked as tiny and insubstantial as dinghies.

'That is the biggest boat I've ever seen.'

'They can be bigger. That one, *The Tiphys*, is about the length of two football pitches—two hundred and sixty metres, to be precise.'

She blinked. 'How on earth do you know that?'

Was there some kind of marine equivalent of trainspotting? Although it didn't seem likely it would be Achileas's cup of tea.

Next to her, Achileas was silent. Then, 'See that logo on the bow? That's an Alexios ship. It's owned by Andreas Alexios.'

She had heard the name. Anyone not living under a rock had heard of the Alexios Shipping Group. Alexios was a name like Onassis or Niarchos. A name that conjured up images of proud, dark-eyed men standing on the decks of their shimmering oversized yachts, dictating the mood of the Aegean like modern-day Poseidons.

'Is he a friend of yours?'

He shook his head. 'Not a friend, no.' There was a short, taut pause, and then he added coolly, 'He's my father.'

His father. She stared at him in confusion. His father was *that* Andreas. Why, then, was he not Achileas Alexios?

Beside her, Achileas was still, but there was a kind of anticipatory tension vibrating in the air, like in that moment before the magician pulls a rabbit from a hat. Glancing up at his proud profile, she knew why he had not taken his father's name. Achileas was exactly the kind of man who would want to prove himself, want his success to be his own and not the result of any nepotistic bias.

'He must be very proud of you,' she said softly. 'For achieving so much without making use of his name.' Lifting her chin, she smiled a little shyly. 'Actually, I changed my name too.'

'You did?'

She felt his arms tighten around her, felt the first ripple of longing as he drew her closer. 'Well, maybe not changed. Just shortened. My real name is Josephine, but no one's ever called me that. Except the vicar when he christened me.'

'It's a beautiful name. You probably just needed time to grow into it.'

Her heart jumped as he reached out and tucked a strand of hair behind her ear.

'And now you have. So, do you want to come to the ball with me, Josephine?'

The heat in his voice as he said her name shuddered through her, kicking up sparks. 'Yes,' she said hoarsely.

'Then I'll go and make a few calls.' Reaching out, he took hold of her shirt, pinching the fabric between his fingers to pull her against him. 'First, though, I'm going to need this back.'

He undid the top button, then the next one down, his mouth finding hers as the shirt slid from her shoulders, and then he was walking her backwards into the bedroom towards the bed...

CHAPTER NINE

IT WAS ONE of the lesser-known benefits of being very wealthy, Achileas thought, settling back on the sofa, and stretching out his legs, that time became somewhat irrelevant. You could never be late or early, because essentially you *were* the board meeting or the dinner party or the charity lunch. When you arrived, everything started. And whenever you decided to leave there was always a car waiting at the kerb to take you where you wanted to go next.

But, rich or poor, some things didn't change. And that was why he was sitting here fully dressed, waiting for Effie. Or was it Josephine? He liked both names, but if he was being honest what he liked most was knowing that she was *his* Josephine. That nobody else had ever called her by that name.

If he was being honest.

The words rolled around inside his head like a bottle on a bar room floor. Only he wasn't being honest. Far from it.

And maybe at the beginning that had been the right, the only thing to do. He hadn't been about to share the details of his life with some random chambermaid. But there was nothing random about his relationship with Effie now. And he had known all along he would have to share some essential truths about himself with her.

He'd told himself the right time would present itself.

And he'd been correct: it had.

Spotting *The Tiphys* at sea had been not just the right but the perfect time to tell her about his father. To admit the truth of their relationship—if that was even the correct word for it.

Only then Effie had made an assumption...the wrong assumption. She had mistakenly thought that the reason he didn't share a surname with Andreas was down to some kind of noble desire on his part to strike out on his own.

She had looked up at him, those huge amber eyes filled with such wonder, and even though he'd known that it had nothing at all to do with him—that the man she was imagining didn't actually exist—he had been momentarily lost in what it would feel like to deserve that look. If he had truly been that man, instead of one with bitter resentment in his heart.

After that, there had been no way he could tell her that he hadn't chosen to be Achileas Kane. That his father had not just withheld the name of Alexios but denied his paternity, disowned the very existence of his son.

But it wasn't just about him.

Nothing was any more, it seemed.

It was about Effie, too, and she was essentially a good person. If he told her the truth about his father's behaviour, then it would be hard not to reveal that his motives for marriage were a lot less altruistic than he was making out. And for some reason her respect, her believing him to be a good son, mattered.

Mattered more than punishing his father.

His spine stiffened. Was that true?

For longer than he could remember he had wanted to get even with Andreas. To take back what was rightfully his.

All those years he had worked sixteen, twenty hours a day, six days a week, sometimes seven, to build his empire, he had lived and breathed that goal. This engagement to Effie was supposed to be his way of making it happen. Besting his father's lie with one of his own—a better one.

Only each decision he made had some knock-on effect he hadn't considered—like some giant game of cosmic pinball. That was why he had ended up asking her to the Galanólefki Ball…to distract her, and to distract himself from the hidden truths he was keeping.

And a part of him wanted to go, wanted to play Prince Charming to her Cinderella. To see her smile. To make her smile.

But mostly he just wanted to stay here, with her. For it to be just the two of them. He wanted to be able to reach out and touch her, to watch her eyes widen as he found the sweet spot inside her that made her body twitch as if she couldn't control it—

Gritting his teeth against the serrated edge of hunger sawing into his groin, he got to his feet and walked across the room to stand by the open French windows. Maybe he would call it off…tell her he was feeling sick.

Not tonight, Josephine, he thought, a reluctant smile pulling at the corners of his mouth—

'Achileas?'

His heart thudded against his ribs. He still hadn't got used to the way she said his name—as if it was a prayer, or a poem…a promise, even.

But as he spun round, he forgot about his name. He forgot to breathe.

Effie was standing in the doorway.

This time he had told her to choose a dress she liked. No budget. Just something that made her feel comfortable in her own skin.

A slow, crawling tension slid over him. Maybe that hadn't been such a good idea. In fact, he was beginning to think that he should have insisted on a dress that focused on his comfort.

How the hell was he going to keep his hands to himself?

Made of pleated chiffon, her dress was the same blue as the sea where it hugged the coastline. It had a high neck with some kind of ribbon tie, and an ankle-skimming hem, but in between it clung to her body like moss to a rock.

And as she moved towards him, on silver heels that added three inches to her height, he caught a glimpse of smooth, bare thigh and realised that despite its demure length there was a leg-showcasing slit in the swirling skirt.

She stopped in front of him, teetering a little on the thick rug.

He had assumed she would put her hair up. But it was loose, casual, spilling over her bare shoulders in a way that made her look young and fresh and sexy. And then there was that intoxicating but not in-your-face scent she wore, which made all five of his senses shiver at once.

It was impossible to look and not touch and, reaching out, he ran his finger along her collarbone.

'You look beautiful.' *Make that exquisite*, he thought, watching the flush of colour flare along her cheekbones. She really was his Cinderella.

She touched his lapel lightly, one of those tentative, sanity-sapping smiles pulling at her mouth. 'So do you.' Now she bit into her lip. 'I didn't keep you waiting too long, did I?'

'I'd wait all night for you.' It wasn't something he could have imagined himself doing, much less saying to any other woman, but he wanted to say it to Effie.

Her eyes met his. 'Thank you. I was just taking a few photos. To show my mum later.'

He nodded and held out his arm.

Over the last few days, they had talked about her mum,

and he'd learned that before her stroke Sam had been a beautician. And even after her stroke she'd been a good mother. It was Sam who had encouraged Effie to launch her perfume business. And it was Sam who had refused to let Effie take care of her after the second stroke.

She had nothing. No partner to support her. No money. Poor health. But she wanted the best for her daughter.

His chest tightened. Somehow, he didn't think that this sham engagement would come under that heading.

Outside, the helicopter crouched like a dragonfly on a waterlily pad, and he helped Effie climb inside. Was that why he felt so on edge? He stared through the glass at the darkening sky. Possibly. Or more likely it was the thought of being on the mainland, within spitting distance of Andreas's huge fabled waterside mansion.

The old familiar ache spread through his chest like an oil spill from a crippled tanker.

A mansion he had yet to visit.

Not that his father was even there, he thought as the helicopter began its descent. At their last meeting—only the second in his life—Andreas had told him that he had a horse running in the Kentucky Derby and would be watching the race in person.

If Andreas had been coming tonight, he wouldn't even have mentioned the ball to Effie. It was too soon for her to meet the father he barely knew. And it was more than that. Once Effie met his father, their relationship would be like a ticking time bomb. All of this—the two of them together—would have to take a back seat, and he wasn't ready for that to happen just yet.

His father's absence should have calmed him, only he couldn't seem to shake his unease…this nervousness that had never troubled him before.

As the helicopter landed, he felt Effie's body tense and,

glancing through the window, he saw that the red-carpeted steps to the observatory were hemmed in on either side by a phalanx of press and photographers.

Instantly he felt a rush of relief at having found an explanation for his uncharacteristic jitters. Always before he had been with a woman for whom this was the norm, but this was all new and probably terrifying for Effie, so naturally he was worrying about her.

'It's okay.' He reached for her hand. 'They can't go inside.' His fingers tightened around hers. 'And I know it looks scary but it's really quite easy. Think of it as a dance. All you have to do is stop, smile, wave and turn.'

She nodded. 'Okay.'

'Oh, and one more thing.' He pulled her closer and kissed her softly. 'Don't let go of my hand.'

Head spinning, Effie followed Achileas along the covered roped-off walkway. Beneath the tented ceiling it felt like a cocoon, but as she stepped outside white light exploded on every side of her. She flinched, blinking. She had seen people walk the red carpet on TV countless times, but she'd had no idea it was like this—so intense, so intrusive.

'Don't let go of my hand.'

It was the last thing Achileas said to her before the car door had opened. Not that she'd needed telling. Blinded by the camera flashes, she hardly knew which way was up, and his hand, firmly threaded through hers, was the only thing keeping her on her feet. His other hand was curved around her waist, and she let him guide her forward—and then he stopped.

Stop. Smile. Wave. Turn.

'Well done,' he whispered against her ear.

Glancing up at him, Effie felt her stomach flip over in a totally uncontrollable response. There could be no man alive more suited to the clean elegance of a classic tuxedo than Achileas Kane. He looked stupidly handsome—as if an artist had drawn him, each mark, each line perfectly capturing every hard plane.

It had been hard to look away before. Now it was beyond her.

'Are you ready?'

She felt his gaze move over her, the blue gleam against the gold of his skin reminding her of Ancient Egyptian artefacts.

She nodded.

'Then let's go to the ball,' he said softly.

Hand in hand, they walked up a flamboyantly wide staircase, and then they were inside the huge galleried room.

Looking down, she felt her breathing jolt. There were at least twenty white-clothed tables, glittering with silverware, and milling around between them were the guests. The men in dark suits and white shirts and the women in every shade of blue from sky to sapphire and deeper still, to indigo and midnight.

And flanking them on either side of the room was a line of statues. Not of stone or marble, but of cream-coloured flowers.

She breathed in. Roses, to be precise.

The smell was intoxicating.

His hand still locked tightly with hers, Achileas led her downstairs. She had thought this would be the easy part, but outside with the cameras flashing she had been unable to see anything. Now she could see everyone—and they could see her.

But as they moved between the groups of guests she started to relax. Everyone was friendly and there was so much to enjoy and take in. And not just with her eyes. As well as the statues there were ruins created out of jasmine and gardenias, and their scent filled the room so that she felt almost drugged.

Or perhaps that was Achileas, she thought helplessly, because right now everything about him, from his precision-tooled bone structure to his teasing, tempting smile, was making her head spin.

And she was not the only one feeling that way.

All around her she could sense women shifting to look furtively over their partners' shoulders, drawn by the magnetic north of Achileas's masculine beauty.

'Let's grab a drink,' he whispered in her ear.

It was such a normal thing to say, but the drinks here were anything but. Like everything else, the cocktails were colour-coordinated to the ball, so there were white margaritas and sapphire martinis. They looked so pretty Effie could hardly bear to drink hers, and she had only taken a few sips when dinner was announced.

The food was delicious. An astonishing granita using the ingredients of a Greek salad, a pairing of white chocolate and cured fish roe, an amazing lamb and shallot *stifado*, and to finish a lemon and basil mousse with a vanilla biscuit and olive oil ice cream.

'Thank you. Dimitris,' Achileas said as the waiter deftly cleared away their plates. 'It was all wonderful. Could you pass on my compliments to the chef?'

The waiter nodded. 'Yes, sir. I'll be sure to tell him, Mr Kane.'

Effie blinked. It was the first time she had heard Achileas speak in that way—at least to someone like a waiter. Probably he was on his best behaviour because they were here at the ball. Although most of the other guests at their table were talking too loudly to notice.

'What?' He raised an eyebrow.

'Nothing.' She hesitated. 'It's just that it was nice of you. To say that to the waiter.'

'You mean Dimitris?' His glittering blue gaze moved over her face. 'I poached Yiannis from this event a couple of years back, so I thought I'd just lay down a marker. Oh, and a wise woman once told me that waiters were people too. And that they have names.'

She felt as if a hand had reached into her chest and squeezed it. He had done it for her. It wasn't a big deal, or anything, but she could feel it tingling inside her.

At some point an orchestra had arrived and discreetly set up. Now they were playing Gershwin show tunes, and maybe it was the wine and the roses, but she felt like dancing.

'Can you dance?' She looked over at Achileas. 'Or do you just stop, smile, wave and turn?'

'Of course I can dance.' He shifted back in his seat. 'Why? Are you asking me?'

The teasing gleam in his blue eyes made her heart quiver. 'Yes, I'm asking.' Her palms were itching to touch him properly. To feel his hands on her body.

'In that case, I'm dancing.'

She stood up, suddenly impatient, but he didn't lead her onto the dance floor. Instead, he steered her through the couples moving in slow circles out of the ballroom.

'I thought we were going to dance,' she protested.

'We are. But not with all those people around us. I want to be alone with you.'

He didn't mean it the way it sounded—she knew that. He was, she was sure, just relieved to have made it this far, and he was naturally better at all this stuff…especially at saying things that sounded intimate and personal.

That was the part she had skipped. Whereas Achileas was an expert—and you didn't get to be that good without putting in the hours. Something wrenched inside her at the thought of how many women that meant, how many beds, how many kisses—

'What is going on in your head?' Achileas said quietly as he pushed open a door, then closed it behind them. He was staring down at her, his eyes intent, questioning.

'Nothing. I was just trying to work out how many guests there are,' she lied. 'Only maths isn't my strong point.'

'Four hundred. But why count them when you could be counting the stars?'

He clicked his fingers and she gasped as the ceiling above their heads turned into a swirling galaxy of thousands of luminous white stars, sparkling against midnight-blue. His arms curled around her waist, and she leaned into him, staring dazedly up at the spinning night sky.

They were in the planetarium.

'It's beautiful,' she whispered, turning to face him. 'But are we allowed in here?'

He shook his head. 'Not officially, no. But I bribed Manos and Stathis, the security guards, to take a little stroll round the block.'

She laughed, breathless, dizzy with a happiness she had never felt before. 'You know their names too?'

'Absolutely. I'm also on first name terms with Aris. He's the technician. He's in charge of the lights and the audio.'

He clicked his fingers again and the sounds of the orchestra from downstairs filled the room.

'Let's dance,' Achileas said softly.

He wrapped his hand around her waist, pulling her against him, and they waltzed slowly around the room. She felt oddly fragile, and once again she wished that she had more experience. Was this how having sex made you feel about a person? Not just physically close, but as if the other person was a part of you, fused with you in a way that had nothing to do with bodies?

It must be, she concluded. That was why she was so attuned to his every movement, his every breath.

'You're full of surprises Achileas Kane,' she said, tightening her hand against the swell of his shoulder.

'Me?' He frowned. 'What about you? Every time I think I've got you pinned down you kick my legs out from under me. There are those lightning flashes of temper. And this dress...' his gaze dropped a notch '...not forgetting, of course, the body beneath the dress. And now it turns out you dance like Cyd Charisse in *Singin' in the Rain.*'

His hand pressed against her back, and he drew her closer, so that she could feel every detail of his muscular body. She knew the film. Her mum loved it. But surely, he meant Debbie Reynolds?

'I wouldn't have had you down as a fan of old musicals,' she said lightly.

Something shifted in his face, just for a moment. 'My mother loves them,' he said at last. 'I guess I watched them so many times I ended up loving them too. Although obviously that's just between you and me.'

Her heart was beating too fast. It was the first time he had mentioned his mother directly and she wanted to ask more questions, only she could sense a reluctance, a hesitation beneath his words. Then again, most sons were protective of their mothers.

'Of course.' She kept her face serious. 'What happens in the planetarium stays in the planetarium.'

He laughed then, and suddenly she couldn't stop smiling.

'As it happens,' she added, 'my mum loves old musicals too.'

'So, she was the one who taught you to dance?'

Effie shook her head. 'No, that was my dad. He was

into swing and jive, you know, Lindy Hop, that kind of thing. Before everything bad happened, he used to take my mum out dancing on a Saturday night. Our neighbour Mrs Barker would come and sit with me.'

Her fingers trembled against his arm. She had forgotten those evenings—how her dad, handsome in his suit and tie, would let her stand on his shoes while he danced around the tiny flat, her mother laughing and clapping at the edge of the room.

'I'm sorry.' Achileas's face was serious now, his smile gone. 'I didn't mean to upset you—'

'You didn't. It's a nice memory. Usually, I only remember the bad things.' She bit her lip. 'Thank you.'

Beneath the glittering stars, his skin looked like polished bronze. 'You don't need to thank me.'

'But I do. I know my dad is a long way from perfect, but it's been such a long time since I've thought about him in a good way. And it was good sometimes. I think I need to remember that, because it's not a great idea to hold on to the bad. Sometimes you have to grip really tightly to the good, otherwise you get stuck in the past.'

It was probably the longest speech she had made in her life, too long maybe because they had stopped moving now and he was staring at her, breathing a little unsteadily.

'Why do you think I'm holding on to you so tightly?' he said at last. His voice was taut, like a bow before the arrow flew. 'You're a good person, Effie. Good for me. Too good for me.'

A frown pleated his forehead and he muttered something in Greek. Then he lowered his face and kissed her.

His mouth drove the breath from her. There was a white flash, brighter than all the stars above them combined. She felt him slant his head, adjusting the fit of his mouth to hers, and then he kissed her again—kissed her as though it was years, not hours, since he had last kissed her.

And she couldn't get enough. Even if it meant never taking another breath. She wanted to taste him—all of him. She wanted all of his heat and his hardness—

Her fingers bit into the swell of his biceps. 'Can we go back to the villa?'

She felt the muscles along his jaw tighten as he breathed out against her mouth and knew that he was feeling the same shattering hunger. 'Yes. I think that would be a good idea.'

He pulled her closer and she clutched at him, feeling the hardness of him through her dress, and he kissed her again—quickly this time, as though he didn't trust himself to linger.

He led her back through the building, walking so fast and with such a sense of purpose that she had to run to keep up.

'Sorry—' Slowing his pace, he turned and gave her a smile that was both apologetic and shimmering with a need that made her breath dissolve. 'I wasn't thinking of you in heels,' he said, leading her carefully down the staircase. 'Well, I was, but not in that—'

He broke off, and his grip on her arm tightened almost painfully. Glancing up at his face, she felt her breath catch. His smile hadn't so much faded as shifted into a different version of itself, like a tree shedding leaves in the autumn.

'What is it? Have you changed your mind?'

But Achileas didn't answer. Nor was he looking at her. His eyes were fixed on a grey-haired man standing at the bottom of the staircase. Standing…watching. Waiting.

Her breath died in her throat.

She had never seen him before in her life, but he was so

familiar to her. Still handsome, his hair greying now, with straight, symmetrical features and those blue, blue eyes.

The same blue eyes as his son.

Her gaze moved silently between the two men, and she knew without any doubt that she was looking at Achileas's father. She knew because it was like looking through a book of fabric samples where the pattern was the same, but the colour was slightly different.

For a moment, neither man spoke nor moved. They were like two ships run aground on sandbanks.

And then finally the older man inclined his head. 'Achileas. What a pleasant surprise.'

His gaze hovered for a moment where his son's arm curved around Effie's waist, and then it lasered in on her face. She blinked. Beside her, Achileas stood stiffly in silence.

Motivated as much by good manners as panic, she held out her hand. 'Hi, I'm Effie—Effie Price. I'm…' She hesitated, unsure suddenly of how to finish the sentence she had started.

But, reaching out and taking her hand, Andreas Alexios finished it for her. 'Engaged,' he said, tilting the diamond up to the light as he kissed her fingers. 'Congratulations, my dear.' His smile was as smooth and polished as his voice. 'I'm afraid we haven't been introduced. I'm—'

'My apologies.'

With a rush of relief, Effie felt Achileas move beside her, and she turned to him, smiling. But as she looked up into his face, she felt her smile freeze. He was smiling too, but his eyes were as flat and distant as the horizon.

'Effie, this is Andreas Alexios. My father.'

'It's very nice to meet you,' Effie said carefully, try-ing and failing to follow the twisting undercurrents of the conversation. It was clear neither man had expected to see the other—but surely that was a cause for joy, not caution?

As if reading her mind, Andreas tilted his head again and said in the same polished voice, 'We should celebrate.' Turning slightly, he narrowed his eyes across the crowded ballroom. 'Now, where is Eugenie? Ah, there she is—'

Achileas's mother!

Curiosity overcoming her confusion, Effie followed the direction of his gaze. She felt a jab of both admiration and disappointment. Dressed in the palest blue of a dawn sky, the woman talking to a couple at the edge of the dance floor was younger than Andreas, and very beautiful, but she looked nothing like her son. Achileas was all molten heat. Eugenie Alexios was cool and blonde and regal—like a storybook snow queen.

Beside her, Andreas was making one of those small, indefinable but unmistakably autocratic gestures with his hand that had several waiters running across the room. 'I think champagne is in order,' he said softly.

'That would be—' Effie began.

'A bad idea,' Achileas interrupted. His arm tightened around her waist. 'We've had a busy few weeks and Effie is feeling a little done in. We were just on our way home when we bumped into you.'

'A pity.' Andreas frowned. 'But you should certainly go home, my dear. Get some rest. However, I insist you both join us for lunch tomorrow. After all, we have a lot to talk about.'

'Tomorrow, then,' Achileas said, and before she had a chance to say goodbye, he had caught her elbow and was propelling her through the building.

But why were they leaving? He hadn't even spoken to his mother. Nor, as it turned out, was he planning on speaking to her.

On their journey back to the villa Achileas was silent—the kind of silence that was like a heavy, stifling shroud. Her pulse trembled. She knew he was angry. She just didn't know why. Although she suspected it had something to do with his need to be in control. Each time things had come to a head between them, that had been the touchpaper for the ensuing fireworks.

But he had been so abrupt with his father, rude almost and it made her feel as if she had been rude by association. She knew she should be angry too, and she was—only every time she caught sight of his rigid profile the flame of her anger seemed to go out like too-damp kindling.

Back at the villa, the staff who had been waiting for their return took one look at Achileas's dark, dangerous expression and retreated. Effie glanced around the empty sitting room. Now it was just the two of them.

And then there was one, she thought, as he stalked through the French windows onto the balcony.

Taking a breath, she followed him. The sky was littered with stars, just as it had been in the planetarium, only these stars were joined by a huge pale moon.

Beneath it, Achileas was leaning against the rail, looking at the dark Aegean, a part of the darkness, almost. And now he reminded her not of his father, but hers. A man who had gambled big on the horses and lost. Only unless she was missing something this was what he had wanted to happen.

'Do you want to talk?' she said quietly, and at the sound of her voice he turned, as she knew he would.

But not to talk but to blame.

'I think you've done enough talking for one night, don't you?' he snarled, his anger circling her like a narrow-eyed panther.

So, she had been right. This was about her not waiting

for him to make the introductions. But for him to get so angry was not just unreasonable, it was illogical. 'He's your father, Achileas. I could hardly just ignore him.'

'But you didn't have to tell him about the engagement.'

'I didn't. He saw the ring. But why wouldn't I tell him anyway? Isn't that why we're doing this? For him?' She took a step forward, wanting to touch him, to lead him back to that place of closeness they had found. 'Look, I know it was a shock, the two of you meeting like that, and I know you probably had it all planned out in your head—'

'You don't know anything.' He walked towards her, his movements precise with fury. 'You don't know anything about me.'

She flinched from his words as if he had hit her. And she felt as if he had.

It wasn't true. She *did* know him. Or had she simply got lost in the miraculous addictive hunger that gnawed at both of them? Confused that obliterating passion with a deeper understanding of the man standing in front of her with his hands balled at his sides?

'You're right. I don't understand why this is a problem. So talk to me. Tell me what I need to know.'

'I don't need you to know anything. I don't need you.'

'Everybody needs someone,' she said, trying to stay calm, or at least sound it. 'If you can't talk to me then talk to your father. Or your mother.'

The angry creature pacing beside her stumbled, and she felt her heart twist, remembering the beautiful, elegant blonde woman at the ball who was so unlike her own mother. And yet they shared a love of old musicals…

She felt a sudden tilting vertigo, as if she had drunk the champagne Andreas had suggested. Something had occurred to her—something so shattering she could hardly believe it.

. 'Except she's not your mother, is she? Eugenie, I mean?' she said quietly.

He didn't move a muscle. He didn't even tense.

And yet she felt his reaction like a burst of electromagnetic energy, just as if a lightning bolt had struck him and the effects were pulsing from his body into hers.

She was right.

Achileas was staring at her. His breathing wasn't quite steady, and his eyes looked strange, the pupils huge and dark. He had looked at her like that once before, but when?

'Achileas…' she said softly.

But as she reached for him, he turned and walked away without a backward glance, and was instantly swallowed up by the darkness. And now, she really was alone.

CHAPTER TEN

STARING AFTER HIM, Effie felt short of breath as she remembered when she had seen that look on Achileas's face before. It had been back in London, in his limousine, right after she'd accused him of hiding.

And now he was hiding again. Out there in the darkness.

Her head was full of panic. She needed to go after him, find him, but he could be anywhere.

No, not just anywhere.

She felt her heartbeat slow. She knew where he was. He had gone there before, and he would go back there for the same reason. To lift that anger and frustration, the pain he carried everywhere.

The pain of watching his mother being replaced in his father's affections.

Eugenie must be Andreas's mistress. And, knowing that, she felt everything else fall into place. Achileas's frustration with the world, that near-constant simmering anger and the strange weave of tension between the two men when they'd met at the ball.

She was sure she was right, but for the moment it didn't matter. What mattered was finding Achileas.

Even with the full moon it took her fifteen minutes to reach the lagoon. Things looked different at night, and of course it didn't help that she was wearing heels, but finally she found the path down between the sand dunes.

Achileas was not swimming this time. He had taken off his jacket and was barefoot, sitting on the sand, his shoulders slumped like Atlas, his eyes fixed on the barely moving water.

'You shouldn't have come,' he said as she sat down beside him.

He didn't turn to look at her, but she didn't need to see his face. She could read his shoulders, the set of his jaw.

'That's not up to you,' she said quietly. 'Only I expect you'll have to prove that it is, and any moment now you're going to storm off into the darkness again. I can't stop you doing that, but I'm just warning you now that I'm going to follow you.'

'And why would you do that?'

His hand flexed against the sand. But he stayed sitting beside her, and all the time he was throwing angry questions at her he was here and safe.

She stared at his rigid profile. 'You'd do the same for me. You *did* the same for me.'

'That was different. You were upset.'

And you're not? she thought.

He looked up at her, as if hearing her unspoken accusation. 'No amount of talking is going to change this.'

He meant fix this, she thought. But first he had to admit what was broken.

'Maybe not,' she admitted. 'Some things can't be changed. But sometimes they don't need to be. You just need to find a way to accept them and adapt.'

'Accept and adapt?' He shook his head, his mouth twisting into a shape that scraped at her skin. 'And you think I can do that?'

There was tension in his words, and with a jolt she realised that he didn't need to go into the darkness to hide. He was hiding all the time, using his anger and impatience to deflect prying eyes from what lay beneath.

Slipping off her sandals, she nodded. 'I think you can do pretty much anything if you set your mind to it.'

There was something flickering in his eyes that she couldn't follow. 'How did you know?' he said finally. 'That Eugenie wasn't my mother?'

Remembering Eugenie's cool, regal beauty, she said quietly, 'She didn't seem like the kind of person who likes old musicals.'

'Probably not. Truthfully, though, what would I know?' There was a tightness in his voice that made it sound flat, detached, as if it belonged to another man entirely. 'I've never met her. But then up until six months ago I'd only met my father once.'

Effie stared at him in confusion. Was that a joke? Surely it must be. But one look at his face told her that he was being serious. Mute with shock, she groped in her mind for some kind of logic that would explain his words.

'I don't understand…how is that possible?'

He shifted—a miniscule squaring of his shoulders. 'My father had a one-night stand with my mother. I was the result.'

Effie tried to make her next question sound casual. 'So they were never married?'

His face was like carved stone. 'He was already married.'

Married for seven years, she thought, mentally subtracting Achileas's age from the length of Andreas's marriage to Eugenie. Her heart started to pound. She had got it back to front. His mother had been the mistress—not Eugenie.

'How did it happen?'

His hands flexed against the sand again.

'At some party. Back in the day, my mother was a model. She was young and pretty. My father was on his own in New York. It was never meant to be anything but a fling. He had a wife…children. When my mother got pregnant, he sent some lawyers to see her. They got her to sign an NDA and he paid her off.'

His shoulders rose and fell.

'Oh, and he made her agree to keep his name off the birth certificate, which was a nice touch.'

Effie stared at him, appalled. It was a detail, but there was an efficiency about it that was breathtakingly cruel.

With an effort, she cleared her throat. 'And he never got in touch?'

Achileas shook his head. 'Never. I didn't even know who my father was until I was twelve. Whenever I asked her, my mother was always so vague I used to think he was a spy, and then out of the blue she told me I was going to boarding school in England. I didn't want to go, and we argued, and she told me that I had to go because that was what my father wanted.'

His mouth twisted. 'It was one of his demands. That and learning Greek.'

Picturing a younger Achileas, Effie felt her pulse jerk. It must have been so baffling for him, and hurtful, having to comply with the dictates of a faceless stranger who cared so little about him that he had never bothered to introduce himself.

'But you did meet him eventually?'

'When I was thirteen. It was the summer term of my first year.'

She watched the muscles tighten beneath his shirt.

'I was playing rugby in the final of an inter-school tournament. We were winning, and then at half time one of my teammates told me that a Greek billionaire was presenting the cup. Some shipping tycoon called Alexios.'

The ache in his voice echoed in the darkness.

'I knew it couldn't be a coincidence. That he was there to see me. And when we walked back onto the pitch, I couldn't stop looking for him in the crowd. Of course he wasn't there. He was being wined and dined by the head teacher. But I totally lost my concentration, and we lost the match.'

Effie swallowed. His face was tight, and she knew that he could still remember it now: the nervous anticipation of finally meeting his long-absent father, the panic that it might be a big mix-up—a different Greek billionaire called Alexios.

'We had to line up to get our runner-up medals, and when I saw him, I was shocked and excited, because we looked so alike. I knew I was right. That he must be there to see me. And I was so certain he'd say something.'

He hesitated, and now his hands were still, the knuckles white.

'Only when my name was called out, he just handed me the medal and shook my hand. As if I was just some random boy. As if I was nothing to him.'

Achileas felt his stomach clench. Even now he didn't know how he had managed to walk away as if nothing had happened. As if his whole world hadn't just spun into the crash barrier like a jack-knifing truck.

For days afterwards he had been mute with shock, and he had felt this pain—as if something had torn inside him and wouldn't heal. Eventually he'd learned to live with it, but as the pain had dulled his rage had intensified. Rage at his mother for getting pregnant. Rage with his father for rejecting him. Rage at a world that turned a blind eye to the careless, hurtful behaviour of people who were supposed to know better.

And he'd been furious for such a long time now.

He felt Effie's fingers curl around his, her small, cool hand pulling him back, calming his heartbeat.

'And after that?' she asked.

'After that I didn't see him again until six months ago.'

It had been late—around ten. Would he have picked up the phone if he had known it was Andreas? Probably. His father was like the sun to his earth. Distant, but impossible to live without. And he had tried—tried so hard—had spent so long trying not to care, hating Andreas. But even though he had wanted to hang up, to reject his father as Andreas had rejected him, he hadn't been able to do it.

'He called me at home in New York. Said he was in town and asked if I could come and see him. I wasn't going to. I was so angry with him. I'd been angry with him for years. But I still couldn't not go.'

'What would have been the point of not going?' Effie asked quietly. 'Not seeing him wouldn't have stopped him being your father.' Her fingers tightened around his. 'I'm guessing that's when he told you he was ill?'

Achileas nodded slowly. 'He has prostate cancer, and now it's spread. He's been fighting it for years and I don't think there's much else they can do. So, he wants to set his affairs in order.'

The ache in his chest had spread to his limbs. They felt heavy and immobile. His hand in Effie's was a dead weight.

'He has three daughters, but they have nothing to do with his business, and anyway he wants his empire—his legacy—to pass down the male line.' He couldn't keep the bitterness from his voice. 'Basically, that's why he got in touch. To let me know that he was ready to acknowledge me as his son and heir, but—'

He didn't want to admit the next part—to acknowledge that his father's acceptance came with a condition attached. That for him, entry into the fabled Alexios clan came with strings.

And maybe he didn't have to. He had already admitted so much—too much. Only the effort of hiding the truth was suddenly exhausting.

Glancing over at Effie's small oval face, he felt a mix of impatience and admiration. She wouldn't give up. She would sit and wait, or if necessary, follow him to the ends of the island—probably to the ends of the earth.

'But you had to get married?' she said quietly.

His eyes found hers. They were brown beneath the moonlight, but he could still see the flecks of gold in the irises. 'Yes. And I know you must hate me—'

She stared at him. 'Why would I hate you?'

'Because I lied to you.'

'Yes, you did—for the same reason I lied to you. Because we didn't know each other, and the truth is hard for us to share with anyone, let alone a stranger.'

She spoke in that soft, precise way of hers that he found so soothing. Only he didn't want to be soothed; he didn't deserve to be.

'But I kept lying to you even after I knew how badly you'd been hurt by your father's lies. I let you think I was doing a good thing. That I was a good person—'

She frowned. 'You *are* a good person.'

'Why? Because of this? Us?'

'Yes.' The word echoed around the silent beach as she nodded. 'You're marrying someone you don't love for someone you do.'

Something wrenched inside him, and he pulled his hand

free of hers and got to his feet, backing away from her as she stood up too.

'No, you're wrong. I don't love my father. I *hate* him for what he did to me—what he's still doing to me.'

The old familiar anger was rushing over him like a dark storm surge, and it was both a relief and an agony. 'I'm sorry to disappoint you, Effie, but I'm not faking this marriage to make him happy. I'm doing it to get even.'

There it was. The truth, the whole truth and nothing but the truth.

And it felt good to admit it finally.

It had been a long journey. In the beginning there had been only pain, and then afterwards that all-consuming rage. He'd understood that his father's rejection was the cause of it, but understanding hadn't eased the pain or calmed his fury. He'd known he needed to do more—needed to find some way to balance the equation or feel that way for ever.

And then suddenly the solution had been there. And the best part was that it had been his father who had inadvertently presented it to him.

'I'm going to take away his name. Do to him what he did to me. I'm not giving him heirs. The Alexios name, and his legacy, will die with him.'

It had to. Because he had no idea how to be a father.

Effie was staring at him as if she didn't know him. For a moment he felt like a stranger to himself, but of course it was strange, finally saying out loud what he'd been thinking privately for years.

'And that's what you want?' she asked.

He nodded. 'It's what I've wanted ever since he handed me that runner-up medal.'

There was a long silence that stretched out into the darkness, and then her eyes found his and she said quietly, 'I don't believe you.'

Around them the air seemed to tremble at her words. As if a storm was approaching. Only the sky above was clear and cloudless.

'You think I'm lying? After everything I just told you.'

There was another silence, and then she took a step forward. In the moonlight her face was as pale and serious as it had been that first day outside the Stanmore, when she'd told him he should apologise to her.

'Yes, I do. But only because you're having to lie to yourself. Look, we both know patience isn't one of your virtues, Achileas. If you really wanted to punish your father as badly as you say, then you would have been desperate to get on with it. As soon as you saw Andreas you would have told him about the engagement. But you did the opposite—'

'It wasn't the right time.'

'Of course it wasn't.'

Her voice was gentle—too gentle—and something inside him…something that had always been hard and impermeable…started to crumble.

'It's never going to be the right time. Because you don't hate your father and you don't want to punish him. You love him and you want to get to know him.'

His heart was a dark weight in his chest as he felt her hand touch his.

'He reached out to you.'

Taking a breath, he forced himself to speak. 'I'm just a means to an end for him.'

'Maybe.' She was silent for a moment. Then, 'Or maybe he needed a reason to reach out. He's old and ill, but he's also proud. He made some choices when he was younger than you—wrong choices—and maybe forcing this marriage on you is his way of trying to right those wrongs without losing face.'

She stroked his cheek with her fingertips.

'I don't know for sure, but I think you have more in common with Andreas than just your looks.'

She was so certain of the goodness of his motives, so certain that there was good in the world. He envied that belief and he wanted to prove her right.

But she was wrong.

Wrong about the world.

Wrong about him.

'You're right.' Watching her face soften, he hated himself for what he was about to say, but he couldn't pretend— not to Effie…not now. 'Andreas and I gave up on each other a long time ago. Me marrying you can't change that, and it won't. You see, I can't forgive him, and I don't love him. I don't know how to love, and I don't want to know.'

He couldn't put himself in the position of needing someone. Couldn't risk yet more rejection, more pain.

'I'm not like your father,' he said. 'I can't gamble my happiness on someone else's throw of the dice. And I know that's not what you want to hear but I don't want to lie to you. Not now. Not anymore.'

In the moonlight, her eyes were like polished amber stones, vivid like flames against her flushed cheeks. He leaned forward and kissed her softly, feeling his own body flame in response. But as he moved to deepen the kiss her hands pressed against his chest and she backed out of his arms.

'Effie…?'

He watched her turn and walk slowly towards the water, and then she reached around and undid the ribbon around her throat. His heart missed a beat as the blue chiffon fluttered down her body onto the sand.

His gaze sharpened.

She was completely naked, her head to one side as she gazed down at the tiny waves rippling over her feet. He swallowed, dry-mouthed. Silhouetted against the moonlight, her body was the single most erotic sight he'd ever seen.

'What are you doing?' he said hoarsely.

She didn't look back at him. 'I'm going for a swim.'

Now she was in the water.

Frowning, he took a step forward. 'But you told me you couldn't swim.'

The water was up to her shoulders. 'I can't. But that doesn't change the fact that I'm here…going for a swim.'

He was already running into the waves as she disappeared beneath the surface, and then suddenly she was in his arms, her hair slick against her head, her eyelashes splayed like starfishes.

Swearing loudly, he hauled her against him. 'What the hell are you playing at?'

Her hands gripped his shoulders and her beautiful eyes locked onto his. 'I just wanted to prove to you that when things can't be changed, you can accept them and adapt.'

'By drowning?'

She bit into her lip. 'I wasn't drowning. I was waving, so you knew where to find me.'

'I know where to find you, Effie. You're by my side.'

The truth in those words tore him in two. He had imagined a woman who would be able to fake a marriage with him, but Effie was so much more than that. She would risk her life for him. Only what about now? Now that she knew the truth?

He might not know about love, but he knew Effie. He knew how much it hurt her to lie, and that she had only done so because she'd thought his motives were good.

Something twisted inside him. If this arrangement was going to continue it would have to be her choice.

'But maybe that needs to change,' he said slowly. 'Because I can't. I can't adapt or accept what Andreas did to me. To my mother. I need to do this. I need to win.'

His need for revenge was like a living, breathing shadow—always at his heels, night, and day. And nothing could change that.

There was no sound except their breathing. Around them the universe was silent, as if shocked by his words.

'I know that's how you feel.'

Her face was pale, but her voice was grave and certain, and he felt a rush of relief that he hadn't managed to push her away like everyone else.

'I know why you feel that way. And that's enough for me. Nothing's changed.'

'You still want to do this?' He'd been so scared she would quietly refuse to go any further.

For a moment she didn't reply and then her eyes found his. 'We still have a deal, don't we?'

The sudden reminder of the reason Effie was there was like a physical blow. But he knew it was irrational to feel that sting beneath his ribs.

He nodded. 'Yes, we do, but—'

'Okay, then.'

Glancing down, he caught sight of her bare breasts and their rosy-tipped nipples. Instantly the sting beneath his ribs was forgotten as heat rushed through him.

'How did you know where to find me?' he asked.

Her lashes flickered up. 'I saw you the other morning... swimming.' A pulse began to beat wildly in her throat. 'You were naked.'

There was a moment of sharpening silence and then he

drew her against him, his body tensing as he felt her bare, wet skin slide over his soaked clothes.

'And now you are,' he said softly.

Their eyes locked for a full sixty seconds and then he jerked her against him, taking her mouth as if he owned it, parting her lips and kissing her hungrily. She moaned softly, curling her hands around his neck, wrapping her legs around his waist, and he lifted her again, pushing forward through the water.

Reaching the sand, he laid her down, kissing her high on her neck, then low on her jawbone, feeling her body shudder.

'Wait a minute.'

He leaned back and wrestled his soaked shirt up and over his head. Keeping his eyes trained on her face, he yanked his trousers open, his jaw clenching as she freed him from the wet fabric of his boxers.

He was already so hard…

Sucking in a breath, Effie wrapped her hand around his smooth, straining erection, her nipples tightening painfully as Achileas lowered his mouth to her breast and licked first one and then the other.

His hand was moving between her thighs, parting her to the cool night air and she moved against his hand, arching her back away from the wet sand, lifting her body, maddened by his touch, needing more of him. Her pulse accelerated as she felt the hard length of him dig into her stomach. So close to the soft, slick heat between her thighs.

But not close enough.

Grabbing his hips, she pulled him closer, and he grunted, grabbing himself, sucking in a breath.

'I haven't got a condom, Effie.'

Her stomach clenched. She stared at him in shock. She

hadn't thought this through. But then she hadn't been thinking at all—or at least not in any logical way.

Her head had been spinning from everything Achileas had told her, and she'd been fighting the weight of his anger and pain. Her pain, too, for failing to help him—just as she had failed to help her father with his demons. But then he'd kissed her, and she had kissed him back, and that had been unthinking too…instinctive.

Necessary.

Only she had forgotten about protection.

'I'm due my period any day, so I should be safe…' her hands stilled against his chest '…but maybe we should go back to the villa.'

The risk of pregnancy was almost non-existent. But she had heard the tension in his voice when he had spoken about not giving his father heirs.

'No.' The muscles in his face were tight. 'I want you now.'

'I want you too,' she said hoarsely.

He rolled over, taking her with him so that she was straddling his hips, and she shivered inside and out as his hands caught her by the waist and he lifted her, sliding the blunt head of his erection against her clitoris back and forth, until she thought she would die from pleasure.

She leaned forward, pressing her forehead into his, and now he pushed inside her, thrusting deeply and then withdrawing to thrust again, in a hard, intoxicating rhythm that made her moan against his mouth. It was coming. She could feel her body starting to fray around him, unravelling faster and faster, in time with his hips.

And then her muscles tensed, and she was shuddering against him, feeling his stubble rasping against her cheek as he lunged forward and his body spilled forcefully into hers.

CHAPTER ELEVEN

LEANING BACK AGAINST the leather banquette seat, Achileas stared across the blue water, his heart pounding in time with the thump of the launch's hull as it bounced over the waves. It was finally happening. Today, for the first time, he was going to step inside the Villa Thymári—Andreas's waterside mansion.

In his head it had become a mythical place. A kind of Greek Camelot.

His shoulders tensed.

Guinevere's failure to produce an heir had, in part, led to the fall of King Arthur's legendary home. Did he still want that to happen to the house of Alexios?

He had thought so. In all the years he'd spent plotting his revenge, it had been the yin to the yang of Andreas's rejection. The ultimate sting in the tail.

But if that was the case, why had he had unprotected sex with Effie on the beach?

Short answer: because he hadn't wanted to wait.

Long answer…

He frowned. Was there a long answer? Basically, he had wanted her, there and then, and she had seemed certain it was safe, and he had trusted her.

His eyes shifted to the woman sitting beside him as he tested that sentence inside his head. It was true: he did trust Effie. But it had still been a stupid risk to take. He didn't want children. He didn't have the right instincts. How could a fatherless boy be a father?

And yet he couldn't seem to get the idea out of his head that she could be pregnant. That a baby…their baby…might be forming inside her.

And for some reason it wasn't freaking him out.

There was a reason, he told himself firmly. He'd waited so long to get even with his father and now the moment of reckoning was finally here, so naturally he was feeling completely off-balance.

His chest tightened. It wasn't just that.

When Effie had told him that he loved his father and wanted to get to know him, not punish him, it had been as if she had thrown a light switch and spun him round in the darkness. And now he didn't know up from down.

She was wrong, but it had knocked him off course like a rogue wave, sweeping away all the recognisable pointers.

Not all of them, he thought, gazing at the woman sitting beside him. Effie had made her way to him in the darkness. And remembering the moment when she'd sat down beside him on the sand, he felt calm again—safe, like a ship in a storm seeing the beam of a lighthouse marking out a safe path through the rocks ahead.

On impulse he caught her arm, turning her and pulling her against him.

'We haven't really talked about what happened last night. I know you said you thought it was safe, but I want you to know that you don't need to worry,' he said quietly. 'I'll look after you. I mean, if you are—'

'I won't be,' she said quickly. She smiled stiffly. 'My period is due in a day or two, so I'm completely safe.'

Safe in that she almost certainly wasn't pregnant, Effie thought as his eyes locked with hers. But she wasn't safe from the hunger in his narrowed blue gaze, or the softness of his mouth, or the hard, insistent press of his body...

Wasn't that why they were having this conversation? Because he made her reckless? Made her want things... need things? Made her lose control. Made her walk into the sea even though she could barely swim.

His touch made her shiver inside—made her feel so hollowed out with longing there was nothing else. Certainly no common sense.

What other explanation could there be for what she had let happen—no, conspired to make happen? Sex without protection was beyond reckless—it was crazy.

What if it hadn't been that time of the month? Would she still have taken the risk? It was one thing lying to other people, but they couldn't lie about their relationship to a child. A child Achileas didn't want. And yet he had been as reckless as her.

Stomach cartwheeling, she stared ahead to where a huge, pale house sat like an opal on a ring beside the shimmering aquamarine water. Why would he take a risk like that?

Of course the answer to that was obvious. Clearly his head had been all over the place. But in time, with her support, that could change—

In time? With her support?

She wasn't safe from that either. That instinct, inherited straight from her mother, to hope for the best, to go with the flow however bad things were, however painful it was for her to do so, and wait for things to change.

Last night all of the above had crowded in on her, and that was why she had walked into the water, then had unprotected sex with a man who didn't want children.

But it wouldn't happen again.

There would be no further risk-taking.

What had happened last night had been a one-off. Everything had been so raw, so painful, and sex had been both a balm, and a place to get lost. A place to hide from the swirl of emotions churning inside her. Pushing aside all those confusing and confused feelings, she had chosen to embrace her need and his—because it had been all either of them could handle.

That was their truth. That dark, mesmerising hunger. That shimmering fire.

Achileas hadn't been ready to accept the other truth. That he loved his father. Andreas's rejection still hurt him too much.

She gritted her teeth. She was doing it again. But this wasn't her problem to fix. She wasn't going to be like her mother, clinging on to something that would break her. She wouldn't and she couldn't be that woman.

That wasn't what she'd signed up for, and from now on she was going to stick to the script.

As the launch came to a stop Achileas helped her disembark, and she gazed up at Andreas's villa. It was more like a palace, really, and Achileas was like the prodigal son, returning home to sit at his father's table.

Albeit with conditions attached.

Her stomach clenched. It still shocked her that Andreas could have treated his child so ruthlessly and was manipulating him even now. Yet she was sure that there was more to it. Sure that Andreas was too proud to admit to his mistake, much less apologise for it, and that this was his way of making amends without losing face.

Not your problem, she told herself firmly as a uniformed maid stepped forward, smiling stiffly.

'Welcome to the Villa Thymári. Please, if you would follow me?'

'Thank you,' Achileas said beside her.

'Yes, thank you,' Effie added quickly.

It was stupid, but the maid's black dress and white apron felt like an omen. A reminder of that version of herself she had left behind in London.

Or she had thought she'd left behind.

The interior of the house was stunning. Walking through it, Effie felt less like Cinderella and more like the Little Match Girl. With a mix of statuary and modern art adding texture and colour to its soaring high-ceilinged rooms, the villa was cool and pale and exquisitely beautiful.

A lot like their hostess, Effie thought as Eugenie rose to greet them.

'How lovely to meet you,' she said quietly. 'Andreas has been so excited about you coming.'

If Andreas was excited, he hid it well. But perhaps if you belonged to the exclusive top one percent of the richest men in the world there was very little left to excite you. He greeted both her and Achileas in that same polished marble voice, his blue eyes moving over them like a searchlight.

'Are you recovered, Ms Price?'

'Yes, thank you, Kýrios Alexios,' she said carefully. 'But please call me Effie.'

He inclined his head. 'And you shall call me Andreas. Now, Effie, shall we have that glass of champagne? And then we can eat.'

As she'd expected, the meal was delicious. A sea urchin and artichoke salad, followed by roasted lamb that fell off the bone and aubergine with a feta crust. To finish there was traditional Greek *kadaifi* and pink peppercorn ice cream.

The conversation was just as sophisticated. They discussed the ball, Greek political issues, and their English and American counterparts, and then Andreas and Achileas talked about something called long short equity.

Andreas seemed perfectly at ease, as if having lunch with his estranged son was something that happened every day. But although Achileas might look handsome and relaxed too, with his hand curving easily around the stem of his wine glass, there was a taut set to his body—as if he was holding a kite steady in a high wind.

And that was understandable. He was in his father's home. Finally. She could only try to imagine what that would feel like to the boy who had been handed a runner-up medal by the same man over two decades ago.

A man who had silver-framed photos of three beautiful blonde women prominently displayed on every surface. Three sisters. His daughters. Achileas's half-sisters.

Their mother, Eugenie, was also on edge. Outwardly the older woman was the perfect smiling hostess, polite and attentive to their every need. Occasionally, though, her serene smile seemed to slip a little, as if it was an effort to keep it in place.

Not that Effie could blame her. How must it feel to be confronted by living proof of your husband's infidelity and betrayal? Had she known what Andreas had done at the time? Did she know what he was doing now?

It was impossible to tell. It was as if she was trapped beneath glass.

After dessert, they moved outside. Eugenie had been called away to the phone, so it was just the three of them sitting on the wide leather sofas beneath a huge white canopy.

'Your coffee, Ms Price.'

'Thank you.' Effie smiled up at the maid—different maid, same uniform—feeling again that twinge of unease.

'Achileas tells me you were in the hospitality sector

before you decided to set up your own business.' Andreas leaned back, his blue eyes moving with deceptive carelessness over Effie's face. 'Working as a chambermaid.'

'Yes, I was. I worked at the Stanmore in London,' she said, lifting her chin. 'I would have liked to concentrate on my perfumery sooner, but I needed to work to pay the rent.'

Andreas nodded. 'Everyone has to start somewhere. And you were working at the hotel when you met my son?'

'She was.' Achileas leaned forward and picked up his coffee cup, positioning himself between her and his father. 'But she wasn't at work when we met again and got to know one another.' He turned, his blue eyes resting on her face, his gaze fierce and unwavering. 'That was later.'

Her chest tightened—no, that was wrong. It felt more as if it was being stretched…stretched almost to its limits… by something building inside her that she couldn't name.

There was a beat of silence and Andreas smiled. 'Achileas… I left some paperwork on the desk in my study for you to read through. I wonder if you might take a look.' He glanced over his shoulder and instantly the maid reappeared. 'Show Mr Kane to my office.'

Watching Achileas leave, Effie felt her heart start to beat faster. She had thought this meeting today would be an opportunity for father and son to talk. Now, though, it appeared that Andreas wanted to speak to her.

But to what end?

Still smiling, Andreas got to his feet. 'If I may, Effie, I'd like to show you the rose garden. I think you would enjoy it. We have both the Turkish and the Damascene varieties which I believe are used extensively in perfumery.'

Naturally, she agreed, and the garden was beautiful. Arranged in a spiral, like the shell of a snail, the roses at the centre were the oldest and rarest. The smell was extraordinary—as delicate as fine wine with notes of sweet apricot, green apple and honey. It was hard not to simply stand and breathe.

Andreas seemed pleased by her reaction. 'So, has perfumery always been a passion of yours?'

Effie nodded. 'Always. My mother was a beautician, and she encouraged me when I was very little to make potions and perfumes. My idea for the business grew out of that. Although it's still at a very early stage,' she admitted.

'That might be a good thing.' The older man's eyes moved past her to the beautiful house. 'Being an Alexios comes, if you'll excuse the pun, at a *price*. Clearly there are huge benefits and privileges. Less obviously, sacrifices have to be made.'

She cleared her throat. 'What kind of sacrifices?'

'This family is a job in its own right. We are patrons of charitable foundations. We endorse political candidates. We fund and support the arts and scientific research. On top of all that, you would have a home to run—this home in the future.' He paused. 'And, of course, a family to raise.'

Remembering that moment on the beach, she felt her pulse stumble.

'I think it might be a little early to be talking about having a family.' She smiled stiffly. 'We're not even married yet.'

'But you will talk about it, I hope?'

She stared at Andreas, startled. Not by his desire for grandchildren—many parents felt the same way, her mum among them. But because Andreas had disowned his son before he was even born.

'Wouldn't it be better to wait a little?' she said carefully. 'I mean, you and Achileas have only just met. You might like some time to get to know one another.'

Andreas smiled, and there was something tyrannical

about his smile. A Zeus-like disregard for the wishes of lesser mortals—even those related to him.

'Achileas understands. He knows the importance of legacy to a family like ours. I've explained to him that the name Alexios is a privilege to hand from father to son, and from son to grandson,' Andreas continued smoothly.

Father to son…son to grandson. It sounded like a prayer, and she felt a wave of pity for the old man sitting opposite her. He had lived his life always one step ahead of the pack, but he was slowing down now, and it must be hard for him to know that at some point he would stop.

But Achileas had lost so many years with him already. He needed this time with his father even if he didn't know it himself.

'I can see why you would think that, but I disagree,' she said.

Andreas frowned, and he looked so much like his son that her breathing momentarily lost its rhythm.

'I'm not sure I understand, Effie.'

'The word "privilege" makes it sound as if you have to deserve the name in some way. But I think a name is something you live up to. And on that basis, you don't need anything more from your son,' she said, her voice catching as she pictured Achileas's taut, arrogant face because his was an arrogance that masked the hurt that had shaped his character, his life. 'You should just be proud of the man he is. He's a strong man. A good man. And I—'

Her blood was pounding through her veins like the music had last night. The scent of the roses was making her feel dizzy. Except it wasn't the roses. It was something else entirely. Something that made her feel as if the garden was a boat adrift at sea. She could feel herself filling with a warm golden light, brighter than the sun, deeper than the sea, and it was in that moment, staring into Andreas's blue eyes, that she realised she was in love with his son.

But of course she was. It seemed so obvious now. Love was the reason she had followed him into the darkness last night. And the reason why she had opened her body to his without barriers. She had wanted him to know that her love was different. That it came without conditions to meet or hurdles to cross. That it was fierce and partisan and limitless.

Steadying her breathing, she said quietly, 'Achileas has worked hard his whole life to build a business of his own. He didn't need the Alexios name. What I'm trying to say is that he doesn't need your name now.'

The air seemed to still.

'In your opinion.'

Andreas's voice didn't alter, but she saw his jaw tighten.

'I'm not sure Achileas feels the same way.'

Effie stared at him, a spark of anger flaring inside her as she remembered Achileas's face in the moonlight. 'You don't know what he feels. You hardly know him.'

Andreas's blue eyes—Achileas's eyes—moved to rest on hers. 'Of course I know him. He's my son. My flesh and blood.'

Behind him, the breeze was lifting rose petals and sending them into the sky like confetti. She shook her head. 'No, that's not enough.'

Now Andreas's face was flat with shock and an anger of his own. 'Not enough? My dear, it's an unbreakable bond.'

'It should be—yes,' she agreed. 'But you broke that bond. You didn't give him a chance to be your son. You erased yourself from his life and you hurt him. You're still hurting him now…putting conditions on your acceptance.'

She felt tears burn in her eyes.

'He would do anything for you because he loves you.

And I would do anything for him. I'd have any number of children with him if that was what he wanted, because I love him.'

The words left her mouth before she could check them, but she barely noticed. All that mattered was making Andreas understand what Achileas needed.

'But we won't be having a child any time soon. Not until you put him first and become a father to your son.'

'Effie—'

She spun round. Achileas was standing in the sunlight, staring at her. She pressed her hand against her forehead. How long had he been there? How much had he heard?

He was still staring at her, his eyes fixed on hers. His face was unreadable, but she could feel his anger, and his shock. Breathing shakily, she watched his gaze shift to his father, and then he was walking towards her, and her pulse slammed into her skin as his hand caught her elbow, his grip firm, precise, impersonal.

'I think I should get you home.'

Up close, she could see the tension in every line of the body she knew better than her own, and memories of that day in London tumbled through her head. Only that had been the beginning, and this felt like the end.

'Achileas…' she whispered.

But he ignored her, turning again to his father. 'Please thank Eugenie for a wonderful lunch.'

Still holding her arm, he guided her away from the house, moving swiftly and silently. She wanted to speak, to apologise, to tell him that she loved him. But the words kept slipping away like rose petals in the wind.

They reached the launch and he helped her on board.

Her heart jolted. He had stepped back onto the jetty. 'What are you doing? Aren't you coming with me?'

His face was shuttered. 'I have to talk to my father.'

'Then let me come with you—'

He cut her off. 'I don't need you to come with me.'

'I know, but I want to apologise—and I want to be there for you.'

Her stomach lurched as he shook his head slowly.

'I don't want you there.' His voice was clipped, harsh. Irrevocably final. 'Go back to the villa. I'll see you when I see you.'

'But I love you…' It was all she could force past the lump in her throat.

He stared at her in silence. 'I know,' he said finally, and then the launch started to move, and he was turning and walking back to the huge white house.

CHAPTER TWELVE

IT WAS EXACTLY the same as before, Effie thought dully as the launch bumped lightly over the waves. Except the last time Achileas had bundled her into a waiting vehicle he'd got in beside her. This time she was alone.

Back on the island, she made her way to the villa. Every step, every breath was an effort. Finally, she reached her bedroom and collapsed on the bed. She felt numb—almost as if she was floating outside of her body, watching herself.

If only that were true; then she might not have made such a mess of everything…

Her breath caught in her throat as she thought back to how she had wished for more experience. Now she had it. From a declaration of love to heartbreak in ninety seconds. Even though she had warned herself to stay detached. Told herself not to get involved.

But logic and sense were no match for love.

Love was blind, unthinking.

And in her case unrequited.

His lack of love for her was as obvious and undeniable as her love for him. And it didn't matter that they shared this exquisite bewitching chemistry. Sex wasn't love. It was a part of it, but love was about so much more than bodies moving in harmony.

It was about more than *'I'll see you when I see you.'*

A pain such as she had never felt before, that surely didn't have a name, clawed at her insides, and she got to her feet and stumbled onto the balcony. Outside the sun was softening and she breathed in deeply, the salt-scented air calming her as it had that first day.

The first day...

She could still remember that mix of panic and exhilaration as she had stood looking out across the Aegean. Everything had been ahead of her then—a future filled with possibilities. And for the first time in her life, she had been a part of those endless variables, doing more than just conjuring up adventure in a bottle.

She was living it, sharing it with Achileas. Except she wasn't. Not then, not now, not ever.

Her hands gripped the rail. Was that what it had felt like to her father? That yearning, unshakeable conviction that you were different...that the odds didn't apply to you. She had seen it so many times with Bill—the same trajectory of fervent, unquestioning belief, the euphoria as his horse nosed ahead of its rivals, and then the stunned disbelief as it lost.

She had never expected to feel that way herself. She'd always thought she was like her mum, and she had got dangerously close to following in Sam's footsteps, but she wasn't going to make the mistakes that Sam had made with her father, caring for a man who lied to himself his whole life.

And Achileas was lying. She knew he wanted, *needed* Andreas's love, but she wasn't going to wait and watch the lies he was telling himself destroy him. *And her.*

The ring on her finger caught the sun, sending a rainbow of dancing light across the pale stone. Reaching down, she tried to pull it off. She might as well get used to not wearing it.

But the ring wouldn't budge.

It was too much.

Emotion choked her, and she covered her mouth with her hand and gave in to the tears she'd been holding back ever since Achileas had walked away from the jetty.

But she couldn't cry for ever.

Two hours later, she splashed her face with cold water and stared at her reflection. She had never loved anyone before, but she knew she would never love again as she loved Achileas. There was no other man like him.

Her mouth trembled. Just thinking that made her legs buckle, but even though she had lost him she still had a life to live. It would be less of a life in so many ways, but she had her mum, and her friends, and thanks to Achileas's investment she would have the chance to make her dream of creating her own perfume brand come true.

She wasn't going to take all the money. Just the amount the bank would have given her if she had made that meeting and got the loan. Obviously, she would leave the ring behind too. Soap would get it off…

She turned towards the bathroom.

Her heart stopped.

Achileas was standing in the doorway, his blue eyes still, his face taut in the hazy light.

'Are you okay?'

The tightness in his voice made her hands ball into fists. She wanted to reach out and touch him, but he wasn't hers to touch any more. He never had been.

'I'm fine.' She forced herself to keep looking at him, even though it hurt to do so. 'Are *you* okay?'

He nodded, his eyes moving past her to the suitcase on the bed. 'You're packing.'

Not a question, a statement. In other words, he wasn't going to try and talk her out of leaving.

She nodded. 'I'm sorry, but I think it's for the best.'

'You're reneging on our deal?' He walked towards her, moving with that devastating masculine grace that made her unravel inside. 'I'm not sure you want to do that. You see, there are consequences. But perhaps you didn't read the small print?'

She had seen him angry many times before, but this felt like an entirely different emotion. She could feel it rolling off him in waves, so that it made her feel unsteady on her feet. But he could threaten what he liked. She had nothing to lose.

'I didn't. But it doesn't matter. I can't do this. I won't do this. I'm sorry if that is difficult for you to accept.'

His eyes locked on hers. 'I don't accept it.'

She wrapped her arms around her body, trying to hold in the pain that was threatening to capsize her. 'You're not being reasonable.'

'I guess not,' he agreed. 'Then again, I'm not a reasonable man. I'm selfish and arrogant and impatient. For most of my life I've been angry. And unhappy.'

Achileas tilted his dark head backwards.

'More than unhappy. I felt cursed—and then I walked into you outside the Stanmore, and everything changed. Only I didn't realise. I just kept telling myself the same lies about why I needed a wife. Why I needed you to be my wife. I told myself that I was doing you a favour.'

'You were,' she said quietly.

He wanted to laugh then—because it was laughable, ludicrous.

'No, I really wasn't. All I did was give you money, and I have so much money I could give half of it away without noticing. But you changed me. You made me look at the world in a different way.'

Watching Effie's eyes fill with tears, he felt as if his heart would burst.

'Only I didn't realise that either. I kept clinging to the past, holding on to the hate. Because I'm not just selfish and arrogant and impatient, I'm stupid too. So when you told me that I didn't want to punish my father, that I loved him, I didn't listen.' His mouth twisted. 'But the truth is, Effie, that you were right.'

She had seen beneath his anger. Seen the need to love and be loved that he had struggled against all his life.

He thought back to when he'd walked into the Alexios house. It had been the moment he had waited for all his life, and he had expected it to be transformative…seismic.

Instead, he'd felt sad, and oddly worried about the man he had hated for so long. A proud, stubborn man who was growing older and frailer. A man so much like himself.

And in that moment, he had known that some things couldn't be changed, that he needed to find a way to accept them. That it was time to accept that he wanted more than the Alexios name.

He took a step forward. 'You made me see that I had a choice. I could do what I planned—take revenge and stay angry—or I could accept that my father had already been punished enough by the stupid, selfish decision he made more than three decades ago. Only I had to do it on my own.'

Walking away from her had been the hardest thing he had ever done. Harder and more painful than walking away from Andreas at that rugby match all those years ago.

'It had to be just me and him. Can you forgive me?'

She shook her head. 'I don't need to forgive you for reaching out to your father.'

'But I hurt you.' Heart clenching, he reached out and

touched her face…her sweet, serious face. 'And I'm sorrier for that than you can imagine. But if you won't let me apologise then at least let me thank you.'

'For what?'

'For everything. You made me look at myself and see who I really was beneath the suits and the stubble. Who I wanted to be. You lifted the curse. You're such a good person, Effie.'

Her lip wobbled. 'Not in the garden, I wasn't. I was rude and cruel. He's an old man, and he's sick, and he wants his family around him.'

Achileas brushed away the tears that were spilling from her beautiful amber eyes.

'He has his family. He has two sisters, and he has Eugenie and three daughters. And he has me.'

She breathed out shakily. 'So you made it all right with him?'

He shook his head slowly. 'Actually, no. I told him that you and I weren't real. That I'd set the whole marriage up because I wanted to punish him.'

Her eyes widened with such horror that he started to laugh.

'And then I told him that I didn't want or need what he was offering. That I knew what love was and that it didn't come with conditions.'

He pulled her against him, wrapping his arms around her waist, holding her close.

'It's okay. He was shocked and angry at first. You were right about us having more in common than just looks. He's got a pretty impressive temper. But then…then he apologised.'

Remembering Andreas's face, the sudden softening in his voice, Achileas heard his own voice falter. 'He said that he has regretted what he did every day. And that whatever it took, he wanted me in his life for the rest of it.'

'I'm so pleased for you.' Effie's eyes filled with tears again.

'Yeah…seems you were right about that too. I guess in the future I'm just going to assume you're always right. It'll be easier that way.'

'The future?'

Effie felt her heart skip a beat as Achileas framed her face with his hands, forcing her to look at him.

'What you said to my father… Did you mean it? About loving me?'

There was nowhere to hide from his deep blue gaze. But she didn't want to hide ever again. Instead, she dived right in. 'Yes. Every word. I love you.'

'And I love you—'

His voice cracked as he struggled to speak, and now her heart was in freefall.

'And I know you said that you didn't think it was very likely, but if there is a baby, I'll love him or her too. I'll love every baby we have, Effie.'

'Every baby?' Her hands gripped the front of his shirt, tears of happiness and joy spilling from her eyes. 'Shouldn't we get married first?'

'Yeah, about that…'

His mouth curved into one of those smiles that made her blood turn to air.

'I know I asked you to marry me before, but I want… I need to ask you again. Will you be my wife for real, my sweet Effie…my darling Josephine?'

Searching his eyes, she saw a man in love. A man wanting to love and be loved. She saw that the hardness, the anger, was gone.

'Effie?' he prompted, frowning, and she started to laugh. The impatience hadn't gone though.

'Yes,' she said quietly. 'Yes, I will.'

And, reaching up, she kissed him—softly at first, and then more hungrily—and he kissed her back, his arms tightening around her, holding her close with all his strength and all his passion.

* * * * *

COMING SOON!

We really hope you enjoyed reading this book.
If you're looking for more romance, be sure to
head to the shops when new books are
available on

Thursday 4th
August

To see which titles are coming soon, please visit
millsandboon.co.uk/nextmonth

MILLS & BOON®

Coming next month

INNOCENT UNTIL HIS FORBIDDEN TOUCH
Carol Marinelli

"Seriously?" His deep Italian voice entered the room before he even walked in. "I do not need a PR strategist?"

"A Liason Aide, Sir," his Aide murmured.

Beatrice stood as she'd been instructed earlier, but as he entered, every assumption she'd made about him was wiped away.

Prince Julius brimmed, not just with authority but with health and energy. It was as if a forcefield had entered the room.

She had dealt with alpha males and females at the top of their game – or rather – usually when they crashing from the top.

Not he.

He was, quite literally, stunning.

He stunned.

"It's a pleasure to meet you," she said and then added. "Sir."

"Likewise," he said, even if his eyes said otherwise.

God, he was tall, Beatrice thought, it was more than just his height, he was the most immaculate man she had ever seen.

Beatrice swallowed, not wanting to pursue that line of thought. The issue was that at most interviews she had found most people were less in the flesh.

He was so, so much more.

Continue reading
INNOCENT UNTIL HIS FORBIDDEN TOUCH
Carol Marinelli

Available next month
www.millsandboon.co.uk

MILLS & BOON

THE HEART OF ROMANCE

A ROMANCE FOR EVERY READER

MODERN

Prepare to be swept off your feet by sophisticated, sexy and seductive heroes, in some of the world's most glamourous and romantic locations, where power and passion collide.

HISTORICAL

Escape with historical heroes from time gone by. Whether your passion is for wicked Regency Rakes, muscled Vikings or rugged Highlanders, awaken the romance of the past.

MEDICAL

Set your pulse racing with dedicated, delectable doctors in the high-pressure world of medicine, where emotions run high and passion, comfort and love are the best medicine.

True Love

Celebrate true love with tender stories of heartfelt romance, from the rush of falling in love to the joy a new baby can bring, and a focus on the emotional heart of a relationship.

Desire

Indulge in secrets and scandal, intense drama and plenty of sizzling hot action with powerful and passionate heroes who have it all: wealth, status, good looks…everything but the right woman.

HEROES

Experience all the excitement of a gripping thriller, with an intense romance at its heart. Resourceful, true-to-life women and strong, fearless men face danger and desire - a killer combination!

To see which titles are coming soon, please visit

millsandboon.co.uk/nextmonth

LET'S TALK
Romance

For exclusive extracts, competitions
and special offers, find us online: